TODAY'S BLOCKBUSTER— TOMORROW'S HEADLINES

"Holds rapt attention to the very conclusion . . . dramatic and suspenseful, a many-faceted spellbinder which is headed straight for Hollywood."
—*Columbus Dispatch*

"A spine-tingling, edge-of-your-chair story in the tradition of *Airport* and *Hotel*."
—*Sioux Falls Argus-Leader*

"Builds suspense by the paragraph."
—*Richmond News Leader*

"A testament to the blatant peril surrounding every urban cliff dweller."
—*San Francisco Chronicle*

"Gripping . . . will make one helluva singeing flick."
—*The Kirkus Reviews*

THE GLASS INFERNO
was originally published by Doubleday & Company, Inc.

THE
GLASS
INFERNO

by Thomas N. Scortia
and Frank M. Robinson

A POCKET BOOK EDITION published by
Simon & Schuster of Canada, Ltd. • Markham, Ontario, Canada
Registered User of the Trademark

*All of the characters in this book are fictitious
and any resemblance to actual persons, living
or dead, is purely coincidental.*

THE GLASS INFERNO

Doubleday edition published 1974

POCKET BOOK edition published December, 1974
2nd printing........October, 1974

This POCKET BOOK edition includes every word contained
in the original, higher-priced edition. It is printed from
brand-new plates made from completely reset, clear, easy-
to-read type. POCKET BOOK editions are published by
POCKET BOOKS, a division of Simon & Schuster of Canada,
Ltd., 330 Steelcase Road, Markham, Ontario L3R 2M1.
Trademarks registered in Canada and other countries.

Standard Book Number: 671-78768-3.
Library of Congress Catalog Card Number: 73-18909.

For Martha, Emilie and Richard
—in appreciation

ACKNOWLEDGMENTS

No project of the size and scope of THE GLASS INFERNO can be the sole product of the authors. From May 1972, when the project was first conceived, to the present, a great many people have contributed their time and technical information to the book. Errors, nevertheless, do creep in and for these we assume full responsibility. In some instances we have taken auctorial license, particularly in minimizing the smoke hazards of high-rise fires.

THE GLASS INFERNO is not intended as an indictment of architects or contractors—there are no such villains in the book—but rather as a comment on the nature of human error and the economic pressures inherent in modern building technology. The city is nowhere identified since all modern cities and towns, to a greater or lesser degree, face the same problems in fighting high-rise fires. The Glass House itself, as the reader might expect, is a composite of many such buildings. And, of course, the characters of THE GLASS INFERNO exist only in our imaginations, and any resemblance to real people, living or dead, is not intentional.

We would like to thank Inspector James I. King of the San Francisco Fire Department, Architect Rob Hult and Researcher Gene Klinger for valuable technical information and for reading and commenting on the final manuscript. We are also indebted for specialized technical information and help to retired Fire Administrator Warren Pietro, Anchorman Bob Marshall of KGO-TV, helicopter pilot and Chief Warrant Officer Gerald W. Fisch, Attorney David Hodghead, and Marion Cole of the National Fire Protection Association. Special thanks for thoroughness go to our research assistants, Kathy Fast and Tom Passavant. Finally, a bow of appreciation to two very patient ladies: Jan McMillan, who often worked into the night hours on manuscript drafts, and our editor Diane Cleaver who, with others at Doubleday, was more than kind and helpful to us.

—Thomas N. Scortia and
Frank M. Robinson

Early

Evening

Every beast has a time and place of birth.

For the fire, it was late afternoon in a small room deep within one of the newer high rises that dotted the city. The room had purpose and importance—though it was never pointed out during the frequent tours of the building—and an indefinable odor, characteristic of rooms of its type. It was also a little more cluttered than the usual.

It was shortly after five o'clock when the door to the room opened; thereafter the overhead fluorescents flickered on. There was a long pause, the slight shuffling sounds of something being moved, then the snap of a switch as the lights extinguished. Eyes blinked in the glow from the open doorway, casually inspecting the room for a few seconds. Then shoulders briefly obscured the light from the corridor, the door closed, and the room lost itself in darkness.

But not total darkness. A small spark glowed in one corner of the room, nursed by a frayed cotton strand—the umbilical cord for the beast.

The temperature of the room was a little less than 70 degrees and starting to fall, mirroring the chill autumn air outside the building.

∽◦∽

1.

By four-thirty Wednesday afternoon, the long-expected Canadian cold front was passing north of the city. On Lee Avenue, the young saplings in front of the National Curtainwall Building, stripped of their autumn foliage, whipped violently against the surrounding wrought-iron grills. Low banks of clouds scudded across the sky and the fine rain turned into a biting sleet. Workmen, decorating the street lamps with plastic Santa Clauses, clutched desperately at their ladders as ice began to coat the rungs. Clerks and secretaries, dismissed early for the Thanksgiving holidays, deserted the middle of the sidewalk for the narrow safety offered by building fronts, or else scurried for the security of subway entrances, repeatedly losing their footing on the slick of water and melting ice.

Six blocks away, Craig Barton leaned impatiently against the steering wheel of his rented car and nervously chewed the end of an unlit cigarillo. The traffic had slowed to a halt and an occasional wisp of cold air seeped into the car's interior, cutting through the feeble warmth from the defective heater. The perfect ending for a lousy day, Barton thought. Stacked up over the airport for an hour, then a lemon for a driveaway, and finally the traffic jam as a capper. He couldn't get to the office now before everybody had left; there'd be no chance to double check on why Leroux had sent for him in the first place. He'd be walking in cold and Wyndom Leroux was no man to have a conference with if you were unprepared.

It wasn't going to be a pleasant evening in other ways either. Jenny had paged him at the airport to relay Leroux's sudden invitation to dinner and it was obvious that it hadn't set well with her—not that anything *did* set well with her these days. And if the dinner lasted long enough and the weather worsened, they'd probably wind up spending the night in a hotel instead of with Jenny's parents in nearby Southport. That was sure to bring tears

4

and recriminations from Jenny. It would never occur to her that he might have his own resentments about being called back to headquarters in the middle of delicate negotiations.

The light turned green and the crowds at the corner surged across the street, spreading out to thread their way through the close-packed automobiles. Darting in and out of the noisy tangle of traffic, like water beetles skimming across a crowded pond, messenger boys sped by on single-speed Schwinns, their baskets loaded with records, stacks of print-out sheets, and rolls of blueprints. For a second, Barton's nostrils flared at the memory of the faint ammonia odor of the prints, a smell that always excited him with its associated visions of buildings yet to be built.

He leaned forward, suddenly curious, and glanced out the window at the city's skyline. Even in six months, there had been changes. The Traveler's Building had been topped out and the Curtainwall was two thirds of the way up: psuedo-Mies van der Rohe inspiration that unfortunately didn't have the clarity of detailing that was the hallmark of a van der Rohe project. A hundred yards north, the new Fireman's Insurance Headquarters loomed in the sleet. It was a more sensitive structure, though the site itself was bad—so small that the building seemed crammed onto it and the plaza in front looked the size of a child's sandbox. The Kohnke Insurance Building next to it didn't help; it resembled a downtown motel more than an office building.

The lights changed again. Barton toed the accelerator and lurched forward another thirty yards across the intersection before he came to a stop. Now he could see the Glass House—the nickname for the National Curtainwall Building—a few blocks away, its tower etched against the dark clouds. He caught his breath. *God, it's beautiful!* He felt the same sudden sweep of pride that he had felt when he flew in for the dedication three months before —sans Jenny, much to her annoyance.

He clamped harder on the cigarillo and stared intently at the building. Damnit, he had a right to be proud—and so did Leroux. Sixty-six stories of gold-tinted glass panels and gold-anodized aluminum. The location on the north side of the financial district had been selected so there would be no buildings for several blocks around that could challenge it. There had been no compromise on the size of the site itself—the plazas on each side of the building were spacious and inviting; you didn't feel crowded as you strolled across them to the building's entrance. Sixty-six stories—thirty commercial and office floors and thirty-six of apartment floors—straight up with no setbacks. On the southern exposure, a shear wall marked the utility core and served as a golden backdrop for the scenic elevator to the Promenade Room at the top. Barton squinted; he could just make out the tiny spot of light crawling slowly up to the rooftop restaurant. They hadn't done too badly, he thought; the most popular post-cards in the local drugstores were those of the Glass House at night. It had become a symbol of the city.

The traffic was easing now and a few minutes later Barton was driving down the ramp that cut through one of the plazas into the basement garage. He caught a glimpse of the plaza just before the building overhang blocked his view—a broad expanse of buffed terrazzo and native fieldstone on which white ceramic planters holding young conifers were scattered. Wide fieldstone and terrazzo steps ascended to the lower lobby, curving around a gleaming, free-form sculpture of gold-anodized aluminum and Plexiglass rods. At night, the rods were the light pumps of multiple-colored bulbs hidden in the base so that the delicate webwork of rods and wires was bathed in a slowly changing pool of light.

He wheeled the car to the parking attendant's booth and stepped out into the welcome warmth of the building.

"How long you going to be, sir?" The car hiker slid into the seat he had just vacated.

"Not sure—probably until about eleven. Fill up the tank while you're at it, will you?"

"They sure don't do much for you at the airports these days, do they?"

"Hell, they don't even empty the ashtrays any more."

Barton walked past the gas pumps and caught the elevator up to the lower lobby. Just before the doors closed behind him, he heard the roar of a jack rabbit start and then the screech of tires. He smiled to himself; at least some things in the world never changed.

The lower concourse looked more finished than when he had last seen it. The shop windows glistened with displays of jade and Christmas cards, imported cameras, and stereo components. One display, intended for holiday vacationers, featured men's sport shirts and shorts in a riot of Hawaiian colors. Barton paused for a moment to look at them. Two years of working for National Curtainwall and he hadn't yet found time for the traditional two weeks in August. His resentment started to build; then he shrugged. Next year for sure, he promised himself, and stepped on the escalator to the main concourse.

Barton felt another wave of pride as he walked into the first-floor lobby; for a brief moment he felt like taking off his hat, as if he were in a cathedral. It didn't have the overwhelming vastness of the lobbies in the newer hotels, but it was still a superb utilization of space. The proportions of the floor area were almost classical in their relationship and the exterior tinted glass walls extending two stories up gave a feeling of openness. At the far end of the concourse stood the tall, bronze doors of Surety National while at the opposite end, jutting into the lobby itself, loomed the tiled mural walls of the square utility core that held the elevator banks and the numerous electric, steam, and gas lines that served the building. The scenic elevator pierced one side of the core near the entrance, soaring up the shear wall, the external face of the utility core, to the Promenade Room.

Barton recalled that Jenny had never ridden in it. He made a mental note to use it after dinner; the ride might take the edge off the evening for her. The elevator cage was darkened during its ascent or descent—the lights visible from the street were in the base—and the illusion of hanging suspended in space over the city below was breathtaking.

The lobby was filled with employees leaving for the

evening and for a moment Barton felt like a salmon swimming upstream. The office population of the building was close to three thousand and they all seemed to be trying to leave at once. The lights flicked off in Surety National, dimming that end of the lobby. He shoved his way through to the information desk opposite the bank of elevators that served the business floors. The dark-haired girl behind it, dressed in a chic gold-and-red uniform and wearing a little pill-box hat, looked vaguely reminiscent of "Johnny" in the old Philip Morris ads. She flashed him a stewardess-type smile.

"I'm sorry, sir, but the Promenade Room is booked solid for the evening."

Six months away and already he looked like a tourist, Barton thought.

"On a night like tonight?"

The smile became tentative; she was afraid he was going to be difficult. "It's the start of the holidays, sir, and we seem to be the 'in' spot in town." She tried to soften the blow. "Another night, perhaps?"

"I'm with Wyndom Leroux's party," Barton said shortly. "Did he leave any messages?"

She looked impressed and shuffled through the papers on the desk. "His reservation's not until eight o'clock but I don't see any messages. Is there anything . . . ?"

He turned away. "Thanks anyway." The best idea would be to drop his bag in the offices, freshen up, and head for the Promenade Room bar. He was almost to the elevator bank when he spotted Dan Garfunkel, the head of security, talking to a young guard. Garfunkel was a thick, heavy-set man in his fifties. He had spent twenty years with the police force and another ten with the Burns Detective Agency. He was dressed in a plain, dark suit, his only badge of office being the two-way radio attached to his belt on the left hip; there was no mistaking his position, however. Everything about him spelled out "cop," Barton thought. He was balding, with a thin fringe around the sides like a monk's tonsure, and had a beard so heavy that Barton guessed he shaved twice a day when he was on the job. He had a quiet, intense way of talk-

ing and was one of the few men whom Barton had ever
met who could chew somebody out in a whisper. He was
doing just that as Barton approached.

"I know it's not your shift but I'm short two men and
you're the last one on the roster, so that makes it your
baby. You don't like it, I'll find a cop who wants to
moonlight. Remember that the building officially closes
at six and you start to check ID's then. Any reservations
for the Promenade Room, send them over to Sue. Any
difficulties, call me on your two-way. Don't get smart with
the people, you're as much public relations as you are
security. And I don't want to hear any more complaints
about kids in the lobby."

The guard nodded, stony-faced, and walked away. Garfunkel stared coldly at Barton for a second and then a
mind that never forgot a face found an identification to
go along with it. He shook his head, relaxing. "He's a
good man—four years in the MP's—but I swear to God
nobody wants to work any more, Mr. Barton; they all
want a free ride. A little sleet and suddenly everybody's
sick or their car won't start or their great-grandmother
dropped in unexpectedly from Dubuque."

Barton looked sympathetic. "How shorthanded are
you?"

"A third of the shift didn't show—it was Sammy's
great-grandmother from Dubuque, believe it or not. Which
means I'll have to spend the evening in the monitoring
room, watching the idiot tubes with Yates. Helluva way
to handle security, especially with all the shoplifting,
burglary, and petty vandalism we've been having—Christ,
we even had a rape last month. I've been after the super
to install infrared sensors in the stairwells so we'll know
if we've got trespassers, but nobody wants to spend the
money."

"How's the leasing going?"

Garfunkel shook his head. "Almost all of the commercial and office floors are leased," he said, ticking them off
on his stubby fingers. "Fifty through sixty-four are still
nearly empty, though some of the suites aren't finished
yet—you should try and make the rounds through that

mess. And then there's this guy Quantrell and his broadcasts. He's really got it in for the boss and a lot of people watch him and get skittish. Me, I think Mr. Leroux ought to sue the bastard."

Barton had heard a little about Quantrell and his telecasts out in San Francisco. But mention of the apartment floors brought another thought to mind.

"How's Jernigan coming along?" Harry Jernigan had come from Burns along with Garfunkel. A handsome, athletic black in his early thirties, Jernigan was deputy head of security and responsible for the residential floors. Barton had met him once and the man's natural sense of dignity had impressed him.

Garfunkel smiled. "Harry's doing great, just great. Some of the older tenants called him 'boy' at first; then they found out he had a master's degree in fine arts and that ended that. A lot of the women give him the eye but he doesn't let it get to him. If they could see what he's got at home they'd all turn green. I feel sorry for Harry, though; he's got more relatives sponging off him than Standard has oil wells. He's a good man, Mr. Barton. If I ever left here . . ." He shrugged. "Yeah, and someday the meek will inherit the earth."

"Times are changing, Dan; he'll do okay."

"Maybe *you* think so and *I* think so but a lot of people out there, *they* don't think so. Otherwise, he would have been able to use that master's."

The lobby was emptying rapidly now. A few people milled before the information desk, checking on reservations. A group of cleaning women, most of them Puerto Rican, waited by the elevators, chattering away in soft Spanish. Garfunkel left to start his security rounds; Barton picked up his bag and walked over to the elevator bank. He nodded to one of the women whom he had met while working overtime during the dedication: Albina Obligado, a graying woman with a startling amount of gold in her white teeth. She was so pleasantly Earth Mother that he felt a small pleasure at seeing her again.

One of the elevators emptied out and the cleaning women crowded in, Albina holding the doors open for

Barton. He signaled for her to go ahead and pressed the call button for the end cab. Then something about the marble cladding around the elevator bank caught his eye. The grout around the slabs was already crumbling. Sloppy workmanship, he thought, irritated. Then he frowned and took a closer look. It wasn't real marble after all but a polyester synthetic. He'd never noticed it before, but then the synthetics were excellent visual copies. Still, he was damned sure it wasn't what the architectural team responsible for the interiors had called for. Somewhere along the line, somebody had been sold a bill of goods.

Another man joined him at the elevator and Barton nodded. One of the early commercial tenants whom he knew slightly; he and his partner ran an interior decorating shop on the floor below National Curtainwall's executive offices. Brian—no, Ian—Douglas, a large man who always seemed to dress a shade too elegantly for his size; he was the type who had probably been a swimmer in college and was now tending to softness. About forty-five, Barton decided, a good ten years older than his partner, whose name Barton couldn't recall.

"Lousy night," Barton said idly.

Douglas started. "Oh, yes, dreadful," he mumbled. He didn't say anything more and Barton decided something was on his mind. Business was probably bad and he was working late after having gone out for a quick supper. Too bad, if that were the case. Barton rather liked the big man, though his younger partner seemed a little self-consciously . . . what did they call it, "butch"? Well, everybody had their hang-ups.

The elevator doors slid silently open and they stepped in. Barton punched 18 for his floor and 17 for Douglas. The doors had just started to close when suddenly a tall, rail-thin man in a wrinkled janitor's uniform hurried toward them. "Hold it, fellas—hold it, will ya!"

Barton stuck out his foot to intercept the photoelectric-eye beam at the bottom of the elevator doors. They slid open again and the thin man scurried in, still puffing. "Thanks a lot, Mr. Barton."

"Any time, Krost," Barton said indifferently. He had

never liked Michael Krost, who was maintenance super-visor for five of the office floors, including those of National Curtainwall. A sour-looking, middle-aged man with a thick head of coarse, graying hair, there was a furtiveness about him that put Barton on edge. Word had it that Krost was a lush and had once been caught drink-ing on the job. For some reason, Leroux had interceded to save him. Probably for old time's sake, Barton thought. Krost had come over from the Melton Building where National Curtainwall had been headquartered until they moved into the Glass House.

"Sure good to have you back aboard, Mr. Barton," Krost said. "Just the other night I was telling Daisy that you were out there on the West Coast showing them how a big architect and a construction team operate. Mr. Leroux must think a lot of you to send you out on a project like that."

Douglas retreated to the far end of the elevator to avoid the odor of stale beer and faintly mildewed clothing that hung around Krost like a fog. Barton ignored it. "What floor, Krost?"

"Make it twenty for me, Mr. Barton." Yellow teeth showed through in a thin smile. "Got to ride herd on them cleaning women up there, yes sir."

The cab stopped at seventeen and Douglas got out, obviously grateful to get away from Krost. Then it was Barton's turn, Krost shouting after him: "Daisy and I, we both hope you have a good weekend, Mr. Barton!"

National Curtainwall's offices occupied the entire floor, as well as a portion of the two above it. The entrance to the executive suites was at the far end and normally one ran the gamut of three secretaries before entering. Tonight, all the anterooms were deserted. Barton shucked out of his topcoat and draped it on the tree before enter-ing the inner suite. A few lights glared in the Credit Union area, as well as some of the other offices. He might luck out and run into somebody with some solid information after all, he thought hopefully. The Credit Union people, of course, would be working on accounts. NC employed close to five hundred people in the local offices alone and a lot of them must have withdrawn money or cashed paychecks for the long weekend.

Barton snapped on the lights in his office, dropped his small suitcase on the floor, and stepped over to the window to stare out at the darkening city, half hidden by clouds and pelting sleet. They'd be spending the night in a hotel for sure; he wouldn't drive out to Southport after supper for all the tea in China. And it might be a good time to talk to Jenny, to set some things right that had been going very wrong these last two years.

He loosened his tie and hung his suit coat in the small office closet; then he started down the hall to see who might still be around. Lights glowed in the architects' division. He walked into the first office, knocking on the door as he entered.

"You ought to be home watching the tube, Joe, how come so late?" he asked. Joe Moore had left Wexler and Haines the same time he had and was one of the few men at NC with whom Barton felt genuinely comfortable, probably because he wasn't a company man. Five years younger than himself, Moore was a crackerjack architect whose only character flaw—if it could be considered a flaw—was that he preferred to spend his evenings bowling and his Saturday afternoons golfing rather than putting in overtime doing and dying for dear old Curtainwall. It wasn't a lack of ambition, but rather a sense of proportion about life, an attitude that Barton admired.

Moore shifted his chair away from the drawing board so Barton could see better. "Leroux's new brainstorm. Take a look."

Barton glanced over his shoulder at a superb color rendering of a new high rise. "It's for a site in St. Louis. The property was acquired and cleared last year and next month they start excavating for the foundation." Moore paused. "Once they start, it should go pretty fast in spite of the weather."

There was something in his voice that made Barton bend closer to the board. It was a beautiful building, he thought; it would be a credit to any city. Then he felt the back of his neck go red.

"You know," Moore said slowly, "it's the same kind of similarity you find in housing developments where all the homes are built from the same master plan and only the exterior trim and the details differ—the garage is on the left side instead of the right or maybe there's a car porch instead. Why shouldn't St. Louis have a Glass House? Color it blue instead of gold, put the scenic elevator on the northern exposure, make a few minor changes in the curtainwall . . ."

"The industry would laugh at him," Barton said in a flat voice.

"You think so? Start figuring the savings, the speed in construction. You practically eliminate the architectural expense. You know most of the problems in advance—you crank them out like the houses in a subdivision. He'll be selling a beautiful building at a cut-rate price and he'll still make a killing in time savings alone."

"You're not kidding me?"

"That rendering cost five grand, that's no joke."

"He doesn't need a renderer, he needs a retoucher." Barton felt feverish. "Leroux knows I won't go for this."

"Maybe he thinks he can sweet talk you."

"On something like this?" Barton was outraged. "Come on, Joe!" He sat down on a nearby chair. "Who's supposed to be the chief architect?"

Moore was silent for a moment, staring down at the rendering, then looked directly up at him. His voice was flat. "It came with a promotion and a title and a lot of money. I couldn't turn it down."

"You won't be doing any drafting," Barton said contemptuously. "You'll be making tracings."

Moore kept a poker face. "If it helps any Beth's been sick and I really need that money. Leroux's always resented that I wasn't one of his boys, then he saw his chance and made his move. So now I'm his—body, soul, and talent, come rain, shine, or the Inverness Open."

There wasn't anything to say, Barton thought. Moore had to play the hand that was dealt him, he didn't have any choice.

Moore fumbled for a cigarette. "How's Jenny?"

"Okay. She flew in yesterday, stayed with the Lerouxes last night, and spent today shopping with Thelma. We're having dinner in the Promenade Room at eight. Command performance."

"She'll hate that."

"I expect I'll hear all about it." Barton thumbed the rendering. "What does the old man want to see me about? This?"

"He'll probably mention it but I don't think it's the real reason. Ever hear of a TV newscaster named Quantrell?"

"Garfunkel told me about him downstairs."

"He's running an exposé series on Leroux and the Glass House. It's too popular."

Barton felt puzzled. "What's that got to do with me? I don't know the man, I've never met him, I've never even seen his show. What's the deal?"

Moore spread his hands out in appeal. "Look, all I know is what I hear. You were good friends with the first assistant fire chief, Mario Infantino, right? He's also a division chief, right? You used to sit it on fire-code meetings with him, right? And you and he buddied during army reserve meetings back here, right?"

"So?"

"Leroux thinks that Infantino is feeding Quantrell information about National Curtainwall—confidential information."

Barton stared. "I still don't get it. One, Mario wouldn't do it and two, where would he get the information?"

"I guess that's why Leroux wants to talk to you," Moore said quietly. "Or so the rumors go."

"You've got my sympathy on Beth," Barton said stiffly. "Thanks for the gossip—don't work too late." He stood up and walked down the hall to the executive washroom, ignoring Moore's shouts behind him. He needed cold water, a lot of it.

For a moment, the room took his mind off himself. It was a sybaritic dream, the Florentine marble and gilded wrought-iron basin fixtures in the shape of dolphins, plus a solid wall of mirrors. It was the sort of john that

Douglas would probably have designed, Barton thought, then smiled at his own prejudice.

He turned the taps to run water into the basin, thinking of what he might say when he saw Leroux later. When he had first met Leroux, he had been chief architect for Wexler and Haines; the Glass House had been their account. He had liked Leroux and had deliberately impressed him with his knowledge of architecture and construction techniques. Leroux had offered him a junior vice-presidency in National Curtainwall. He had accepted and at the same time had broken up with Quinn Reynolds to court and marry Jenny, whom he had met several months before and with whom he had fallen in love.

It now looked like he had made a mistake, he thought grimly. Two of them. He cupped the cold water in his hands and sloshed his face with it, coming up gasping.

His major disappointment had been that he hadn't been given the chance to oversee the construction crews on the Glass House, that Leroux had not appointed him site supervisor. Instead, Leroux had transferred him to Boston for a year and a half and then to San Francisco to make a preliminary survey for a high rise to be built in the wharf area near the Embarcadero freeway. It was a tricky assignment, not only because of the building code problems attendant to any construction near the San Andreas fault, but also because of growing civic opposition to high rises. Then Leroux had called him two days ago, in the middle of his preparations for an appearance before the Board of Supervisors. He had to see Barton as soon as possible about various vague problems. It wasn't like Leroux and something in his voice had made Barton uneasy.

He dried his hands and face and adjusted his tie in the mirror. The face that stared back shocked him. The graying at the temples, the slight puffiness to the jowls, the faint lines etching themselves around the eyes . . . He was thirty-eight and no amount of squash playing at the club, no number of steam baths seemed to take away the slight sag to the chin line, the faint pudginess that was slowly softening the trim outline of his body. Even Jenny—or perhaps, especially Jenny—had remarked on the change in him.

On the other hand, Leroux was made for the business; he thrived on it. He was in his early sixties and looked fifty. He claimed to be a self-made man, though Barton doubted that; somewhere in his background there was a prep school or an eastern college. But the self-made bit fit his own myth as a drifter who worked in the oil fields of Louisiana, then married Thelma, and bought her father's construction firm on an extended note. It had been a small company but with Leroux at the helm, it had grown rapidly. He branched out into general contracting and formed National Curtainwall when he built a small high rise in downtown Raleigh after the end of the Korean war. And now Leroux was on his way to becoming . . . what?

And what about himself? Barton thought. The problem was simple. He wanted to be his own boss; he didn't want his buildings stolen from him. *So what was he going to do about it?*

He felt the anger rise in him, shrugged if off, and walked back to his office. It was five minutes to six, too early even to go to the Promenade Room to get drunk enough so he would have the guts to do something he could be sorry about later.

He turned on the television set on top of the office bookcase, sat back in his swivel chair and lit up another cigarillo. The news would be coming up at six o'clock. Now was his chance to watch Quantrell and see what all the shouting was about.

2.

Jeffrey Quantrell leaned forward in his seat and said, "Look, cabbie, if you can't make it any faster than this, then drop me off in front of the Towers rather than at the side entrance; I'm late now."

"Sure thing, Mr. Quantrell—it's all this holiday traffic, a lot of people have been let out early."

Jeffrey Quantrell leaned back, letting the heavy fur collar of his coat cradle his head and neck. It wasn't everybody in town who would be recognized by their cab driver, he thought; one of the advantages of having a six- and an eleven-o'clock time slot—and something to say on it. KYS-TV was great for fame, if not so good when it came to fortune.

The cab braked to a halt in front of Clairmont Towers, its tires sliding for an instant before they found new purchase. Small puddles of water were freezing on the asphalt and the sidewalk. The holly wreaths decorating the main entrance of the Towers had already grown inch-long fingers of ice.

Quantrell shivered, pulled his hat low over his ears, and threw open the taxi door. He thrust a bill at the driver, yelled "Keep it!" and slammed the door behind him. For a moment he fought for a footing against the wind and the driving sleet, then sprinted for the entrance, skidding every few feet on the sidewalk slick. He made it to the revolving door and pushed his way in, his glasses immediately fogging in the warmth of the building.

"Helluva night, isn't it, Mr. Quantrell?" Frank, the ancient newsboy just inside the entrance, had his paper ready for him. Quantrell grabbed it, tucked it under his arm, and flipped him a quarter. "Yeah, it sure is," he said and ran for the express elevator, pushing the button repeatedly with his thumb. He could probably run up the stairs faster, he thought. He fumbled in his pocket for a handkerchief and dabbed at his glasses, only succeeding in smearing them by the time the elevator doors opened. The studios of KYS-TV occupied the thirtieth floor, with the affiliated AM and FM stations taking up the floor below. The Clairmont Towers itself was forty stories high, with the penthouse the private warren of William Glade Clairmont, the elderly millionaire who owned both the building and the stations, as well as a dozen other enterprises throughout the state.

Quantrell left the elevator and plunged down the hall toward the newsroom, ignoring the greetings from the people he passed. He was in no mood to be sociable, particularly with fellow workers who, he knew, had no special love for him anyway. Well, you never got ahead by playing nice guy, he thought. Success bred its resentments; the supporting cast almost always resented the star.

The newsroom was the typical bull-pen madhouse of jammed-together desks, a dozen typewriters chattering away, a few monitor screens mounted halfway up the wall, and little cubicles off to one side for the anchormen and a few top investigative reporters like himself. That had been the first battle he had won at KYS. To him, covering the news meant more than filling out a film information sheet and then having some editor/producer write his story and an anchorman do the wrap-around while he himself might appear on screen for all of thirty seconds. He had won a position as an investigative reporter and the minor skirmishes fought since had established the relative freedom with which he could work. He had won all his battles, he thought proudly, dating back to the days when he had worked for the local station in Tuscaloosa, covering Governor Wallace barring the doors of the university during the early days of integration.

Christ, there had been casualties along the way, he reflected. He was now one of the most hated—and respected—men in the business. But this time he wasn't fighting a battle; he was fighting a war. When it was over, he would have bested one of the largest businessmen in the city, built up the ratings of the station until they topped anyone else's in the state, and put himself in line for a network anchorman spot.

He took off his hat and shook the ice and water off on the floor, then unbelted his coat and hung it on the hook that was reserved for him only—the sole fringe benefit that KYS offered.

"Hey, Quantrell, if you want to play the abominable snowman, why don't you go back outside? How would you like it if I clouded up and rained all over your copy?"

He deliberately gave his coat an extra shake, murmured, "Sorry, Ed," and sauntered over to the small, glassed-in office with the news tickers. Outside of the weather, there was no major story on the wires, which meant that his series might be allotted even more time than usual. Fine, he certainly had enough to fill it.

He poured himself a cup of coffee, tasted it and found it bitter, then added a heavy helping of cream, despite what it might mean in the long run to his lean and hungry image on camera. He was staring moodily into his cup and mentally rearranging his thoughts for the program, when Sandy came in with the script that he had dictated earlier over the phone.

"All through," she said brightly. "Should I give a copy to Bridgeport?"

"Sandy," he said quietly, "executive producers have no authority to censor my scripts. Since they don't have the authority, there's not much sense in showing them a copy, is there?" She had a date for tonight, he thought; she had ladled on the eyeshadow like mustard on a bun.

"Going out?" he asked softly.

She hesitated at the door, looking at him with the same combination of attraction and revulsion that he imagined a bird felt for a snake. "I had sort of a tentative date after the eleven-o'clock news," she admitted nervously.

It wasn't that he found her attractive, Quantrell thought. Like most small women in their late twenties she had already acquired a slight double chin that would broaden in another few years to give her a baby-doll look. But she was infatuated with him and he knew she hated and despised herself because she couldn't help it. In any event, she was much too valuable for him to let her go so easily. "That's too bad, Sandy, I was hoping we might have a bite together after the broadcast." He shrugged. "If it's important, please keep it; I don't want to be accused of being a Cupid killer."

She fought with herself for a long moment and he watched the struggle with clinical interest. Finally she said in a low voice, "I could probably get out of it, have a headache . . . something like that."

He looked grateful but not too much so. "Thanks a lot,

Sandy, I really appreciate it." He resolved to pay more attention to her in the future. It was always useful to have a personal hold on his female assistants, and Sandy was certainly one of the more efficient ones he'd had in the past few years. She heard all the rumors practically before they started and several times in the past he had managed to head off political brouhahas with the staff simply because of her advance knowledge of what was happening. He hoped the date hadn't been serious; now was no time to lose his Girl Friday in a hearts-and-flowers routine.

"Did Infantino call?" he asked.

She looked surprised. "Did you expect him to?"

"Yes," he said thoughtfully, "I did." He had phoned earlier for some information on the fire codes and had expected Infantino to call back.

"I can get him at home. He's off shift now."

"Don't bother. With his kids whooping it up in the background, it'd be like trying to discuss existential philosophy in a boiler room." Besides, he thought, for what he had in mind, it would be just as effective if First Assistant Chief Mario Infantino could not be reached for comment.

He glanced quickly through the script, made a few notations on it, then pulled a sheaf of notes from his pocket, and handed them to her. "Those are last-minute inserts; you want to type me up a clean copy? I'll need the final in half an hour."

She ruffled through the notes. "That's quite a bit."

"Sandy, when have you ever let me down?" He gave her hand a gentle squeeze.

She started to leave, then suddenly turned. "Oh—Mr. Bridgeport is looking for you."

"I'll bet he is," Quantrell murmured. Herb Bridgeport was the station's news editor as well as the executive producer of Quantrell's show, a soft, pudgy man who lived in mortal terror of a frown from the station manager or a bolt of lightning from the Olympian heights of W. G. Clairmont's penthouse. A frightened man, Quantrell thought with contempt, which was the whole problem with television news these days. Too many so-called reporters who were satisfied to be collectors of handouts and press releases, commentators on second-hand information. Very few newsmen conceived of their jobs in terms of investigative reporting. Which was where he was unique. He had seen the need for it within the framework of television news coverage and had managed to outline his ideas to old man Clairmont himself. Clairmont had been intrigued, and Quantrell had been assigned a small staff and budget and given carte blanche to roam the city and dig up stories. It was paying off for the station now —and, in particular, it was paying off for him. The dailies had even dubbed his small group of legmen "Quantrell's Raiders." Catchy phrase, he could do a lot with it at some future date.

He glanced at his watch. Time to make-up and shave before he went on the air. He took the electric razor from the bottom drawer of his desk and headed for the washroom. His beard was heavy and he always liked to shave just before a broadcast. If he didn't, the slight shadow of beard gave his thin features a sinister and devious look. He guided the buzzing head of the shaver over his jowls and quickly reviewed the more important points of his evening broadcast, occasionally making subvocal sounds as he turned a particularly pleasing phrase. It was the right profession for him, that was certain, Quantrell thought. Possessed of a deep, resonant voice and a wry humor to his delivery, he also had the knack for ferreting out the people who always seemed to know where the bodies were buried. In the case of the Glass House, it was Will Shevelson, the former construction foreman who had been axed two thirds of the way through the final construction period and who hated Leroux's guts. And then, of course, there was Infantino himself. A man with a mission, he thought—the kind who was most dangerous to himself. Infantino was bucking the whole Fire Department establishment; all he had to do was keep shooting off his mouth to reporters and in another month he'd be back to being a hose jockey.

Quantrell scrubbed at the patch of hair under his chin,

noting with displeasure that the fold of flesh just under the bone was becoming a shade too thick. He always photographed too full-faced, which meant that he had to diet constantly to maintain the hollows in his cheeks and the intense angularity to his face. Camera make-up took only a minute.

He finished and slipped into his shirt, carefully knotting his broad-patterned tie. Conservative mod, he thought; youthful, without forcing the youth image. The viewers liked it; it made him look very much one of the "now" generation, whatever that might be. He ran his comb carefully through his hair, wishing he had a hair dryer here in the washroom, then flicked off the fluorescent mirror lights.

Ten minutes before air time. He stepped from the washroom and almost ran into Bridgeport. The chubby man was breathless. "Jeff, I've got to talk to you."

"Later, it's almost air time."

"The old man's very concerned," Bridgeport insisted, almost tearful.

"Catch me after the broadcast," Quantrell said coldly. "I don't have the time now." He walked off, wondering if Bridgeport might have seen the script. Not likely; Sandy wouldn't cross him. If she had turned it over to him, Bridgeport would be one helluva lot more disturbed than he actually was. For a moment, Quantrell felt a twinge of pity for the man. He produced Quantrell's show but had gradually lost his authority to censor Quantrell's scripts. It was a slap in the face for Bridgeport and caused him endless worry. This was one time when it should, Quantrell thought.

He reached in his pocket and realized he had left his cigarette lighter beside the washbasin. He went back in and picked it up, his mind flashing back to the ceremony when he was leaving Greenville, South Carolina, after a two-year stint at the boondock station and management had presented him with it. It was a handsome lighter. He thumbed it and lit his cigarette, then watched the dancing flame for a moment.

Flames. He turned and looked out the window of the

washroom toward the Glass House, a thin shaft of gold against the lowering sky. That was it, he thought, the key to a network spot. He raised the flickering light and sighted along it at the distant building. One plus one, he thought, the simplest of all equations.

Suddenly he could hear Sandy outside the door. "Five minutes, Jeff."

For another moment he looked at the flame and past it, at the distant tower of the Glass House.

"Right on," he said softly.

3.

Mario Infantino felt on edge. Even the smell of minestrone and roast beef that seeped out of the kitchen didn't make him feel any more at ease. A dozen minutes until the six-o'clock news and five would get you ten that tonight would be the blowoff. Quantrell had been building up to something for the past two weeks; hardly a day had gone by that he didn't call, despite the fact that Mario had kept recommending that he contact public relations. Mario had been glad to talk to him at first, even in front of the cameras that had tracked him down to one or two small fires. But the way it was coming out on the air had made him look publicity hungry and things were strained enough in the department as it was.

He punched Channel 4 on the TV set and settled back to watch the tag end of a movie that preceded the news. At the sound from the set, three boys came boiling out of a distant bedroom and raced into the living room. "Hey, Dad, can I watch *The Far West?* Can I?"

"Dad, I don't wanna watch *Far West,* you promised last week I could see *Hanrahan, Private Eye!*"

"He didn't, he said I could watch *Galactic Rover!*"

Infantino sighed. Down at the firehouse, where his division headquarters was based, he often referred to his sons as "the menagerie" and kept telling David Lencho, a rookie hoseman in his company, how it was a full-time job to "tame the menagerie." Lencho dreamed of getting married and Infantino delighted in describing the horrors of raising a family to him. It wasn't that he didn't love the boys. There were just those nights when he would have been perfectly willing to auction them off on the block. Tonight was one of them.

"Look, kids, none of you are going to watch anything —I'm going to look at the news. You want to see something, turn on the set in the playroom in the basement."

"But it's black and white!"

Jerry, the oldest, mumbled something about Quantrell, and Infantino caught his arm in a tight grip. "You use that kind of language in front of your mother, young man, and I'll guarantee you won't be able to sit down for a week." The boy winced and Infantino let go, suddenly ashamed of himself. He was tired, he thought, too tired. "Doris!" he yelled.

She came in from the kitchen, wiping her hands and brushing damp strands of hair out of her eyes.

"Doris, get your kids out of here, I want to watch the news."

She shooed them into the basement, then said, "They're all mine? You didn't have anything to do with it?"

He laughed. "Okay, okay—I was half responsible. When do we eat?"

"Right now." She glanced at the set and her eyes strayed to the clock on the mantel. "I can set up the TV tables and we can eat in here; the kids can serve themselves."

Infantino nodded. "Why don't we do that; I want to see what the bastard has to say tonight."

She looked concerned. "Did he phone you again today?"

"Yeah, but I wouldn't take the call."

"I wish you hadn't taken any of them."

He glanced up at her, annoyed. "Don't start in on me, Doris; don't you think I wish the same?" She squeezed his shoulder lightly and went to the basement steps to announce that dinner was ready. That was something else Quantrell had screwed up for him, Infantino thought. He liked dinner at home—there were few enough that he had away from the firehouse—with all the kids sitting around the table, noisy as they usually were, and Doris bringing in huge plates of pasta from the kitchen or her own special lamb stew, which he never ceased to brag about. There was something about Doris, small and efficient in her crisp apron and with just a touch of make-up, that he found highly arousing. The movie stars were for somebody else, he liked to think; show him a woman who could keep a house and raise the kids and still not let herself fall apart and she was for him—you could have all the rest.

Now supper was a different affair, noisy but hurried if it was before the six-o'clock news, and slow and usually deadly quiet if it was after. There was a special tension during the dinner hour and Infantino resented it and blamed Quantrell for it.

Doris set up the TV tables and he started to nibble at his food as the parade of news slowly passed by. And then Quantrell appeared on the screen with that look of special concern that his viewers found so charming and heartwarming.

"I don't think he really gives a damn at all," Doris said in a low voice.

"Doris, please."

On the screen, Quantrell started with a statistical approach, supported by a series of graphs flashed on a board behind him. The population of an average high rise during the working day, the difficulty of evacuating so many people down the stairwells in case of a fire, the hazards of using the elevators, the fire dangers from modern furnishings, and the impossibility of policing what tenants might bring into a building. Some film clips of fires in South America and Japan, including one particularly terrifying segment on the high-rise fire in São Paulo, Brazil. Then it was time for a commercial break and Quantrell's request to stay tuned in because the next five minutes would be devoted to a story proving that if some of the developers in the city were not above the law, neither were they incapable of changing it.

"You haven't touched your dinner, Mario."

"I'm not hungry."

"Is what he says true?"

Infantino nodded slowly. "I wish it weren't but it is. I'd give a lot to be able to say he was lying."

And then Quantrell was back again, this time standing in front of a huge blowup of the Glass House.

"People have accused me of picking on the building you see behind me. They maintain that there are dozens of high rises throughout the city which are inherently fireproof shells that have been filled with enough combustibles to turn them into tinderboxes. And they're absolutely right—the city has dozens, hundreds, of such buildings. There are measures, of course, that can be taken. One is an extensive sprinkler system. But sprinkler systems are frequently unpopular with tenants because they're unsightly and unpopular with builders because they're expensive. Some progressive builders have nevertheless installed sprinkler systems throughout, perhaps in return for lower insurance rates. But our local building codes do not require a building to be completely sprinklered and until they do, competition will deprive most high-rise tenants of that protection.

"The Department of Building and Safety, however, is not completely blind to the hazards of high-rise fires and the fire codes have other requirements that builders have to follow; granted that adherence in these codes is often a matter between the local contractor and the building inspector. The vast majority of inspectors are honest men who are paid relatively small salaries for the work they do. But it would be too much to expect all of them to be above temptation. However, the construction of the tall buildings that dot our skyline involves huge amounts of money, and big money frequently has methods of getting its own way besides the obvious but crude one of bribery.

"For instance, consider the city code requirement that all buildings above a certain height have stairwells that are pressurized to keep out smoke and thus serve as a safe, interior fire escape for tenants. This is a vital, relatively cheap protection for the occupants of our skyscrapers. Listen to what Mario Infantino has to say about them. Mr. Infantino is the youngest and most knowledge-able of our city's division fire chiefs as well as first assis-tant chief fire engineer."

Infantino cursed and felt Doris' hand on his shoulder. Quantrell had faded from the screen, to be replaced by Infantino's own image in a street interview that had been taped weeks before. He leaned forward to catch the words of his television alter ego.

". . . Well, of course, the pressurized stairwell is an obvious and straightforward approach to confining the spread of smoke during a high-rise fire. It offers invalu-able protection to the tenants of such buildings at a minimal cost. As a protective device, it's probably next in importance only to sprinkler systems—and in buildings that are only partially sprinklered, it may be even more important for the safety of the average tenant."

Quantrell's image reappeared on the screen.

"It may come as a shock to our viewers that the build-ing code requirement requiring pressurized stairwells was repealed by the City Council shortly after construction began on the Glass House, well after its building permits had been issued. Coincidence? Perhaps."

Behind him appeared an architect's drawing of a por-tion of the Glass House. The date under the National Curtainwall logo was quite clear.

"These drawings from the earliest design period for the Glass House show that the plans never included a pressurized stairwell, despite the fact that at the time National Curtainwall's architects were designing the Glass House, our building codes clearly required such stairwells. Prior knowledge that this requirement would no longer exist when the building was finished? A wish? A mere hope? The management of National Curtainwall, as usual, had nothing to say. Nobody at City Hall seemed to know the answer. And when we called the Fire Department, the usually knowledgeable Division Fire Chief Mario Infantino could not be reached for comment.

"Nevertheless, the conclusion is inescapable that some-body knew. We repeat: Big money is a law unto itself;

it has a way of writing its own codes. Good night and may God watch over all of us—particularly those of you who live high in the sky."

Infantino stalked over to the set and abruptly switched it off. "He's a goddamned muckraker. That was just a warning to me—play ball or I get tarred with the same brush he's using on everybody else. I wasn't ducking his question, I was just ducking him. Everything I say to the bastard gets twisted."

"He's causing trouble between you and Chief Fuchs, isn't he?"

Infantino shrugged. "He's not helping any. Fuchs thinks I'm trying an end run behind his back. I don't know what the hell he'll think after tonight."

"Don't talk to that TV man at all then," Doris said pragmatically. "What you don't say can't hurt you."

Infantino shook his head, exasperated. "As far as opening my mouth goes, it's damned if I do and damned if I don't. I've been an idiot, I've said too much in the past. If I clam up now, it'll look as if the department has muzzled me, or worse yet, that I've been bought off."

There were sudden noises from the basement and the three boys came boiling back into the living room; the program they had finally settled on was over. In a moment they began to roughhouse, rolling around on the floor and bumping against Infantino's chair.

"Look, kids, I've got a lot on my mind—how about taking it easy on your old man?"

"It's not too early for bedtime," Doris warned.

There was a sudden silence and then a plaintive "But tomorrow's a holiday!"

"All right," she said. "You can go back down and watch for another hour—but only on condition that you don't bother your mother and father."

"We promise!" And they were gone like wind-blown leaves back into the basement.

Infantino sank back in his chair, shaking his head. "My God, I don't think I can stand the silence."

Doris suddenly came over and sat on his lap. "I think the dishes can wait," she half whispered. He wrapped her small waist in his thick arms and pulled her to him, delighting in the softness of her body against the muscles of his midsection. Her hair was moist against his face, still smelling faintly of the perfume in the hair spray she used. He buried his face in it, breathing in the scent, and then his hands were moving gently over her body as they kissed.

"The children," Doris said quietly.

"They won't bother us for an hour, you know that. You sent them away, remember?"

She laughed and he kissed her on the ear and then on the mouth, then gathered her in his arms and stood up. She was light and warm and moved gently against him as he carried her into the bedroom. She kicked off her shoes as they entered and shoved the door closed behind them. He let her down on the bed and then lay down beside her, running his fingers through her hair. She seemed so small and fragile against his bulk, too small to have borne him three boys, he thought.

They touched and quickly the ritual of removing clothing, undoing each other's buttons and snaps and zippers, pausing every now and then to kiss and hold each other. He was terribly excited now, part of the thrill being the slow, tender way they went about touching each other, each of them enjoying the delicious tension of anticipation.

Later, when they were unclothed and he was making love to her in the darkness of the bedroom, he thought how very lucky he was. For a second, Quantrell intruded on his thoughts and he wondered how the newscaster had obtained the architect's drawing, how he had known about the possible code violation. Then all thoughts of Quantrell faded from his mind and Mario Infantino lowered himself into his wife, his muscular body spasming in her arms as her nails raked light streaks through the sweat that coated his back and buttocks.

4.

"I think that's the most ego*tis*tical man I've ever seen," Rosette said. "Know what I mean, Harry? He really thinks he's something when he's in front of that camera!"

Harry Jernigan was about to answer when a red light lit up on the switchboard behind him and he picked up the phone. "Security, Jernigan here." He listened for a moment, made a wry face at Rosette, and said into the mouthpiece, "No, ma'am, there are no fire escapes on the outside of this building. In case of emergency, stay in your room until we notify you or take the plainly marked fire stairs at the end of the corridor. No, ma'am, don't take the elevator. Yes, I know it's forty-seven floors." He winced. "No trouble at all, ma'am."

He put the phone down and Rosette leaned over the counter, her maid's blouse stretching taut across her breasts. "Somebody else was watching besides us, huh?" Jernigan turned off the small portable TV and put it on the floor behind his counter, out of sight. It had been a slow night and for the first time he had been able to take in all of Quantrell's broadcast without being interrupted or having to hide the set while he played Mr. Cool. *"Everybody* else was watching. That was Mrs. Klinger in 4710. She wants to know how come we don't have fire escapes." He shook his head. "The more money they've got, Rosie, the less brains they have to go along with it."

"I want to know what you thought, Harry." Something in her voice told him the broadcast had worried her.

"What did I think? I thought he was a bastard, same as you did." Jernigan had a possessive feeling about the Glass House and resented criticism of it from outsiders. "Why the hell pick on us? There must be a dozen buildings in the city, a hundred, that are real firetraps and he keeps pointing the finger at this one." He shrugged, irritated. "It's got to be a pay-off of some kind."

31

Rosette looked at him shrewdly. "You believed some of it, huh?"

Jernigan leaned back in his chair, his hands clasped behind his head. "Yes and no. In some ways, Rosie, he doesn't know the half of it. If I were to wander around some of the unfinished floors, for example, you sure as hell wouldn't catch me smoking any cigarettes."

"You ever been in some of the furnished apartments?" She looked thoughtful. "It must be nice to have the money to buy all that furniture and the drapes and the woolly rugs that some folks got, but if that guy on the tube is right, all you'd have to do is drop one match and *foof*, it'd all go up." She cocked her head at him. "Harry, if there should ever be a fire here, how in the hell would you get out? I'm serious, the reason I'm asking is I keep wondering how the hell *I* would get out."

"You'd get out the same way I'd get out, Rosie—you'd walk out. Look, you fly airplanes, don't you?"

"You know I got a brother in Nashville and I visit him every couple of months."

"What would you do if something happened to the airplane?"

She grinned. "Why, I'd just flap my wings and fly on home alone."

"Well, you could do the same thing here—you're high enough up. Now be quiet, I don't want to talk about it any more." Mrs. Klinger hadn't been the only one who called him for evacuation instructions. Every time Quantrell was on the air, he'd get a couple of phone calls from tenants wondering how they'd get out if anything should happen. And wondering how they'd get out was just one step removed from moving out.

"How's Marnie?"

He looked up at her sharply. "You've got nothing to do but stand around and talk?"

Her eyes were innocent. "It's the Thanksgiving holidays and I'm off duty—so you're right, I've got nothing to do but stand around and talk. How's Marnie?"

"Fine, keping busy—not like some people I know."

"Leroy still call you the house nigger?"

Jernigan's lips thinned. Leroy was his younger brother, a college dropout, who had dropped in with a militant group and now spent most of his time hanging around the Black Knights bar a block from the house, daydreaming about what he'd do to Whitey when the revolution came. Cursing Whitey out also included not working for him or even applying for unemployment compensation. Jernigan remembered with some satisfaction the night he'd set the table with pumpernickel instead of white bread and Leroy's muttered complaints until he suddenly got the idea and left the table boiling mad.

"He hasn't changed much."

Rosette looked sympathetic. "How about Melvin and his wife?" Melvin was a few years older than Leroy and didn't have his hang-ups but was still a born loser when it came to finding work. His unemployment checks had run out three months before, though his wife, Estella, almost made up for it—she had a job as a secretary downtown and helped Marnie with the kids and the cooking.

"Yeah, Melvin's still there, too." Jernigan took a brief call and then turned back to Rosette. "You forgot to ask about Jimmie."

"He hates your guts—"

"—and wouldn't be caught dead living with me if I was the only relative he had. Thank God for small favors."

There was the slight sound of elevator doors *whooshing* quietly open and Jernigan turned, his face professionally blank. For security reasons, among others, the sky lobby was the necessary transfer point between the commercial and residential floors. Any tenant or delivery man who wanted to go to the apartments above the thirty-first floor had to change over to the bank of residential elevators in the sky lobby. It was Jernigan's job to pass them if he knew them or if they had the proper identification; in the case of strangers, he would call the apartment and ask for clearance.

"Miss Mueller!" His sudden smile faded slightly and a tingue of formality returned to his voice. "And Mr. Claiborne. Good evening, sir."

He turned his attention back to the stocky woman who had just stepped out of the elevator, red-cheeked and faintly perspiring. Of all the tenants in the building, Lisa Mueller was probably his favorite. She was sixty but looked a good ten years younger, a retired schoolteacher from St. Louis—the kind of teacher Jernigan had often wished he had had when he was a kid. "Out walking in this kind of weather?"

She made a face of mock surprise. "There's something wrong with this weather, Harry? Nonsense, it's good weather—though Harlee doesn't agree with me, do you, Harlee?"

Harlee Claiborne was a slender man, maybe five years younger than Lisa, though he looked older, with a carefully trimmed white mustache and the waxy appearance of a store-window dummy. Jernigan glanced at him and couldn't help smiling to himself. Claiborne looked a little wilted right now: damp, winded, slightly grouchy, and trying hard not to show any of it. "I think you should take better care of yourself, Lisolette; many more walks like this and I'll be visiting you in the hospital."

"A good brisk walk is good for you, Harlee; it tones the muscles." He looked skeptical and she squeezed his arm sympathetically, causing him to wince, then suddenly turned to Rosette, all concern. "You're not working this evening, are you, Rosie? The holidays start tomorrow."

Rosette was as pleased as Jernigan to see her. "No, ma'am, Mr. Harris said I could leave at seven and I was just talking with Harry for a few minutes before changing and going home."

"Are the Harrises going to be home this evening?"

Rosette nodded. "So far as I know—when Mr. Harris gets home from work, he usually doesn't care to go anyplace."

"I wanted to drop in to see Sharon—I've got an extra ticket for the ballet, the Leningrad-Kirov." Lisolette glowed. "She'll love it, don't you think?"

Jernigan felt slightly uncomfortable. Like most women her age who had no family, Lisa was very lonely and for all practical purposes had adopted fourteen-year-old

Sharon Harris. It was fine for Sharon, who shared many of the same cultural enthusiasms that Lisa did and which the older woman did her best to encourage. But he wasn't sure that Sharon's parents approved. He caught Rosie's eye and knew she was thinking the same thing.

"I'm sure she'll like it very much, Lisa." Ten-to-one her parents wouldn't let her go, he thought to himself. Aaron Harris was a cold fish and his wife wasn't much warmer.

"The Albrechts," Lisa added suddenly. "Are they in, too?"

Jernigan held out his hands helplessly. "I think so, Miss Mueller, but you know I can't ring them; they'd never hear me. I don't have them down on my checkout list, though."

"That's really too bad about them," Rosette interrupted, "being deaf and dumb like that. I can't imagine what it would be like not being able to talk to my husband."

Jernigan smiled. "I bet he can't imagine what it would be like, either, though I bet he'd give a lot to find out." He suddenly became serious. "They can't hear or talk to their three kids, either—that must be pretty rough."

"That's not true," Lisolette objected. "They all know sign language, even the youngest."

"That's not quite the same, Lisolette," Claiborne said, slightly testy. He suddenly sneezed.

"You know sign language, Miss Mueller?" Jernigan asked.

"A little. It's not hard to pick up and it can really be very expressive." She grew thoughtful for a moment. "And when there's a lot of love in a family, perhaps you don't have to say so much." She glanced at her wrist watch and made a slight sound of dismay. "My, I had no idea it was so late—Schiller will be expecting his dinner and he'll be angry." She turned and walked briskly toward the elevator bank. "Have a pleasant evening, Rosie. You'll call me at nine, Harlee? And you've made reservations at the Promenade Room?"

"Of course, my dear—we're hardly going out on a night like tonight."

A moment later, Lisolette Mueller was gone, the faint odor of lilacs and Ivory soap hanging in the air like mist.

"Remarkable woman," Harlee Claiborne murmured quietly, "a truly remarkable woman."

"She's really something," Jernigan agreed. He had mixed feelings toward Claiborne and wasn't altogether happy that Lisa had apparently picked him as a companion. Did they call it dating at their age? he wondered. Well, why not. He noticed that Rosie was sticking around by his desk, glancing at Claiborne from under lowered lids—which meant that she knew something he didn't and would tell him as soon as Claiborne had left.

"From St. Louis, isn't she?" Claiborne asked casually. "Retired schoolteacher?"

"Didn't she tell you?" Jernigan was carefully distant.

Claiborne grew confidential. "It must be difficult for a woman her age to make ends meet. Inflation eats away at your pension and it's difficult to get along unless you have a little something extra put away, or a small inheritance, that sort of thing."

"I wouldn't know, Mr. Claiborne," Jernigan said formally. "Miss Mueller doesn't spend her money foolishly."

Claiborne snapped his fingers as if he had suddenly remembered something. "She did say something about the family business, a brewery, I believe, that was absorbed by a larger company."

Jernigan suddenly decided to let his education show. "I really wouldn't know," he said coldly. "The tenants' personal lives are their own; I don't intrude or ask questions."

Claiborne realized, too late, that he had gone too far. "Yes, of course, that's the only proper attitude." He started for the elevators, then abruptly turned before he reached the bank. "She's a fine woman," he said simply. "I like her very much." It was a half apology for his deliberate questioning and Jernigan was startled by its unexpected sincerity.

After he was gone, Rosette snorted indignantly. "I bet he likes her—likes her money, he means. That deadbeat hasn't paid his rent in two months; he's nothing but a gold digger."

"Gigolo," Jernigan corrected. "Gold diggers are women." He suddenly looked at her accusingly. "Been snooping again, Rosie?"

"Harry, he's got three shirts and one good suit and a bureau full of dust! Now you tell me, what is he? Don't you think I've met guys like him before?"

"I didn't know you went for the older types, Rosie." Jernigan looked up at her, curious. "How come you know all this about him?"

"The head housekeeper's a friend of mine and Captain Harriman was wondering whether Claiborne was going to skip or not so one day when Harlee was out, she let herself in to check."

Captain Harriman was a good manager, Jernigan thought. Which meant that a credit check in depth was being conducted on Claiborne right then, and he probably had less than a week to go before he was tossed out on his ear. Lisa might be hurt but in the long run it would probably be for the better.

Rosie suddenly leaned closer and lowered her voice. "Time for me to split, handsome; here comes Miss America of 1964. See you later." She turned and smiled, said, "Good evening, Miss Elmon," in a loud voice, and disappeared into the elevators.

Deirdre Elmon was tall, red-haired, and looked like she had stepped out of a 1950 movie, Jernigan thought. Big chested and big hipped, she walked like a windup version of Marilyn Monroe. Great if you liked the type. He didn't. She had done something with her hair to give it a metallic sheen and for a moment he wondered if red was the real color. He smiled to himself. He really didn't give a damn, which would probably upset her if she knew.

"Good evening, Harry." Her voice was husky and deliberately throaty, right out of the late-night movie. If the rolled-up copy of *Variety* that she invariably carried with her during the day was any indication, she wanted to be an actress. It was a little sad, he thought; for what she had to offer, she was ten years over the hill. Like his brother Melvin—in her own way, she was a born loser.

He turned the checkout book around for her to sign. "Big date tonight, Miss Elmon?"

"Big enough. Dinner at the Plaza and a movie. I'm not sure when I'll be back, so be a sweetheart and take any messages for me, will you?" She looked up at him and for just a fleeting second he thought he saw the real Deirdre Elmon, the sixteen-year-old with too much of a desire to make it big to leave any room for serious thoughts on just how to go about it. She suddenly smiled. "It's too bad you're married, Harry—or maybe I should say it's too bad you're married and loyal." And then she was onstage again, the slight hint of wistfulness buried beneath her make-up, making her grand exit framed in the open door of the elevator. "If you ever change your mind, handsome . . ."

"I won't—but thanks for the compliment."

"Enjoy it, honey, compliments don't cost a thing." And then the doors had closed.

She wasn't even vaguely his cup of tea, Jernigan thought sadly. And she wasn't just a bad actress; she was —pathetic. He stared after her for a long moment, wondering who was keeping her. She had no job that he knew of, but then again, he had never seen her bring anybody home.

And then he realized that it had to be somebody in the building with access to an executive suite so they could shack up there. She wasn't going out to dinner, he thought. She wasn't going to see a movie; she wasn't even going to leave the building. She wasn't dressed for the weather, but then she never was. She probably never even bothered to look out the window to check what it was like. Whenever she returned from one of her big dates, whether it had been a steady downpour outside or a regular blizzard, her coat was always dry; her shoes had never been touched by water or slush, and her brittle hairdo had never been blown by the wind.

You couldn't help but notice these things, Jernigan thought. Not if you had been a cop for ten years.

5.

Deirdre Elmon took the residential express down to the garage level, then quickly crossed over to an elevator servicing the commercial floors, her heel taps ringing against the tile. It would have been faster to have taken a commercial elevator from the sky lobby directly down to Bigelow's floor, but she didn't want Jernigan to wonder —he probably suspected too much as it was.

Not that she gave a damn if anybody knew, she thought grimly, but it had taken a long time to get Bigelow past the worry-wart stage and there was no sense in running risks that might expose both herself and him. He isn't much, honey, she told herself, but at the moment he's all you've got. And he wasn't all that bad . . . Getting gray and a little chubby around the middle, but he worked out and was still what the society pages called "ruggedly handsome." And most important of all, he was . . . generous.

She buzzed for the elevator, hoping it would be empty when it arrived. It was and she thumbed 21, then leaned against the wall of the cab. John Bigelow III, vice-president of Motivational Displays, and someday when his older brother died or retired, he would be the president. Not a large company, but one of the largest devoted to putting on trade shows for commercial clients. She had first met him when he had hired her through a model agency to staff a client's booth at a Consumer Electronics show. He had been friendly and attentive and when another show had come up, he had asked for her specifically. The affair had grown from there.

The cab started to slow and Deirdre took a quick

glance at her compact mirror. She was thirty-one—her most carefully kept secret—but could pass for a woman in her middle twenties. It was tough to do, she thought grimly, and with every year that went by, it got tougher. Then the elevator stopped and the door started to open.

He was waiting for her, pulling her inside the front door as soon as she rapped lightly three times on the frosted glass. He swept her into his arms and nuzzled her neck, kissing her casually and then more passionately. She closed her eyes. He wasn't bad, she kept thinking to herself; he wasn't bad at all—maybe he was right out of the late-night movie but she was honest enough to admit that so was she. His only real drawback was a wife to whom he had been married for twenty-five years and two kids, none of whom he loved—or so he said—but that made no difference in the larger equation. His wife had family money and he was never going to divorce her. So little Deirdre got the emotional leavings, plus the regularly paid rent on a one-bedroom apartment in the Glass House and a generous allowance. *And* the promise of an introduction—someday—to a friend who was a producer.

I believe in the Easter bunny, too, she thought, then let herself go and returned his kisses with just the right amount of enthusiasm. "You've been away a long time, hon. I've missed you," she said.

"Business," he said briefly and she instinctively doubted him. He cupped one of her breasts and she let him paw her for a moment, then gently pushed him away. He took her hand. "Let's go on back," he urged, whispering. "I've got some surprises."

She shrugged out of her fox wrap, draping it over an arm, then followed him through the storage area just beyond the small outer office. It was a large, almost cavernous room stocked with polystyrene displays that usually reflected the season of the year. Tonight the room was filled with phalanxes of plastic Santa Clauses and fleets of reindeer and small armies of elves and gnomes. She couldn't help giggling. It was the season of the year that she loved best and the displays made her feel young, almost childish. If there was a storeroom for Disneyland, she thought, this had to be it.

Then they were in the dark of the executive suite with Bigelow closing the door behind him and fumbling for the light switch. He found it, but the fluorescents built into the wall didn't come on—instead a small Christmas tree set on the coffee table in front of the sofa bed flared into brilliance. Deirdre gasped, then said, "Wait a minute," and found the pull for the draperies behind the couch. A moment later she had drawn all the draperies so the lights from the tree blended in with the spectacular view of the city visible through the picture windows set in the outside walls of the room.

It was beautiful, she thought, really beautiful, and for the first time in years she almost felt like crying. Then Bigelow had snapped on the fluorescents, dimming the small lights of the tree and blanking the scene outside. "I thought you'd like it," he said proudly. And then, "There's more. Look under the tree." He hesitated. "Or do you want a drink first?"

"In a minute," she giggled, "but not this very moment." There were several packages beneath the tree and an envelope. She opened the small, flat package first. A string of cultured pearls. Not the most expensive—but expensive enough. The other package contained a small, gold-banded wrist watch. Again, not the most expensive, though hardly cheap. The envelope contained a check for $638.90. She caught her breath. The odd figure struck her as funny—probably something to do with taxes, which would be typical of the practical-minded Bigelow—and she laughed, then stood up and ran to Bigelow, who was leaning against the side of the small, built-in bar. She threw her arms around him, then found his tongue. She could tell he was already a good three drinks down but it didn't matter.

"There's still more," he said quietly.

Deirdre froze. There couldn't be more, she thought wildly. He wasn't going to divorce his wife, she knew him better than that.

"Julien will be in town next week," Bigelow continued.

"I've told him about you. He's holding auditions for a Simon play and he thinks you might fit one of the parts, one of the smaller ones." She stared at him and something in his eyes gave him away. He knew the instant she read it and abruptly drained his glass of scotch and poured himself another. There was only a trace of slur in his voice when he added quietly, "After that, Deedee, well, it's been fun but we both knew it had to end."

She stood stock still for a long moment. The odd figure on the check—two months' rent in advance. And a couple of presents to salve his conscience. Merry Christmas to Deirdre Elmon, who would be Deedee Carsons again the moment she went back to the model agency. She stalked back to the couch and took the pearls and the watch and dropped them into the small wastebasket nearby, already filled with the gift wrappings.

"You're a real bastard," she said softly.

He came around so he was framed against the window. "Am I? I never promised you a thing, Deedee. You start something like this, you don't exactly sign a contract. What did you think I was going to do? Divorce my wife? Disinherit my kids?"

"You don't love them," she said sullenly.

"I fell out of love with my wife after the first year," he admitted thickly. "With you, well, I never did give you a hearts-and-flowers routine."

"Somebody else?" she asked, knowing the answer.

"Might be," he said. "I can't help having an eye for a good-looking chick."

She showed her contempt. "You sound like a dirty old man." That made him angry.

"Why not? I can afford to be," he snapped.

She picked up the wastebasket and threw it at him. Then she ran for the door. He caught her, twisting her arm up behind her back but not enough to really hurt. His breath was heavy with the scotch. "You always do the dropping, don't you, Dee? Or at least you used to— you're getting a little too old for that now. I could have liked you more, Dee, but you never gave value for value received. For a mistress, you always withheld desire on your part. I was always the one who had to want you. A woman can be either a good whore or a good mistress, Dee, but you didn't bother trying to be either one." His face was brutal with contempt.

He let her go then and she sagged back on the couch. He wiped the damp hair away from his eyes and unconsciously brushed each shoe tip against the back of the opposite pant leg; a nervous reaction with him. Deirdre was trying hard not to sob; she had never fully realized the college athlete that was buried beneath the thirty extra pounds of lard.

"You always use people?" she asked, but the line lacked bite.

"Me? I suppose you don't? What would you have done with me if I had introduced you to Julien right at the start? Would you have taken the time to let me down gently or would you have dumped me right away?"

"You hurt my arm," she said finally.

He sighed. "You're a lousy actress, Dee. Julien's not going to thank me."

She started to lash out at him, then, to get even. "You're no youngster, you ever look at yourself? You're fat, you wear a wig—you couldn't keep a young girl."

"I get what I pay for, Dee," he said sourly. He changed the subject then and became almost fatherly. "Look, why should this surprise you? It had to end sometime. I had hoped it wouldn't end too painfully. If I hadn't gotten tired of you, Deirdre, you would have gotten tired of me and found somebody else sooner or later. Come on, admit it." He walked over to the wastebasket and plucked out the pearls and watch and dropped them on the coffee table in front of her. Then he went to the bar and came back with a wad of Kleenex. "Here, you'll want to fix your make-up."

Not even time to cry, she thought. She automatically opened her purse and took out her compact and started retouching her skillfully constructed face. It would have had to end sometime, like he had said, she thought. And he hadn't been ungenerous. . . .

Ungenerous, hell, he was paying her off. Like buying up

a contract. If she had any pride, she'd walk out; the pearls and the watch hardly meant that much. But then there was the matter of the check; it would be easy enough for him to stop payment on it. And there was Julien.

It was then she realized that Bigelow had completely disarmed her and she wondered if he knew it. She was never going to make that audition. She had been kidding herself all her life and deep down she had known it. There was an old saying that you should never take away a person's song, she thought, but neither should you force him to sing. She had no talent, never had had any, but now she couldn't even pretend. That in itself was reason enough to hate Bigelow. She stood up.

Bigelow was looking at her curiously. "You don't have to leave. I told my wife I'd be away for the weekend and I thought we could spend most of it right here."

She flared. "You've got your goddamned gall! You say it's all over with and then you ask me to spend the night. I don't get you."

"Maybe it's because I want the one piece of yourself that you never gave me before," Bigelow said quietly. "I want you to stay because *you* want to, not because I want you to."

She felt an unreasoning hunger for him then, composed of equal parts of humiliation, a secret admiration for his sudden and unexpected strength, and the realization that, in one sense, it would be a small victory for her. Regardless of how he phrased it, he wanted her, if only for the night. And staying would take some of the sting out of the rejection. Or had he figured all of that out, too?

She sat down. "I could use a drink," she said, "And please turn off the goddamned lights except for the Christmas tree." She sat in the darkness for a few moments and in her mind's eye watched a whole parade of Christmases go by. Her fingers strayed to the pearls. It could have been worse. . . .

"I was going to get you a pair of Guccis for Christmas," she said suddenly.

"Thanks for the thought." He abruptly started to swear. "Damned refrigerator is out of order. No ice."

"It doesn't matter, I'll take mine straight up."

His voice was a snarl. "The hell you will; at the rent we pay, things should be working. I'll call maintenance and have them send somebody up."

Deirdre felt vaguely alarmed. "They'll send up Krost. He's on the night shift."

"What's the matter? Can't he fix a refrigerator?"

She shrugged. "He's a snoop with a dirty mind." She snuggled down into one arm of the couch and watched the lights on the Christmas tree mix with the lights of the city below. It could have been worse, she thought, sleepy. It could have been a whole lot worse. . . .

6.

It had started out as a bad night for Michael Krost the moment he had come on duty. He was in the maintenance locker room changing into his uniform when Malcolm Donaldson, the night maintenance supervisor, stormed in, spotting his brown paper bag before he had had a chance to slip it under the bench or hide it in the locker itself.

"What's that you've got there, Krost—come on, let's see it." Krost tried to slip it behind him but the short, burly Scotsman had bounded around the bench and grabbed it. "Open up the bag, Mike, or I'll take it away from you and open it up myself!" Krost reluctantly revealed the contents of the bag and for a moment Donaldson was ominously quiet. "Four star. Your drinking taste is improving, Krost, or maybe you got a raise I didn't know about—and which you damned well didn't deserve!"

"I was taking it home to Daisy as a gift," Krost had said sullenly.

The thin wreath of reddish white hair that encircled Donaldson's thinning hair bristled as if it had become electrified. "A little gift for the little woman," he said sarcastically. "You sure it wasn't a gift for yourself, to be presented, say, sometime between ten o'clock and midnight? What do you take me for, man? Do I look that much the idiot? You better thank your blessed saints the seal isn't broken or I would have your job and I'd have it now, be damned how friendly you are with Leroux!"

He thrust the bottle back in the bag and handed it to Krost who clutched at it nervously. "It was going to be a gift, I swear it, Mr. Donaldson." He licked his lips. "You know I wouldn't—"

"I know you wouldn't what?" Donaldson roared. "Drink on the job? If there's anything I know you would do, it's that! Well, I'll let you off easy. Just get it out of the building. Give it to some poor deserving soul on the street— there must be a lot of them out there in this weather— and I'll forget I ever saw it. Otherwise, you go on report and this time I'll make it stick if I have to put my own job on the line!"

Donaldson fumbled in his locker for his small brown bottle of ulcer medicine and Krost edged away, hastily buttoning his shirt. Donaldson erupted again, misinterpreting the movement. "Don't dump it now, you ninny! Wait until I get through talking." He took a swallow of thick liquid from the bottle and wiped his mouth with the back of his hand. A few moments later he seemed calmer. "We're shorthanded, in case you haven't heard yet, so you'll be working the floors from seventeen through twenty-five. You ride herd on those women of yours and I don't want to hear any more complaints from tenants about wastebaskets not being emptied or bottles left in the hall, like last weekend. How many of your young ladies showed up tonight?"

Krost smiled weakly, trying to please. "Pretty many all of them, Mr. Donaldson. I've got a pretty good crew, they don't often miss, no sir." He was already making up his mind where he would hide the bottle.

" 'Pretty many all of them, Mr. Donaldson,' " Donaldson mimicked. "How the hell many is 'pretty many,' Krost?"

"All but two," Krost said, now surly. "We can get along."

"Counting the other crews, that means we're down about 15 per cent throughout the building," Donaldson complained, more to himself than to Krost. "Christ, you can't depend on anybody these days." He took another gulp from the bottle and turned back to Krost. "I want your floors spotless when the tenants come back on Monday, you understand me? Last week everybody and their kid brother was on my tail and, so help me, if it happens this time, it's not going to be my fault."

He turned back to his locker to change and Krost watched him out of the corner of his eye. Donaldson was showing his age and with his guts acting up—well, he might have to go on the early retirement list. All he had to do was wait, Krost thought. Donaldson's formerly brilliant red hair had receded to a fringe of dirty pink and his eyes seemed weaker and more watery every day, isolated in a pale face that more and more resembled a piece of paper that somebody had crumpled and then tried to smooth out.

I could have had your job, Krost thought to himself. *All I had to do was ask Leroux and it would've been you playing nursemaid to a bunch of old women who can't speak English instead of me. But when we came over from the Melton Building, I played nice guy and let you have it.*

Donaldson was tying his laces, puffing while he did so. "Don't go doing one of your fancy disappearing acts tonight, Krost; stick around where I can get hold of you."

"Sure thing, Mr. Donaldson," Krost said. "Just give me a ring and I'll come a-running."

Donaldson looked at him contemptuously. "How the hell can you be an Uncle Tom when you're white? Go to work, Krost—and get rid of that bottle!"

Krost scurried out, making a mental note to avoid Donaldson for the rest of the evening. There was an easy way to do it, since Donaldson seldom checked the Apex Printers' utility room on the twenty-fifth floor. He had hidden there from the maintenance super on more than one occasion when he had wanted a little time to himself or a chance to catch a nap.

He paused at the escalator and glanced back. Donaldson was standing in the door of the maintenance locker room, hands on hips, glaring at him. Sonuvabitch, Krost thought, I really ought to fix his wagon. The right word to Leroux . . . And then he decided it was better not to push things. Leroux might remember the two formal complaints that Donaldson had already lodged with Captain Harriman about Krost drinking on the job. There was no need to remind Leroux of those, no need to give him a chance to put two and two together. No sir, no need for that at all.

But there was no need to get rid of his bottle, either— at least not the way Donaldson intended. He crossed over to the elevator bank in the main lobby and caught a car going up. A few minutes later, the bottle was safe and sound in one of his numerous hiding spots around the building and he was back in the lobby, buying a copy of the evening paper. The women would be on duty now, he thought; he'd checked them early so he could have time off later on. Despite the extra floors, it shouldn't be too hard a night.

There was an elevator going up and he made a dash for it. Douglas, the fag decorator, and one of Leroux's bright boys, an architect named Barton, were on it. He buttered Barton up for a minute—never know when that might come in handy—then got off on twenty, automatically checking the doors of the offices along the corridor to make sure they were locked. The cleaning women had keys, but it was good insurance to be able to say that somebody had forgotten to lock up, just in case anything was ever missing. He stopped for a moment to talk to Albina Obligado, who was vacuuming the north corridor. She was a small, olive-skinned woman who understood practically no English and perhaps because of it really never knew just where Krost stood in the managerial hierarchy, aside from the fact that he was very important. Krost ordinarily didn't care for Puerto Ricans but Albina was, obviously, different. She was deferential, looked at the floor when she spoke to him, and hadn't missed a day in the six months that she had worked at the Glass House.

"You let Dolores do the south corridor," he told her, automatically raising his voice. "You understand? Dolores does the south corridor." He'd have to spread the help around tonight.

Albina nodded without looking up and nervously tugged the vacuum cleaner a few feet farther down the hall. "I understand, yes sir, I understand."

Krost turned back to the elevators and for a moment considered going up to the sky lobby and talking with Jernigan—he wasn't too bright but not a bad sort, for a colored man—then changed his mind. He could also go to his own official cubbyhole on the twenty-first floor and wait for Donaldson to check him out. But the "office" was bare and uncomfortable, outfitted with a desk, a phone, a tablet, and overhead fluorescents so bright they gave him a headache. Or he could look up the bottle —no, that was for later on, to welcome in the holidays in the right way! Which left the twenty-fifth floor and the Apex Printers' utility room, a nice, cozy place to relax on a night when the city was being coated with freezing sleet. Well, why not? Besides, if he remembered correctly, he had left it stocked from a previous visit and there was no sense in letting that stock go to waste, no sir!

He caught the elevator up to twenty-five and looked up and down the hall when he got off to make sure that Donaldson wasn't around. You could never tell . . . When he got to the entrance of the utility room, Krost checked the corridor again to make sure Donaldson hadn't materialized out of thin air to keep an eye on him, then quickly opened the door and entered, closing it behind him even before his hand had reached the light switch.

The room itself was small, perhaps 12 by 18, part of it taken up by a small locker containing toilet and cleaning supplies, and the rest of it by a battered desk and easy chair, a small skid of printing paper, packages of mimeo and reproduction bond, and drums of inks and thinners. Somebody had used one of the drums recently and failed to close the spring-loaded valve tightly. Krost grabbed a rag from under the sink and wiped up the spill; the rag came away black and greasy. He wrinkled his nose. Better have Albina or one of the other cleaning women in here later in the evening. He tossed the rag into a nearby metal container, almost full to the brim with other such rags. Have to clean that out, too; the super was touchy about solvent rags.

Krost inspected the cleanup with satisfaction, then went to the door, took a final look outside, closed and locked it. He walked back to the locker and opened it. The top shelf was fronted with rolls of toilet paper which Krost kept constantly replenished so the owners of Apex would never have to fish around in the back looking for a final roll. Now he carefully took two rolls from the front and reached in back and pulled out a mug, a small immersion heater, a jar of instant coffee, and a bottle of powdered cream substitute. A good cup of coffee on a night like tonight would go just right, he thought. He placed them on the chipped, porcelain-topped metal table next to the slop sink, then filled the mug with water and stuck in the aluminum-coil immersion heater, plugging it into the electrical outlet midway up the wall. He unscrewed the top of the coffee jar, then realized he hadn't taken the spoon out with the rest of the fixings. He went back to the locker and, standing on tiptoe, felt around behind the rolls of tissue. He found the spoon and then his hands brushed against another bottle. He fought with his conscience for a moment and gracefully lost. It was a cold night outside and a bitch of a night inside and a man could use a little something to warm his guts.

He pulled out the spoon, along with a Windex bottle. The contents of the bottle were a light brown, rather than the usual blue. If Donaldson ever found it and went to the trouble of smelling the contents, Krost thought, it would be all over but the firing—unless he figured an employee of Apex owned it. At any rate, there was no disguising the aroma of good brandy. A few days before, he'd helped himself from the bar in Consolidated Distributors on the twenty-second floor; it was good aromatic

Portuguese brandy that danced smoothly over the tongue and seemed to vanish before it ever reached the throat. He unscrewed the cap, sniffed appreciatively, then up-ended the bottle and let a few drops dribble into his mouth. Man, that was fine stuff! He smacked his lips and set the bottle down beside the coffee cup. Already the water in it was showing a swirling motion around the aluminum coil.

Krost rubbed his hands together, realized he still had some grease on them from his cleanup around the solvent can, and walked over to the sink to wash. His hands were wet and soapy when the phone on the wall beside the door rang. Damn, he thought, no paper towels. He dried his hands on his blue chinos while the phone continued to ring. Finally, he took it off the cradle, automatically said, "Krost here," and not until then realized he had made a tactical blunder. Donaldson's voice was enough to blister the paint right off the wall.

"What the hell are you doing up there, Krost? Running off a winter seed catalog? I spend half my goddamned time trying to track you down!"

"I was checking supplies, Mr. Donaldson," Krost said lamely.

"Since when are Apex supplies any of your business?"

"They asked me to some night . . ." Krost's voice trailed off.

"You want me to check that, Krost?" Donaldson asked coldly. "Finding you makes me feel like a rat catcher—one with lots of experience. Damn it, I told you to stick around where I could get hold of you!"

"Is something wrong, Mr. Donaldson?" Krost was oozing contrition. "If there's anything you want me to do . . ."

Donaldson cut him short. "Yeah, for once there's something you can do. Go down to Motivational Displays on twenty-one."

"But they're all gone for the weekend!" Krost bleated.

"Bigelow, their v.p., just called from their executive suite. You know where that is?"

"The little apartment with kitchenette at the opposite

end of their offices?" He remembered it well; the bar there was usually well stocked.

"The refrigerator's out of order and Bigelow's entertaining a client."

Krost was offended. "They want a refrigerator fixed at this time of night?"

"Don't ask questions, just go down there and fix that box. Then get back to me—I want to know where you're going to be goofing off next."

"Sure thing, Mr. Donaldson." Krost hung up. *Screw you, Mac, you're not going to pin me down that easy.* Next time when the phone rang, he wouldn't bother answering. Let Donaldson try and chase him down; he didn't know all the hidey holes.

He finished wiping his hands on his pants and flicked off the light switch, then locked the door after him. He idly wondered who the hell Bigelow could be entertaining at this time of night.

7.

So much money, Lex Hughes thought—more money than the Credit Union had had in its vault for as long as he could remember. Not enough to make a man independently wealthy but thirty thousand dollars was still nothing to sneeze at. He made a final entry in the ledger before him, then his pudgy fingers gathered up a number of larger bills and with a lover's touch added them to the stack before him. He wet his thumb, jogged the stack so the bills were even at the short edge and flicked his thumb slowly across them, counting as he went. Another thousand. He wrapped a paper band tightly around the bundle and laid it gently in the nearby tray. It was the Christmas Club that accounted for the additional funds, he thought. Next week the accounts would mature and there would be numerous withdrawals for holiday gift buying.

"How're you doing, Lex?"

"It's going to be a long night, Carolyn." He grouped another stack of bills in front of him and started counting, then suddenly glanced up at the camera overhead. The Eye was what they called it in the Credit Union, the all-seeing, ubiquitous Eye that constantly scanned the railed enclosure and the open vault behind it. He had been down in the security monitoring room once and Garfunkel had shown him the small television screen that was tied into the Credit Union camera, as well as the indicator for the small impulse sensor that registered the body heat of anybody near the camera itself. It had given him an eerie feeling and now whenever he saw the camera approaching him on scan, its small, red "on" light glowing, he felt queasy inside, as if the camera could read his thoughts.

Once, when he had been a child, they had a kitchen calendar showing a huge, disembodied eye floating in clouds and underneath the legend "Thou God, Thou Seest Me." His mother had been a strong fundamentalist and her firm belief in a personal God who was aware of your every action had obsessed him since childhood. Occasionally, he would remember the calendar and as the camera sweep approached him, he would think: *Thou Seest Me.*

"Lex, do you have the credit vouchers from the Fifth Street operation?"

Hughes started guiltily, he had momentarily forgotten that she had been working in the vault behind him. "Just a minute," he mumbled, "they're here someplace." He searched his desk and handed them to her. At twenty-eight, Carolyn Oakes somehow seemed a decade older, he thought with a trace of pity. It wasn't that she had aged prematurely; it was more her manner and the way she dressed—low-heeled, "sensible" shoes, her carefully brushed brown hair gathered at the back, an almost total lack of make-up. She was actually rather attractive, Hughes thought, but she rarely dated and seemed to have given up on the constant quest for a husband that motivated so many of the girls who worked in the Credit Union. One thing he had to give her—she was dependable and had a precise, mathematical mind that was ideal for the job she held.

She leaned against his desk and kicked off a shoe so she could massage her instep. "God, what a day—I'd like to go home and soak in the tub half the night after we wind up this mess."

He continued banding the money in front of him, his fingers doing it almost automatically. "So why don't you?"

"I've made plans for the weekend. My sister is picking me up tonight and we're going upstate to spend the weekend with my uncle. I wish now I hadn't promised."

"Better give her a call," Hughes said after a moment's thought. "What with the early payday because of Thanksgiving and the Christmas Club money, we'll be here another two hours at least."

She slipped her shoe back on and started going over the ledgers at a nearby desk. "The foremen aren't exactly underpaid, are they?"

Hughes was silent for a moment while he counted, then banded another bundle. "They sure as hell aren't." They had a lot more to show for their years of work than he did, he thought. After twenty years he was fifteen hundred in debt and had a wife who couldn't resist a bargain and a son who was a dummy and wasn't even making it in the local junior college. . . . Any union man on a construction job took home twice what he did. He knew, he saw their paychecks when they cashed them at the Union. Granted that envy was not a Christian trait, nevertheless it . . . just . . . wasn't . . . fair.

The phone on Carolyn's desk rang and she answered, then turned to Hughes, her hand covering the mouthpiece. "It's your wife."

"Do you mind, Carolyn? I'll only be a minute."

"I've got some entries to make in the vault anyway," Carolyn said.

Hughes leaned over and took the phone. "I'm sorry," he said after a moment. "I know it's the holidays but I just can't walk away from the job." He listened in silence for a second more, then said, "I'll make it home as soon as I can," and hung up. He didn't have much to show for his home life, either, he thought. You made a mistake when you were young and the sap was rising and you spent the rest of your life regretting it. There was a brief time, after he had graduated from college, when he had tried his hand at acting in New York. If he had only been able to give it another six months . . . But he hadn't and that had been that. It actually hurt to see a play now, particularly if it was a revival and he knew some of the lines. He'd sit in the audience and mumble them to himself, anticipating the actors onstage. He'd sold out his hopes, he thought, for a woman who didn't love him and whose only ambition in life was to spend the type of money he could never hope to make. Who was it who said we all lead lives of quiet desperation?

He opened his bottom desk drawer and ran his fingers over the travel folders he kept there, his mind's eye visualizing the exotic countries they described. Japan, Greece, the Near East . . .

"Why don't you go someday?" Carolyn asked gently, coming up behind him.

"Yeah, sure, someday. You know, I saw a little of Japan when I was in the service. Not much of it—when you're in the Army, somehow you never really see much of the country you're stationed in. A friend of mine who was in the Navy said the only thing he ever saw overseas were the little steak-and-egg restaurants around fleet landing that catered to the sailors." He looked at her thoughtfully. "You ever been overseas, Carolyn? Ever been to England or Germany or Greece?"

She nodded, feeling oddly sorry for him. "I belong to a tour group and every summer we go someplace. Last year it was Greece and I saw Athens and Piraeus, the Acropolis, that sort of thing. You ought to join one—it's cheaper than flying from here to the Coast."

He took off his glasses, closed his eyes, and kneaded the bridge of his nose for a moment. "You know, I think I could really use about two months on the Italian Riviera. By myself." He sighed. "I suppose that surprises you?"

She shook her head. "No, I wouldn't say it does. Except

that the Italian Riviera suffers from a lot of pollution now and the Mediterranean isn't quite as blue as it looks in the travel folders." She was sorry she had mentioned it when she saw the look on his face. "The Adriatic coast is the place where everybody goes now," she continued, trying to make it up to him. "It's less expensive and even more beautiful—it's not as commercial, not as touristy."

"The Adriatic? I'll have to look into that. Someday, maybe . . ." He closed his eyes for a moment and sighed, then asked: "Have you got all the vouchers entered?"

"Yes." She glanced at her watch. "I better call my sister."

"Carolyn . . ." Hughes hesitated a moment. "Look, why don't you go ahead and take off? I can finish up here alone."

She shook her head. "You know the regulations. Got to have a watcher to watch the watcher."

"Afraid I'll grab the money and run off to the Adriatic coast?" He laughed. "Not that it isn't a thought."

"No, of course not." She knew her face was slightly red. "But I'm in charge of the vault and if anyone found out . . ."

"Don't sweat it, I'll cover for you." She still hesitated. "Go ahead, Carolyn, get out of here—there's not that much left to do anyway."

She reached for her coat which was draped over a desk chair and said, "You sure you don't need me?"

"Of course I need you but why spoil both our evenings? Besides, the weather's getting bad and if you wait any longer, you won't be able to go at all. The guys in the architects' division left an hour ago."

"Thanks a lot, Lex." She paused at the door. "Anybody ever tell you that you're a very nice man? Thanks again."

He touched an imaginary cap with his forefinger and said, "My pleasure." She had talked about the trip all last week and had mentioned several times that the son of her uncle's best friend was also visiting and that her uncle had wanted her to meet him. She had made fun of the idea—she had no hopes, none at all, but then, who knew? She deserved a last chance. Besides, his evening was nothing to look forward to even if he went home.

With good luck, Hughes thought, Carolyn would do better with her uncle's visitor than he had done with Maggie. Maggie. How had it all happened, anyway? The year in New York, the chance with the show—for peanuts, of course, but a chance nonetheless. And then Maggie had told him she was pregnant. One could barely live on an Equity salary in those days; it was absolutely impossible for two. So he had done the decent thing and married her—abortion was out—and got himself a clerk's job, the type of work he had done ever since. And Maggie hadn't changed. Still giddy, with a vivacity that was charming in a girl of twenty and appalling in a woman of forty, and an absolute conviction that clothes made the woman—if the price was high and the labels right.

He finished the last entry and began to run the totals. When he was through, he picked up the tray of money to take it to the vault. So much money, he thought again, more than thirty thousand dollars—a lot more, closer to forty. And there was more money in the vault, plus negotiable securities and bonds that some of the officers kept there. If he were a dishonest man, now was his chance. And that was the irony of it all, he thought. He couldn't be a thief if his life depended on it, his early training had laced him into a moral straitjacket.

Hadn't it?

He glanced up at the camera eye scanning him. Of course it had.

Thou Seest Me.

The spark has grown stronger now, fanned by the faint breeze from the ventilator. It glows brightly, like a firefly in the evening shadows. The strand of frayed cotton, slowly eaten by the spark, feathers into a light gray ash that falls as dust to the floor below. The spark has nibbled its way two inches up the wispy hair of cotton to two threads, the warp and woof of the fabric above it. The new supply of food is too much for the spark and it slowly starts to darken, dying of indigestion. The threads at the juncture point blacken, pulling heat away from the spark. It's now too weak to burn past the slight pressure point where the two strands of cotton meet. It dims some more; the beast is dying before it's ever really had a chance to live.

The temperature in the room has continued to drop and somewhere in the depths of the wall, near the ceiling, two dissimilar metals of different coefficients of expansion twist in a common embrace, reaching out in their struggle to touch a cadmium nickel contact. A brief electrical flash marks the tripping of a relay many floors below and a fan deep in the bowels of the building slowly sobs to life. Overhead in the room, warm air abruptly floods from the ventilator grill. The sudden displacement of air in the darkened room blows away the smothering layer of combustion products and fresh oxygen swirls around the fading spark. It flares under the sudden gust of air and leaps the juncture of the two threads. In the next instant, the juncture separates and two sparks glow in the darkness where only one had glowed before.

The flow of warm air from the ventilator grill in the ceiling grows stronger. The sparks grow brighter.

The infant beast now has two arms.

8.

Well, the old saying was sure right, Krost thought to himself. It took a real drinker to recognize another drinker. He smiled half crookedly with secret knowledge and said, "Mr. Donaldson said you got trouble up here, Mr. Bigelow?"

Bigelow stared at him with red-rimmed eyes and read the same message. "Back there," he said curtly, jerking his head in the direction of the executive suite. Krost padded obediently after him through the storage room, glancing curiously about at the styrofoam Santa Clauses and reindeer; it looked like the toy section of a huge department store, he thought. Then they were in the suite itself and Bigelow was pointing an accusing finger at the refrigerator in the kitchen nook. "How the hell can a man entertain a client without any ice? I don't know what's wrong with the damned thing, the light won't even come on."

"Yes sir, it sure must be inconvenient, but we'll have it fixed in a jiffy, Mr. Bigelow." His eyes were darting about the suite as he was talking. If Bigelow was entertaining, there wasn't much indication of it; he was the only one present in the suite, there were no coats on the sofa or business papers scattered over the coffee table or brief cases leaning against it.

Krost knelt down by the refrigerator. "I don't know what's wrong with companies any more, you get things right from the factory and you'd think they'd do a quality check or something before they shipped them out but, no sir, they never seem to touch the things, it's just sell 'em and forget 'em." What was wrong was that the plug had been pulled out of the wall in back but it was hard to get at and not immediately noticeable. You'd have to get down on your hands and knees and fish around in the dust behind the unit, but Bigelow didn't look like the type who would be willing to wrinkle his trousers or get grease on his fancy, thick-heeled shoes. "Should have it fixed in a moment, Mr. Bigelow; doesn't look like anything major."

Bigelow was nervous and getting more so. "Just go ahead and fix it, don't talk my ear off about it."

"Yes sir, Mr. Bigelow, like I was telling Daisy the other night, you really can't concentrate on anything difficult if you're talking at the same time. If silence isn't golden, at least it sometimes pays off."

Krost spotted it then. The closed door, probably the bathroom, *had* to be the bathroom. And not a sound from it. He had left a pair of pliers on the counter and stood up to get them. Two glasses in the sink, one with a thick smear of red around the rim. Well, it just had to be that way; who would be entertaining a client on Thanksgiving Eve? Maybe Donaldson was dumb enough to think so but he certainly wasn't.

He made noises with the pliers for a moment, then pushed the plug into the wall socket and blinked at the sudden flood of light from the refrigerator in its darkened nook.

"I guess that'll do it, okay, Mr. Bigelow?" He'd give a lot to know who was up there; Bigelow didn't look like the hooker type. Maybe one of the secretaries who worked in the building; that'd make for a nice scandal, maybe even a profitable one. He slipped the pliers in his rear pocket and backed out of the nook.

"Yeah, that'll do it," Bigelow muttered, holding open the door at the other end of the suite. Then Krost caught something out of the corner of his eye and turned slowly to admire the view of the city through the huge windows. He was right—a copy of *Variety* wedged between a couch cushion and the armrest. He wasn't in any hurry to leave now.

"You sure do have a beautiful view from up here, Mr. Bigelow. Never seen the city look so nice before, even if it is raining."

Bigelow stared at him for a second, then pulled out his wallet and found a five-dollar bill, folding it into Krost's hand. "Thanks a lot for fixing the refrigerator," he said grimly. "I really appreciate it."

Krost looked down at the bill. "Why, there's no reason for you to go doing this, Mr. Bigelow! We maintenance people don't charge for our services; it all comes with the rent . . ." He still didn't move and Bigelow slowly pulled out another five, this time holding it just outside the door.

"I know what it's like to be pulled away from your regular duties for something like this. I'm sorry I've kept you this long." His looks were murderous and Krost knew the game was over, though he considered he had done rather well in playing it out for an easy ten.

"Thanks again, Mr. Bigelow." Once in the hall, Krost thought: Who did the dirty old bastard think he was kidding with that story about a buyer from out of town? If there was any buyer, it was Bigelow himself and the price he was paying was probably pretty steep. Women like Miss Elmon didn't come cheap, that was for sure. Hell, he hadn't asked Bigelow to give him any money, he thought self-righteously; that was all Bigelow's idea—his guilty conscience speaking. Then he remembered his electric lantern; he had left it on the kitchen counter. He thought of going back for it, then figured it wouldn't be wise. Not right then, at any rate.

He took the elevator back up to twenty-five and paused before the door of the Apex utility room, fumbling for his key. God, he could use a drink right now; the least Bigelow could've done was to offer him one. Probably have saved him ten bucks in the bargain, but, of course, that had been guilt money. . . .

It was then, with sudden panic, that he remembered the coffee cup with the immersion heater. *Sweet Jesus, not again!* He could feel the sweat start to pop on his forehead. He thrust the key in the lock and slammed into the room, to lean against the door with a sigh of relief. The cup was just where he had left it, the heater leaning against the inside edge. Then he noticed there wasn't any steam coming from the cup. He leaped for it, but not soon enough.

Krost reached for the wall plug at the precise moment the heater exploded. It was at that second in time that all the water in the cup boiled away and with no water to cool the coils, the aluminum covering melted and slumped. The coils promptly short-circuited and the aluminum covering itself erupted in a shower of metal sparks. One of them hit the back of Krost's hand and he swore and jerked his hand away, knocking over the Windex bottle. The brandy spilled out on the porcelain table top and in a flash, the surface of the table was covered with flickering blue flames as the burning brandy spread.

Krost hastily tried to smother the flames with his bare hands, scorching the hair on the back of his knuckles. The flaming brandy was now dripping on the floor in front of the table and running in blazing little rivulets toward the solvent locker. Krost stomped frantically on the flames, then ran to the mop sink and grabbed up the mop leaning against it and swung the head against the fiery streams. The blue flames had just started to dance around the bottom of the locker when he brought the damp strings down on them, extinguishing them more by the violence of his action than by the faint moisture in the mop.

He turned back to the table. The puddle of brandy was already drying, the alcohol having burned itself out, but there was still some liquor in the tipped-over bottle. Flames were puffing from its throat as the alcohol vaporized and burned at the mouth. Panicky, Krost lifted the mop and swung it down on the bottle, knocking it off the table to shatter on the floor. The brandy was all gone now, the last of the alcohol dying in a faint burst of azure.

Krost stood there gasping, frightened now by the heavy beating of his heart. It had almost been the Melton Building fire all over again but, thank God, this one he'd caught in time. He looked around. Jesus, what a mess . . . He got a broom from the locker and swept up the little pieces of glass, then wet the mop and scrubbed the floor and the table top. A flat piece of cardboard served as a dustpan. He brushed the shards of the cup and fused remains of the immersion heater onto it and started to dump them into a nearby trash barrel, then hesitated. That'd be a dead giveaway. Instead, he wrapped the debris in paper towels from the locker and stuffed the thick wad into a pocket—he'd dispose of it on another floor.

Finally, he stood back and inspected the room. Except for the several burned spots on the table where droplets of hot metal had splashed, there wasn't anything to indicate there had been a fire. He put the spoon and the jars of coffee and dried cream back in the top locker and then washed out the mop. Nobody'd ever know, he thought. The faint odor of brandy and the smell of burning metal had already disappeared into the air-conditioning ducts.

Now, sweet Jesus, he could *really* use a drink. The brandy was gone but there was more where it had originally come from—the wet bar and liquor display in Consolidated Distributors on the twenty-second floor. Well, why not? He had to check on the cleaning women anyway and he could get rid of the cup pieces and the fused heater up there, too.

Or . . . He teetered in the doorway, uncertain. He could always go back to where he had left the bottle he had brought to work. He considered it for a moment, then thought *hell no,* grinning to himself. It was too early and, besides, he'd save that for dessert. Consolidated was out of anything of real quality and along about midnight, he'd be in the mood for quality.

Krost was starting on a bender but as well as he knew himself, at that particular moment, he didn't realize it.

9.

The duty roster read like a crossword puzzle with half the words missing, Garfunkel thought, annoyed. Mirisch in particular had a checkered attendance record; he was a moonlighter and didn't actually need the job, which probably explained it. He'd show up the next duty shift with some elaborate excuse but it was a cinch he wouldn't show tonight. Garfunkel was damned if he would call him; that was Mirisch's obligation. Well, there were plenty of men on his waiting list; he'd pick a returned vet the next time—they needed the work and they were usually reliable. Better to hire a new man and go to the trouble of breaking him in than have a man continue to crap out just when you needed him. You had to be a hard nose, Garfunkel thought, or you'd get it jammed up your butt every time.

He picked up the copies of the check lists that Jernigan and the lobby guard had given him and ran his eye quickly down the names. Not many people were working late, which was understandable, and it looked like the bulk of the tenants had gone away for the weekend. He would've headed south himself and spent the holidays at his sister's if it hadn't been for the mass truancies among the guards.

He took a final glance around the lobby—the dinner crowd was showing up in force now—then walked up the short flight of stairs to the surveillance room. It was a small office, about the size of offices in automobile agencies, with one wall lined with sensor indicators for heat and smoke, plus about a dozen monitoring screens that covered the sensitive areas of the building—the lobbies, the garage, the tellers' cages in the bank as well as the vault area in National Curtainwall's Credit Union, and similar stations. Ordinarily he'd have two men on duty to spell each other at the screens and make fire patrols, but Sammy was also out for the evening.

"Things under control, Arnie?"

Arnold Shea twisted in his chair and said, "Hi, chief, glad you're here. You know, I almost think we're going to have a heist in the Credit Union."

Garfunkel quickly moved in to look at the scope. On screen, Hughes was counting money and banding the bundles of bills, occasionally looking up at the camera with a thoughtful glance.

"I don't like it, chief, if I ever saw a guy who was planning on beating it with all the money, that's him."

"You're out of your mind. Give Lex Hughes a chance and he'll quote the Bible at you until it's running out of your ears; he's a member in good standing at one of those revivalist churches."

"They're not above passing the plate in church, are they?"

"If Hughes saw you drop a penny on the sidewalk, he'd run a mile to give it back and you better believe it. I made the mistake of showing him the screens once and he turned white; probably thinks it's the eye of God watching him and every once in a while he can't resist watching back. The time to worry is when he starts talking to it. Not a bad guy otherwise; poor bastard's stuck with a wife who's forty and thinks she's still sixteen."

Shea smiled. "What've you got against women, chief?"

"Nothing—I was married to one once, wasn't I?" Garfunkel glanced at his watch. It was close to seven o'clock and in a few minutes the electrical locks would be activated on the stairwell doors and the whole building would be buttoned up. If he wanted to, he could head for home after that; Arnie could handle the scopes and Jernigan the residential floors and he had three other men scattered throughout the building, which should be enough to cover everything. And it would sure as hell be nice to be able to take his shoes off; physically, as well as professionally, he had become the complete flatfoot.

Shea was yawning. "These things can really hypnotize you. I've damned near fallen asleep a dozen times; it's different when you've got somebody here to talk to."

The bastard had read his mind, Garfunkel groaned to himself. It was part of a plot, anything to keep him from being able to wriggle his toes in the privacy of his own apartment. He couldn't trust Shea to last until the next shift, let alone be sure that the next shift would even show up.

"I don't know," Shea said thoughtfully, back at the screen again. "I tell you, Dan, that guy's got the South America look in his eyes."

"He's probably thinking of the Virgin Mother Mary," Garfunkel grunted. "I told you, he's the most honest guy in the building—with the exception of myself." He sat down on a nearby chair and glanced through the tenant lists again, matching them up with the Promenade Room reservations. Quite a few were eating upstairs, including Lisolette Mueller and Harlee Claiborne—now there was a deadbeat for you. But he couldn't blame them; it would be nice to eat out on Thanksgiving Eve but not with the kind of weather that was blowing up outside.

Shea suddenly tensed. "Hey!"

Garfunkel was immediately at his shoulder. "What's up?"

Shea was relaxing now but still obviously uneasy. "The lobby screen—thought I saw somebody running across the far corridor. Just caught it out of the corner of my eye." They both watched the screen for several sweeps of the lobby camera. Only tourists, Sue, and the guard. "It was probably nothing," Shea said. "Maybe a phantom image, something like that. Or maybe my eyes were playing tricks on me."

Maybe they were and maybe they weren't, Garfunkel thought, but that settled it for sure—he wasn't going home. They were too shorthanded for one thing. And for another . . . With Quantrell's broadcasts, it would be just like some nut to pick this evening to try and torch the building.

10.

The lobby of the Glass House was more crowded than Jesus Obligado could ever remember. He breathed a silent prayer of thanks as he pushed through the revolving doors. For a moment he just stood inside, absorbing the warmth and shaking some of the water off his thin windbreaker. It was a real bitch outside, he thought, no kind of weather for his Levis and light jacket. But he had sold his heavy leather one weeks ago, along with the watch

that his father had left him when he died and the color
TV set that he had told his mother had been stolen.

He started to shiver again; sweat coated his forehead.
The cramps and the vomiting would start next and the
lobby was no place to be when that happened. As it was,
if he hung around very long it wouldn't be more than
a few minutes before the guard would spot him among all
the women with their fur coats and their husbands all
dressed up for the night. There were a few kids with their
parents but nobody his age. The only ones allowed in the
lobby after six were people who worked in the building
or those going to the restaurant at the top and who the
hell his age had enough money for that?

The guard was standing by the reservations desk, paying no attention at all to who came through the doors,
and Jesus felt a little of the tension drain out of him.
It wouldn't be easy but given a little luck, he could make
it; he had before. He looked around for the camera at
the far end of the lobby, near the doors of Surety National, and spotted it panning slowly over the crowd, working
its way toward him. He was too obvious, standing by the
doors. He loped forward a few feet to mingle with the
crowd and then worked his way toward the door leading
to the stairwell. He had to be on the second floor before
seven, when the electric locks activated and the floors
were sealed to anybody who might come up the stairwell.
He glanced at the clock on the marble wall near the bank
entrance; he had a few minutes but not very many.

The people in the lobby crowded toward the reservations desk and the guard was momentarily preoccupied
trying to form them into a line. If he was fast enough,
Jesus thought, he could make it. The camera was now at
the far limit of its scan. He edged quickly around the
periphery of the crowd; people were too intent trying to
push their way to the head of the line to pay much attention to him. Finally he was out in the open, a good twenty
feet from the door. The guard was still issuing instructions
and trying to handle the crowd, but the camera had
started on its way back. Jesus chanced it and half ran
toward the door. The guard was busy with an elderly

couple who seemed lost and confused in the lobby tur-
moil. Jesus wasn't sure if the camera had spotted him or
not.

Then he had tugged open the metal door and slipped
through, hearing the automatic door closer sigh above him
as it pulled the panel shut. He was in the bare concrete
stairwell now, its walls showing the imprint of the plywood forms into which the concrete had been poured. He
leaned against the wall for a moment, the gray steps rising silently above him. He was going to be sick; he could
feel the contents of his stomach start to pump and then
the taste of bile in his mouth. He wouldn't, he thought
—he couldn't. He didn't have the time. He kept his
mouth clamped shut and fought it down, the sweat dripping down the stubble on his chin. When the cramps
came, he wouldn't be able to help himself then; there
wouldn't be anything he could do. They were unpredictable but it wouldn't be more than an hour. He had to find
his mother, get the money, and then reach his connection
before they started.

Oh God, he thought, feeling his knees start to sag, he
was going to be sick. He gagged, caught it in time, and
wiped his mouth with his sleeve. Spinner, his connection,
was a sonuvabitch; he wouldn't wait in the alley for more
than ten minutes past the agreed time. The bastard had
drained him dry the past month, but he wouldn't wait an
extra ten minutes even if there was a full grand in it for
him. Spinner had been busted twice for pushing and the
narcs had told him the next time he came back, they
would throw away the key if they didn't find a way to
kill him first.

His mother, Jesus suddenly thought in panic. She
worked on floors seventeen through twenty, but he was
never sure where she might start or how long it would
take her to work through the various floors. The only
thing to do was go through them all and when he found
her, try and borrow a twenty. She'd have her wallet with
her. She never left it in the lockers, none of the cleaning
ladies did. Otherwise, he wouldn't bother looking her up
at all. Twenty would get him through the night and to-

morrow would have to take care of itself. Right now, tomorrow was a hundred years away.

He didn't have much time, he thought frantically. He had to get through the second-floor stairwell door before seven and it must be close to that now, if not past it. But no, he hadn't heard the electric door locks click. He scrambled up the steps to the landing, had to stop again to fight down the urge to vomit, and then he was up to the second floor and pushing through the door. He was halfway through when he heard the slight buzz that meant the electric locks had just been activated. Another second and he would have been locked out. He'd have no money and that meant puking his guts out in some alley or shivering with nausea and the cramps on his stinking cot back home or maybe over at Maria's house.

He darted through the door to the elevator bank and frantically buzzed for an elevator. A moment later the doors hissed open and he thumbed the call button for the seventeenth floor. Blessed Mother Mary, make her be there, he thought, almost sobbing. He wouldn't have the strength nor the time to search all the floors and Spinner wouldn't wait; the prick would never wait.

He got off on seventeen and slipped quietly down the corridor, passing several commercial shops, their windows dead and lifeless. He rounded a corner and spotted a frosted glass door up ahead glowing with a dim illumination—Today's Interiors, with the names *Ian Douglas* and *Larry Uhlmann* in fancy printing below it. They were the two faggots who ran it, he thought. Douglas, he remembered, was the older, barrel-chested fat man; Uhlmann was younger and thinner. He had run into them once before when he had come up to see his mother after hours and had pretended that the guard had given him permission. Neither one of them had been very friendly but there had been something in the older fairy's eyes. Interior decorators, Jesus mused thoughtfully. They sold the fancy stuff that rich people put in their houses, expensive stuff. He hesitated a moment by the door listening. There weren't any sounds and he guessed by the dimness of the light that whoever was there was probably working in the back. It might be worth a try, he thought suddenly. There wouldn't be any customers there and if the owners were in back, it might be possible to rip something off. Maybe he could make a trade to Spinner—then instinctively he knew that was unlikely, that his mother was the best bet.

He padded quietly down the corridor. The lights were on in the National Curtainwall offices; he had been in there once, too, when his mother was cleaning up. But there weren't enough lights on to indicate the cleaning women were inside; only a few toward the rear, where they had a safe and kept a lot of money. His mother had told him it was what they called a Credit Union and that a lot of employees banked there. Maybe they had a lot of money there, he thought—it was just before the holidays. For a moment he wished he had a gun and then shrugged the thought aside. He was too chicken for that; guns scared him. When he was a little younger he had been in gang fights where they fought with knives and chains; then one night somebody had shown up with a gun and one of his buddies was killed, and he got creased in the side and bled like a pig for half a day. His mother had managed to get a Puerto Rican doctor to stitch him up, a doctor who knew enough to keep his mouth shut and hadn't asked Jesus how it had happened. But Jesus had steered away from gangs after that; the next time he might not be so lucky.

He started to get panicky. He was nearing the end of the corridor and there were no signs of the cleaning women. All of the sand-filled ashtrays lining the corridor were still filled with butts and none of the remaining offices showed any lights. Maybe another corridor . . . He broke into a run and a few minutes later realized that he had been right, none of the cleaning women had gotten to the floor yet. Christ, what was he going to do? He could feel the first hint of a cramp and paled beneath his olive skin. Maybe she had been sick. Maybe Martinez, her new "husband," had slapped her around too much and hurt her so bad she couldn't go to work. That *macho* pig, he thought, someday he'd stick six inches of steel into him and see how *macho* the greaser was then. . . .

She was probably working on another floor, he thought hopefully. He ran back toward the elevators, then paused for a moment outside Today's Interiors. The lights were still on in back and he hesitated by the door a moment, then tried the knob. It turned easily in his hand. He silently opened the door about six inches and glanced inside. There was nobody around, though now he could hear faint movements from the rear, like somebody working an adding machine. They were busy, he thought. It was worth the chance. He pushed through into the darkened outer shop, letting the door close quietly behind him. For a moment he stood in the darkness, waiting for his eyes to adjust, then glanced quickly around. At first, there didn't seem to be much that would do him any good. A desk against the wall that might have a cash box in it . . . He walked quietly over and cautiously pulled open the drawers one by one. Paper and envelopes and what looked like a folder of bills; no money except a few pennies in the narrow top drawer, along with some stamps, rubber bands, and paper clips.

Shit. There were bolts of cloth in the corner and stacked against the far wall, and fancy, delicate-looking furniture that wouldn't last a week in his house. Suddenly curious, he walked over to a couch and sat down, first bouncing on it, then wriggling his narrow hips against the upholstery. It wasn't even comfortable; who would buy crap like that?

Then he spotted it. A section of glassed-in shelves standing in shadow against the far wall. He lit a match, the sound of the striking surprisingly loud in the room, and held the flame up to the shelves. They were of gray, tinted glass and one of them held a group of small figures that looked like they might be of ivory. He could cram a number of them in his pocket; maybe Spinner would give him a dollar apiece on credit. Then his eyes lit up. Next to the figures was a small, antique clock with a lot of painting and what looked like a gold band running around the clock face itself. That had to be worth money, at least twenty dollars all by itself. Even Spinner should be able to see that.

He slid the doors quietly open and had just started to lift out the clock when suddenly the room blazed with light and a deep voice growled, "What the hell do you think you're doing?"

Jesus jerked back, his elbow brushing against the shelf of ivory pieces which crashed to the carpeted floor.

"You little bastard, my netsukes!" The fat man leaped for him and Jesus ran for the door, still clutching the clock. The fat man got there first and Jesus suddenly realized just how large and heavy he was. A good 250, maybe 6 feet 2. He literally towered over Jesus' own 130 pounds and 5 feet 8. Jesus backed away, then suddenly turned and kicked at the small ivory carvings, scattering them over the floor.

The fat man yelled and fell to one knee, trying to catch the pieces bouncing over the rug. Jesus bolted for the door and was halfway through when a heavy hand closed on his ankle and jerked him back. He fell, dropping the clock, which promptly shattered. He rolled like a cat trying to scramble to his hands and knees, and suddenly thudded up against the wall. The big man had him immediately, clutching him by the shoulders, his thick fingers sinking almost to the bone. Jesus' right hand snaked to his pocket but the big man beat him to it, hooking his fingers in the pocket's edge and ripping the cloth down so the switchblade fell harmlessly out on the floor.

"Dirty little street bastard!" The man yanked him to his feet and pinioned his arms behind him, one hand holding both of Jesus' thin wrists. He had seemed like a soft man at first but the belly pressing against Jesus' hip was hard and ridged with muscle and the hand holding his wrists felt like iron.

"You're hurting me, man!"

"Then stand still or I'll hurt you one hell of a lot more," the man said, his voice thick with anger.

"Let go, man; I ain't going anyplace." He stopped struggling and the man relaxed his grip a little.

"What's your name?"

Sullenly. "Jesus. Jesus Obligado."

His eyes snapped quickly about the shop and the big

man said, "Don't try it. You're a goddamned burglar and I could probably kill you and nobody would say anything."

Jesus leaned back against the wall, massaging the sting out of his wrists. That was a frigging lie, he thought; the big man might hurt him but he wasn't going to kill him. Jesus had met the type who might kill him and whatever the big man was, he wasn't that. He relaxed a little. The big man would probably call the cops, but he could always say that he had been looking for his mother and had seen the lights and walked in, thinking his mother might be there since this was one of the offices she cleaned. And if that didn't work . . . Suddenly he had an even better idea. He could say the big man had invited him up and offered him money. The cops would believe that; the big man was obviously swish. He began to feel cocky.

"What's so funny?" the big man asked.

"You going to call a cop?"

"Any reason why I shouldn't?"

"Sure." Jesus was defiant now. "You call them and I'll tell them you asked me up here, that you wanted to fuc . . ."

He didn't even sense it coming. The big man's hand caught him at the side of the face and he staggered and almost went down; the slap had been so hard his teeth hurt.

"You're in the wrong state," the big man said coldly. "You're too old. Sodomy's not a crime but blackmail is." He looked at Jesus closer. "What're you after? What did you want?"

"Money," Jesus said sullenly. "What the hell you think?"

"What for?"

Jesus suddenly yanked up his long sleeves and held out his thin arms, vein side up. "Take a look, man; take a good look. You never seen tracks before?"

Something flashed in the man's eyes for a moment; Jesus wasn't sure what it was.

"Christ kid, you're killing yourself," the big man said softly.

Jesus was suddenly angry, angry at the city, angry at his mother for not being where she should have been, angry at the big man. "You think I should go to the clinic, right? There's a waiting list at the clinic, man, there's a fucking waiting list for six weeks!" His voice rose in pitch. "What do you think I should do? Go cold turkey in my stinking little apartment? My mother, she doesn't even know! Her boy friend would throw me out on my ass!"

He was starting to feel sick again, the sweat creeping back. He started to shiver, his teeth chattering.

"Look, man, you know me; okay, I know you, too. Twenty dollars, I need twenty dollars." He arched his back slightly against the wall, pushing his pelvis forward. "Twenty dollars. You want me?" His voice was almost a plea. "I'm good. I've hustled before. I don't mind. There's nobody here; I ain't going to say nothing. Twenty dollars, you can have me, man!"

Again, there was something in the man's face that Jesus couldn't read. "What makes you think I want you?" he asked finally.

"I know you," Jesus said simply.

The big man shook his head. "I don't want *you*," he said quietly. For the moment he seemed to be thinking of something and Jesus realized he had lowered his guard. He lunged forward, jamming his shoulder into the man's belly, then made a dash for the door. He could feel the big man reach for him but a second later he was out in the corridor, racing for the far end. Once around the corner he stopped and listened for a brief second; nobody was following him. He crept to the elevator and pressed the button. Fuck him, Jesus thought, feeling the vomit start to well up again. Fuck him in the ass . . .

He found his mother on the eighteenth floor, at the end of the hall near the fire stairwell, dragging her wheeled mop bucket along the corridor. He hadn't seen her for a week; she looked dead tired. Too bad, he thought, she was tired and he was sick.

She looked up, startled, when she heard his steps. "Jesus!" She broke into rapid Spanish. "What are you doing here? You shouldn't be here!"

He was shivering again. "For Christ's sake, Mama, speak English. I don't understand you." He paused for a moment to control his stomach. "I need money, Mama."

"No money," she said firmly. She bent to lower the mop into the bucket.

He kicked the bucket away from her.

"Mama, I don't wanna hurt you." He licked his lips. There wasn't any other person he could turn to; there was no other place to go. "Mama," he repeated quietly, "I need money."

She backed away from him. "I said—no money."

He was on her then, clutching at the shoulders of her blue uniform and shaking her. *"You crazy old spic lady, I need money! I need it now, right now!"*

11.

Dan Garfunkel said: "Arnie, I think I'm going to make a fire patrol."

The guard let his eyes stray from the monitor tubes a moment to stare at Garfunkel. "You checked in at eight, chief; that's going to make it a long day for you."

Garfunkel picked up the small clipboard he used when on fire patrol and started for the floor. "We're short-handed and what else is there to do? Go home and watch the tube? There's nothing worth watching anyway except cops and robbers. See you in an hour; give me a call on the two-way if anything comes up."

All of which was at least half a lie, he thought; he would've given almost anything to be able to sink back in an easy chair and loosen the laces of his shoes. *C'est la vie. . . .*

The long night ahead, however, didn't bother Garfunkel half so much as the thought of a four-day-holiday weekend, the only thing worse than a three-day-holiday weekend. He and Ellen had never had children and when she had died, it seemed like his job had assumed more and more importance in his life; he only felt alive and needed when he was at work, surrounded by the hundred and one problems that came up during the day and vicariously living the lives of those around him. Jernigan's family, he had once admitted to himself, were more real to him than his own relatives, though he had met Marnie only once and the rest of Jernigan's family not at all.

He was, he had realized with growing bitterness, a lonely man.

Garfunkel took a long flashlight from the rack just outside the office and then checked the lobby briefly before catching the outside elevator up to the Promenade Room. Diners pressed in around him, exclaiming either in delight or fear as the city dropped away below them. Garfunkel watched the scene clinically—it was one he had seen a hundred times before—and stepped quietly out into the waiting room on the sixty-fifth floor, most of his fellow passengers lining up to check their coats.

"You're not going to be eating here tonight, are you, Dan?" Quinn Reynolds, the young hostess for the room, had come hurrying over the moment she spotted him.

Garfunkel smiled and shook his head. "Couldn't afford it, Quinn—just on fire patrol. Looks like you're going to have a full house tonight."

She nodded. "There'll be some no shows because of the weather so actually we're booked over capacity." She turned back to the entrance to the dining room. "Take care, Dan—have a nice holiday."

Garfunkel found the exit stairs and walked up to the sixty-sixth floor, the floor that held the unoccupied penthouse and the room that housed the motor generators for the residential elevator bank. He flashed his light around the motor room, automatically searching for anything that didn't seem to belong there—cans, packages, anything that might be a potential bomb or an arsonist's rig. It wasn't that he expected to find anything, though they had had more than their share of bomb scares, and building management had turned down all consular headquarters as possible tenants. But you never knew. . . .

He didn't turn on the wall switch in the penthouse living room but stood in the middle of the empty room and closed his eyes, letting himself "feel" the building as much as possible. It was really blowing outside, he thought after a moment; he could sense the slight sway of the building itself. Other than that, there was the faint pulsing of the motors and electrical machinery below, the vague mechanical whisper that was the building talking to itself as it got ready for the evening. There was a difference between the dark and the daylight in the noises that the building made; there was a difference between when she was awake and when she was settling down for the night.

He opened his eyes and flashed the light around the empty rooms. It would be easy for somebody to come up to the Promenade Room to eat and then slip up the stairs, he thought. But then, when it came to arson, any part of the building was vulnerable. . . . He climbed back down the stairs, ducked in the restaurant kitchen for a moment where one of the chefs forced a chicken leg on him, then down to the observation deck, a circular sea of glass just beyond which the city below twinkled in the sleet and rain. The deck itself was like a huge circular moat. On the other side of the inside wall, hidden from the tourists, were the gigantic tanks of water that acted as reservoirs for the internal standpipes as well as for the air-conditioning system and the sprinklered areas. Garfunkel let himself in and gave the room a cursory inspection, then walked down to the utility deck just below, a machinery room filled with generators and motors and huge fans, a ceiling laced with conduits and the walls lined with meters indicating water pressures, steam pressures, excess smoke, and heat indicators, air flow gauges and the like. The room was manned during the day; during the evening, duplicate meters and other indicators in the basement engine room were read hourly by the night crew.

Returning to the stairwell, he sensed again the overwhelming feel of metal encasing him. He thought, tenants in their apartments never fully realize the presence of the spiderweb of steel girders that hold up their carpeted cocoons. Then he was striding along the corridors of unfinished apartments on the top floors, making notations on his pad as he went. Maybe it was the holidays, maybe it was just that people didn't care any more. Loose lumber and sheets of plywood lying around, drums of paint and varnish—at least one of them open, stacks of asphalt and plastic tile, open crates still half filled with excelsior . . . Christ, when was the last time the captain had been through? He'd report it in the morning except that Harriman was on vacation and the pipsqueak filling in for him was the type who would never talk back to a construction foreman. But somebody sure as hell had better start . . .

The fire stairs slowly got wider as he went down and the floors themselves quickly assumed a more finished appearance, with carpeting and wallpaper in the corridors and neatly varnished doors to apartments instead of narrow sheets of plywood leaning against gaping holes in the concrete-block walls. Each door had a small plaque on it and Garfunkel stopped to read one. Odd, he thought; as many times as he had been through the halls, he had never noticed them before. *What to Do in Case of Fire.* He chalked it up as a first; probably less than one tenant in ten was even aware of the plaques. If anything ever did happen, it would be the old Navy dictum all over again: *When in danger, when in doubt, run in circles, scream and shout.*

The next stairwell, something about the standpipes and their attached hoses caught his eye and he stopped for a moment to investigate. Somebody had slit one of the two-and-a-half-inch cotton fire hoses halfway through. Vandals, Garfunkel thought, infuriated—reason number one why firemen preferred to lug their own fifty-foot lengths of hose up flights of stairs. Probably kids who had access to the stairwells during the day, the same kids who would "steal" elevators for joy riding and have to be keyed down to the main lobby via the fireman's override switch.

The next stairwell opened out on the sky lobby. Jernigan was at his desk, staring at a point just below the counter top. The early movie, Garfunkel thought. "Hi, Harry, how's it going?"

Jernigan looked up and smiled broadly, snapping off the set. "Just goofing off as usual, Dan—but I'd rather be inside than out, that's for sure."

"Anything worth reporting?"

"If there had been, I would've. Slow night." He paused for a moment, obviously in doubt as to whether he should mention something or not. "Hey, Dan, you got any plans for tomorrow?"

"Damn right—take off my shoes, open up a can of beer, settle back, and watch the game. Why, what's up?"

"Marnie, you know how much she's always cooking . . ." Jernigan hesitated a moment and Garfunkel realized with sudden panic what was coming. "There's going to be more than enough and I can't stand a steady diet of turkey sandwich lunches. I thought you might be willing to help out."

"Hey, look, Harry, that's damned—"

"White of me?" Jernigan grinned. "Look, boss, you're more than welcome."

"Well, ah, I really appreciate it, Harry, but I had sort of . . ."

"Want to be by yourself?" There was something in Jernigan's voice that Garfunkel had never heard before. Softly: "Come off it, Dan."

"I'll think about it," Garfunkel said slowly. "It's really nice of you, Harry, I appreciate it."

Jernigan looked down at some papers behind the counter. "There's this secretary who works with Marnie. She's white, middle thirties, husband died a year ago. Marnie thought she'd invite her, too." He held up his hands. "It's no setup, no Cupid playing. But I figure if there's two of you honkeys at the dinner table, Leroy will freak out and maybe he'll move." He added what he hoped would be the clincher. "She's a foxy chick, Dan; we don't allow dogs in the house."

Garfunkel couldn't meet his eyes. "I'll think it over, Harry—it's really nice of you and Marnie, I mean that."

Jernigan read the refusal in his voice, shuffled some papers on his desk, and switched the TV set back on. He didn't look up. "Call me in the morning if you think you can make it, Dan. Marnie would love to have you."

It was two more flights down before Garfunkel could bring himself back under control. The perversity of human nature, he thought. What made you reject friendship when it was offered and was something you wanted badly? And it hadn't been easy for Jernigan to make the offer, least of all to have it rejected. Garfunkel sighed. He couldn't go—it would be pushing himself in, and there had also been an element of pity to the offer which he couldn't acknowledge. Or was he being masochistic about it all?

On the twenty-eighth floor he paused for a moment, suddenly alert and suspicious. The faint smell of smoke. He tracked it down the corridor and let himself into the offices of Johnson Tours. The slight wisp of smoke was coming from an overflowing ashtray that hadn't been emptied; during the day somebody had crumpled up several sheets of paper and dropped them into the tray, on top of a not-quite-out cigarette butt. The papers and the other butts must have been smoldering for hours. At least once a night, the fire patrol found something like that, Garfunkel thought. If it wasn't an ashtray fire, it was a hot plate that had been left on, or a wastebasket that somebody had dropped a lit cigarette into. . . . He got a cup of water from the cooler and doused the tray, making notations on his clipboard to send the company a memo about the building's fire regulations. It would be the second memo, if he remembered correctly. Who the hell was in charge of the cleaning women on the floor anyway? Krost, of course, it would have to be. That lush couldn't smell smoke in the middle of a burning garbage dump. Jesus, if only he were in charge of hiring and firing for one day . . .

The twenty-first floor was completely dark except for a few lights in the back of Motivational Displays. Somebody using the executive suite, he thought, then remembered that Bigelow had checked in perhaps an hour earlier. Which didn't make sense; he had checked in alone, he didn't have a girl with him. The next three floors were National Curtainwall's and the lights were on in their executive offices, which wasn't unusual. The Credit Union was working late, of course, and recently their architectural division had been burning the midnight oil. There had been rumors of a new project on the part of Leroux, something supposed to revolutionize building.

Seventeen was dark and Garfunkel walked slowly down the corridor trying the doors of the various offices to make sure they were locked. He rounded a corner and was about to try the utility-room door when he noticed that Modern Interiors was lit up and Ian Douglas was standing in the doorway, looking toward the other end of the hall. He hurried over.

"Something wrong, Mr. Douglas?"

The big man whirled and let out a sigh. "Sorry, you startled me."

Garfunkel looked at him closely. A shade too white, too pinched around the nose, breathing a little too hard. "You sure there's nothing wrong? No trespassers?"

"What?" Douglas' eyes went wide and he shook his head. "No, no, nothing like that. I just thought I heard a noise, it was nothing."

"You're sure?"

A flash of irritation. "Yes, I'm quite sure. If I had seen anybody I would have called."

Garfunkel nodded, his face impassive. "Have a good night, Mr. Douglas."

Now why the hell should Douglas have lied? Garfunkel wondered, after having made a thorough search of the floor. Nobody was there now, but there were heel marks on the waxed floor tile near the end of the corridor, where somebody had obviously been running and skidded around the corner. He felt uneasy. He was too understaffed to launch a search party and reluctant to call in the local police; chances were whoever it was had left the building by now anyway.

A dozen floors more and he was in the shops' section —the stores and little boutiques that were open to the public. It was the only part of the building that was sprinklered, he noted—according to the fire codes, all public gathering places had to be. He slipped through the main lobby, unnoticed by the guard who was checking in customers for the Promenade Room, and took the stairwell to the lower concourse and parking level.

"Everything okay, Joe?"

The car hiker wiped his hands on a mechanic's rag, then turned back to counting his parking stubs. "Everything's fine, Mr. Garfunkel, but I think we've got a house full of no tippers."

"It's not that they don't want to, Joe, it's just that after eating supper in the Promenade Room, they don't have any money left."

The attendant started jogging toward a car that had just rolled down the ramp. "You're probably right—the luncheon crowd's usually good for a quarter to half a buck."

Garfunkel glanced around and made a mental note to tell Joe to be more careful when he was pumping gas; there were signs of spill all around the gas pumps. But what the hell did he expect, he thought; the floor functioned as both a parking lot and a gas station. The only difference between this and a regular station was that a regular station was out in the open and here it was all enclosed.

Another floor down and he was in the basement boiler room. As usual, it was neat as a pin, in contrast to the unfinished floors and the parking space.

"What's the matter, Dan—nobody showed up and you have to make the rounds now?"

"Partly that and partly I thought I'd just come down to see you, Griff."

"Don't BS me, Garfunkel. You know where the coffee is. Help yourself; I ain't gonna wait on you."

Garfunkel poured himself a cup and then pulled a chair over to the battered desk that was Griff Edwards' office. Edwards was fat, graying, and with a slightly pocked skin that made him look like an old "B" movie villain. Garfunkel teetered back on both legs of the chair until the back met the concrete wall, holding the mug with both hands and letting the steam drift up into his face. The coffee was burned but then beggars couldn't be choosers.

He glanced around at the huge boilers and the rows of meters against the far wall, the log book hanging at the end of the rows. "How's it going?"

"That's a dumb question, Garfunkel—how's it supposed to be going?" Edwards got to his feet with a wheeze and waddled over to the coffeepot. "Find any raging infernos upstairs?"

"Sure, one ashtray—hardly enough smoke to set off any of your smoke detectors." Garfunkel took a huge sip of the coffee and almost gagged. It was hot as hell and thick enough to spread on bread. "You been watching any of Quantrell's TV programs, Griff?"

Edwards sighed. "Yeah, I've seen a few. Nothing in them that wouldn't apply to almost any new building." He looked at Garfunkel quizzically. "What do you want me to say, that they don't build 'em like they used to? They don't build anything like they used to, you know that."

"What's down here that might help us in case of a fire?" Garfunkel asked curiously.

"The telephone, so we can call the Fire Department."

Garfunkel laughed. "I'll remember that." He buried his nose back in his coffee cup, watching with interest as Edwards poured sugar into his own mug. It wasn't good for him; Edwards was too fat now and had once complained of angina. "Put in any more, Griff, and it'll turn to fudge."

"So then I won't drink it, I'll eat it with my fingers." He looked at Garfunkel shrewdly. "You worry about too many people, Dan, you gotta stop that—you'll kick before I do."

"Can't help it—who would I talk to if something happened to you?" He blew on his coffee. "I understand the Old Man took a week's vacation, starting today."

"Why not? Why stick around over the long weekend?"

"That means Crandall's in charge then, right?"

Edwards shook his head wonderingly. "Regular little old gossip, aren't you? What're you fishing for?"

"Just wondered what you thought of Crandall."

"Finest example of the Peter principle that I've ever seen, except that he reached the level of his incompetence several levels ago. Outside of that, he's a boot licker, unfriendly and vicious. If anything ever goes wrong, it's always somebody else's fault. If it wasn't, it will be. Now, why are you carrying on about him?"

"Upstairs," Garfunkel said shortly. "The unfinished area. The place is a mess—tools, wood, cans of paint all over the place. Ought to be reported to somebody and I guess I'll have to turn the report in to him."

Edwards thought about it for a moment. "Captain Harriman would do something about it immediately; Crandall's going to hate you because then he'll have to talk back to the construction foreman and Crandall being Crandall, he'll probably get flattened on the spot. And then he *will* hate you. But you don't have to worry about that."

Garfunkel looked at him curiously. "What do you mean, I don't have to worry about it?"

"Because Crandall really ain't in charge." Garfunkel raised his eyebrows and Edwards leaned back in his chair, smiled like the Cheshire cat and took a big swallow of his coffee. "The weather got to him; he went home at noon with a cough and a runny nose and eyes so red he looked like he had been on an all-night bender."

"So who's in charge?"

Edwards glanced up at him benignly. "Griff Edwards, senior engineer—look it up in the chart of organization. If Crandall's really down with the bug, I'll probably run the whole shebang until the captain gets back. Just turn your little old report over to me, I've been aching to chew somebody out for a month now. It'll be a pleasure."

"You couldn't have told me right out, could you?"

Edwards looked wounded. "What fun would there have been in that? The expression on your face was worth it all, Dan."

Garfunkel grinned into his coffee cup, then turned serious. "Griff, you know Jernigan?"

"Sure, good man." Edwards looked at him sharply. "He's not thinking of quitting, is he?"

"No, no, nothing like that. He and his wife, Marnie, have invited me over for dinner tomorrow."

"What's wrong with that? I already know you got nothing against his color so why not go?"

"They've invited over a woman who works with Marnie, too. Harry said that she was—you know, a real looker."

"On second thought, don't go. Let me fill in for you."

Garfunkel frowned. "Griff, I want to go and yet I know I won't. I know I'd enjoy it and yet I keep thinking I really just want to be by myself."

Edwards nodded. "The holidays got you down already? Don't answer that, I hate 'em, too, and may the good Lord forgive me, I can remember when I used to look forward to the chubby little man with the whiskers and the sack full of toys." He was silent for a moment. "How's your coffee—you ain't drinking much tonight."

"I drank enough of it to keep me awake until Monday. Save it for when you have to clean the wax off your floors." He stood up to go, then paused for a moment at the door. "Griff, seriously, what would happen if a good fire got started in the building here? Your honest opinion?"

Edwards brought his chair down on all four legs with a crash. "Oh, for chrissakes, Garfunkel, quit acting like an old woman! You really want to know, we'd go up like a Christmas tree, like a blooming Christmas tree! Now, are you happy?"

12.

Douglas ran to the door but the hall was empty; Jesus had abruptly vanished. He was still staring down the empty corridor, lost in thought, when Garfunkel came up behind him and asked what was wrong. When the security chief mentioned the possibility of trespassers, he grew unreasonably annoyed. It wasn't until after he returned to the office that he realized he hadn't wanted the boy caught.

He wasn't sure why, at first. The kid would undoubtedly have made some wild accusations. After all, how had he gotten past the guards and into the building? Wasn't it logical that Douglas had taken him upstairs for all the obvious reasons? It wouldn't wash, of course; he had signed in alone, and Barton, whom he had met in the elevator, could verify he had been by himself. But there would still be the half smiles that said silently: *"You know what queers are like."* He had been through that type of hassle before. Well, he had faced the possibility of blackmail years ago and had sworn he would never give in to it, regardless of the price he might have to pay. No, fear hadn't been it; there had been something about the kid himself. . . .

He replaced the glass shelf and stooped to gather up the scattered netsukes, the small ivory carvings used as ornaments for obis, the wide sashes that bound formal Japanese kimonos. It was a few minutes before he found the last one, a startlingly realistic carving of a water buffalo. It was his favorite and he fingered it lovingly. The artist had etched the hair onto the body of the beast with such accuracy that you'd swear you could see each individual strand. The face of the buffalo was placid and bovine.

Douglas replaced the piece with the others, feeling a quiet sense of pleasure at its beauty. The thought of selling the buffalo was abhorrent to him and he had steered more than one would-be purchaser away from the carving. There would come a time, he knew, when just the right person would be charmed by it and then he would part with it. But by that time the piece would be so engraved in his memory that the mere thought of it would be as satisfying as the reality.

He walked slowly through the shop, past the small models of rooms with their own miniaturized lighting and the broad teak table upon which were the books of fabric and carpet samples. Matching chairs of teak faced the table and on the wall behind it hung a print of Larry's favorite Picasso, "La Minotaurmachie." Douglas had given it to him on his thirtieth birthday.

The office in back had little of the comfort and charm of the showroom. Taking up a sizable fraction of the room was a Herman Miller desk with an electronic computer on top and scattered scraps of paper and open ledgers surrounding it. There was a businesslike atmosphere to it all that chilled his heart.

That was it, he thought. His whole life could be summed up in the figures in the ledgers, all forty-four years of it. He absently ran his fingers through his thinning hair, then sucked in his stomach and placed his hands between his belt and belly, feeling the flesh push back against his palms. I'm getting old, he thought, and that was the real problem. Without the resilience of youth, minor problems became major tragedies, and you discovered the strength you thought you had, had slipped away during the passing years. You didn't welcome challenges any more; you just felt tired and inadequate, or simply beaten.

He and Larry were going broke; the ledgers, the computer didn't lie. They were going broke in ways other than financial, too. He glanced at the small Kodachrome under the glass working surface of the desk. It was of him and Larry, taken a number of years before at Fire Island. They had both gone there on a lark; they hadn't bothered with the obviously gay sections, spending most of their time on the beach or alone with each other. The world was young, relatively speaking, and they would never grow old.

Only that was ten years ago, Douglas thought, when he had been a vigorous thirty-four. Now he was a thicker, tired forty-four. On the other hand, Larry, who was naturally slender and saved from being too pretty by an almost insignificant thickening of the bridge of the nose and a slightly heavy cast to his chin, had matured into a striking man of thirty-two.

Too striking, Douglas thought. Larry, he was convinced, had developed outside interests. Douglas had always assured him that he had complete freedom in that respect; he had never believed that a man and a woman could be completely monogamous over the long haul, let alone two men. Recently Larry had been coming in late at night with no explanations offered—not that Douglas would have asked—and a week ago when Douglas had been walking along the street hurrying to an appointment, he had spotted Larry through the window of Belcher's having lunch with a man in his late thirties. The stranger had the tanned, athletic good looks of someone who had the leisure and the money to spend a good deal of time in the sun and to keep his body in condition. He had reminded Douglas of himself a number of years before.

Douglas sighed and sat down with the ledgers again, then abruptly closed them and pushed them to one side. The shop had been a gamble, one that they had lost. They had thought they would attract a good many clients from among the obviously affluent tenants of the Glass House, but it turned out that most of the tenants were older and more conservative in their design philosophy. Those who were younger preferred to boast that their apartments had been done by Peck and Wuncraft; Today's Interiors was very *déclassé*, very unstylish.

He pushed his chair back and walked into the store-room where they kept bolt after bolt of expensive drapery fabrics with delicate weaves and bright patterns, as well as quantities of thick, nubby upholstery materials with intricate traceries of metallic threads. Many of them had been ordered for jobs that had failed to materialize or had been canceled. On the other side of the narrow aisle were stacks of polyfoam decorator cushions and sheets of polyurethane foam that they used in some of their in-house upholstering jobs. Most of their upholstering was subcontracted but occasionally Larry liked to re-cover some of their stock pieces, altering the lines into something new and striking. Douglas ran a hand gently over the surfaces of the cloth. When they liquidated, most of the materials would bring only pennies on the dollar, hardly enough to satisfy their creditors.

He walked into the showroom and picked up the small ivory carving of the buffalo. Just fondling it gave him a momentary peace of mind. And then he remembered Jesus again. The skinny little Puerto Rican kid . . .

It hadn't been lust . . . he was far removed from that. It had been what? Pity? Probably. A good deal of identification, too. One loser spotting another. It was easy to recognize the telltale sign: It was when you gave up. He sat down on the couch for a moment and kneaded his forehead with his hands. You had to be strong to get by in the world. With a little strength, you could face failure or perhaps summon up that final bit of effort to save the game at the last minute. But this game was finished.

He went back to the office and started the long, painful process of checking the figures once more. Funny to see himself mirrored in Jesus, he mused. Maybe he should have told Garfunkel about it; God knows what the kid might get into. But no, he thought, he'd thrown a scare into him. He was probably long gone by now.

13.

The sleet had changed to a wet, driving snow and just outside the window, a watery ice formed on the ledge. Barton stared out the glass for a moment longer, then shivered and turned away, flicking off the yammering from the small television set. It was close to seven-thirty and the bar of the Promenade Room would be a better place to reflect upon his sins than his darkened office.

He straightened his tie and slipped into his suit coat. The lights in the architectural division were now out; Moore had gone home for the evening, probably still hurt by his attitude. He'd call him tomorrow, Barton thought; if they had the time, he and Jenny might even drop out and see how Beth was coming along. He took the elevator to the sky lobby, nodded briefly to Jernigan, who seemed as if something was bothering him and he didn't want to talk, and changed over to the residential elevator up to the Promenade Room. A few moments later he stepped out into the foyer of the restaurant, alive with the soft murmur of diners and the clink of silver and glassware.

As always, the setting and the view were breathtaking. The room was candlelit, the dancing flames playing over the polished, black marble floor. The tables were set with damask linen and on each there was a vase with a single red rose. The walls were of a smoke-colored glass, allowing a darkened view of the promenade outside and beyond that, the lights of the city itself.

"Craig?"

He would have known the voice anywhere. He turned, almost indecently glad to see her.

"Quinn! How long have you been working here?"

Her light blue eyes looked up from under long lashes in a familiar, almost puckish glance. "You helped me get the job, you ought to know. Three months, all of them good ones."

"I knew you were working here, of course, but"—he shrugged helplessly—"it slipped my mind or I would have come up earlier."

The candlelight from the foyer seemed to flicker in her eyes. "Forgotten me already, Craig? Fine thing!" She waved at the crowded dining room behind her. "If you're going to be in town long, drop up some weekend afternoon—it's slow then. And by all means bring Jenny, I'm dying to meet her." There was no jealousy in Quinn, Barton thought, despite the fact that he had broken off with her when he met Jenny. Quinn and he had had something of an understanding and the breakup had been very close to a jilting. "Two years is quite long enough to keep her hidden, Craig." She hesitated a moment, then asked seriously "How are things, really? I hear rumors; I won't deny I've always kept track."

"Things could be better," he said frankly. "Maybe it's something everybody has to go through. I'm a lot older and—"

"And Jenny has to grow up, that it?"

He smiled. "I guess. How about yourself?"

Her laugh was throaty, almost a whiskey laugh. "You show me yours and I'll show you mine, Craig. His name's Leslie, he's an architect—I seem to be consistent—and sometime within the next month I suspect he'll try to convince me to marry him."

"Do you love him?"

"If he tries to convince me he'll be shocked at how quickly he'll win the argument!" She squeezed his arm. "Come back on the weekend and bring Jenny. Incidentally, your table won't be ready until eight, but I assume you know that. Showdown at the O.K. corral, right?" She laughed. "Don't look so shocked, the walls at NC have ears." She picked up several menus from a nearby foyer table and swirled toward a couple waiting impatiently at the dining room entrance. If Jenny had half her poise, half her maturity, Barton thought . . . But the comparison wasn't fair; Quinn had almost ten years on Jenny and you learned a lot about humility in ten years.

The right-hand quarter of the dining room was devoted to the bar, separated from the main room by a wall of the smoke-colored glass faced with a row of tall, potted ferns. It was a shadowy alcove of small booths and a mahogany bar with swivel chairs upholstered in rich, black leather. He had just started to slide into one when a voice from one of the darker booths said quietly, "Care to join me, Craig?"

"I'd be delighted, Wyndom."

Leroux was standing up when he came over, a tall, lean aristocrat with high cheekbones, an aquiline nose, and a faint bluish gray to his sideburns. Barton had never known Leroux's age but guessed that the man was in his middle fifties, maybe sixty; not past his prime but well within it, a man whose finely hewn features and deep-set eyes radiated an enormous sense of physical power. Caesar, Barton thought, the noblest Roman of them all. Leroux should have gone into politics rather than business; he had the sort of face that was made to be stamped on a coin. Barton shook the proffered hand and sat down. "Where are Jenny and Thelma?"

"They're getting a view of the city from the promenade." Barton glanced at the darkened walk just beyond the restaurant walls. A hundred feet away, two women were silhouetted against the night sky, gazing down at the lights of the city far below.

Leroux motioned to a waiter. "The usual scotch with a twist?"

"That'll be fine." Barton guessed that Leroux kept a Farley file on his top employees and refreshed his memory at regular intervals as to what they preferred to eat and drink. He'd see what happened when they ordered dinner.

Leroux had relaxed in the back of the booth, his face almost lost in the shadows. "Sorry to have called you back so suddenly, Craig; I realize what an inconvenience it must have been."

"Some," Barton admitted. "We were about to go before the Board of Supervisors with the proposal and I had to ask for a delay in the hearings; it will be another two weeks now."

"That shouldn't be fatal. How does it look?"

Barton hesitated. "The Citizens' Committee is pretty strong when it comes to height limitations along the waterfront."

"The popular feeling?"

"That they have a point."

"Your feelings?"

"I don't think they matter," Barton said slowly.

Leroux hunched forward over the table and Barton sensed an annoyed hostility behind the outer show of geniality. "They do. Let's say I'm curious."

Barton took a breath. "I think they've got a point, too.

The buildings are too large for the site. They'll block the view of the bay from quite a large section of the city. I don't think we'll get the project past the Supervisors, but I think we'll make a lot of enemies if we try."

There was a long silence. "If you didn't believe in the project," Leroux asked finally, "why did you agree to work on it?"

Barton felt like a small boy being reprimanded by his father. "It was my job; it was what you had hired me for. Once I got into it, things didn't look the same. Regardless of my personal feelings, I don't think my efforts suffered any."

"You don't? But you've just told me you don't expect success."

"That's right, I don't."

Leroux thought about it for a moment, then dismissed it with a wave of his hand. "It'll have to go to accounting and they'll figure out the ratio of lower income against lower capital investment. I can't do it in my head. So we don't build as high, it was worth the attempt." He took a sip of his drink. "You're a good friend of this division chief in the Fire Department, Mario Infantino, aren't you?"

Right down to it, Barton thought. The real reason why he had been called in. "I'm a friend of his, I don't know how good. We were in the same reserve unit when I lived here; we've sat in the same fire code meetings together. That's about it."

"You don't know a newscaster named Quantrell?" Leroux's eyes were very cold.

"I've never met the man, I've never even watched his show until tonight."

Leroux laughed shortly. "What did you think of it?"

"I think he's a muckraker. And I think somebody's been feeding him inside information."

"That's right. Somebody is."

"And you think it's me."

"I didn't say that. I suppose it's a possibility."

The drink was helping, Barton thought. He signaled for another. "You gave me a good job, Wyn; you gave me opportunity. In retrospect, I'm not so sure I should have taken the job, but at the time I appreciated it. And you think I would repay you by acting the informer?"

"Why not? It happens every day. Few businesses operate on gratitude and those that do don't operate very long."

"I don't have the motivation," Barton said dryly. "And furthermore, I don't have the information. I never worked with the construction team—you pulled me off and sent me to Boston, remember? If I had been here, they sure as hell wouldn't have used synthetics for the cladding around the elevator banks. I assume you knew about that."

"Why ask me? It sounds like a cost factor; accounting handles that." He changed the subject. "Why should Infantino have a knife out for us? If he's such a good friend of yours, why is he stabbing you in the back—which is what he's doing when he teams up with Quantrell."

Barton could feel the anger start to build. That was fine, he thought, let it. "You're being a little paranoid, Wyndom. Who told you that Infantino had teamed up with Quantrell? I know him well enough to know that he wouldn't do that; he wouldn't sell out."

In the darkened alcove, Leroux's face almost looked satanic. "Anybody will sell out if the price is right. All you have to know is the price—and it isn't always money."

The situation had rattled Leroux, Barton thought, more than he had figured it could have—or should have. "All right, how bad is it?"

Leroux twirled his empty glass in his hand. "If it were just the Glass House, we could probably ride it out. But newscasters in other cities have picked up the Quantrell broadcasts; they think we're vulnerable, that Quantrell wouldn't be saying what he is unless he actually had something. Now it's monkey see, monkey do. We're under attack in half a dozen cities where we have major projects building or on the boards. In some areas, the pressure has been enough for the city to launch an investigation. Usually we're suspected of circumventing local building codes or we're accused of shoddy workmanship. Here, the leasing of the Glass House has come to a halt—in fact, we're starting to lose tenants. You want to read the balance sheets? You're welcome to; they'll provide you with quite an education."

"Why me, Wyn?" Barton asked at last. "I come into town and everybody knows that I'm the guy under suspicion. They wouldn't think that if *you* didn't think that."

"Circumstantial," Leroux admitted. "If you didn't know the information, you still had access to it. And I would say that you don't show good judgment in your choice of friends."

Three drinks down and he had come to a conclusion, Barton thought. It was one that he had been a long time arriving at but now that he was there, he wasn't sorry. "Wyn," he said slowly, "I've got a few things to admit but they're not what you think. First of all, I'm tired of this discussion. I personally think you're tired and upset, otherwise you would have thought all this out before sending for me. Second, I've been too goddamned busy to run around feeding information to Fire Department division chiefs or rating-happy TV reporters. You can believe me or not on that score; I don't give a damn. And, finally, I guess I'm tired of my job. You did me a favor in giving it to me and now I'm doing myself a favor in giving it back to you. I don't like the political in-fighting in a corporation. And now, through no fault of my own, I find myself in the middle of it. I'm not a politician or a CPA or a public relations man; I'm an architect and it occurs to me that you're never going to use me as one. From what I saw of Joe Moore's latest assignment, you're not in the market for architects anyway. So my recommendation to you is that you go out and hire yourself that politician and that CPA and that PR man—I've just resigned all three posts."

Barton drained his glass and stood up, a trace unsteady. "That's all I've got to say. To be honest, I thought that when it came down to it all I would say was 'I quit.' I guess we're never too old to surprise ourselves."

Leroux was smiling. "Sit down, Craig, before you fall down. You might as well have dinner—you could use it —and the food here is good. Besides, don't forget that you didn't come alone, though perhaps you would just as soon." His smile faded. "I believe you . . . I believed you before you got here. Frankly, I can't do without you. Maybe that's what hurts. That and the fact that after twenty years in the business, your blood gets replaced by computer read-out sheets from accounting. Business is a game, Craig, and it's not how you play it, it's whether you win or lose."

Barton sat down. The charming self-pity of one of the most powerful men he knew. I need you, son, was what Leroux was saying and he could feel himself responding. It was that—and what he knew Jenny would say if she thought the whole trip had been for the purpose of turning in his resignation. She'd never understand, he thought, not in a million years.

"About Quantrell," Leroux continued. "I've taken steps to muzzle him that I think will be effective."

Barton leaned back in the booth and sighed. Here went the old ball game but there were some questions that he had to ask, too; answers that he needed to have.

"Do you want to muzzle him because he's wrong—or because he's right?"

Leroux looked at him with a friendly openness, the tension of the earlier conversation gone. "You want my frank opinion of his charges?"

"If you want to discuss them."

Leroux smiled. "I'll be delighted to, Craig—I was hoping you would ask me."

The faint glow in the darkened room has brightened to the point where an observer, if he were present, could make out the shadowy forms of three fifty-five-gallon drums and half a dozen carboys, as well as metal shelving extending along one wall. Some of the shelves have louvered steel doors; others are open and display rank on rank of metal cans and bottles, their labels smeared from careless pouring.

The glow is coming from a thousand tiny sparks nibbling at a stack of quilted cotton pads, the kind movers use to protect the surfaces of valuable wooden furniture. The pile of pads, stacked untidily against the wall beneath some of the metal shelving, is almost five feet high; in places, cotton batting shows through holes torn in the worn fabric covering. The sparks are feeding on the charred threads of the third pad from the bottom.

The smoke sensor in the ceiling has so far failed to detect the curling tendrils of smoke; the accompanying heat sensor will not sound an alarm until the temperature in the room reaches at least 135 degrees. The temperature is still somewhat on the chill side and warm air blows gently from the ventilator grill, fanning the sparks below.

In the center of the charred cloth and blackened cotton, intricate chemical processes have finally yielded enough energy for the threads to reach the kindling point. The bed of sparks suddenly glows brighter and a tiny flame abruptly appears like some sinister yellow butterfly emerging from its cocoon. It dances over the rapidly charring fabric and is quickly joined by others.

The infant beast has learned to walk.

14.

Jeffrey Quantrell stood quietly in front of the huge blowup of the Glass House, favoring the unseen audience with his "sincere" smile while the network sign-off credits were matted over his on-screen image. As soon as the red light above the Number One camera winked out, he threw his script on the desk and leaned back with a sigh, fishing for a cigarette. One of the cameramen looked at him and made a gun-at-the-head motion with his finger. A moment later, a technician stuck his head out of the control booth and asked, "You sure you know what you're doing, Jeff?"

"As sure as I've ever been."

"It was a sensational bit but . . ."

Quantrell smiled. "I'll drink to that. How about joining me for a quickie, or are you on duty?"

"Got time for a short one; Reynolds can handle the movie."

They ducked out for half an hour, Quantrell's favored procedure immediately following a show. The chill air cleared his head and the two drinks gave him time to do some subconscious thinking about the eleven-o'clock follow-up, which was usually laced with viewer response from the first show, letting him editorialize more than he normally could on the earlier slot.

After coming back, he started to jot down some notes for Sandy to transcribe. Once the broadcast was over, he thought, he'd take her out to the Stationbreak for drinks and a steak and then it'd be her place or his. His good deed for the day, he thought to himself.

"Do you have time to talk now, Mr. Quantrell?" The note of formality in Bridgeport's voice caught Quantrell off guard and he glanced up sharply. Trouble, he thought. Bridgeport was too poker-faced; ordinarily his chubby features were a blackboard on which were written the woes of the world, or at least of the station.

"Can't it wait until morning? I've got to shape up the eleven-o'clock show."

"I didn't mean with me," Bridgeport said with mock deprecation, a hint of a triumphant smile tugging at the corners of his mouth. "I meant with Mr. Clairmont. You remember; he's the station manager."

Quantrell stared at him for a moment. The Old Man's nephew had inherited the station manager spot after graduating from college and spending a year holding down various secondary positions. Everything that could be said against nepotism applied to Victor Clairmont except for the single important fact that he was a man of some intelligence. Quantrell knew that Clairmont didn't like him, but it was the Old Man who had given him carte blanche and young Clairmont had gone along. He jammed his notes in his pocket and stood up. "Where's he at?"

"In his office." Again, the hint of a malicious smile. "He's been waiting for you ever since the end of the show."

"Too bad I didn't know sooner; we could have had a drink together." Quantrell unfolded from the chair and followed Bridgeport as he waddled down the hall. There wasn't much doubt that Bridgeport was pleased at the turn of events, Quantrell thought, but he doubted that the news director was behind it. It wasn't like him to invite a head-on confrontation . . . he was more the weasel type. He'd sweat and worry and wring his hands but he wouldn't do anything—that is, until somebody higher up had expressed his displeasure and then Bridgeport would dart in for the kill. So if it hadn't been Bridgeport, then it had to be somebody else. In the organization itself? Not likely, he thought, nobody had that kind of authority. More likely it was pressure from the outside, and if that were the case, then the source was obvious.

Clairmont's spacious office was paneled in mahogany with signed photographs of celebrities lining the walls and a huge globe set in a floor frame for those moments when Clairmont might want to spin it and play God. Victor Clairmont was sitting behind his pool-table-sized desk, a neatly tailored twenty-five with a carefully trimmed mustache that worked valiantly but in vain at trying to make him appear older. "Please sit down, Jeff."

"Thank you, Victor." There was one chair near the desk and Quantrell made himself comfortable in it, leaning back in the deep cushions, well aware that he looked every inch the experienced telecaster. He had the appearance and the voice and he knew how to use both. There was no other chair nearby and Bridgeport stood nervously by the desk, trying to make up his mind what facial expression might be the most appropriate. Quantrell smiled to himself.

"Jeff, I won't beat around the bush; this isn't going to be a friendly conference. I've never liked your series about the Glass House and Wyndom Leroux. After tonight's show, I like it even less."

Quantrell nodded. "You've always been frank in that respect. My carte blanche for the series came from your uncle. He said I could do as I wished and I took him at his word."

"I never agreed with him," Clairmont continued, his face serious. "I never thought it was good for a reporter to be completely independent of management. Basically, your idea was viable—an exposé series to improve the slipping news rating of the station." He glanced at Bridgeport who flushed and looked like he was sorry he had stayed for the meeting. "Unfortunately, I now think a personal element has crept into your series, I think you've turned your carte blanche into a vendetta."

"There's nothing personal about my series on Leroux," Quantrell said easily. "The facts are as I've stated them; they're easily documented."

Clairmont's voice sharpened. "Are they? A few broadcasts back you mentioned that the floors and walls of the Glass House had been breached by the utilities people, making it easy for smoke to spread throughout the building in case of fire."

"That's right. The phone people have breached walls and floors to run their lines through. The same is true of the firm that installed the security TV system. Even the

HVAC—heating, ventilating, and air-conditioning—people have broken through the floors and walls. You can go over there and see for yourself."

"I've done that. One of Leroux's assistants took me on a complete tour. Granted that the fire walls were broken through at one time, since then they've been completely resealed."

"Not in every case. In any event, plaster is about as useful in preventing the spread of fire as wrapping paper."

Clairmont stared at him for a long moment. "I've talked to different contractors throughout the city, Jeff. It may not be a good practice but it's a common one. Why crucify Leroux for it?"

"I wasn't aware that I had," Quantrell said coldly. "I can't cover every building in the city; the Glass House is one of the newest and biggest, it makes a good example."

Clairmont seemed about to say something more, then apparently changed his mind. "I assume you've got good sources for what you've had to say."

"Of course."

"Would you mind telling me who they are?"

Quantrell laughed. "You're not a congressional committee, Mr. Clairmont. Even if you were, I'd rather go to jail than tell my sources. Other newsmen have, I'm no different in that respect."

"Then we have to take the accuracy of what you say on good faith?"

"If you don't want to, then you should never have hired me. Presumably you took me on because of my reputation as a good newsman; you were willing to pay the salary I asked for because you wanted to improve your ratings. I've succeeded in doing that; in return, I have every right to believe I have the backing of management."

Clairmont looked uneasy. "Look, Jeff, let's quit fencing. I've got a problem . . . the station has a problem. And because of that, you've got a problem."

"I'm dying to hear what it is."

"For openers, a multimillion-dollar libel suit. That's why I asked about your sources. If they're not top-notch . . ." He shrugged. "We couldn't afford the beating we'd take."

"Then you've got nothing to worry about," Quantrell said, beginning to relax. "My sources are the best."

"But you won't tell me who they are?"

Quantrell hesitated and decided to make a concession. "Not just yet; perhaps later."

Clairmont didn't look impressed and Quantrell felt genuinely worried for the first time. There was something else.

"I said that was just for openers. Our station license is up for renewal in two months. Ordinarily the FCC would grant such a renewal as a matter of course. This time, we're being contested on two grounds. One, that we've failed to serve the community interest. Two, that we're an effective monopoly in this area. We own the leading AM and FM radio stations; we publish the largest newspaper circulation-wise, and of course we own KYS."

Out of the corner of his eye, Quantrell could see Bridgeport leaning forward like some pudgy Roman emperor, anticipating the kill in the arena before him.

"You intend to fight, of course?" Quantrell asked.

"No, we don't," Clairmont said quietly. "It's not worth it when it comes down to dollars and cents."

"Your opinion or your uncle's?"

"Both."

Anger flooded Quantrell then. "When I came here," he said, biting off his words, "your news division was at the bottom of the heap in ratings. It wasn't hard to figure out why—bad management or, more accurately, management meddling in what it knew nothing about. There's damned little journalism left in television for the simple reason that the writing and the gathering of news are managed by men who have no background in it. You dictate what we cover and how we present it, but the fact is that you're salesmen, not newsmen. Continue to run your station that way and you'll get exactly what you deserve—you'll lose your audience because they'll tune to a station where they do know what they're doing."

Clairmont brushed it aside. "Leroux's one tough cookie,

Jeff. He's threatening the libel action because of the dropoff in rentals at the Glass House. And as you could guess, he's also behind the formal challenge to the FCC —on both counts."

"I told him to soft-pedal that story," Bridgeport suddenly whined, smarting from Quantrell's attack on station management.

"Herb, for Christ's sakes, stay out of this," Clairmont said, annoyed. "The point, Jeff, is that we find ourselves in serious danger of losing a major investment because of you. And it isn't worth it. That's it, pure and simple."

"You want me to back off the story?"

"You misunderstand me," Clairmont said dryly. "We've decided to terminate your contract."

"It's still got two years to run," Quantrell said tightly.

"I'm sure your attorney and the station's can reach some equitable agreement. In the meantime, I'd suggest an indefinite leave of absence—starting tonight."

As easy as that, Quantrell thought, stunned. He hadn't stood a prayer from the moment he had walked in. "What about the eleven-o'clock slot tonight?"

"I've got a story we could substitute," Bridgeport volunteered. "One of the regular anchormen could handle it."

Clairmont hesitated. "If you want to go on tonight, Jeff, that's up to you. But no coverage on the Glass House."

"Frankly, I don't think I could do a stint in front of the cameras tonight," Quantrell said quietly. "I think I'm going to be sick."

"All right, if you want it that way, Jeff. I'll see that your recommendations are excellent." He stood up and held out his hand.

Quantrell ignored it. "With your permission, I'll spend the rest of the night cleaning out my desk." He turned and strode out, ignoring Bridgeport standing at the door, no longer trying to hide his smile of triumph.

He stalked through the silent newsroom—the word had already spread—and sat at his desk for a long moment before touching anything on it. Firing him would be an admission of guilt, he thought slowly; Leroux could go ahead with his libel suit even after he had left the station and his own dismissal would weigh heavily against management. Surely the Old Man could see that; his newspaper hadn't won its Pulitzer prizes by running away from stories. The Old Man—

He buzzed for Sandy and a moment later she appeared in the doorway, looking slightly apprehensive. The expression was mixed with something else, something that he wasn't sure he could read but something that he didn't like. Well, it could wait; he didn't have the time to figure her out now.

"Sandy, get me Old Man Clairmont, will you?"

Her mouth dropped and then she said quietly, "Yes, sir." A minute later his intercom buzzed and Sandy said, "It's Mr. Clairmont on line two."

He leaned back in his chair, suddenly confident again. "Mr. Clairmont," he said into the phone, "this is Jeffrey Quantrell. I know it's late and I've already talked to Victor but I think you owe me ten minutes of your time."

The elderly voice at the other end of the line was polite but firm. "There's not much to talk about."

"In all fairness to me, you owe me the time," Quantrell insisted. "There are some facts of which you're unaware, facts that I didn't tell your nephew. I think you ought to hear them. I have no wish to argue the point, only to present the facts to you as I see them." He paused for effect. "You owe me the time, sir, as one gentleman to another. It won't take long."

There was a short pause. "Very well, come on up. Ten minutes, though, no more."

"I'll be right there." Quantrell hung up the phone in mild triumph. He was counting on the elder Clairmont's newspaper background, something his nephew lacked. He had momentarily forgotten how the Old Man had won his Pulitzer. With good luck, somewhere within the withered husk there was still the old-time reporter, the man whose Pulitzer had been based on the exposure and conviction of a politician who had been his best friend.

15.

Lisolette Mueller—she often wrote her last name in the umlauted form as Müller—was delighted. Her evening dinner with Harlee would be the perfect ending for a wonderful day. It had started with a quiet morning during which she had played the "Pastorale" in massive, thundering cadenzas that literally rattled her apartment windows and, finally, in a fit of bittersweet nostalgia, she had unearthed her worn but precious 78 rpm records of Madame Schumann-Heink in a recital of ponderous lieder.

It had been a marvelous way to spend the morning of one's sixtieth birthday. She had wept a little, too, remembering the old days in St. Louis, the girls she had known in the *Turnverein*—and the boys, too, many of whom had made charming fools of themselves over her —and the thousands of students who had passed through her gym and history classes at South St. Louis' Goethe High School. It had been a full life, she thought, rewarding enough so that at sixty she still felt young and a part of the world and the people around her.

Not that she actually looked sixty, she assured herself. In one sense it made little difference to her if she did or didn't, but she had a residual pride in her stocky and still athletic figure—with no trace of a double chin, she reminded herself. Her hair had silvered at the temples and there were gray strands mixed with her natural brunette, but the over-all effect was not displeasing to her eye. Or to others, she added mentally, thinking of Harlee Claiborne. Granted that his attention was compounded of business interests as well as personal ones, but she was quite sure that he found her attractive.

By evening, after a long walk in the park, her mellow mood had developed into a sort of *Volksfreude* and she felt the urge to visit some of her friends in the building. She busied herself in the kitchen for a moment and then called into the living room, "Schiller, come here and

105

see what Lisa has for you." The gray tomcat, whom she kept against all rules of the building, arched his back at the mention of his name, purred, and sauntered into the kitchen. "Isn't that splendid? See the kidneys that Lisa has chopped up so nicely for you?" The Harrises were still home, she thought, and she had promised to look in at the Albrechts before going to dinner. "Schiller, we aren't going to be able to use our extra ticket for the Leningrad-Kirov—Gertrude has to work that night—and I'm sure Sharon would like it, don't you?"

Schiller, who had almost finished his dinner, purred but made no other comment. No fool Schiller, Lisolette thought. "And I think Sharon would appreciate Prokofiev's 'Cinderella,' too," Lisolette continued. "Not that I really approve of the modern Russians but Prokofiev should have been German."

Schiller was now full and drowsy and could sense the chill of the brewing storm outside; he padded back into the living room and curled into a tight ball in his favored corner of the couch. The cushions were warm and feline dreams were only moments away.

Lisolette found a light jacket in the hall closet, one that she had knitted herself and was properly proud of. In her younger days—at fifty, for instance—she had won several blue ribbons at the Missouri State Fair in Jefferson City for her knitting and crocheting. She slipped it on, scratched Schiller absently under his chin, and left. All three of the elevators were in operation at the moment and she waited impatiently. She suspected that the Harrises were planning on going to the movies tonight and she didn't want to miss them. They were a nice, though somewhat stiff middle-class couple who, she suspected, looked upon her as something of a busybody, particularly when it came to Sharon, whom she regarded as the real flower of the Harris household. Sharon, at fourteen, was the middle of the three Harris children, Irene being seventeen and Danny—Daniel, as his father, Aaron, insisted on calling him—being eleven.

Lisolette was fond of all three of the children but had a special liking for Sharon, who was quiet and given to introspection and filled with a questing intelligence. She appealed to the schoolteacher in Lisolette—and also reminded Lisolette very much of herself at that age. Lisolette had met Sharon and her mother in the park one day, surrounded by three teen-age boys who had been taunting them and working up their courage to snatch the mother's purse. With Lisolette on the scene, the odds had suddenly reversed themselves and the boys had fled while Lisolette had escorted home a frightened Sharon and her badly shaken mother. To her delight, they also lived in the Glass House, a block from the park.

It was an unusual family, Lisolette thought. Ruth Harris was portly and round-faced, almost a caricature of the Jewish middle-class housewife. Gregarious in the extreme, she was very proud of her husband and the three children. Lisolette had liked her instantly, though she wasn't quite sure that her friendship was returned. Tolerated, perhaps, she thought sadly, but she was a shade too German to be completely accepted either by Ruth or her husband, Aaron, who was president of an over-the-counter clothing company and on the board of directors of two small corporations. He was verging on being both fat and balding but had a hearty manner and occasionally, Lisolette thought, you could see the small boy hiding within the large bulk of the man.

The elevator finally came and a moment later she was knocking on the door of the Harris apartment. Ruth opened it and Lisolette said, almost apologetically, "I hope I haven't caught you at a bad time but I had to stop by and see Sharon."

"We were just getting ready . . ." Ruth started, looking harried, then suddenly swung the door wide. Lisolette could almost imagine her mind flicking back to that day in the park. "Come on in, Lisolette—we were going to go out but there's always time for a cup of coffee."

Aaron Harris came puffing in from the bedroom, a bow tie canted at an odd angle on his throat. "Ruthie, you know I can't tie this damned thing. . . ." He noticed Lisolette and frowned for a moment, then slid automatically into the role of good host. "You caught us at a bad time, Lisolette; we're trying to make the early show. We'll be a few minutes, so help yourself to a cup of coffee; it's in the breakfast nook."

"I'll only be a minute," Lisolette apologized. "Is Sharon home?"

Irene, the eldest daughter, came in from the kitchen holding a glass of milk. "Honestly, Daddy, we'd better hurry or we'll be late." She nodded at Lisolette, "Hello, Miss Mueller, congratulate us—we finally got Dad to take us out for a night on the town."

"Some night," Aaron protested.

"Sharon's baby-sitting tonight," Ruth Harris said, busy with the bow tie. "She's with Danny in the family room."

"I have this extra ticket to the Kirov's 'Cinderella,' " Lisolette explained tentatively. "It's for next Thursday night and I thought she might like to go."

Ruth Harris hesitated in the middle of tying the bow. "That's a school night," she said, suddenly doubtful. "How late will she be up?"

Lisolette felt uncomfortable. "Rather late, but one doesn't get a chance to see the Kirov every day."

"Don't be such a *kvetch*," Aaron said, the small boy suddenly surfacing. "Let her go. In the meantime, tie the tie and no back talk."

"Sharon!" Ruth called, turning her attention back to the tie.

Sharon's voice floated in from the family room. "Oh, Mama, it's just at the exciting part!"

"You've got company!" Aaron shouted. Then, "For heaven's sake, Ruth, you're strangling me!"

Sharon appeared in the hallway, pale-faced and shy; Danny was half hidden behind her.

"Lisa, Lisa!" Danny suddenly chanted, breaking away from his sister. He ran into the room and clutched at Lisolette's skirt. She laughed and rumpled his hair.

"Mind your manners, Danny," Ruth said sharply. "How many times do I have to warn you about mauling people?"

"He's a boy," Lisolette said indulgently, "and boys are like that, right, Danny?" Too late she caught Ruth's thin-lipped silence and reminded herself that she wasn't, after all, a member of the family. She turned to Sharon, keeping her voice more formal. "How are you, Sharon?"

"I'm very fine, Miss Mueller." For a second she was all seriousness and then, abruptly, all smiles. "Oh, it's ever so good to see you!"

Lisolette told her about the ticket and she turned immediately to her father. "Will it be all right, Daddy?"

He was busy fastening the ornate links into his cuffs. "Why ask me, ask your mother. With me, it's okay."

"It's all right. Sharon," Ruth said, a trifle reluctantly. "Only you'll have to go to bed early the night before; we can't have you losing your rest."

"I'm going back to watch TV," Danny announced, realizing that none of this concerned him.

"Good night, Danny," Lisolette said. He was too preoccupied to notice. She turned to the Harrises and made her good-byes, hugging Sharon and doing her best to be nice to Ruth. The rest of the family liked her, she knew well enough, but Ruth was jealous of her position within it and obviously didn't like the possibility of having a strange maiden aunt grafted on the family tree.

Outside in the corridor she straightened her jacket and suddenly realized that Danny must have been eating chocolate before he came in. His hands had left thick dark stains on the nubby wool. Boys will be boys, she thought, and sighed wistfully. She missed teaching school, missed all of the children. They had been such a wonderful part of her life. . . .

She glanced down at her small diamond studded wrist watch and hesitated. She had promised the Albrechts that she would stop in but she had taken more time at the Harrises than she had planned. She would have to hurry if she was going to see the Albrechts and still have time to dress for dinner with Harlee. He was a delightful man, she mused, with a worldly poise and sense of culture that suggested he might have been a bit of a roué in his time. It was one of the things that made him attractive, she thought; that tiny thrill of danger and distrust. It was too bad that after tonight their brief and pleasant relationship would probably end, though she had learned long ago to accept the bad with the good. . . . She made up her mind. She would drop by the Albrechts; Harlee was the sort of gentleman who would expect his ladies to be fashionably late. In any event, she thought somewhat sadly, tonight he would probably be more than willing to wait.

Tom Albrecht met her at the door in silence, his sensitive hands and fingers signaling his welcome. She replied in the same manner. He could read lips as well as could his wife, Evelyn, but Lisolette preferred to use sign language. He was inviting her in for coffee; her own stubby fingers conveyed her acceptance.

Evelyn was sitting in a kitchen chair, knotting a macramé mat. She glanced up, smiled, and rose to greet Lisolette. Suddenly there was a wild whoop from the living room; that would be Chris, Lisolette thought, their five-year-old son. The whoop, as well as the immediate scolding by their daughter Linda, was lost on the Albrechts themselves.

Lisolette motioned to Evelyn that she could not stay long and followed the two of them into the dining room. The three children—Chris, Linda, aged seven, and Martin, the baby of the family at three, were sitting around the table having their evening meal. Evelyn had spread the table top with place mats and Linda was playing mother and having her hands full. Lisolette knew that Evelyn preferred having the mealtime split in two, since Tom's job as an engineer for a local electronics firm often kept him away until late at night, and the evening routine had gradually divided into two separate dinner hours.

Evelyn set a plate for her at the table and Lisolette said, "Hello" to the children, reserving a special kiss for Martin and receiving a taste of baby food in return. They were a beautiful family, she thought, the noisy dinner table marred only by the silence of the parents. From his high cheekbones, Lisolette suspected that Tom had Amerindian ancestors someplace in his background. Evelyn had more delicate features and looked the prom-girl type that television advertisers loved. They got along so well among themselves that you frequently forgot that they were deaf mutes; they even attended the ballet occasionally, though they could not hear the music. One of the few times that they themselves had become bitterly aware of their handicap was the time they had been trapped in a San Francisco fog so dense that neither could see the other to communicate. Evelyn had told Lisolette of the panic they had felt, and the fear.

They finished their coffee and Lisolette with swift fingers told them she must be going. Both expressed honest regret. "I have a gentleman friend calling." Lisolette signaled and could feel herself blushing. Tom smiled broadly and motioned, "A lady such as you must be very careful."

She laughed and spelled back, "At my age, there's no longer anything to be careful about." She promised to baby-sit with Linda and the other children on the following Tuesday and then excused herself.

Outside the door, she glanced again at her watch and realized she was running very late indeed. What wonderful people, she thought, hurrying to the elevator bank. Then she remembered Harlee. If she really hurried, she thought, she wouldn't keep him waiting very long at all. She hadn't, she reflected, running over ancient history, kept a beau waiting yet. And then she caught the idea appealing to her.

At her age, she chided herself. She was becoming a flirt. . . .

16.

One of the few good things about being poverty-stricken, Harlee Claiborne thought, was that when it came to going out for the evening, it reduced the time you took to decide what to wear. For a suit, the choice was simple—it was either the blue or the brown. For shirts and accessories, the choice was almost as easy. He opened the top drawer of his bureau and inspected the contents within.

Three drip-dry shirts, two of them with French cuffs, and two neckties, fashionably wide. Again, one blue and one brown, both with the paisley patterns he preferred.

He picked out one of the shirts and the brown tie and laid them out on the bed. Harlee Claiborne—"gentleman," as he liked to think of himself—was about to go to work. He had already showered and applied a trace of cologne to his face, and then a drop or two on his wrists. His military brushes were on the top of the bureau, neatly clipped in their leather traveling case, and he took them out to run through his hair. He was in his late fifties and wore his longish, white hair in the latest style. It was one of his few conceits, partly because his wife of many years ago had always been fond of it. Pragmatically, he realized, it was one of his more important assets, along with a naturally lean figure that had never seen either a handball or a tennis court but somehow suggested that he was a former expert at one or the other. Another asset, he was frank to admit, was a faintly British mid-Atlantic accent. He had acquired it as a commercial agent in the Bahamas years ago and when he discovered how charming women considered it to be, he had cultivated it assiduously.

Along with his appearance—that of an aging, handsome gentleman in the pink of condition—his carefully modulated, accented voice had been of inestimable value in his business: that of meeting and subsequently conning middle-aged and lonely ladies of affluence. He didn't consider himself as either a fake or a predator but more as an actor whose stint on stage might last several weeks or several months and who invariably gave value for value received. He had once even gone so far as to marry one of his ladies some ten years before, a delightful woman who had inherited a printing and engraving shop. He had managed it for several years, even learning the intricacies of the technology, before being forced into bankruptcy through no fault of his own.

Adele had died soon after, but the knowledge acquired at the shop had stood him in good stead when the memory of her had faded and he had gravitated back to the company of lonely but well-off matrons. It was the trade for which God had apparently chosen him and he no longer debated the morality of it with himself. He prided himself on his charm—and on the interest he could drum up in an otherwise useless stock certificate. For years he had favored lumber stocks but more recently he had switched to those dealing in metals, especially uranium. But whichever they were, all of his certificates were works of art.

He lit a cigarette from the still burning butt in the ashtray and pulled open the bureau drawer just below the one that held his shirts. Its only contents were a thick kraft envelope containing the best examples of his work to date. He opened the envelope and gently pulled out the certificates, inspecting the engraving critically. The corporate seal impressed on gold foil in the left-hand corner was a masterpiece; he'd hand-cast the die for the seal himself. United Power Metals. It was impressive and if one were to go so far as to check, there even was such a corporation in California. The ambiguous title was what had attracted him, though the company in question dealt in purified alkali metals such as sodium and calcium, a far cry in the Table of Elements from uranium.

He carefully slipped the certificates back into the envelope and walked to the closet. His good blue suit, much sponged and pressed, was there on a heavy wooden hanger he had taken from the Hyatt Regency in San Francisco several months before. The suit had been tailored for him in St. Paul years ago and the lapels were somewhat narrow by current fashion standards but the tailor had made sure he could carry the large kraft envelope in the suit coat without ruining its lines. After all, you didn't go to dinner lugging along a brief case. The tailor had been a genuine craftsman; it had been a pity to have to leave St. Paul so soon after the suit had been delivered, but it would have been a mere matter of hours before the tailor discovered that his credit card had lapsed the year before. Computers had definitely made his life more difficult, even the primitive ones back then.

He would be leaving the Glass House soon, too, he

thought; he was behind in his rent and the business office was getting a bit stiff in its demands. The long weekend would probably see it, unless he was exceptionally lucky or could persuade Lisolette to be of some help.

He put on the trousers, following it with the coat, slipped the envelope into place, then swore to himself when he realized he had dribbled ashes onto the lapel. He took a clothes brush off its closet hook and began to scrub at the faint gray powder stains, in the process knocking off more of the hot ash from the cigarette dangling between his lips. A coal lit on some fluff on the closet floor and glowed brightly for a moment before he stomped it out. Coughing slightly, he returned to the bedroom and took another cigarette from the pack on the bureau. He would have to quit; at his age, he smoked entirely too much. Lisolette had chided him about that in her schoolmarmish way and for an instant she had sounded like an echo of his long dead wife who had constantly nagged him, saying, "Harlee, you're rotting your lungs out with those things." Later, he wondered if she had been prescient; she had been at it long before the Surgeon General's warning.

In many respects, Lisolette reminded him of her. Heavier, of course, but the same sparkling eyes, quick wit and broad, cultural interests. He had found her fascinating from the start and there were times when he regretted his baser motives in seeking her out. But one had to live and the rule of the world was still eat or be eaten. He knew from the discreet inquiries he had made—granted his questioning of Jernigan tonight had not been discreet; indeed it had been a serious mistake—that she had a teacher's pension and a small inheritance. The amount of money that Lisolette would be willing to "invest" would probably be small, but he had no intentions of pushing it, of leaving her destitute or even badly inconvenienced. That was one of the rules of the game: You never sheared the sheep so close it hurt. They seldom went to the police then, but he liked to think there was a touch of altruism to it as well.

He carefully knotted the blue paisley tie and then inserted the tie tac, looking in the mirror as he centered the latter. He carefully shot his cuffs so the proper fraction of an inch was exposed, then stopped. Smoke. For a moment he thought it was the butt of his earlier cigarette which he had failed to scrub completely out, then realized the odor was of burning cloth. He carefully inspected the rug on the floor, kicking the nap this way and that, then thought, panic-stricken, that it might be coming from his other suit, the brown one. He ran to the closet, pulling the suit off the hanger and spreading it out on the bed for a quick inspection. Nothing. He returned to the closet where he had stomped out the coal earlier, searching through the slight whorls of dust and hair on the floor. Then he spotted the faint haze of smoke. A spark from his cigarette had lodged in the seat of one of his good pair of slacks and smoldered to the point where there was a charred spot the size of a dime in the top of the inseam.

He pinched the fire out, momentarily feeling both disgusted and depressed. They were his best trousers, expensive double knits that he had purchased only a year before. He might be able to mend them but he doubted it. That was the trouble with knits; it cost a lot to have them rewoven and, in any event, he had little enough money remaining as it was.

Well, there was no helping it now. No matter how fond he was of Lisolette, the burn in the trousers had underscored the fact that he was broke and tonight he would have to score. Perhaps, if she didn't go for stocks, he could manage a small personal loan. "My dear, I'm terribly embarrassed but my financial man hasn't forwarded my monthly check and . . ." Lisolette would undoubtedly be softhearted enough to sit still for a loan.

All of his ladies had been very generous.

The fire races over the surface of the charring fabric and digs deeply into the cotton batting underneath. Burning linters fall to the tiled floor. Flames burrow beneath the mats, charring the interiors. The air above the mats shimmers as smoke and heat rise from the flames. The temperature of the metal shelving over the mats climbs —first a mere ten degrees, then another ten, climbing until the battleship green of the underside of the shelf turns olive, then dark brown. Bubbles of gas form under the paint, pushing it out in glowing blisters that char even as they grow. The paint is leprous now, bubbling outward, charring and flaking away to fall on the mats below.

On the shelf itself, a metal can suddenly pops its seams as its flat sides distend in the heat. The liquid squirts out from the vapor pressure inside. Nearby, the paper label of a gallon jug, half filled with a murky opalescent liquid, begins to brown. Glue flakes away from the underside of the label and falls in brittle fragments as the label curls off the side of the bottle. The curling label chars, blackens, and abruptly dissolves in sparks. The next instant the bottle cracks apart like a shattered egg and liquid gushes from its interior onto the shelf, running along the retaining edge that acts as a dam. Then the liquid reaches the end of the shelf and thin streams spatter down on the matting below, almost extinguishing part of the fire before the liquid itself vaporizes. There is a brief pause as the flammable vapors spill down over the matting, then a small whooshing sound as the liquid blazes up.

In the machinery room near the top of the Glass House, several panels light up with red strips and there is the siren of the smoke sensors. There is no one on duty to hear. In the basement, Griff Edwards curses his age and weakening kidneys and the blackness of his coffee and goes to the washroom down the hall. When he finishes, *he hesitates a moment, then climbs to the lobby in hopes that the bulldog edition of the morning paper is now out; the crossword puzzle helps pass away the long hours of the night watch. The stream of diners to the Prŏmenade Room has lessened for the moment and he stops to talk to Sue. She is a pretty girl with personal problems and Griff is a sympathetic listener; she has little to fear from him and he is flattered by her confidences. In the basement, the heat panels light up a brilliant red and the smoke sensors whine for attention. The direct connection to the Fire Department has buzzed briefly. Then a faulty solder connection has parted and the signal has died. The trouble light on the panel has been inoperative for a week without detection. The man on monitoring duty who had glanced up at the first signal has gone back to jotting down figures from an endless row of meters, the momentary signal forgotten.*

In the room, the beast grasps at the thin streams of liquid and climbs them like a boy going hand over hand up a rope. The pool of liquid on the shelf ignites with a small roar of triumph. Other metal cans make loud pang-ing sounds as their contents overheat and the cans themselves explode. Two more bottles shatter and liquid cascades down over the flaming mats below.

The surface of the shelf is completely aflame now and metal cans are rupturing in a deadly sequence. The shattering of gallon and quart containers sounds like corn being popped for a birthday party. Which, of course, it is.

The beast is now three hours old.

~~⌒⊙⌒~~

17.

The trip in the scenic elevator had been spectacular and even frightening and Lisolette had not been shy in clinging to Harlee most of the way up. As they stepped into the foyer of the Promenade Room, she couldn't resist saying, "As many times as I've had lunch here, I've never come up this way. It's like my cousin in New York who's never been to the top of the Empire State Building."

Claiborne was flattered, as he suspected Lisolette meant him to be. He offered his arm and Lisolette took it firmly, allowing him to guide her toward the reservation desk. "My dear, you can't imagine what a pleasure it is to have such a charming dinner companion to show off."

"Many compliments like that and you'll turn my head, even at my age, Harlee."

"I would consider myself lucky if I could." He paused before the desk and waited for Quinn Reynolds, the hostess, to return. "Odd," he said, "I've always wondered why they didn't have a maître d' up here."

· "It's the luncheon trade, Harlee—the clientele is mostly women who have come to do their shopping down below. I imagine they feel more at ease with a hostess and waitresses." She looked through the windows of the dining room to the thick clouds outside. "Thank goodness, we don't have to go out to dine on a night like tonight."

Quinn Reynolds approached from the dining floor and Claiborne smiled at her somewhat warily. "Good evening, Miss Reynolds, reservations for two?"

For a moment Quinn seemed to hesitate and Claiborne felt his stomach start to knot. She knew, he thought. Quinn glanced down at her reservation list and then up at Lisolette, who was still holding tightly to Claiborne's arm, glowing with pleasure at the prospects of the evening ahead. "Of course, Mr. Claiborne." She broke into a smile. "It's good to see you again, Miss Mueller. Won't you come this way?" She picked up two black-edged

118

menus and led them down the steps to the dining floor and a far table near one of the windows. Claiborne helped Lisolette out of her coat, which Quinn took, then held her chair while she seated herself and draped the huge, white bird of a napkin carefully on her lap.

Before Claiborne had a chance to sit down, Quinn said easily, "I wonder if I might see you a moment, Mr. Claiborne? We'll have to make a substitution on the wine you asked to have chilled and my only available list at the moment is at the desk."

Claiborne shrugged. "Of course." He knew perfectly well what she wanted. He made apologies to Lisolette, and followed Quinn back to her desk.

"I'm terribly sorry, Mr. Claiborne," Quinn said quietly, once out of range of Lisolette's hearing. "I know this is embarrassing but your bill here is now almost two hundred dollars. Accounting has notified me not to accept your signature until that has been settled." She was uncomfortable in telling him, Claiborne could tell, but determined.

"My dear," he said, patting her hand, "you're a charming girl and I have no desire to cause you embarrassment. I'll take care of my account tomorrow. It's just that I've encountered a temporary cash flow problem; all of that is cleared up now."

The muscles jumped in Quinn's cheeks and her voice chilled. "I'm sorry, Mr. Claiborne, but I have my orders. Frankly, I wish I could accept your signature tonight. I'm quite fond of Miss Mueller and I realize your embarrassment would be hers as well. . . ."

"No matter, my dear," Claiborne said lightly, "I'll be very glad to take care of the bill by cash tonight."

Quinn smiled. "That will be fine, Mr. Claiborne—I'm sorry these things happen. Do have a pleasant evening."

"I'm sure we will, Miss Reynolds." He retraced his steps to the table, thinking grimly: It has to be tonight. Much as he liked Lisolette, there was no other way out —he might even be evicted from the building tomorrow. He was sure, when the time came to pay the bill, that he could pretend he had left his wallet below. Miss

Reynolds wouldn't cause a fuss, if for no other reason than out of deference to Lisolette. But she would report it to the manager. And, of course, there would be no chance that he would be seated in the future.

Lisolette looked up at him as he sat down. "Any trouble, Harlee? You were gone so long . . ."

"Trouble? Of course not, my dear, no real problem at all. You'll have a cocktail, of course?"

"You're trying to lead me astray," Lisolette said, her eyes sparkling.

He laughed. "Perhaps." She ordered a frozen daiquiri and he hesitated a moment, then asked for a double martini. "The chill," he said, pointing out the window. "I need the fortification."

There was a doubt in her eyes which she quickly masked. "You seem distressed," she said noncommittally.

"Not really," he said, choosing his words carefully. "I suppose I'm basically a tragic man—in the midst of pleasure and the joys of good companionship, I remember how soon these things must end." The drinks came and he sipped his while she tasted her own.

"The Germans have a word for it," Lisolette said. "They call it *Weltschmerz*—world weariness."

He laughed. "That's too grand a term for it."

"Perhaps it's something more on the order of what Sudermann once wrote about. Are you familiar with Sudermann?"

"I'm afraid I'm not," he said, somewhat wary. This was a side of Lisolette that he hadn't quite expected and wasn't prepared for.

"Well, he was once a most popular writer. I was thinking of his *Frau Sorge,* which translates roughly as *Dame Care.* It's about a boy cursed throughout his life with care and sorrow. Sudermann was much like Thomas Hardy in his outlook—*Frau Sorge* is actually the Germanic counterpart of *Jude the Obscure.*"

She was beyond him, he thought. His ladies had been gentle and charming and generous but seldom intellectual. He felt like somebody who was fond of white wine and had just been introduced to champagne. "Poor Jude," he laughed. "No, Lisolette, I'm afraid that even there I don't stand up to such a grand comparison. I'm not a sorrowful man by nature—rather an optimistic one, in fact."

"Very much like my father," she said thoughtfully. "You would have liked him. He was a master brewer in St. Louis, at the Schwartz Brau Brewery. He was a very fierce, and very loving, man."

"He produced a lovely daughter."

"No obvious flattery, Harlee." She laughed, then was thoughtful again. "He was . . . formidable. He came over here from Frankfurt am Main—*Sud' Deutsch* and very proud of his cultural heritage, something he passed on to me." The shadow of a more tragic memory passed over her face. "He was a very brave man, too; he almost died for it in the late thirties."

"Oh?" Claiborne said gently. She obviously wanted to talk and he was perfectly willing to let her.

"Those were the days of the German-American Bund and they were very strong in South St. Louis. One could go to the Schwartzwald, the Black Forest, and see swastikas and oak leaves all over the walls and men marching around in brown shirts with armbands, belts, and SS caps —all of that dreadful type of costume." She suddenly seemed depressed.

"That was a long time ago, Lisolette."

"Perhaps not to me. Papa and I went to the park one time—I must have been twenty-one or -two at the time. . . . I was just getting into my graduate work—and there were a group of them marching and doing close-order drill. Papa called them a disgrace to the land of Schiller and Beethoven and he got into a dreadful fight with their officer . . . then the rest of them started beating him. The police came but it was too late and Papa almost died."

"Did they hurt *you?*" Claiborne asked after a moment of silence.

Lisolette smiled; for once it wasn't a kind smile. "There was a metal stake thrust into the ground near a trash can. I pulled it up and attacked one of them who was trying to kick Papa with his foot. I put him in the hospital." There was a somewhat sad triumphant look in her eyes. "Perhaps it was a terrible thing to do but I couldn't let them do that to Papa, could I?"

He looked at her and suddenly remembered his long dead wife, Adele. Both Lisolette and Adele were possessed of the same sort of fierce pride. It was exactly the sort of thing Adele might have done. A formidable woman, he thought. He toasted Lisolette silently and she joined him, her eyes misty with memories. "I've missed Papa over the years," she said slowly. "Mama died when I was very young and he was . . . quite important to me all of my life."

"Did you ever marry, Lisolette?"

She shook her head, staring down at her drink. "Papa never recovered from the beating; I had to take care of him. It wasn't that I was never asked, you know." She looked up, the sparkle back in her eyes. "Would it surprise you if I said I'm not a virgin?" She smiled warmly. "Do I shock you?"

"Hardly," he said, laughing.

"Well, I'm not," she said proudly. She pressed a hand to her mouth. "A little alcohol and I say too much—you must excuse me, Harlee. Nevertheless, it's true and I feel pleased that I knew what love was. But there was Papa, and, of course, the children . . . all the dear children I taught, all the fine young girls and boys. I suppose that became my life instead."

Remarkable, he thought, there was so much within her that he found himself admiring. So much strength. She seemed giddy at times, but underneath there was that raw-boned strength.

"Now tell me about your stocks—before they bring the food so that we can enjoy our dinner."

She had taken him by surprise; he had almost forgotten why he had asked her to dinner. "Perhaps later on," he stalled.

"I think now would be better," she said. "There's so much you'll have to explain to me."

He took out the envelope and spread the contents on

the table. She listened attentively, taking it all in, but for some reason his heart wasn't in it. Her obvious trust in him made him feel uncomfortable; it took away the pleasure of the game, of the conquest.

"Now, Lisolette, you must remember that stocks of this sort—most over-the-counter stocks—are highly speculative."

"But if you think the chances are good, Harlee . . ." she began.

"You really should give it a great deal of thought," he said seriously. What the hell was wrong with him? he wondered. He was blowing the whole pitch.

"You know I trust your judgment," she said simply. She fingered the certificates in front of her. "They're very pretty, aren't they? Very impressive." She glanced at him, her face open. "What should I buy, Harlee? You'll have to tell me."

"The metal stocks," he began. He could feel the sweat in his armpits and on his forehead.

"Yes?"

Suddenly he was very angry with her, with himself. "You trust me completely, don't you, Lisolette?"

Her face was suddenly quite serious. "Of course."

"Why should you?" he asked slowly. "Why should you trust my judgment—or me either, for that matter?"

She looked flustered. "You're angry. Did I say something wrong?"

"You're trusting, Lisolette," he said grimly. "Much too trusting."

"Is there any reason why I shouldn't trust you?" She looked perplexed.

He leaned back in his chair and took a long drink of the martini. His ex-wife, he thought, he had forgotten how much he had loved her. And Lisolette was her duplicate. Adele had trusted him with the business, with her bank accounts, and she had left him everything in her will. She had loved him, too.

"Lisolette," he said slowly, "what if I told you that these stocks were absolutely worthless, that they're not worth the parchment they're printed on. I should know—

I printed most of them myself." He touched one of them. "You're right—they're beautiful, but worthless. They're fake." He looked up at her. "So am I, Lisolette. I don't have a dollar to my name, I'm two months behind in the rent; I can't even pay for our dinner tonight."

Lisolette frowned. "When one is in desperate straits . . ."

"You misunderstand," he said impatiently. "This is my way of life." He hesitated. "You aren't the first one; I'm sure there are a dozen warrants waiting for me around the country, although most of my ladies are too well bred to bring charges."

"Your ladies," she said, smiling.

"My ladies," he said, suddenly unaccountably sad. "My poor ladies."

"You're a very sensitive man, Harlee."

He looked at her sharply. "You haven't heard a word I've said, have you?"

"Of course I have. Every word."

"You don't seem surprised."

She made a gesture. "Why should I be? I knew all this long before tonight; it was very easy to check."

He stared at her, shocked, and then suddenly angry. "And you let me go ahead and make a fool of myself?"

She reached out and took one of his hands. "That's not it at all. You're a lovely, gentle man, and I wouldn't hurt you for all the world. I wouldn't have missed the money— and you have given me so much more."

"You would have gone ahead with it, let me take your money?"

"If it had come to that—though perhaps not as much as you wanted."

"Lisa," he said, for the first time using the diminutive form of her name, "you're really an astonishing woman."

She smiled. "No, just a woman who has lived a long time and still has an eye for the gentlemen." Suddenly she was overcome with delight at her judgment. "Would it surprise you if I knew you would tell me all about the stock certificates, the truth about them? I told Rosette that you were the most honest man I had ever met!"

He laughed quietly. "God, I wish I had known you

earlier." And then he realized that he had, and that he had married her. Adele. She was Adele all over again.

"Now," Lisolette said, suddenly very matter-of-fact, "while you were trying to convince Miss Reynolds that she should allow us to eat here, I took the liberty of ordering chateaubriand and a bottle of Château Lafite Rothschild, '64. You see, I *do* know what gentlemen like!"

"Why . . . ?"

She shrugged. "I knew what she must be saying to you —and I wanted you to enjoy the evening with me."

How like Adele, he thought. How much like Adele. And yet—how uniquely Lisolette Mueller.

18.

Thelma and Jenny had shown up and Barton and Leroux, not wishing to talk business in front of them, had gone for a stroll on the promenade. There were still ten minutes before their table would be ready. Time enough to ask Leroux questions that Quantrell's TV program had brought up—more than time, probably; considering how crowded the room was and that nobody was in a hurry to venture back outside. The table would undoubtedly be late anyway and with less tension and hostility on Leroux's part. Barton was beginning to enjoy himself. He was inside where it was warm and smelled pleasantly of food, and relaxed enough to admire the beauty of the soft snow drifting past the windows. It was almost a ghost snow— light, puffy flakes that clung to the glass for a moment before dissolving into tears of water that trickled down out of sight.

"Craig, you've been around architecture and construction long enough to realize there's no such thing as a fire- proof building, the best we can build is a fire-resistant one," Leroux was saying. "Almost anything will burn; it all depends on how hot it gets. That's your basic premise. After that, we get into time—how long will a piece of wood or a strip of rug resist charring, resist breaking into open flame? And at what temperature? Almost anything that goes into any building has a fire rating—it's the law. And then there are building codes that every construction firm has to follow. We're no different from the others. We do our best to compete; we cut unnecessary corners and frills —that's the name of the game. But we don't break the law. The city has inspectors; the Fire Department has inspectors; the insurance companies have inspectors. If they don't approve of the construction of one of our buildings, we can't open it up for tenancy. It's as simple as that."

Barton swirled his drink for a moment and thought that it was anything but as simple as that. Leroux was pitching him and he wondered why the older man was making the effort.

"What about insurance trade offs? Quantrell implied that a builder could completely sprinkler his building, for example, and perhaps get a reduced rate from the insurance company that would help pay for the sprinkler system. True?"

Leroux laughed. "That's almost a knee-slapper. He might actually find his insurance rates going up; there's always the chance that something will set off the sprinklers accidentally and if they're in a shop area with goods below, you've got one expensive, unholy mess on your hands. And few tenants would go for unsightly dropheads in their ceiling. What might happen is that you might get trade offs from the city in the form of relaxation of other parts of the fire code. For the majority of high rises, however, there's not much chance of lower insurance rates. Insurance is dirt cheap to begin with—there are something like four hundred companies out there bidding for your business. Frankly, the annual light-bulb bill for the Glass House will run to more than our annual insurance premiums."

Barton drained his glass. Good, but they had included everything but ice cream in his Ramos fizz. He signaled for another. "How come it's so cheap?"

Leroux looked angry. "Because, despite everything that

Mr. Quantrell implies, fires in high-rise buildings are scarcer than tits on a boar hog. Sure, they happen—so do airplanes crashes. But, relatively speaking, the annual fatalities are so low as to be nonexistent. How much insurance can you buy for fifty cents at the local airport—fifteen thousand dollars' worth?" He calmed a little. "All the public areas in the Glass House are sprinklered—they have to be. Install them throughout an entire building and the expense would be so high you'd no longer be competitive. Sears Roebuck did it in their headquarters building, as much for public image as for safety. But we're not Sears —at least not this year."

Maybe he was tired, maybe it was because Leroux was trying too hard, but Barton didn't feel convinced.

"Craig, look out there. That building about two o'clock to your right. the one with the small red beacon on top. The Penobscot Building. National Curtainwall was the developer there. And on your left, about the same relative position—the Hanson Building is ours, too. There are half a dozen more in town, all ours." For a moment he was lost in thought. "In a sense, Craig, we're the original ecologists. Mankind can't go on expanding his living space forever, cutting down forests and leveling the hills. Los Angeles houses a population two thirds that of Chicago in twice its space. We can't afford suburbia forever; we have to get back to the city, the city that was invented as a trading center, as a manufacturing center, designed so the worker could be close to his job." He flicked the ash off his cigar. "We build cities, Craig—it's not a mean occupation."

He wasn't Caesar after all, Barton thought. He was Ramses; he was a pyramid builder.

"You mentioned earlier that you had seen Joe Moore's project," Leroux said. "Do you know what's behind it?"

Barton suddenly felt stone sober. "No, but I'd like to. For some strange reason, Wyn, I can't see a country full of replicas of the Glass House."

Leroux smiled. "You might see one or two, probably no more than that—local conditions vary too much from city to city. But I wouldn't deny that you'll see some that

are remarkably similar, that might differ only in external
detailing or such things as size of site, height—you could
list the variables. And you'll see parts of it incorporated in
buildings that might, to the untrained eye, seem radically
different. I wish I could claim the original idea but a hotel
chain beat me to it. Their flagship hotels are all designed
after the same general model—a shell of rooms surrounding an enormous interior lobby, complete with 'outside'
elevators running the height of the lobby, fountains, plaza-
type restaurants, the works. The lobbies may vary in size
and shape but they're still the same idea. For the most
part, the basic problems of cantilevered floors and the
like have all been figured out; you make the modifications
you want and the building goes up in nothing flat."

Leroux was leading up to something, Barton thought
uneasily. He had said earlier that he couldn't do without
him, which was ridiculous, but there had to be a reason
why Leroux thought so.

"Construction is a hazardous occupation financially,"
Leroux continued. "It's one where time is often the most
critical factor. As a developer, we first have to arrange
for interim financing, usually with a bank or a real estate
investment trust, where the interest rates are high—banks
don't like to tie up their capital for long periods of time,
for one thing. And the building itself represents a risk, it
exists only on paper and a lot of things can go wrong between the rendering and the completed project. God help
you if you run into trouble putting in your foundations,
for example. When the building is finished, we arrange for
permanent financing, usually with an insurance company.
The finished building is much less of a risk and the rates
are lower. One of your obvious expenses, of course, is
how long you tie up the initial capital."

"You taught me all of that in the first six months,"
Barton said shortly. "You've been a good teacher."

It was Leroux's turn to signal for another drink.
"Developers and builders naturally try to beat that problem. The first thing was to junk the traditional method
of acquiring the site, having the architectural firm prepare
a complete set of working drawings, then calling for bids.

Unfortunately, there's the time factor—the time to turn out the drawings, the time required for contractors to plow through all the drawings to make their bids. You can lose six months, perhaps close to a year. So most high rises are 'scope' jobs or built by 'fast-track' methods. You usually don't ask for bids. As soon as the initial shape is pinned down, we start construction of the basic building the foundation, frame, skin, basic mechanical, the core with the fire stairs, elevators, and the like. You work from the shell inward, essentially doing a lot of your designing at the same time you're building, though granted that much of your basic designing may have been done before the rendering. You do an estimate of the quantity of materials you'd need, even though you may not have decided on a specific use for them at the time of the estimate. There's an element of waste involved but you save on the most valuable commodity of all—time."

"You're leading up to something, Wyn; what is it?"

"The idea is to have a proven product, Craig, like the hotel chain I mentioned. Or the Glass House. It's a beautiful building; we'll market it in various permutations and combinations—again, like the hotels. But because there's so little risk with a proven product, there's no need for risk capital, for interim financing, and the high interest rates. You eliminate the middle man financially. Which cuts the expense of the building to the eventual owner."

"The only thing he doesn't get is something that's uniquely his own," Barton said bitterly. "Something that's an expression of his own corporation or business."

Leroux waved his hand at the skyline. "There are a lot of buildings out there, Craig. How many of them strike you as beautiful? One out of ten perhaps? Or is that a highly inflated figure? What's wrong with a Glass House here and a slightly different version of it in Milwaukee? Nobody lives in two cities at the same time; the natives would hardly be offended."

Leroux had sold Moore on the idea, Barton thought. That's what he had sensed and that's what Moore hadn't wanted to admit—that he had actually considered Leroux's idea to be a good one.

"You're telling me this for a reason, Wyn. I gather there's some role you have in mind that I'm supposed to play?"

"That's right." Leroux suddenly looked troubled, unsure of himself because of Barton's lack of enthusiastic response. "This isn't something that's going to happen several years from now; it's in the works already. United Insurance has agreed to finance all National Curtainwall buildings—at permanent financing rates. We'll be developer, designer, do the general contracting, decorate, and manage. We'll be hard to beat."

"We'll turn out buildings like GM turns out cars, that it? Complete with a five-year guarantee?"

"That's one way of looking at it," Leroux said coldly. "It isn't mine."

"And me?"

"You were right earlier—I don't need your talents as an architect . . . I already bought those. I need managerial talent; I need somebody to help me run the show. I hand-picked you and I hand-trained you during the last two years. You're the man I want—you're the only man I've had time enough to teach. That was probably a mistake."

Barton turned back to the window. Opportunity . . . again. New title, new salary, success with a capital "S" because if Leroux had figured it right, in a few years National Curtainwall would be one of the largest developers in the country. But opportunity had come when he didn't want it, when he had already made up his mind as to what he was going to do. Leroux kept opening doors for him that he didn't want to walk through.

"The concept isn't quite as narrow as you might think," Leroux continued persuasively. "The Glass House is only one example; there'll be other . . . models, if you like."

The snowflakes were getting finer, Barton thought idly, and coming down with greater force. The wind must really be howling around the building.

"It's a big job," Leroux added, irritated. "Maybe you're not a big enough man for it."

"Oh, for Christ's sake, Wyn, cut it out—I'm not twenty

years old. I didn't say I wouldn't take it. I want time to think it over." Jenny would be delighted, he thought bitterly.

Suddenly Quinn was at their elbow, saying softly: "Your table's ready now—would you follow me, please?" She was pleasant but decidedly formal, probably because of the presence of Leroux, Barton thought.

They followed her into the dining room where Thelma and Jenny were already seated. Barton gave his drink order—black coffee and preferably immediately—and squeezed Jenny's hand. She was unresponsive and distant, a slim, dark-haired girl in her middle twenties whose classic beauty was marred only by a too-thin nose. At one time, Barton thought morosely, she was full of life, relaxed and outgoing. That had been one of the things that had attracted him to her; in so many ways she had been like Quinn, only a younger version. Tonight, as usual lately, she was withdrawn and remote; she wouldn't have ten words to say throughout the entire meal.

He turned his attention to Thelma Leroux. The enigma in Leroux's life, he thought. A woman he would probably never quite understand, but one whom he instinctively respected. Younger than Leroux, though perhaps not by much. Like Wyndom, she was from North Carolina and still possessed a lingering trace of southern accent and charm. A naturally warm, self-confident woman who had somehow endowed matronhood with sensuality. She was slightly chubby—just enough to prevent the crepe from forming under her throat—with pale, smooth skin and frost-tinged hair. And despite her sophistication, there was still an earthiness about her. She could probably mingle with construction foremen as easily as with dowagers and still be herself, he thought.

"You know," Thelma said, "as long as the building's been open, I've never eaten here."

"That's Wyn's fault," Barton said. "He should have taken you here long before now. Curtainwall could even pick up the tab as a business expense."

"Like hell it could," Leroux interrupted. "The IRS watches us like a hawk."

"It's a beautiful place, Craig, and the service seems delightful, too." Thelma's eyes sparkled with a hint of mischief. "The hostess seemed to know you. Is she somebody out of your past?"

Barton smiled. "Quinn's an old friend I once dated a long time ago—before I met Jenny."

"How long before, Craig?" Jenny's voice was small and stiff and there was sudden silence at the table.

"As a matter of fact," Barton said curtly, "*just* before I met you. You and she were much alike—I told you about Quinn."

"She seems older than I had expected," Jenny said coolly.

"More mature," Barton corrected shortly. Irritated, he whipped his place napkin off the table, his elbow knocking over the carafe of water in the process. It shattered on the floor and he swore softly to himself, almost not hearing Thelma's quiet "There's no damage, Craig—the waitress shouldn't have left it so near the edge." Quinn was already sending over a bus boy with a small broom and several napkins to soak up the water.

Barton turned to the table behind him at which a middle-aged, rather stout woman and an elderly, dapper man were sitting. "I'm sorry if you were splashed, I'll make good the cleaning. . . ."

"No, no, I wouldn't think of it," the woman said, smiling. "It's only water. *Mein lieber Gott*—think how wet we would be if we were outside! Isn't that right, Harlee?"

"Quite right, my dear. Don't trouble yourself, sir, it's trifling. I assure you." He was brushing at some spots on his suit and there was a tone in his voice that made Barton wonder if his response would have been the same if his wife hadn't spoken up first.

He turned back to the table. It was going to be a long night. he thought, and Jenny had apparently made up her mind to make it even longer.

"It must have been rough flying weather today," Thelma was saying, spreading a thin oil of conversation over the troubled waters. "Or does the weather bother you when you fly? I know it would me, particularly if I had to leave San Francisco to come here."

Barton couldn't help smiling. Thelma into the breach, he thought. He envied Leroux.

19.

Time was running out and Jesus was beginning to feel panicky. He had followed his mother from office to office as she methodically emptied wastebaskets into the large canvas bag in the frame she wheeled behind her, begging and pleading for money. Her answer had always been a mumbled "no." He was angry one minute and sobbing the next and then he started to get increasingly mean. He was already very close to the time when Spinner had planned on meeting him. Twenty minutes more and Spinner would have left; he had other appointments. Besides, Spinner had been nervous ever since his last bust; if Jesus stood him up, he might get suspicious and turn Jesus off completely. After all, he had a record and Spinner might think the cops were using him to entrap dealers. . . .

Jesus felt the sweat dampen his armpits and ooze over his forehead. Spinner would think that, in fact it would be the first thing that Spinner would think. Jesus was constantly fighting nausea now and instinctively knew the cramps were only minutes away.

"Mama, you've got to help me!"

She shook her head. "No. You help yourself."

"You want I should do something terrible?" The top of his upper lip was soaked and he was beginning to shake.

"I have no money," she said stoically, tugging at her cart.

"Mama, I got to meet this man, I got to have the money. You don't know what it's like. If I don't make this connection, it could kill me."

Her eyes suddenly flicked at him. "Connection?"

He licked his lips, then ripped at the buttons on his sleeves and pushed the cuffs up over his knobby elbows. He held out his arms with the veins showing. "You see these, Mama?" he asked thickly. "They're tracks. From needles. I'm hooked, Mama; I'm hooked on heroin. I need a fix. You know what I mean? I need a fix, Mama; if I don't get it, it could kill me."

"Kill you? You kill yourself."

He grabbed her shoulders then, his thin fingers digging into her flesh. She winced with pain and pulled free. "Maybe you kill me instead," she said angrily. "Is that what you want to do; kill me, maybe? You want twenty dollars. I don't have twenty dollars. Ask as much as you like, I don't have it."

She was lying, he thought, she had to have it. "You don't care what happens to me!" he yelled angrily. "Maybe you want me to go out and rip off some mark in an alley, is that what you want? A brick in a sock and there he is and all I have to do is go through his pockets. Or maybe I hit him too hard and he never wakes up. You never think I hurt anybody, Mama? You never think I hide in an alley and wait for somebody to go by? You don't know me, Mama, you never knew me!"

She emptied a basket into the cart, followed it with the contents of several ashtrays, and wiped them out with a damp rag. "Turn yourself in," she grunted. "Maybe that can help you." He didn't see the tears that were forming at the corners of her eyes.

"Mama," he said slowly, the strength draining out of him as he felt the nausea build again, "I don't need to ask you. I can go down on the street and get money. I can sell myself, Mama; I can let old men use me like a girl." His voice was almost a sob now. "They pay me, Mama; I'm good at it. I don't want to, but I got to."

Her back was to him and the tears stood on her cheeks like raindrops. "So you're a girl," she said. "You're not a man." Her voice was close to breaking, but he didn't notice.

The nausea passed and he came around the desk and pushed her back against it. "Maybe I should report you to welfare, Mama," he hissed. "You're living with Martinez, only you ain't married to him. I turn you in and they take you off the lists; they don't know about your job here. You want me to do that? I will, Mama; I swear to God I will! They'll throw you out of that dump you live in and you ain't ever going to find another place that cheap to stay!"

"Jesus!" For a moment her emotions showed and then they were washed away in silent tears. "I have another floor to clean tonight. Maria didn't come to work." She huddled inside her uniform. "Leave me alone, Jesus, just leave me alone. I got to do my job."

He leaned over and swept a desk clean of its files and letter trays and telephone, sending them clattering to the floor. "Why should I care about your goddamned job? What's it mean to me?" He suddenly struck a match and held it over the canvas bag in the waste cart, filled with the scrap paper from a dozen offices. "Your goddamned job . . . I'll burn down your goddamned job! You want to see me do it? I will, Mama, you know I will!" She was now thoroughly frightened and reached for a phone on another desk to call security. Jesus batted it out of her hands, his eyes wild. "Mama, I want money, you understand me? I want it now!"

He could feel the weakness start again and he began to gag. "I know you've got money, Mama," he said faintly.

Out of the corner of his eye he could see her clutch almost automatically at her pocket. "I knew it, goddamnit!" he shouted. He came slowly around the desk, holding out his hand. "Gimme the wallet or I'll break your fucking arm!"

She tried to run, to reach another phone, and he pounced on her, knocking her against the desk and pulling the phone out of the floor connection. Then she was running for the office door. He tripped her, grabbing at her smock. She held her hands over the pocket containing her wallet but his fingers were already there, pulling, tearing.

"Please, Jesus, *por Dios!*"

"Speak English, Mama," he sneered. The next instant he had torn the wallet from her pocket and was leafing through the contents. Oh, Christ, sixteen bucks . . . Maybe Spinner would consider it on account, maybe half a bag would get him through. He pushed past her and had just opened the door to the hall when the first of the cramps hit him and he abruptly doubled up, gasping for breath and gagging at the same time. He sagged against the door frame, fighting for strength.

Albina was running toward him now, her face wet with tears but an angry look in her eyes. Jesus turned his back to her to fend her off and then she had seized the wallet and money from his hand and he was too feeble to resist. "Mama, don't . . ."

She was running for the elevator bank and he started after her, a little of his strength returning. She pressed the call button, then glanced at him coming toward her and changed her mind and ran for the stairwell door. He caught her when she was half through, grabbing her wrist to twist the cash out of her hand. They were making too much noise, he thought, and if that fat faggot Douglas had called security, the guards would be on them any minute. His mother had started to cry for help and he clamped a hand on her mouth and at the same time tried to pull the money out of her hand. She fell backward, pulling him with her, and they tumbled through the open door onto the landing. The door started to swing inexorably shut and Jesus leaped for it, shouting, "Catch it!" His fingers scrabbled at the edge of the metal and then he heard the lock click into place.

"Goddamnit, see what you've done!" Jesus snarled, whirling on his mother. "We're trapped!" She huddled, sobbing, on the landing, her back to the wall, clutching the wallet to her breast and trying to stuff the crumpled bills back into it. For a moment they stood glaring at each other and then Jesus felt something else suddenly grip his stomach. It wasn't nausea . . . it was the smell of smoke. He turned to look down the stairwell.

The air in the well below was already hazy with it.

In the machinery room at the top of the Glass House and in the subbasement, the whine of the smoke sensors has stopped and the glow of the heat indicators has faded. The electrical connections to the instruments have been burned through, the sensors themselves twisted or melted lumps of metal. Griff Edwards waddles back to his desk, spreads out his paper, and tries to think of a two-letter word that is a composing room term; he is uncertain whether the last letter is an "n" or an "m." Since the panel trouble light isn't working, he does not realize the futility of his vigil.

A number of floors above, the beast is feeding hungrily and raging around the confines of the room. It is now brilliantly lit—a storage room filled with rows of shelves and lockers holding drums and bottles of solvents and waxes, half-open cartons of toweling and toilet paper. The majority of these have started to char, ready to add more fuel to the flames surrounding them.

Most of the bottles on the shelves above the burning mats have burst in the intense heat, dribbling their contents over the mats below. Close by, a locker suddenly bursts open as a five-gallon drum inside explodes. A few feet away, the flames are clawing at several fifty-gallon drums resting on their sides in a metal rack. The drums contain a stripping solvent, trichloroethylene, for removing old wax from tile floors. The stenciled letters on the lower drum have begun to fade into the surrounding char as the paint on the drum blisters. The solvent inside begins to vaporize, building up pressure to the point where the ends of the drum are bulging with a terrible pregnancy.

The walls of the room, except for the one that doubles as the wall of the utility core, are of dry-wall plaster. The paper surfacing of the wall panels has already charred and the plaster in the paper-plaster sandwich is steaming, breaking down under the heat and buckling from the in-

137

ternal pressures of carbon dioxide being driven from the plaster itself. Overhead, the perforated acoustical tile has buckled and torn loose from the ceiling. Under ordinary circumstances, the tile is relatively fire resistant but the tile itself is now charring and disintegrating as its binder decomposes under the intense heat. On the floor below, the asphalt tile, protected somewhat by its heat absorbing contact with the concrete floor, is nevertheless melting on the surface and in many places, bulging. Where the tile bulges and curls away from the floor, it melts, slumps, and begins to burn with a smoky flame. Near the ceiling, a stringer holding a fifteen-foot fluorescent light fixture gives way and the fixture, still suspended from the other stringer, falls, smashing into the surface of melted tile.

The pressure in the nearby drum of trichloroethylene has finally become too great and the spigot shoots across the room, propelled by the internal pressure. A moment later, the drum erupts. At normal temperatures "trichlor" is not flammable, but in this heat the liquid spatters over the room, vaporizes, and ignites. The other drums have sprung leaks rather than exploding, and the superheated liquids flood across the floor to join the fiery deluge.

The beast is now raging in its prison, plucking at the concrete ceiling overhead, pushing the walls, clawing at the metal door, twisting and warping it but momentarily unable to burst it from its hinges. The liquids on the floor push toward the crack at the bottom of the door and a blazing finger thrusts underneath and finds fresh tile and paint just beyond. Another finger follows and instantly the blazing flood is seeping underneath the metal panel.

The beast has learned cunning.

20.

Credits, debentures, unpaid bills, canceled orders . . . the whole sordid history of a business failure—it was like walking onto a battlefield after the war was over but the corpses had yet to be buried. Still, somebody had to do it, Douglas thought, and Larry had no head for figures. He could add a column six different times and come up with six different answers. Not that he wasn't bright, but his knack for business lay more in public relations and sales.

Douglas leaned back in his chair and rubbed his knuckles into his eyes. For a moment his mind wandered back ten years to when he had met Larry at a football game in Oakland. Douglas had been working for another decorating firm then and the local client had invited him to the game. Larry had some sort of butt job in the front office of the Forty-Niners and the client—what had been his name, anyway?—had introduced them during half time, probably intentionally matchmaking. He and Larry had liked each other instantly. It had been an odd sort of courtship, with no apologies offered and none expected. When it came to love, whatever they had been looking for, they found in each other. Larry's career depended very much on his being circumspect and yet, with Ian, he had seemed to grow almost overnight into a fully functioning human being with no hang-ups and few regrets. Two weeks later, Douglas had returned home, but they continued to correspond and then one morning Douglas had received a telegram from Larry asking Ian to meet him at the airport. Larry had never returned home.

But all of that was over now. Douglas suddenly snapped his pencil and threw the pieces against the wall in sudden decision. He may have grown too old for Larry, who now had other interests, but he couldn't continue to drift, couldn't continue to be weak and indecisive about both

Larry and the business. He couldn't continue to live as a weakling.

He reached down and pulled open the bottom drawer of the desk. There was a group of manila folders stacked upright within it and in the last one he found what he was searching for. Edged in green curlicues, it looked very impressive. The title said: "Comprehensive Fire and Liability Coverage."

He thumbed through it for a moment and nodded to himself; it was the simplest solution. They would split the payments and go their separate ways. The cash wouldn't amount to much, perhaps fifteen thousand dollars each after their creditors were paid. But with that, he could go to California or Oregon and perhaps start all over again, build a new life. There would be no Larry in it—nobody could fill that void and, in any event, he was too old and too tired to look. It had been very good while it had lasted; it was asking too much to expect lightning to strike twice.

What one needed in life, he thought, were courage and determination. He stood up and went into the outer shop, almost bumping his knees against a charcoal-colored settee over which had been arranged some draperies; they were of shantung with thin threads of gold woven throughout the rich silk. It was the perfect place to begin, he thought. He found the lighter fluid in a table drawer and stripped the spout from it with a pair of pliers, then began to dribble the fluid over the drapery fabric and the settee upholstery. He tossed the can in a wastebasket, fumbled out a pack of paper matches, struck one, and threw it on the couch. It flickered and went out. He tried a second, feeling his resolve begin to fail. It lay for a moment on the soaked couch, guttering, and then caught. A smoky flame raced from the match and leaped at the drapery fabric. A few seconds later the entire surface of the couch with its burden of drapery fabrics was blazing. The room started to fill with a greasy, black smoke, and the flames brightened.

For a moment Douglas watched the flames with all the fascination of a child, and then the seriousness of what he was doing suddenly hit him. "My God, oh my God!" The radiant heat from the couch felt hot against his face and even as he watched, the flames leaped higher, filling the room with rolling clouds of smoke. The wooden arms of the settee were charring now as the fire ate into the flammable varnish. The polyurethane foam upholstery began to swell and smoky flames raced across its exposed surface; the smoke from the foam was thick and acrid and made Douglas gag. A few minutes more, he thought, and the whole shop would be blazing.

He suddenly turned and ran back to the storeroom to look for the carbon-dioxide fire extinguisher. It wasn't hanging in its usual space on the wall and Douglas could feel the panic start to build inside. He should run into the hall and sound the alarm but there would be questions. . . . Then he remembered that Larry had taken the extinguisher down to repair its bracket. He found it at the foot of a pile of throw rugs. He grabbed it and ran back into the display room.

The foam upholstery was blazing as if it had been soaked in gasoline. Douglas aimed the black cone of the extinguisher at it and thumbed the trigger. Clouds of frost-flecked carbon dioxide spilled out over the flames. They shuddered for a moment and then leaped higher. Douglas moved in on them, firing burst after burst from the extinguisher. He finally had one end of the settee under control and worked toward the other, then attacked the flames already creeping up the side of a bolt of drapery goods leaning against the couch. If there was only enough charge in the extinguisher . . .

The last of the flames finally died and he grabbed up a sample of Fiberglas draperies to beat out the remaining sparks. He hurried back to the office washroom and filled a large flower holder with water, throwing the blooms on the floor, then returned and doused the wisps of smoke still coming from the charred settee and upholstery, returning for more water until the furniture and the fabric had ceased to smolder altogether. Then he sank down into a nearby Empire chair.

The reaction from the fire made him weak and for a

moment he thought he would vomit. The fumes from the upholstery had been nauseating and this, coupled with the heavy charge of adrenalin in his system, had left him shaking. He might have been trapped, he thought slowly. Another minute and his exit would have been blocked by the flaming draperies, and after that there would have been no way out. The upholstery, he thought, still breathing heavily, the foam had burned far faster than he had believed possible.

He sighed after a moment and began to pick up the charred fabrics. There were heavy vinyl bags in the storeroom and he could fill them with the charred materials, though the showroom would still be a mess. There was little he could do about the settee frame itself—possibly knock it apart and pack the pieces in bags as well. But the smoke had permeated the shop and the fabrics themselves; the cleaning bill alone would break them and there would be explanations to be made to Larry. He flinched inwardly. Half the shop was Larry's but he hadn't acted that way; he had made all the decisions, as if Larry's opinions were worth no more than those of an office boy.

He sniffed the air, realizing the smoke was still very heavy in the display room in spite of the air conditioning. Opening a window might help air out the shop and he walked over and pulled aside the draperies. The windows were completely sealed; there was no way to open them. It was because of the air conditioning, he thought; he could not open any one of the windows, short of shattering it, though presumably maintenance might have a way. He looked closer, spotting the recessed slot in a corner of the frame, and recalled that the window could be released with a special tool. But no such tools had been issued to the tenants; he would have to call the maintenance people, which he wasn't about to do.

He returned to the showroom and finished bagging the remaining scraps of charred cloth. There was no way he could explain this to Larry, he thought, agonized. The burned settee, the ruined fabrics, the sodden cloth, and the smell of smoke throughout.

The smoke was still very intense and he suddenly stopped and sniffed. It wasn't the humid, after-odor of smoke and water, the smell of something that had been burned. His watering eyes and face told him that this smoke was warm, that it wasn't coming from the doused ashes of a dead fire but from a fresh one, a fire that was still burning someplace. He dropped the vinyl bag that he had been holding and went back to the settee, searching for some stray spark, some piece of charring fabric that he had missed.

No, everything was out. Only now he was sure that the smoke was becoming more intense, and that the odor was somehow different. In place of the acrid, poisonous odors from the upholstery, this smoke had a thinner quality with a trace of volatiles that had not been characteristic of the smoke from the earlier fire. It reminded him just a little of the odor of the lighter fluid that he had used to start the fire in the first place.

Abruptly, he located the source of the smell and ran to the corridor door and opened it. The hallway was already filling with smoke. At the far end, several doors beyond the elevator bank, was the storeroom for the floor, its door now framed by white smoke. He had wandered past several times when the cleaning women or Krost, the maintenance super, had been in it and knew that it was filled with huge containers of waxes and solvents, as well as cartons of toilet tissue and stacks of moving pads.

Smoke was oozing out from the wide crack under the door and even as he watched he saw the first small finger of solvent flow from under the door, blue flames racing across its surface. It was joined by another and then a pool of flaming liquid was flowing out from under the door. The corridor ceiling above the storeroom door had already begun to blacken and he knew it was only moments before it would be blazing.

He slammed his office door, his heart beating wildly. An accidental fire, the very thing he might have prayed for. A solution to his own problems and without any assist on his part; in fact, once the fire crept down the hall, it would cover the evidence of his own folly. The catch, of course, was that there were more people in the building than just himself. He reached for the phone on the nearby table and dialed security's three-digit number. Garfunkel answered and he blurted, "Mr. Garfunkel, this is Ian Douglas. We have a fire up here in the corridor storeroom. It smells like a solvent fire. . . . I'd say it's too late for fire extinguishers, my guess is that the whole storeroom is blazing—it looks like the ceiling tile is ready to go."

Over the phone, Garfunkel's voice was crisp and authoritative: "Mr. Douglas, get the hell out of there. Understand? Don't try to take anything; get out now." There was a sudden click at the other end and once again Douglas felt panicky. He started for the door, then hesitated by the glass display case. He opened it and plucked out the small netsuke of the water buffalo. He couldn't leave it behind, he thought; of all the things in the shop, it had the most sentimental value for him. It, and Larry's "Minotaurmachie." He lifted it off the wall and tucked it under his arm, then raced for the door. The odor of smoke was now intense and for the first time, he felt real fear.

He threw the door open and a chill suddenly ran down his spine. The far end of the hall was now burning furiously and the pool of flaming solvent was flooding swiftly toward where he stood.

It had already cut him off from the elevator bank.

21.

"What are you thinking about?"

Mario Infantino stirred in the darkness, savoring the lassitude that comes after sex. He felt Doris stroking his head, her nails lightly touching his scalp and tousling his hair, and for a moment his thoughts seemed completely disassociated from his body. It was like drifting down some quiet river with the occasional wave laving his hand when he let it trail in the water.

"Of how much I love you."

Soft laughter in the darkness. "I mean really, Mario." She shifted slightly on the bed so she was on her side and facing him.

"Of Quantrell, I suppose. He could hurt me, Doris. Badly." He hadn't wanted to say it but she should know; the weeks ahead might be very difficult ones, for her as well as for him.

"I guessed he could," she said quietly. "I'm not sure how, yet."

He put his arm around her, his hand caressing the light strands of her hair. "Too much exposure, Doris, I'm too much in the public eye. I'm the youngest first assistant chief in the city's history and there's resentment, some jealousy, too, I suppose. Quantrell makes it look like I'm a publicity seeker."

"And Chief Fuchs?"

The thought of Fuchs made him feel uneasy. "We have differences of opinion."

"He could make you keep quiet any time, couldn't he?"

He kissed her shoulder. "It's a paramilitary organiza-tion . . . I take orders like everybody else. So far he hasn't said anything, but I don't think he likes it. Hell, *I* don't like it. But Fuchs is in a bind; if he tells me to shut up, then Quantrell would accuse him of having me muzzled." He hesitated. "That's going to happen anyway; I won't be giving Quantrell any more interviews. But you saw what happened when I wouldn't talk to him on the phone. Damned if I do, and damned if I don't."

She was thoughtful for a long moment. "You said you and Chief Fuchs disagreed. How?"

"We don't really disagree, Doris. It comes down to the budget and how it's spent. We could probably get all the heavy, new, modern equipment we wanted to fight high-rise fires—the people who own those buildings have power and influence, they'd want the finest—but salaries, equipment to fight brush fires or house fires, that sort of thing would probably be hard to get then. City Hall would look at the over-all budget and say that we had enough. It's a question of balance."

She stirred uneasily. "I'm not sure I follow where you and Chief Fuchs disagree."

"Fuchs has been fighting for higher salaries—the department's beginning to lose men. But we also need newer and more modern equipment: lighter respirators, more two-way walky-talkies, reflective fire clothing, high pressure pump units . . . equipment that's specifically designed for fighting fires in tall buildings. Fuchs is afraid that if we go hat in hand and get the equipment, when he goes back for salaries, he'll get turned down on the grounds that the department was already over budget." He hesitated a moment. "I feel for the old man," he said slowly. "He'd like both if he thought he could have them; so would any chief engineer, I guess. And the fact remains that far more people are killed in home fires, far more property lost in brush fires."

"He can't compromise?"

He let a hand trail down her back until it was cupping one of her buttocks. "He's getting old, set in his ways, I guess. He's been fighting his fight too long; he can't see anybody else's viewpoint. When he made me first assistant chief, he assigned the problem of tall buildings to me. I guess I'm like him in some respects; I see my argument more clearly than his. I would rather see a few men leave the department for greener fields than lose them later . . . for other reasons. He set me up as his technological expert but now he doesn't want to listen to what I have to say." Her warmth was intoxicating to him and he pulled her closer. "Someday we'll have a fire," he murmured, "and it'll turn out to be the daddy of them all, and we won't be able to fight it, we'll just have to stand there and let it burn. I have nightmares about that. . . ."

Someday Fuchs would order him to shut up, he thought, and he wondered what he would do, then. Would he be a good soldier and follow orders, worry about his position in the department, his pension? He wasn't sure, but he knew that a clash was coming. Fuchs was becoming almost less than civil in their meetings, although he could probably blame Quantrell for a lot of that.

"The children," Doris said quietly.

He glanced at the clock on the night stand. There was less than half an hour to go of their favorite program and then they would be back upstairs, raiding the icebox and looking for him to roughhouse with. He shivered slightly; the draft from the open window was turning colder; the weather was closing in rapidly. But there was still almost half an hour yet. . . .

Doris stirred again and he cupped her full breast and glanced down in the half light to admire the gentle swell of her belly and below that the intense black of the triangle of her pubic hair. There was so much life in her, he thought, and he lived too close to danger and sudden death. He moved his hands gently over her body and she arched her back and turned slightly, touching him along the full length of his body. He was aware of her pressing against his hairy thighs, of her small toes tracing chills against his calves, of the touch of her gently rounded belly against his own muscular one.

He had hiked himself up on one elbow and was turning into her when the phone on the night stand began to ring. He was scarcely aware of it, a part of him waiting for it to stop. Only it continued to ring, gradually interrupting his thought and physical concentration.

He reached for it and Doris caught his hand. "No," she whispered fiercely. "Not now."

But there was something insistent about it and he felt the hair on the back of his neck begin to rise. A vague premonition insisted he should answer and he sensed that Doris felt it, too. He pulled slowly away and she said softly, "Oh."

He kissed her deeply and then reached for the phone.

22.

"May I take your coat, sir? Mr. Clairmont's waiting for you in the game room."

Quantrell turned over his coat and hat. "Thank you, Pepé." He had been in Clairmont's penthouse apartment several times before, but always accompanied by the young Clairmont or Bridgeport. He followed Pepé down the hall, admiring the subdued recessed lighting and the polished slate tiles. Above a gilt table, an oval mirror with an intricately carved frame threw his reflection back at him. Just outside the game room, he paused to examine two small paintings on one of the side walls; each was not more than ten inches square. Original Matisses, he noted.

"It's a pleasure to see you again, Jeffrey."

William Glade Clairmont was waiting for him at the entrance to the game room, an ornate, ivory inlaid pool cue in his hand. "I've ordered drinks. Pepé reminded me that you're a scotch drinker—very long memory, Pepé's. I see you like my Matisses?"

"Exquisite," Quantrell admitted. "They must be worth a fortune."

"Fine art has a value, Jeffrey—it's a pity so many people confuse that with price."

Quantrell turned to face Clairmont who stood half a head shorter than he, though he carried himself as though he were a head taller and physically more powerful. He had aged, Quantrell thought, even in the relatively short time he had been with the station. A few more lines in the face, hair that was turning silver instead of gray, a gauntness about him, and a tendency for his clothes to hang. And when he was gone, young Clairmont would be the power behind the dynasty. But not until the Old Man was dead and buried, he thought.

"Well, come on in and make yourself comfortable," Clairmont offered. "I know I said only ten minutes, but

I'm an old man and not many people visit me and I'll be frank, I like visitors these days." He walked back to the pool table in the sprawling game room. "If you play, we might drink and talk while we have a game." He looked oddly hopeful. "Do you?"

"It's been a long time," Quantrell said. "My bank shots aren't what they used to be." He suddenly smiled. "I'm not being hustled, am I?"

"Frankly, yes, but I don't very often get the opportunity—I wouldn't take your money in any event. Willie Hoppe taught me; he was a rather good teacher."

Just then Pepé came in and set a scotch and soda and a gin and tonic on a nearby table, then silently vanished. Clairmont took a sip, offered Quantrell a stick as elaborately inlaid and basically fragile as his own, and racked up the balls. "The cue sticks are a work of art, too, Jeffrey, though not always recognized as such. They're from England and the workmanship is superb; a present from Prince Philip." He chalked the end of his cue. "Do you want to break?"

Quantrell nodded and leaned over the table. It was a bad break and he shrugged.

"You're quite a hell raiser," Clairmont said.

"Sometimes hell has to be raised."

Clairmont nodded and stroked a ball into a side pocket. Quantrell had the feeling he was going to make a run of the table. "That's true, I've done enough of it in my day. However, age has taught me some caution. It's inevitable with age, I guess. Perhaps the older you grow, the more you realize you have to lose."

"I'm familiar with your career," Quantrell said quietly. "That's why I find it hard to believe you would back away from a fight."

Clairmont looked at him gravely. "I never back away from my fights, Jeffrey. This is a fight that you picked for me; I'm not so sure I like that."

The game was momentarily forgotten. "The last time I was here, I explained my ideas for a new kind of investigative video journalism," Quantrell said. "You bought the idea, as I recall. I figured that when you did, my fights became your fights."

"I haven't forgotten that, though I must admit that I'm now sorry I said it. I don't like to be caught in a position where I can be accused of going back on my word." He paused a moment to take another shot; the old man was very good, Quantrell thought with momentary admiration. "I don't like to interfere with what's going on downstairs, though I'm not happy with it. Someday I suppose I'll have to clean house, get rid of the deadwood. But the point is that there's a lot more at stake than a simple lawsuit or a few outraged citizens who think we should be doing a better job of running the station."

"Victor told me of the libel action and the license challenge before the FCC."

"They're serious, though not that serious. Both will be dropped with the dropping of your series."

"You trust Leroux?"

"Of course." Clairmont looked faintly surprised. "I don't particularly care for the man, but he's a man of his word. Frankly, if I were in his shoes I would do precisely as he's done."

"Why not fight it out?" Quantrell asked, "I'm surprised that at your age you would let yourself be intimidated."

"Intimidated?" Clairmont was less cordial now. "I said that it was your fight, not mine. I've had Leroux checked out privately; he's an honest, legitimate businessman and I see no reason to pillory him. There are dozens of other buildings in town, all of them constructed in much the same way as Leroux's. Frankly, the Glass House is probably the best of them to date. Why attack Leroux and his building instead of some of the others?"

Quantrell carefully made his shot and had the satisfaction of seeing the ball drop in a side pocket. "Precisely because it is a new building, Mr. Clairmont, and has supposedly been built with the most advanced techniques available in the last decade. It should have been the best and safest. It isn't."

Clairmont was cold now, leaning his cue against the

table and fixing Quantrell with his aging blue eyes. "I know all about privileged sources, Mr. Quantrell, but you had better have some authority for that statement besides your own opinion."

That was it, Quantrell thought. This was why he had come over to see Clairmont. "I do."

"Who?"

"The construction supervisor on the job, the man who was fired by Wyndom Leroux because he objected to shoddy workmanship, inferior materials, violations of the fire codes that he knew damned well would never be caught, cost cutting to the point where it cut into the bone, let alone the flesh. His name is Will Shevelson. Any time you wish to confirm anything I've said, I can set up an appointment with him."

"Would it shock you, Mr. Quantrell, if I said I didn't give a damn?"

Quantrell stared at him. It was totally unexpected, it didn't fit the picture he had of Clairmont at all. He was beaten, he thought, and he didn't have the faintest reason why. He turned and walked over to the huge picture window looking out over the city, grasping the pool cue behind him with both hands. "Yes, it would shock me, Mr. Clairmont," he said bitterly. "I would be curious as to just why you don't give a damn."

"It's very simple," Clairmont said behind him, and for the first time Quantrell could detect the tremor of age in his voice. "You could call it posterity, if you wish, or blood is thicker than water. I want to leave something to my descendants and if your present series keeps up, I may not be in a position to leave much of anything. The threat to the station is bad enough, as is the libel suit. There are other factors. I own Clairmont Towers, Mr. Quantrell, and I have substantial interest in a number of other high-rise buildings in this city. Your series isn't only hurting rentals in the Glass House, it's hurting rentals in practically every tall building. In addition, there are dozens, hundreds of businesses that lease space in such buildings. They buy ads in newspapers and on the air. Lately, they haven't—at least not in our newspaper and not on our stations. We're facing a spontaneous boycott and it's been hurting—far more than I thought such a boycott might."

"It comes down to a matter of money, then, is that it?"

In the window, he could see the ghostly reflection of Clairmont behind him, nodding. "Pretty much. A great deal of money. If I were a younger man, perhaps I might have a different attitude. But I'm not a younger man." His voice sharpened. "Aside from all of that, I have my doubts as to just what the story is worth—as a story. I'm afraid potential disasters are never quite as gripping as the actual ones. The extra sand in the concrete bridge is of most importance when the bridge collapses. Until then, who really cares? You're dealing with a potential story, Mr. Quantrell, not a real one. It hasn't been worth the time we've given it." He hesitated. "I'm well aware of your ambitions. The most that can be said about your exposé is that it's been self-serving. I'm sorry I let you get so far with it."

Quantrell, still facing the window, felt the back of his neck grow warm. There were things that he wanted to say and he choked them down. It would do no good to antagonize Clairmont; the Old Man's anger would follow him wherever he went. The injustice of it all ate at him like acid. Barely half a mile away from his picture window stood the Glass House and if it wasn't the story of the last ten years, it was at least the story of this one. He stared at it, gleaming in the lights of adjacent buildings as well as bathed in flickering oranges and reds by its own colored floodlights set in the four corners of its plaza. There was even a last flicker of sunlight. . . . He squinted at the sky. That was impossible, the cloud cover was too heavy, the sleet and snow now too thick. And it was too late; the sun had long since dropped over the horizon.

He stared back at the building and sucked in his breath.

"I'll do what I can for you in recommendations," Clairmont was saying behind him, his voice now audibly trembling. The billiards game had exhausted him. "I'm not quite so opposed to you as I may have sounded; ambition in a young man is hardly a crime."

Quantrell's hands suddenly tensed and the pool cue snapped. little pieces of ivory flying about the room.

"See here, Quantrell, what the hell do you think you're doing? That pool cue was priceless. . . ." Clairmont hurried over toward him.

"My God!" Quantrell suddenly said. "Oh, my God!" He felt himself floating on sheer elation. "No story? Come here, by God, I'll show you the story!" Clairmont was standing beside him now and Quantrell clutched at the thin shoulder, feeling the aged bone beneath the expensive fabric.

"Look out there!" he exulted, pointing with one of the broken cue halves. "Take a good look! What the hell do you think is happening?"

Etched against the evening sky, the Glass House towered above its neighbors. What Quantrell had at first taken to be a last glint of sunlight against the building had now become a dirty flicker of orange flame about a third of the way up the side of the Glass House. Heavy clouds of black smoke occasionally obscured the blaze and when they momentarily cleared, the flames were brighter than ever.

Quantrell could hear Clairmont gasp, then lean forward eagerly to peer through the glass. The financier had now completely vanished, to be replaced by the newspaperman.

"No story?" Quantrell laughed, almost hysterical. "There it is, old man—the biggest damned story in a decade!"

Late

Evening

＊＊＊

In the storeroom, the concrete ceiling directly above the shelf of solvents begins to spall and flake away. Dust gathered on the ventilator grill bursts into smoky flame; paint on the grill bubbles and burns; the thin metal grill itself slowly twists and warps in the heat. Behind it, the plastic heating duct begins to burn, adding more smoke to the black clouds pushing past loosely fitting smoke dampers into the labyrinth of ducts to other floors.

Outside, in the corridor, the fire licks at the wooden framing around office doors and gouges at the acoustical tile of the false ceiling. The tile contains a large percentage of asbestos fiber and would ordinarily be considered fire resistant, but the superheated air near the ceiling is well past the 600-degree mark. The fire races along the narrow space between the false ceiling and the floor above. Where ductwork penetrates the concrete fire ceiling, the fire rages and tears at the plaster sealing the gap around the duct. Some of the patching material chars and bursts into flame. Concrete patches slowly spall away, plaster calcines and flakes. In a number of places, no attempt at all was made to patch the hole and the fire crawls up into telephone junction rooms and computer terminal assemblies on the floor above, to feast on smears of grease and chew at the insulation on lashed bundles of wiring.

All the drums and cans have now ruptured in the storeroom; all the bottles have burst, and the flood of flaming liquid has flowed around flaming debris under the storeroom door and down the hall, oozing under the doors of other offices. The tide rolls through the outer display room of Today's Interiors and laps at the bolts of upholstery material, the samples of hanging draperies, and the expensive, delicate furniture. It scorches its way into the storeroom, quickly devouring the aisles of upholstery

157

and drapery goods. The legs of the Herman Miller desk char, then flame; the wood-grained formica top blackens, bubbles, and becomes a solid sheet of fire. The ledgers and stacks of unpaid bills puff into small balls of flame that float briefly in the air before turning into bits of black ash, swirling toward the ceiling. The paint on the adding machine browns and blackens; the plastic parts soon blaze, and the metal keys turn red, then white.

The fire loading of Today's Interiors is heavy and in some parts of the shop, particularly above the bales of polyurethane foam used for upholstery, the temperature of the air approaches 1,000 degrees.

In the hall outside, the beast is fast outgrowing its adolescence and is hungrily searching for more food.

23.

The dinner had started on a chilly note but at least it was going to end on a warmer one, Barton thought, thanks primarily to Thelma. She had been all southern charm and courtesy and, by telling little stories on both herself and Wyndom, had coaxed Jenny into a friendly frame of mind. Jenny was fighting it but she gradually relaxed, and the tension at the table slowly slipped away. There was no denying that the obvious good time being had by the elderly couple at the table behind them had been contagious. You couldn't help but overhear part of the conversation. The stocky woman had an endless series of stories about her life as a schoolteacher, some of them slightly risqué and others hilarious. Even Jenny had to smother her laughter at times. After an hour, the pervasive feeling at their end of the dining room was—what would the stocky woman have called it?—*Gemütlichkeit?*

Leroux lit a cigar and offered one to Barton, who accepted it with thanks. He turned to Jenny. "How about an after-dinner liqueur, Jenny?" She hesitated and Leroux coaxed her. "A little Cherry Heering would top off the roast duck—nothing like basting a good dinner with a good drink."

She suddenly smiled and said, "Yes," and Barton knew the storm for the night was probably over. She might even start looking forward to spending the evening alone with him in a hotel room instead of with her parents. At least, the demands on him would be different—and far more pleasant.

He ordered a Drambuie for himself and quietly toasted Thelma when it came. "To a woman who is probably the most charming hostess in America. Thelma, you've made the evening for us."

Jenny reached over and squeezed the older woman's hand. "You've been a dear to put up with me."

159

Thelma looked half hurt. "Jenny, don't ever accuse me of having to 'put up' with you. It was our pleasure to have you for dinner. We dragged you halfway across the continent and we owe you a good deal more than this."

He heard it then, but paid no attention. The far-off wail of fire sirens, coming closer; it was almost lost in the murmur of conversation in the restaurant.

"Have you made up your mind, Craig?" Leroux was looking at him shrewdly, half hidden behind a haze of cigar smoke. Striking while the iron was hot enough to be malleable, Barton thought.

"I'll let you know tomorrow, Wyn," he said casually. He didn't want to make a big thing of it for fear Jenny would be at him about it for the rest of the night.

Leroux nodded, as if he were sure what the answer would be. "Take your time, Craig; enjoy the weekend. I can reach you at Southport if I have to?"

"Yes—you've got the number." He ordered another Drambuie and had almost worked up the courage to tell Leroux he had a lousy taste in cigars—Wyn couldn't be allowed all the victories that night—when Quinn Reynolds hurried over. Barton froze for a moment, wishing desperately that she had chosen another time to visit. Then he caught the expression on her face.

She leaned over the table, keeping her voice low. She nodded to Leroux but spoke primarily to Barton. "Craig, I hate to interrupt your dinner but Dan Garfunkel just called. We have a fire down below. He knew from the reservation lists both you and Mr. Leroux were up here and thought you should be notified immediately."

The sirens, he recalled. They had come closer and closer and then abruptly stopped. His only thought had been that the fire must be nearby. "What floor?"

"The seventeenth—it's a storeroom fire."

The sense of shock building up within him lessened a little. Storeroom fires were hardly that rare and control was usually a matter of minutes. "How bad?"

"Dan says it's serious."

There was a momentary flash as his eyes met Leroux's.

The older man had gone white underneath his athletic-club tan. "Are they trying to fight it inside the building?"

"Yes. Dan said some of the maintenance men led by Malcolm Donaldson and Griff Edwards took portable extinguishers and went by elevator to seventeen. They were driven back immediately. Heavy smoke and flames . . . too heavy to handle with extinguishers."

"Anybody hurt?"

"Mr. Edwards . . ." Quinn bit her lip briefly. "They've called an ambulance; we don't know. Smoke inhalation, possible coronary from the exertion."

It would be like Griff, Barton thought. Nobody or nothing was going to take his building away from him. There was a moment's silence at the table. He could suddenly feel Jenny's hand squeezing his, hard. "The standpipe in the stairwell . . . did they try to fight the fire from the hose out there?"

Leroux cut in. "It wouldn't have done any good, Craig. Maintenance men aren't trained to handle it; it would take professionals."

"Somebody called Dan with the information about the fire," Quinn said. "Mr. Garfunkel rang the Fire Department immediately."

Barton looked at her, startled. Something had gone wrong. They shouldn't have to call; the heat and smoke sensors in the building had a read-out system connected directly to the Fire Department. Once they indicated the presence of either smoke or fire, four companies were to be dispatched to the Glass House immediately, even if it were only a fire in a wastebasket. "What about the tenants? Has anybody notified them?" He had a sudden mental image of Ian Douglas on the elevator and the lights that were on in the Credit Union . . . though the people there should have left long ago.

Quinn signaled him with her eyes, trying to tell him to keep his voice down. The people at the tables around them had suddenly grown silent and were listening. "Security's taking a building census right now, going through the commercial floors one by one. We've lost telephone communications to seventeen and above, though the residential lines are still working. The switchboard is calling apartment tenants now."

Leroux frowned. "I don't know if that's necessary—it will cause a panic and a jam-up in the elevators, if nothing else. It's a storeroom fire; the firemen are here; it's wildly improbable that the fire will spread beyond the one room."

"Mr. Donaldson reports the corridor is blazing," Quinn added quietly.

"Even so . . ." Leroux chewed on his cigar for a moment. Barton knew what he must be thinking. The more panic, the worse the fire looked, the blacker the headlines in the paper, and the more it would seem that Quantrell had been right.

"Mr. Leroux." Quinn hesitated a moment. "There are one hundred and thirty-two diners plus the kitchen help up here now. Should we try and evacuate them?" There was a thin thread of exasperation running through her voice.

"I don't think so, Miss Reynolds. The diners are probably as safe as they'll ever be, waiting right here." Barton started to object and Leroux glanced at him coldly. "If the firemen can't control it, they'll let us know. There'll be time to evacuate then. If we leave now, we'd have to take the residential elevators to the sky lobby and chances are both the lobby and the elevators are mobbed. I don't think it would do anybody any good to add to the confusion."

"There's the outside, scenic elevator," Quinn said.

"True," Leroux said gently, "but what's the capacity?" She hesitated. "At the most a dozen."

"That would be eleven trips, with the diners left behind getting more and more nervous after each trip. No, I'm afraid if we started to leave now, we'd create a panic. If we have to go, there'll be firemen up here to direct the evacuation—it will make it one hell of a lot easier. As it is, I'd suggest we all stay right here until we're told to leave. Miss Reynolds, how's your wine cellar?"

"It was completely stocked when we opened. We have plenty."

"Break it out—make it on the house." His voice was husky and strained and Barton noticed Thelma watching him like a hawk. A bad heart beneath that healthy exterior? he suddenly wondered. Something else that could be brought on by strain?

A quiet babble began to fill the room. Quinn left the table to circulate among the other diners and reassure them that everything was under control. Barton and Leroux looked at each other in silence, the older man's face blank and unreadable. It must be tough on Leroux, Barton thought. He had lost the game, even if the damage proved to be minor. He had laid elaborate plans to shut up Quantrell, but fate had turned over the wrong card. For all practical purposes, Quantrell's on-the-air statements about the Glass House were now confirmed.

Jenny suddenly turned to him. "Is it really bad?" she whispered.

"I think it's exactly as Quinn told us," Barton said heavily. "But I'm also afraid that she may have only an early report." The sensors hadn't reported the fire to the Fire Department, he thought. That meant there had been a delay during which the fire might really have gotten a foothold. *Had* gotten a foothold; Donaldson and Edwards had been driven from the floor.

"Craig." He looked over at Leroux who seemed like a man who was coming out of shock. His brain was working again and it was obvious he would spend little time with regrets for the past. "I think you ought to take the scenic elevator down to the lobby and act as liaison with the Fire Department. Until such time as I get down there, you're in charge. Some of the tenants who have shops and offices in the building will be showing up; they'll want to talk to someone in authority. I imagine our insurance people will be down there, too."

"Glad to, boss." Barton took a breath. "Only one question: Why don't you go?"

"I'm hardly afraid of facing whoever's down there, Craig. But it would be bad public relations. It'd be too much the image of the captain deserting his ship—not a good idea under the circumstances."

He could buy that, Barton thought, though you could argue it both ways. The papers would get hold of it, or Quantrell, and Leroux could be made to look as if he were not only criminally liable but a coward as well. And then he had another thought.

"Where's Captain Harriman?"

"Out of state for the holidays."

"Crandall?"

Leroux looked pained. "Checked out sick at noon. He wouldn't be any good down below right now anyway."

"All right, I'm it," Barton said. "But just out of curiosity, who follows Crandall in the table of organization?"

"He's out, too," Leroux said gently. "Griff Edwards. He was the oldest man in the organization and I thought it would be a nice gesture; I never imagined it might get down to him."

Barton stood up to go and suddenly Jenny was hanging on his sleeve. "Craig," she said in a little voice, "I think I ought to be with you."

For a moment he was touched, then shook his head. "Jenny, this is probably the safest place in the entire building if you stay behind. If you go with me, I'd insist on putting you in a cab for a hotel as soon as we reach the lobby."

"Then I'll stay right here with our friends," she said, something of a chill back in her voice. Then she caught Thelma's disapproving look and forced a smile. "How often do you get to see this kind of fire from a ringside seat?"

Barton squeezed her shoulder lightly. "Not very often."

He pushed back in his chair and started to squeeze past the table behind him when he felt the stocky woman tap his shoulder. "I couldn't help but overhearing," she said softly. "How serious is it—precisely?"

Barton shook his head. "It's nothing," he reassured her. "A fire in a storeroom. Nobody's been hurt and the Fire Department's already here. There's nothing to worry about—the tenants in the building are being notified. Frankly, if I were you I would drink your wine and enjoy the rest of the evening." He glanced at her escort, who looked slightly pale. "Don't you agree with me, sir?"

"You're quite right, the first rule to follow is to stay put until you can assess just how bad the situation is."

Barton brushed past them toward the scenic elevator. Odd, he thought. The stocky woman had looked quite serious when she had asked him about the fire but when he had said that the tenants were being notified, she had looked even more worried.

Then he was waiting in the foyer for the scenic elevator, along with a few other diners who had abruptly decided to leave. Despite Quinn's reassurances, they were grim and white-faced.

24.

It was odd, Mario Infantino thought, how an evening that had started out so well could turn bad so quickly. The snow was coming down thick enough now that the headlights of other cars were mere fuzzy splotches in the darkness. He could sense by the way the tires lost traction repeatedly that street conditions were bad and getting worse. He ran a red light, then pulled into his reserved space marked "Division Chief" in the lot behind the firehouse and threw his Camaro into park. He yanked the keys from the ignition, tumbled out, and slammed the door behind him. He was halfway across the lot when Chief Engineer Fuchs's official car pulled into the lot alongside his own, its red light flashing. He doubled back and ran toward it.

Fuchs rolled down the window and yelled at him. "It's a hot one, Infantino—made to order for you."

"Dispatch said it was the Glass House. How bad?"

"The whole seventeenth floor and probably the eighteenth by now."

The snow had started to sift down Infantino's neck and

he shivered. "I should be there. That's my district. I should've been notified a long time ago."

"The fire was called in; the heat sensor hookup didn't work." Fuchs spat out the window. "Modern technology, Infantino—it works great when it works and God help you when it doesn't. Incidentally, when you get there, you're in charge—the entire operation."

Infantino stared. "It's customary for the chief engineer to be in charge of an operation this size."

"That's right, and I'll be right behind you." There was a hint of malice in his voice that Infantino picked up immediately.

"Chief, we don't have much time. You better tell me what's on your mind."

"Fair enough." Fuchs got out of his car, pulled his coat up around his ears, and motioned Infantino over to the side of the building. It was cold enough now so his breath came out in little puffs of vapor. "I want you there for two reasons, Infantino. First and most important, you're the only man I've got who's a self-trained expert on this type of fire. I would be doing the department an injustice if I took over when I thought there was a man better equipped to handle it than I am." His voice turned acid. "You might say I'll be there to learn. I'll learn if you can do it and I'll learn if you can't. You've been sounding off on how high-rise fires should be fought. All right, mister, here's your chance to show me."

"You think I've been trying to embarrass you and the department?"

Fuch's salt-and-pepper mustache bristled with fury. "I've seen all of Quantrell's broadcasts; neither I nor the department come out with very high marks. I don't give a damn what's said about me but the department's something else again. It's one of the finest in the country; I've spent my life with it and I've been pallbearer for half the men who started with me as rookies. That television son of a bitch didn't know any of them; he doesn't know how they died and he doesn't care. As far as he's concerned, the department is behind the times, sloppy and possibly corrupt. And a lot of his information had to come from you."

Infantino was red-faced. "That's a goddamn lie! He pumped me and I walked right into it. So I wasn't too bright, what should I have done—shut up so he could accuse you of muzzling me? What the hell motive would I have for undercutting you?"

Fuchs's face was very close to his own, the fog from his breath a small cloud between them. "If I thought you were without personal ambition, Infantino, I would distrust you even more than I do now."

Infantino controlled himself with effort. "What do you want me to do?"

"I told you—run the fire-fighting operations at the Glass House."

"In the hopes that I'll make a mistake?"

The little red veins pulsed in Fuchs's forehead. "If you're half as good as you think you are, then I'm doing the right thing. If you're not, there are boards of inquiry and it won't be my decision alone. But I won't deny that I'd be glad to have you out of my hair."

"I've never complained about the men or the department; it's the lack of modern equipment."

Fuchs nodded wearily. "I know your argument, I've heard it enough times. But no matter what equipment you've got, in the last analysis it's men who fight fires. And a fire is like a cancer—sometimes it takes very little to cure it and other times it's terminal, no matter what you do or what equipment you've got."

"I'll need your cooperation."

"You'll get it."

"Dispatch said four companies are there now. I'll probably want more men."

"We can recall companies as you need them. But I don't want to strip the rest of the city unless I have to."

"Have we got fire sketches on the building?"

Fuchs hesitated. "No," he said slowly. "A team was going over to make them at the end of the month."

"But it's been open for occupancy for three!"

Fuchs exploded. "You expect everybody to see your

problems, but you don't want to see mine, Infantino! You
think every snot-nosed kid wants to grow up to be a
fireman? I've got news for you, friend—we rank far
behind the Police Department and they're not exactly
overwhelmed with applicants! Damned few people are
volunteering for an opportunity to get their brains fried
out—not at the salaries and widows' pensions we pay! I
could have all the fancy equipment in the world, and it
would just sit there and gather dust because I don't have
the men to man it! You've got to have men on the hose,
you've got to have men driving the pumpers and the ladder trucks, you've got to have men to go in with pulldown
hooks and hatchets! Men, that's what you fight fires with!
And we don't have goddamned near enough! We don't
have the fire sketches because I couldn't spare the men
to send over there. Do you understand?" He paused,
shaking with anger. "Most of this city is residential, that's
where most of our fires occur. That's where most people
die. I've concentrated on equipment to fight that kind of
fire and it's cost me blood. Sure, I can get money for
equipment to fight the big ones—then put it in storage
for the rest of the year. But what about salaries? What
about more men? What about equipment designed to
fight the little fires? Your big banks and industrial firms,
they won't come up with the money for that!"

They glared at each other for a moment, the snow falling quietly between them. "There's a difference between
a house and a high rise," Infantino said bitterly. "It's a
factor of ten, maybe a hundred, in the number of possible deaths. They don't have to happen every month, even
once would be enough."

"I'm not without sympathy for your views," Fuchs spit
out. "I resent that you seem to be without any understanding of mine."

"We're talking while the Glass House burns," Infantino
said quietly. "Can we get the blueprints from the Department of Building and Safety? Of if they don't have them,
from the insurance company of National Curtainwall itself?"

Fuchs nodded, his anger spent. "I'll have it checked. Anything else?"

"We'll be sending men into tight, sealed rooms and compartments—we'll need all the respiratory equipment we can get."

"I've already taken care of that." Fuchs turned to go back to his car, his aging shoulders bent against the wind.

"I'm not through!" Infantino shouted.

Fuchs turned. "You've got everything in the city now."

"In this city, yes. I think we ought to contact the department in Southport. They've got new, high-capacity respirators and a hundred-foot tower can throw water to the thirteenth floor."

"I'll put them on the alert, but I'm not going to ask for help at this stage of the game. I doubt we'll need more equipment; I think we can handle our own dirty work."

Infantino nodded. He could understand Fuchs's reluctance to borrow equipment before he absolutely had to. "Thanks a lot, Chief—you've given me everything I'll need."

"You think so?" Fuchs said dryly. "I haven't wished you good luck and I haven't offered any prayers for you —and you need them both at any fire." He turned to walk back to his car. "Can I offer you a lift?"

"No thanks," Infantino said shortly. He hurried into the firehouse, nodding to the housewatchman in his tiny booth near the front of the apparatus floor. The four companies that used the firehouse as division headquarters were gone and, except for the housewatchman, the station was deserted. A skillet with a dozen half-cooked pork chops was on the back burner of the stove in the kitchen, the chops already jelling in their own grease. Scraps of lettuce were scattered over a cutting board.

It took him only a few minutes to slip out of his pants and coat and pull on boots and a turnout suit, fumbling to clip the coat rings tight. He grabbed up a pair of gloves and his high-impact helmet and ran out into the garage to his service car. He fastened his safety belt and flicked on the ignition and the two-way radio. The car was immediately flooded with crackling conversations. He listened for a moment, then roared out of the garage, his siren wailing.

The Glass House was going up much faster than he had thought possible. The weather was partly to blame; the difference in temperature between the air outside the building and the air inside was creating a stack effect. Cold air was heavier and tended to flow into the building through the doors and the numerous small holes and cracks in the curtainwall, then rise like smoke up a chimney.

At the moment, he thought, the Glass House was the tallest chimney in the city.

25.

The engineer in the control room was drawing his hand across his throat: less than a minute for the tag-off. Jeffrey Quantrell turned slightly so that he was looking directly into the eye of Number Two camera. His expression was still that of a concerned citizen, shocked and saddened that the fire he had predicted so long for the Glass House had become reality. There was the slightest tinge of I-told-you-so in his delivery.

"Whatever the outcome of the developing disaster on Lee Avenue, this undoubtedly is only the beginning. In its own way, the Glass House is not unusual—there are dozens like it in the city that, due to poor construction practices and outright violations of the building codes, are firetraps in the sky. In the long run, what can be done about it is up to you. For the rest of the evening, of course, KYS will interrupt its regularly scheduled programming from time to time to bring you the latest on the fire that is currently gnawing at the vitals of the Glass House. Thank you—and good night."

He held his solemn pose until the light winked off and the floor manager signaled him. He had called the shots to the letter, he thought, and he had done a good job of reminding the viewer of just that—without claiming too much credit for himself. He savored the moment for a second longer. Everybody thought he had been crying wolf but here it was—the biggest disaster the city had seen in years. It didn't matter whether they canceled his contract now or not; he could get almost any broadcast job in the country tomorrow if he wanted it.

He straightened his necktie and sauntered out of the studio. The floor manager smiled broadly and waved a friendly congratulation. Quantrell didn't bother to acknowledge it. The bastard would've crucified me six hours ago if he could've, Quantrell thought. Half the personnel in the studio would now be buddy-buddy, and be back to waiting for another chance to sink their knives.

Carter, the director, stuck his head out of the booth as Quantrell walked by and said, "Nice going, Jeff—talk about falling into a cesspool and coming up smelling like a rose."

"Thanks, I like you, too," Quantrell said casually. Behind him, he heard Carter shout, "It's nice to know it hasn't gone to your head!" Another knife out for him but it didn't matter any more; it didn't matter what any of them thought—he wasn't going to be there that much longer, and not by their choice, by his.

He waved to Clairmont's secretary and walked past her desk before she could stop him. He knocked on the door once and walked in. "Hi, Vic, just thought I'd check bases before taking off to watch Leroux's building burn."

Clairmont leaned back in his chair and glanced at his watch. "Well, I lose—I bet Marge it would take you two minutes to get here once you were off the air and it's taken you all of three. What kept you?"

Cool, Quantrell thought. "The autograph seekers in the hall—there's a whole mob of them out here." He took the chair by the desk. "Are you sore because I was right, Vic? I thought you were a bigger man than that."

"You went over my head," Clairmont said tightly. "Do you expect me to congratulate you about that? My uncle called ten minutes before you went on the air; otherwise you would have been playing to a dead camera."

Quantrell managed to look contrite. "I knew I was right and I went to any lengths to prove it. If you're sore, blame fate—I didn't set fire to the building. In the long run, I think my actions and attitudes will be of benefit to the station."

"And to Jeffrey Quantrell's personal ambitions?"

"I didn't know it was a crime to be ambitious. If it is then I'm guilty of it and I imagine you are, too."

"I'll be goddamned if I'll have you running upstairs on every little thing, now that you've pulled this one off," Clairmont flared.

"You wouldn't have done the same thing in my shoes?" Quantrell asked calmly. "I think you would've, especially if you believed in what you were doing as much as I do." He leaned forward. "You didn't leave me any choice, Vic—you had greased the skids for a quick trip back to the sticks and I wasn't going to go without a fight. If it helps, the visit to the Old Man was strictly a one shot— I don't play billiards that well and sooner or later he's going to remember that I broke his favorite cue."

Clairmont half smiled. "He told me about that, too."

Quantrell studied him for a moment. "The story isn't over yet; it will take a lot of work and a lot of cooperation from your end. From now on, it's your story as much as mine and I'll make sure the Old Man knows it."

"Don't do me any favors, Jeff," Clairmont said, but Quantrell could tell his temper had been blunted. The Old Man had never forgiven his nephew for not being a hard-nosed newspaperman. Above all else, the Old Man had wanted to be proud of him and that was the angle to play. So much for the younger Clairmont, Quantrell thought easily.

"What I'll need is the station's complete backing," Quantrell said, realizing wryly that it sounded a shade too pompous for even Clairmont to swallow. He stood up. "Zimmerman is waiting for me outside with his cameraman. With good luck, maybe I'll even get an interview with Leroux."

Clairmont sighed. "Jeff, relax for a moment. We've still got a minor problem. The police have called and want to know your sources for the inside information. Some character on the arson squad—Petucci, you know him?"

"A nebbish. You've got lawyers on retainer; let them handle him."

"Okay." He started to dial his phone and Quantrell got up to go when Clairmont suddenly looked up. "By the way, who the hell were your sources?"

"Your uncle never told you?"

He was too busy talking about you; he never had time to mention anybody else."

"Will Shevelson, former construction foreman. Had a fight with Leroux and got canned."

Clairmont stared at him for a moment, then leaned back and laughed. "Jesus Christ, I might've known! Shevelson!"

Quantrell felt something kick in his stomach. "I don't get it, what's so funny?"

Clairmont shook his head, still half laughing. "I should've guessed it. Six months ago that nut made the rounds of every newspaper and radio and TV station in town trying to peddle his story. I thought he was paranoid and threw him out. You're lucky the building went up; if it hadn't, ten to one you'd be a loser. I wouldn't believe the bastard if he told me the sun was going to rise in the morning."

"The building's burning," Quantrell said simply. "Everything he ever told me checked out."

"Jeff." Clairmont was serious now, all business. "Be careful how you play it. Particularly when it comes to Leroux himself. Plenty of perfectly legitimate businessmen have had fires. Shevelson hates Leroux enough to twist the facts and maybe tell outright lies. If we can make a criminal negligence case against Leroux, that's one thing. But it can't be based on just what Shevelson says. It's sticky now and we'll have to have a company lawyer right here in the office on the other end of your phone line checking out every word of your copy. There's no other way to play it."

Quantrell shrugged. "You've got your responsibilities; I've got mine. As far as playing the story, I intend to use the Glass House only as an example. There are a lot of Glass Houses in the country; the problem is nationwide. Other stations will pick up our coverage."

Clairmont looked thoughtful. "I'm well aware of that. Well, what do you want? What can we do for you?"

"I'll need the Number Two mobile truck and probably the traffic helicopter before it's over."

"They're all yours, though I don't think you'll be able to get the helicopter close enough to do you any good. The downdrafts around the building will be pretty strong."

Quantrell was at the door when Clairmont said quietly, "Got any ideas for an encore, Jeff?"

Clairmont's ace, Quantrell suddenly thought. In another twelve hours or less, the story would be over. It would be yesterday's news, and old news and dead fish stank after the fourth day. He could single out Leroux and make him into a villain, but Clairmont had as much as said he wouldn't be allowed to do that. It would be great story, but in winning for the short term, he had lost for the long one.

"I'll think of something," he said as he left.

Outside, Bridgeport was waiting his turn with the great man. He was uncertain how to react to Quantrell and tried a casual smile first. "Congratulations, Jeff; it was a great show."

"It's always a great show," Quantrell said coldly. "But it takes talent to realize it."

He returned to his office to pick up his tape recorder and then catch Zimmerman who was waiting outside in his car, probably swearing up a storm by now. Sandy was there at the typewriter, her coat on.

He glanced at her. "Where the hell are you going, Sandy?"

She looked at him, half frightened. "You'll be busy covering the Glass House. I called up my date and told him I'd meet him a little later on."

He sat in a swivel chair near hers and took her hands in his. "Sandy, Sandy, I can't have you leave now. I'll be on the phone to you half the night with reports and figures and probably requests for equipment. You're my go-between here; you can't leave me now."

"I've talked to Angie." She bit her lip to keep herself from shaking. "She said she'd cover for me, that chances were you wouldn't have much time to call in at all."

He raised an eyebrow. "I've never worked with Angie, I wouldn't trust her to put a stamp on an envelope. It's you I need, Sandy; you're my personal anchorman back here." He shrugged a shoulder at the newsroom just outside. "You think I would trust the dummies out there to do what I wanted?" He let his voice become softer. "Look, Sandy, tonight I picked up all the marbles—I won the game. And you were as much responsible for my success as I was. I told Victor that, I even mentioned you to the Old Man." He let his shoulders droop helplessly. "If you want to go I can't stop you. But I depend on you, Sandy, I need you. But if you want to duck out for the evening have a good time."

"If you really need me," she said uncertainly.

He squeezed her hand. "He means very much to you, doesn't he, Sandy?" She looked startled and he forced a smile. "You can't hide it, I've known you too long. But if he likes you that much, Sandy, then surely he'd understand about tonight. And when it's all over with, I'll take you both out for a night on the town that you'll never forget. Okay?"

She finally nodded. "Sure," she said quietly. "I'd like that." Her voice held no enthusiasm and he realized it really was hearts-and-flowers time. Well, there were still some bridges to be crossed before then. But losing Sandy right now played no part in his scheme of things.

He squeezed her hand once more, then hurried into his office and found his tape recorder and stuffed a handful of cassettes into his pocket. He checked the recorder to see that it was on full charge, then grabbed his overcoat off the rack and struggled into it. Zimmerman was probably calling him every name in the book.

He brushed quickly through the newsroom, past several girls clattering away at their typewriters and a processing man heading back to the developing room with a reel of sixteen-millimeter film. It was going to be one busy night, he thought. Just before going out the door, he glanced back quickly at Sandy, who was listlessly dialing her phone.

Dumb broad, he thought.

26.

"That mouthy little bastard is the most self-serving son of a bitch I've ever met! And I knew it from the start; goddamnit, I knew it all the time!" Will Shevelson rose from the couch, strode over to the set, and punched the off switch. The image of Jeffrey Quantrell suddenly went mute and dwindled to a point of light. "You want a beer, Marty?"

Marty Hodgehead stretched in his chair, smothered a yawn and said, "Yeah, I could use one."

Shevelson took two cans from the den's refrigerator, tossed one to Hodgehead, and pulled at the ring of his own. "He's a real bastard, Quantrell." Shevelson went back to the couch and sat down, moody in the sudden silence. He was a burly, thick-muscled man in his late forties. Dressed in loose corduroys and an olive work shirt open at the neck, he looked a little like Rodin's "The Thinker." He glanced around the book-lined shelves of his study, his eyes stopping at the small collection of photographs just above his desk. All were of buildings he had worked on in the last twenty years. Several of them were National Curtainwall's, the last an eight-by-ten color print of the Glass House. All good buildings, he thought, even the Glass House—at least from the outside.

Hodgehead had followed his eyes. "Look, Will, forget it. It's all over and done with. They'll put the fire out; this time there'll be a real investigation and Leroux will get his. What more do you want?"

"His skin, so I can tack it up on the wall," Shevelson

muttered. His thick right hand suddenly spasmed in anger and beer geysered out of the can. "Shit, let me get a rag." He came back from behind the bar with a damp cloth and swiped at the floor tiles. "I don't know if I can explain it to you, Marty. The Glass House was my baby, but every day I worked on her, I felt more and more like a pimp who was selling his own daughter."

Leroux kept cutting corners, he thought, and he forced himself to go along. Finally the day came when Leroux showed up on the forty-fourth floor of the unfinished building with the latest drawings spelling out still more changes. Nothing that would hold them up . . . just new specifications for cheaper materials, short cuts in construction. Shevelson blew his stack.

"Did I ever thank you for stopping me from hitting the bastard?"

Hodgehead nodded. "A dozen times." He wiped his mouth on his sleeve. "If you had connected Leroux would have gone right over the edge. It would've been a long drop, Will."

Shevelson nodded. He had replayed the scene a dozen times in his head and hadn't yet made up his mind whether it filled him with terror or regret. He hadn't waited for the official notice of dismissal but had taken the construction elevator down the side of the building, got into his car and driven home. His paycheck had arrived by special delivery the next day, and that had been the end of his career in the building trades. Nobody in the city was willing to risk Leroux's anger and considering the circumstances—in those moments when he was stone sober and cold-bloodedly objective about it—he couldn't blame them. Who would hire a construction foreman who was willing to kill you if you disagreed with him? Leroux himself had never pressed charges, partly because of lack of witnesses.

Shevelson half smiled in remembrance. "I guess I've also thanked you a dozen times for clamming up when Knudsen called you in at the investigation." Knudsen Construction had damn near lost the contract and been sued in the bargain, he mused.

"So you tripped and fell during an argument. It can happen, with all the crap that's lying around on an unfinished floor. But if you had actually connected and Leroux went over . . ." He shrugged. "I guess it would've been a different story. One of the guys would've chickened out, you know that. But it didn't happen, so why worry about it?" He hesitated a moment. "You ain't asking, but I think you should've kept your mouth shut later."

Shevelson nursed his beer and nodded. His feud with Leroux and the Glass House became an obsession the first few months afterward. He contacted newspapers and radio and television stations, trying to tell them what Leroux had done, and was doing, until everybody had figured that he was some kind of nut. There had been a short story or two in the newspapers, a brief abortive investigation that Leroux managed to get quashed, and the story died.

Shevelson went to get another can of beer and turned the TV set back on, staring at tiny figures running across a too-green gridiron. He fiddled a moment with the color and hue controls. "How's that?"

"Looks fine, but it ain't gonna help 'em win."

Shevelson sat back on the couch cushions. "You know, Marty, I think I was disappointed in Leroux as much as anything else. Damnit, the world's run by assholes but I had never considered Leroux to be one; in fact, I thought he was one of the most capable people I ever met. He had knowledge, energy . . ." He searched for the word. "Integrity, too, I guess you'd call it."

"Until it came to the Glass House."

"That's right, until it came to the Glass House." What changed Leroux? he wondered. He really didn't have to make the compromises he made; he wasn't in a money bind. There were compromises to be expected, but there was usually a point past which a man wouldn't go. But Leroux was willing to buy any patchwork scheme that would save a dollar. He was lavish when it came to the external appearances of the building, but the end result was still that Leroux sold his principles and apparently did so without a qualm.

For himself, Shevelson thought . . . well, he'd managed well enough. He finally found a job as building supervisor for this small apartment complex complete with apartment and settled into a quiet life of tinkering around the apartments during the day and drinking beer and watching television at night. After three marriages and three divorces, he had decided that he was a loner and solitude was something he accepted almost with relief.

"How come you ever got tied up with that schmuck on the KYS news show?" Hodgehead asked.

"Because I'm an idiot, because I couldn't leave it alone," Shevelson said, his mood suddenly gloomy. "I got out the blueprints one day and I was going over them and got carried away. So I called up Quantrell and he invited me to lunch and I spilled my guts." He had done more than that, he thought. He had fed the bastard everything he knew of for a certainty and quite a few things he had only suspected.

He grimaced. "It was a cheap shot, Marty . . . you don't have to tell me that. I could have gone to the Building Trades Council; I could have done a dozen other things than what I did. I wanted to hurt Leroux as bad as I could; a slap on the wrist from the Council wouldn't have satisfied me."

"The construction techniques weren't all that bad," Hodgehead said slowly. "Quite a few of them are common practice."

"Whose side are you on, Marty?" Shevelson looked at him angrily, then waved a hand. "Okay, you're part right. But just because something's common practice doesn't make it good practice. One by one, you might defend them. Put them all together and you wind up with a building in which some of the construction techniques or materials haven't been tested outside of a laboratory, a few others that are borderline, and some that you can get away with because your local building code doesn't specifically forbid them." He drained his can of beer and crumpled it in his hand. Something was beginning to surface in the back of his mind. He fished for it but it eluded him. He let his attention drift back to the television screen. Second down and eight to go and the defense was weak; it should be a snap.

"I guess I would have done the same if I had been in your shoes," Hodgehead said. "She was your baby from the start. Let's face it, a building actually belongs to the men who make her, not the men who pay for her."

That's what was wrong, Shevelson thought suddenly. The Glass House had been his baby—and what was bothering him was that it still was. Maybe somebody else had designed it and somebody else had finished it, but with all its faults the Glass House was still his more than anybody else's. It was the most beautiful building in the city and like Pygmalion with his statue, during the slow process of construction, he had fallen in love with it. Now it was going up in smoke and he was just sitting there, drinking his beer and watching the replay of a football game.

With all its faults . . . And who knew them better than he? Not Leroux. To him, the building had been a rendering and a sheaf of figures from his accounting department telling him what it was costing and how much he could save. . . . And not the guy they had called in from the East Coast to wrap up the project after he had gotten the can. So long as he collected his paycheck every Tuesday, the bastard hadn't given a damn. In any event, he had flown back East immediately after the dedication and there was probably no locating him on short notice. The original architect—what was his name, Barton? He had been shipped East before construction had ever begun and the last Shevelson had heard, was working out of San Francisco. The architect who had acted as its site supervisor had since died; probably gone to his glory cursing himself for being too weak to stand up to Leroux. The man had been an ass kisser from the start.

The Fire Department? They'd probably have some diagrams of the location of stairwells and standpipes but they'd hardly know where the bodies were buried.

He made up his mind then and hurried to the closet and grabbed his coat and gloves, making sure the car keys were in his pocket. Crappy weather. Take him half an hour to get there on the freeway, if he was lucky.

"Where the hell you going, Will?"

"To the Glass House, where do you think?"

"After what the prick did to you, you'd help him out?"

Shevelson half smiled. "She's more mine than his, Marty." He was almost out the front door when he remembered and ran back to his study to grab a roll of blueprints from off a bookshelf.

Hodgehead was shaking his head. "Will, they must have a set of the prints down there; you're acting stupid."

"You think so? Quantrell said the fire was on the seventeenth floor. By now it's probably on the eighteenth as well, and that's the headquarters of Curtainwall. They probably can't get at their own set of prints. Sure, they can get the originals from Wexler and Haines—and ten to one they bear as much resemblance to the final set as a car just off the showroom floor has to the same model in a demolition derby." He buttoned his coat and pulled the collar up around his neck. "Marty, I'm probably the only person in the whole goddamned city who has a set of the actual working plans. And Leroux's going to pay through the nose for them."

Fifteen minutes later he rounded a corner of the freeway, fighting to keep his car from skidding off the icy curve. It was hard to tell because of the driving snow, but far ahead in the distance he thought he could make out a faint orange glow on the horizon.

27.

There had to be another bottle around, Bigelow thought; he was sure there was one left over from the staff meeting the week before which had been half meeting and half party. He pawed through the desk drawers in the outer office, then stood up and tried to focus on the room.

Damned room didn't want to stand still, kept circling around him. . . .

He clutched at the edge of a swivel chair, closed his eyes hard, then suddenly opened them very wide. The metal edge of the chair was cold against his naked belly and even that helped some. *God, he was smashed!* He had started drinking early so he would have the courage to go ahead and break off with Deirdre that night. By the time she got there, he was already half a bottle down. Deirdre had promptly joined in so she could forget it all, and between them the drinking had gained a momentum all its own.

Damnit, he *knew* there was a bottle out here someplace! If the room would only settle down. . . . Of *course,* how could he have been so dumb! The little cabinet beneath the bookshelves that they had stocked with plastic cups and a few bottles of mix and a small styrofoam ice bucket for the occasional office party. It had to be down there.

He weaved over to the bookcase, clung to the shelves a moment for support, then knelt by the cabinet doors and yanked them open. Success! He chortled to himself. Any time anybody could hide a bottle on a Bigelow, that would be the day. He pulled it out. Goddamn, only half full. Somebody had been tapping it. He thought for a moment of Krost, then shrugged. Hell, no, that lush had access to better sources for booze than Motivational Displays. He stood up, clutching the bottle in his hand, then suddenly remembered the office party and squinted at the label. Bourbon, and cheap bourbon at that. They had drunk all the good stuff at the meeting and made the mistake of sending out the office boy to pick up a bottle in the building's liquor store.

Bigelow hiccuped once and started for the storeroom leading back to the executive suite. It only proved once again that you shouldn't send a boy to do a man's job, he thought. Funny. But both he and Deirdre were too far gone for quality to matter.

A splinter in the wooden storeroom floor made him yelp and also partly sobered him. He clung to the horns of a polystyrene reindeer for partial support while he stood on one leg and tried to pull the splinter out of the sole of his foot. He ought to have worn his shoes; it had been a dumb thing not to. He managed to focus his eyes and pulled the splinter out. A tiny drop of blood followed it and sobered him even more. He was so drunk, he hadn't felt it go in that deep. Had to be careful. Get too drunk and he wouldn't be able to get it up and that wouldn't do, at least not with Deirdre. She'd never let him forget it. Not that he was ever going to see her again anyway. . . .

He had forgotten to turn off the light in the outer office. He started to turn back, then thought: What the hell? He'd do it later. If he went back now he'd probably pick up another splinter. He threaded his way through the displays and suddenly caught himself thinking that the damned elves and Santa Clauses were a lot of polyester voyeurs. He imagined them looking at him and snickering and he felt his face turn red. It wasn't what you had; it was what you did with it, he reminded himself—then wished, absurdly, that he had slipped into his trousers before going to the outer office in search of another bottle.

He was almost to the door of the executive suite when he heard the sirens. They kept coming closer and then stopped and he wondered idly if he could see the blaze from the windows. They could turn off the lights and watch it like watching a fire on the hearth—only their hearth would be twenty-one floors up.

He felt the bottle begin to slip and clutched it against his sweaty chest. Then he was in the suite and had placed the bottle safely on the bar, next to his trophy. He patted it briefly: It was the only trophy he had ever won in his whole life, awarded to him two years ago for having created "The Most Outstanding Display" at the Small Engines and Motors Show. He stood back a few feet and stared at it affectionately, then made a slight adjustment to the cant of his hat he had dropped on top. Nice trophy. He felt drunkenly sentimental. It was a big mother, he thought, over three feet tall. Win a small one and you had to buy a display case and a small spotlight and . . .

"You jus' gonna stan' there or you gonna pour me a drink?"

Deirdre was sitting on the edge of the now unfolded couch, a sheet wrapped around her. She had turned on the TV set against the wall a few feet away and was staring at it intently. Bigelow glanced at the screen. Old movie, probably one of Deirdre's favorites. She could drive anybody nuts with trivia when it came to the old-timers.

"Jus' hold your horses, Deedee, and I'll pour you two."

He splashed three inches of bourbon over an ice cube in the bottom of her glass and handed it to her. She took it absently, still staring at the screen.

"That good?" Bigelow asked. It was an old Busby Berkeley clinker with hundreds of chorus girls looking very 1930ish. What was it? "When a Broadway baby says goodnight . . ." No, that had been from a song in it, *Lullaby of*—*

"The news a minute ago," Deirdre said. "They cut into the film. Something about a fire." Her words were slurred and Bigelow had trouble making them out. "I didn't get it all. You know, that guy on KYS. A real bastard, I can tell by his eyes. . . ." She sipped at her drink and murmured, "Thanks," and then, "Something about a fire." She frowned again and Bigelow sensed that she was going to go through the whole bit all over. She must be like that when she was learning lines, he thought. He leaned past her and flicked off the set.

"What the hell did you do that for?" She said it with all the huffiness of the local drunk in the corner bar and for a moment Bigelow caught a clear image of what she might be like in the near future. The tiny lines were already forming around her neck and eyes. The elasticity was going from her upper arms and the flesh was dimpling

---

* Portion of lyrics from "Lullaby of Broadway," music by Harry Warren, lyrics by Al Dubin. Copyright © 1935, M. Witmark & Sons. Copyright renewed. Used by permission of Warner Bros. Music.

just below her buttocks. He had been right, something deep within him whispered; it had been time to drop her.

And then he was gulping his own drink, letting the warmth fill his body and chase away his more sober thoughts. He turned out the room light so only the lights on the small Christmas tree were burning. What was the song in *Finian's Rainbow?* "If I'm not with the girl that I love, I love the girl I'm with."* Something like that. He reached for Deirdre in the dusk and she turned and cuddled closer to him. The sheet was no longer wrapped around her. He buried his face in her neck, blowing lightly against her skin.

The phone rang.

"Oh, for Christ's sake!" Bigelow sat bolt upright and grabbed the phone off the end table, shoving it beneath a pillow behind him so the ringing seemed distant and far away. One damned interruption after another, he thought. Who the hell could be calling tonight? Wrong number, probably. He turned back to Deirdre, who was open and waiting for him.

Even while reaching for her, he was dimly aware that for some strange reason his eyes were beginning to water. He automatically closed them. Making love was one of the few activities for which human beings needed no sight, he thought. He was unaware of the slight haze of smoke that was starting to drift out of the suite's ventilation grill high on the wall and was promptly lost in the dusk of the room.

Behind him, smothered by the pillow, the telephone continued its futile ringing.

---

* Portion of lyrics from "When I'm Not Near the Girl I Love," music by Burton Lane, lyrics by E. Y. Harburg. Copyright © 1946 by Chappell & Co., Inc. Copyright renewed. Used by permission of Chappell & Co., Inc.

28.

Lex Hughes was having trouble with the new electronic calculator. The keys on the machine were much smaller than those on the old Monroe adding machine that it had replaced and he was always accidentally punching two keys at once. It must have been something like that which had thrown the totals off by a hundred dollars. A simple mechanical slip, but it had taken the better part of an hour to find the error. It was the sort of thing that was always happening to him, Lex Hughes thought. The story of his life.

He leaned back and sighed. He was very tired, too tired even to feel the usual despair that frequently overwhelmed him when he was working in the office alone at night. For a moment he wished he hadn't let Carolyn go—she was good at finding errors quickly.

It was more than the sense of physical fatigue that he felt; it was the realization that he was devoting his life's work to the handling of other people's money. It was routine; it was drudgery; it was dull—and it was something more than that. *If you're so smart why aren't you rich?* But he would never be rich, he would never even be comfortably well off. He would slowly inch his way up the promotional ladder and by the time he reached the lower executive ranks, there would then be the final banquet and the equivalent of a gold watch. The perfunctory handshake and the unspoken wish that he clean out his desk as soon as possible for his replacement, who would be young and clear of eye and champing at the bit in the outer office. Then a dull retirement and the losing battle against the actuarial charts—accompanied in his golden years by a shrew of a wife who would devote her remaining days to making his life miserable for not having filled hers with charm and excitement and the pleasure of possessions. In her own way, she would finally find a fulfillment that would always escape him.

If he were suddenly granted three wishes, he thought, the first would be that he could be a small boy once again, so he could cry without being thought unmanly.

He got up from his desk and carried the last of the ledgers and his calculation sheets into the vault. He wouldn't take anything home tonight; for once the weekend would be strictly for rest. On the way out of the vault, he stopped and glanced back briefly. The money drawers were like a magnet for him. How many answers to life's problems lay within those deceptively plain metal drawers. . . .

And then, suddenly feeling guilty, he looked up at the Eye, certain that it was reading his thoughts. The red light glowed as the camera slowly panned toward him. *Thou Seest Me,* he thought again. The camera was full on him now and he imagined that he was looking through the lens into unplumbed distances. The sensation gave him a feeling of vertigo. He hated heights and looking into the camera was almost the same as staring down the entire eighteen floors into the security room. He wondered if anybody was looking back.

At that instant, the red light winked out.

His breath seemed to freeze in his throat. No, it couldn't be so. Lights *did* burn out. It was only the light. On Monday, they'd send someone up to replace the bulb, and the camera would follow him again with its implacable red eye.

Only . . . the camera wasn't scanning. At the same instant the red light had winked out, the motor driving the camera stopped and the lens poised motionless, leering directly at him. Now there was no sense of staring down great heights. Intuition whispered that the Eye was dead, that its lens had filmed over and the monitoring screen eighteen floors below had faded into a dull gray, as if a heavy shade had been pulled over the Credit Union area.

He could feel the sweat begin to form under his arms. The room was now completely silent, the barely audible whir of the camera's scanning motor stilled. There was only the sound of his own breathing, of the heavy pounding of his heart . . . and of distant sirens.

Fire engines, he thought, distracted. And they must be very near if he could hear them in the almost soundproof offices.

Suddenly suspicious, he scurried around the rail and ran down the aisle between the rows of desks to the hall door. Once there, he paused for a second in indecision, looking back at the dead camera. It hadn't moved an inch. He turned back to the door, opened it, and peered out into the hall. Nothing, he thought, feeling vaguely disappointed. And then something caught in his throat and nose; the faint, acrid smell of fire. He squinted down the hall at the elevator bank. Lazy tendrils of smoke were floating out of the shafts, bluing the air in the corridor. More smoke was drifting from an air-conditioning duct a few feet farther down.

For the first time he was aware of how close the air in the office had become. Somewhere down below someone had turned off the ventilating fans. There was a fire in the building, he thought slowly. How major a fire, he didn't know. But it had knocked out the camera coaxial and, in effect, drawn a curtain between him and the rest of the world.

He slammed the door and leaned against it, his heart racing. Cut off from the world, cut off from the all-seeing Eye. He ran back to the Credit Union area, feeling the first stirrings of panic. He'd have to get out, but first he'd have to shut the vault doors. They were fireproof and it would have to get awfully hot to damage the contents, but he had read about money being charred within a safe. It could happen. He mopped the perspiration from his forehead and glanced up again at the dead camera. It was up to him; it was his responsibility. The money and the records must be kept safe. It was too bad that the Eye couldn't see how seriously he took his responsibilities, how dependable a man he was in his position.

"You could never find anybody better," he said quietly, not even realizing he was saying it aloud. "No one better," he repeated as though to reassure himself.

The camera said nothing, its dead Eye staring at empty space.

He looked back somberly at the Eye, feeling that if he had been wearing his hat, he should take it off. It was his duty to take the money to a safe place; it was his responsibility.

And then, suddenly, he had another thought. A terrible, frightening thought. What if a distant God had taken pity on him and had given him this one final chance to escape the prison of his life?

But God doesn't work that way, he thought.

Doesn't He? an inner voice asked. Hughes hesitated a moment, then slowly reached for his brief case. He undid the clasp and upended it, letting the few papers within fall to the floor. He couldn't turn his back on this opportunity, he thought, his mind suddenly cold and crystal clear. It was his last chance, the risk was worth it. The deposits were insured. He would be injuring nobody.

He shouldered the vault door all the way open, for one of the few times in his life feeling strong and in complete command of his actions. For the first time in years, he didn't feel obligated to consider the wishes of somebody else ahead of his own. He was *Número Uno,* he thought. This time he came first, this time *his* life was the most important.

He clutched his empty brief case and started to walk into the vault, glancing up briefly at the dead camera overhead. A wild elation filled him. "Thou Seest Me *Not!*" he shouted in triumph.

It felt remarkably good.

29.

Within minutes after Jernigan got the warning call from Garfunkel, the sky lobby started to fill with people. Some of the tenants were dressed for the street, others were in pajamas and slippers with an overcoat hastily thrown over their shoulders. A few were hysterical and Jernigan sensed panic in the air. Faint wisps of smoke were already seeping into the lobby from the elevator shafts. He wondered if the fire below was worse than Garfunkel admitted. He debated for a moment trying to convince residents to return to their apartments and follow the instructions printed on the door plaques. He decided that if he tried, he would have the makings of a riot. It would be the smartest thing to do, but the people in the lobby weren't exactly in the mood for wisdom.

Rosette had arrived. She was watching a television show on a set in the maids' quarters when the movie had been interrupted by the news flash of the fire. She was still in uniform and Jernigan thanked God for small favors. He immediately put her in charge of herding the tenants into the residential express elevator, the only elevator he could safely trust to travel through the fire zone without stopping.

He tried to quiet the tenants. "The Fire Department's already here," he said in a voice loud enough to be heard over the crying and the babble. "The fire's confined to the seventeenth floor; we'll get a little smoke up here but that should be all." That would be more than enough, he thought, and wondered if the fire actually was being confined.

"They never tell us anything!" one woman shrilled. "We were supposed to have fire drills and indoctrination sessions but nobody ever told *me* anything!"

An older tenant turned to Jernigan. "See here, young man, does management have any evacuation plans at all? If so, what are they?"

Jernigan flinched inside. Harriman had planned coffee chats with the tenants, but he had postponed them because of the upcoming holiday season. The tenants couldn't seem to find the time and neither could management.

"This is it, sir, just waiting in line for the express elevator down."

"Didn't they even give the families of employees directions on how to get out?"

"Sir, I don't live here."

The old man laughed shortly. "You're a smarter man than I was."

You had to look at it from their viewpoint, Jernigan thought. There was the lack of communication between the tenants and management and there was also the sense of isolation on the part of the tenants themselves. You had all the privacy you wanted in a high rise; it was worse than the standard apartment house where you seldom knew the people on the other floors unless your kitchen sink overflowed and then you suddenly had the couple downstairs banging on your front door. Here, you didn't even meet people in the hallways. It was more like a hotel: the usually deserted corridors and an occasional chance meeting by the elevators.

Now they were more than just alone; they were frightened as well.

"They'll pay!" a woman added. "The whole apartment will have to be cleaned; I know what smoke damage can amount to!"

". . . See my lawyer first thing Monday . . ."

". . . It's all right, Martha, just a little smoke, we'll be okay . . ."

". . . Whatever happens, hang on to Daddy's coat, don't get separated . . ."

". . . Seen your name on the mail slot, you live right next door . . ."

". . . Al, I'm scared as hell . . ."

One of the down elevators opened and a couple came out with a toy poodle on a leash. Jernigan stared for a moment in fascination, wondering how they had taken the dog in and out of the building with none of the security guards aware of the animal. Lisolette Mueller had her pet cat, Schiller, but that was an open secret; everybody knew it but nobody really objected.

Jernigan helped Rosette form the tenants into lines in front of the residential express to the main lobby; the only stops the elevator was capable of making were the two lobbies and the basement garage. It made no stops at all in the commercial section of the building. Suddenly

Jernigan spotted a beefy salesman type and his chubby wife buzzing one of the elevators in the commercial bank. He moved in quickly.

"I'm sorry, sir, you'll have to wait for the residential express; the commercial elevators are too risky to take down."

The salesman gave him the fish eye. "I don't get it. What do you mean, they're too risky?"

Jernigan had been alerted to the risks once in friendly conversation with a fireman and patiently explained it. "If an elevator is capable of making stops in the fire zone and if the call button on that floor is fused because of the heat, there's a good chance the elevator will be called to that floor whether you want it to or not. Once the doors open, you might never get out alive."

"I don't know what you're talking about, son," the man said. "All I know is Maggie and me aren't going to stay here and broil."

"The fire is fourteen floors below us," Jernigan said calmly. "Look, it's too risky; the elevator might go right to the fire floor."

The lobby was overflowing now. It was going to take time to evacuate the residents and it was going to be increasingly difficult to keep them away from the commercial bank. What none of them realized was that there was a faint blue to the air even now from the smoke. It would get worse, and probably quickly. More people and he would start to lose control. . . .

"I'm buzzing for the elevator, son. I pay my rent; you can't stop me." He was red in the face, trying to work up his anger. Probably because he was scared to death, Jernigan thought. A number of tenants in the crowd had pushed over and would obviously stampede into the elevator the moment its door opened. He could tell by the looks on their faces that they hadn't understood what he had tried to explain to the salesman either.

He raised his voice. "Rosette, make it women and children first, overload it if you have to." There was a safety factor built in that could handle the overloading, particularly with women and children. But even though it wouldn't stop at the fire floor, it was still traveling through the fire zone and the sooner the women and children got out, the better.

He turned back to the salesman, his voice hard. "I'll try once more, mister. There's no call button for the residential express elevator on the seventeenth floor—it won't stop there, it will go right through the fire zone down to the lobby. You take one of the commercial elevators and the chances are it will stop there, even if you didn't press the button for the floor. And once the doors open, you'll cook."

"Don't try to bullshit me, mister. When the elevator comes, I'm going." A few of the tenants behind Jernigan pushed forward in anticipation.

The commercial elevator arrived and the doors slid silently open. Jernigan saw what the salesman did not: The paint on the doors had been slightly scorched. It had probably stopped briefly at the fire floor, the doors opened and closed, and it had then resumed its upward journey. It was almost a sure cinch it would stop there on the way down.

The salesman smiled his triumph. "See you down below," he said and started to get on.

Jernigan grabbed his arm, ignoring the surprised murmurs behind him. "Nobody's taking this elevator!" he said, raising his voice to keep the crowd back that had started to press forward.

The salesman jerked away, raising his fists. "No nigger's going to tell me what I can do and cannot do. We're getting out of here!"

Rosette was watching him, alarmed. Jernigan pointed at the residential elevator which was filling up fast and held up two fingers. She nodded and immediately turned away two women, protesting.

Jernigan reached out and grabbed the salesman by the arm, whirling him off balance. "Sorry, Mac," he said quietly and hit him just below the chin with a quick chop. He caught the salesman before he hit the lobby floor and slapped him halfway back to consciousness, then pushed him toward his screaming wife. "Get him out of here," he said softly. "Right now. There's room for you both in the other elevator but it won't wait." She half carried her husband to Rosette's waiting elevator. The rest of the crowd reluctantly backed away from the commercial bank. Jernigan could tell from the slight sound behind the elevator lobby doors that the cab was going back down, probably to the seventeenth floor.

There weren't too many more tenants coming into the lobby, Jernigan thought, suddenly hopeful; he might be able to clear it out after all. Fifteen minutes later, the crowd in the lobby had thinned noticeably. The next time the elevator came up, several firemen got off, dressed in slickers and helmets. Jernigan motioned them over, away from the crowd.

"How bad is it?"

The older of the two shrugged. "Bad enough, worse than it should be. If we had had an alarm fifteen minutes earlier it might have been a different story. You the guy who's been keeping them away from the commercial elevators?" Jernigan nodded. "Good thinking. How many people left upstairs?"

Jernigan could feel the sweat start to work down the back of his neck; the air in the lobby was getting close. "I'm not sure; I started to log them out and then there wasn't time. I understand the switchboard is trying to notify everybody."

"Sure they are." He made a face. "Two operators on duty, the other two had gone off shift. Your switchboard's jammed with outside calls trying to get in—relatives and friends, probably some crank calls. They're trying to notify the tenants but that takes time. And then there's always people watching the tube with the volume turned up and who won't hear the phone, or who have turned the phone off for the evening, or they're taking a shower, or they've taken sleeping pills and hit the sack. . . ." He shook his head. "We'll have to get more men up here and start going through the floors one by one. Smoke's spreading pretty fast. Thank God the upper floors are empty." He glanced sharply at Jernigan. "What about kids? Any apartments where the parents have gone out for the evening and there's a kid and a baby-sitter?"

Jernigan felt sick. Mrs. Harris and her husband had left for the movies earlier that evening with Irene and he couldn't remember Danny and Sharon going through the lobby when it was emptying out.

"Two Harris kids, boy eleven, girl fourteen. I didn't see them, though that doesn't mean they didn't get out."

"What apartment?"

"Two floors up, I can show you." He called over to Rosette, who was handling the last of the dwindling crowd by the express elevator. "Take over, Rosie, I'll be back in a minute. If I'm not, go down with the last load." The air was distinctly hazy now and it was getting a little more difficult to breathe.

The fireman noticed. "It's not bad enough for masks but you're in a lousy spot here. The utility core has a southern exposure and outside there's a strong north wind. You can't feel it but it works its way into the building and is pushing most of the smoke this way."

Jernigan had buzzed for one of the regular residential elevators going up. "That smoke spread awfully fast."

"Partly the weather—the building acts like a chimney when it's cold out—and partly the building itself. They're trying to reverse the ventilation fans now, suck some of the smoke out. Should've been automatic. Two flights up?"

They caught the elevator and a moment later were running down the hall to the Harris apartment. There was some smoke in the hall but nowhere near as much as in the sky lobby. Probably because the Harris apartment was nearer the north side of the building. He thumped the apartment door with his fist, then fumbled in his pocket for a house key. Crap, he had left it behind at his desk. The senior fireman motioned him to one side and stuck a pry bar in a corner of the door, near the lock. He started to apply pressure when a high-pitched, muffled voice within said, "Just a minute, please."

A moment later the door opened and Sharon Harris looked at them, surprised. "We got a phone call," she said primly, "but we really didn't think you'd be here this soon."

Jernigan followed the firemen into the apartment. There was even less smoke in the apartment than in the corridor. Then he noticed the wet rags around the door. In addition, all the ventilator grills had wet dishtowels and strips of sheeting poked into the holes.

The firemen also noticed and the older one shook his head in admiration. "Who told you how to do it, kid?"

"The telephone operator told us there was a fire and I ran to the door and saw some smoke in the hall. I didn't know how much there might be by the elevators or the stairwells so I thought we ought to stay here until somebody came to get us. Danny has asthma and I was afraid he might not make it. Then I remembered what Lisolette had said about the plaque on the door; she explained it to us." Sharon looked at the firemen very soberly, and Jernigan wondered briefly where he had seen the expression before, and then remembered. "It really seemed like the only sensible thing to do."

The fireman looked over at Jernigan. "Who's this Lisolette?"

"Old-maid schoolteacher—patron saint of all the kids in the building." He wondered briefly how her dinner with Harlee was going and then asked Sharon, "Where's Danny?"

"There." She pointed to the family room. "He's watching the fire on television."

One of the firemen went to the door. "Come on, son, it's time to go."

"Do I have to? This is exciting!"

"Afraid so, son. Get your coat; we've got to leave right now."

In the living room, Sharon picked up one of the wet towels that had been stuffed around the door and gave it to Danny with instructions to hold it over his face and breathe through it. The smoke in the hallway was thicker now and down in the deserted sky lobby, the blue in the air had turned to a dirty gray. Danny started to cough.

"Can you think of anybody else who might not have gotten out?"

"Hell, man, I can't think of any—I sure as hell hope they all got out." The smoke had started to hurt his lungs and Jernigan didn't want to talk. He also didn't want to think about those who might have been left behind. There had to be some, he knew; he'd remember them as soon as he got downstairs and then the night would turn into a living hell for him.

Both Sharon and Danny had started to gag and the firemen shoved them and Jernigan into the residential express. The doors were almost closed when Jernigan violently thumbed the "open" button. He felt like crying.

"I forgot, Jesus, I forgot! There's an old lady and her husband in 3724—name is Richardson. She's a wheelchair case and I know damned well they didn't come through. Maybe they left before the fire but I can't remember seeing them or checking them out." He felt helpless. "I just can't remember."

"That's okay, we'll check it out. When you get down below, try and take a census in the lobby. You got your checkout boards with you? Okay—they've got spare inhalators down there, get one on the kid, just in case."

They caught an elevator going up and then the doors to his own cab had closed and Jernigan could feel the slow acceleration downward. Behind him, Danny was being sick all over the elevator floor.

Back in the deserted sky lobby, the house phone on Jernigan's desk suddenly began to ring. On the little red-lighted switchboard behind the desk, number 3416 was lit up.

Somebody was trying to call the desk from the Albrecht apartment.

30.

Even from where he stood in the doorway, Ian Douglas could feel the heat from the blazing solvent flooding down the hall. It was hotter than he expected, considering the distance. Then he realized with a shock that the distance was narrowing rapidly even as he watched. His eyes were tearing badly from the smoke now; he had to get out. He automatically held up the print to shield his face from the heat and backed quickly down the hall. He could feel the heat on the back of his fingers; the edge of the print frame grew perceptibly warmer.

He wasn't going to make it, he thought, panicked; the fire was traveling too fast. He abruptly turned and ran for the stairwell door, feeling the heat lap against his back. He twisted the knob and yanked the door open, glancing quickly behind him as he ran through. It was like looking into a furnace; the entire corridor was in flames, the blazing solvent only yards away. Then the door closed behind him, its latch making an audible click.

He set the "Minotaurmachie" on the concrete landing, leaning it against the wall, and simultaneously began to cough and wipe at his eyes. His cheeks were wet, as if he had been crying, and his eyes stung. For a minute he held to the iron pipe railing at the edge of the landing, his body shaking violently. Then the coughing spasm passed —it was far easier to breathe in the stairwell and his racing heart slowed as he realized he was safe, at least for the moment. The back of his shirt felt warm. He remembered that it had seemed almost as if it were burning when he ran through the door. Radiant heat, he thought; in the corridor, it must have been intense. The back of his neck was blistered. Then he glanced down at his hands, remembering he had been holding the print before him as he had backed down the hall. The skin on the backs was red and puffy; his knuckles felt like he had brushed them against the burners on an electric stove.

At that moment he heard the sound of sobbing. He cocked his head and listened. It was a sort of whimpering, coming from the landing above him, the one for the eighteenth floor. Somebody was above him and either frightened or hurt, which seemed unlikely since the fire was on his floor. But the smoke had probably carried up. . . . He ran up the stairs, leaving the print behind.

From the stairwell landing, he could see two people partly hidden by the risers. One seemed to be bending over the other. The figure turned and he saw that it was the Puerto Rican kid, the one who had tried to rob his shop! He raced up the remaining steps. He should've reported the goddamned junkie to Garfunkel—what a fool he had been! Then he was on the landing. Jesus looked up at him, startled. Huddled against the wall was one of the cleaning women, trying to stuff some money back into a wallet. Her dress was rumpled and she was crying. Douglas took the scene in immediately. The kid had been trying to mug her for her wallet and she had fought him.

"You goddamned thief!"

Jesus started to scramble away from him. "No, you got me wrong, man!" he pleaded.

"I got you right, you mean!" Douglas caught Jesus along the side of the head with the flat of his hand and sent him sprawling. "What else did you take from her? Did you get her rings, her wrist watch? Anything you forgot?"

"You don't understand!" Jesus blubbered. "I was sick, I needed the money. . . ."

Douglas grabbed him by the front of his shirt and yanked him to his feet. "I ought to throw you down the stairs. I let you go once but I won't make that mistake this time. . . ." His eyes widened. "You set the storeroom on fire, didn't you? It had to be you; there wasn't anybody else around!"

Jesus twisted in his grasp, his eyes wide with fear. "I didn't do nothing, man. I didn't do a goddamn thing; you're outta your mind!"

The cleaning woman struggled to her feet, wincing at

each movement. She had apparently twisted her ankle un-
der her when she had fallen to the concrete. She tugged at
Douglas' sleeve, shaking her head. "My son," she said.
"Mi hijo . . ."

Douglas looked his amazement. "Your son?"

She nodded, her eyes dull. "My son," she said in a
heavy voice.

Douglas loosened his grip and Jesus backed away.
"She's my mother," he said. "She's been working here
since the place opened. I wanted to . . . to borrow some
money from her tonight."

"Borrow, bullshit," Douglas said, disgusted. The kid
would steal the pennies off a dead man's eyes. He probably
tried to shake the old lady down. Douglas began coughing
again and abruptly remembered the fire below.

"We have to get out of here. There's a bad fire in the
building." Albina looked at him, apparently not understanding. She had started to cough herself.

"Fuego," Jesus said, explaining the situation to her in
slightly halting Spanish. Her eyes widened. *"Fuego?"*
Then she turned on him, her manner accusing, the words
pouring from her in a torrent.

Jesus shook his head. "No, Mama, I didn't do it. *I
didn't do it!"*

"There's no time for that; let's get out of here,"
Douglas muttered. He took Albina by one arm to give
her support and slowly started down the stairs, Jesus
following. At the halfway landing, he turned toward the
second flight of stairs, then caught his breath. The flaming
solvent had seeped under the door, setting fire to the
paint. The metal panel itself was blazing. In the next
moment he watched the puddle of burning liquid spread
until it reached the Picasso "Minotaurmachie" leaning
against the wall. The umber-rubbed gilt of the frame
peeled before his eyes, then the glass cracked and shattered into a hundred pieces. The paper darkened and
turned brown. The bull man, contorted in agony before
the maddened crowd of the bull ring, seemed to stare
at him with agony-filled eyes, then dissolved in flames.

The entire landing was now covered with flames. "We can't go down," Douglas said quietly. "We're trapped."

More solvent seeped under the warping door. A sudden wave of heat from the smoky flames drove them back up the steps, away from the landing. A waterfall of fire poured down the concrete risers to the next floor below.

"We gotta get out!" Jesus screamed and ran back up to the eighteenth floor. He hammered at the stairwell door and tugged at the knob. Douglas helped Albina hobble up the steps to the landing; he pulled Jesus away from the door. "Don't be a fool, you can't get in that way; it's locked after seven."

"What the hell are we gonna do?" Jesus demanded. "We can't stay here and fry, man!" His eyes widened. "Oh, God," he sobbed, "look!"

Smoke had started to seep under the stairwell door. Smoke traveled up, Douglas thought. And so did the fire. The eighteenth floor was now probably on fire, as well as the seventeenth. That meant they had to go up—all the way up, to the Promenade Room. Every stairwell door along the way would be locked, every one but the top one. He had dined one evening in the Promenade Room and discovered what he thought had been the men's room door had actually been the door to the stairwell; there had been no difficulty re-entering once the door had closed behind him. Apparently the fire doors at the top and bottom of the stairwell were kept open.

"We've got to go up," he said slowly. "We're cut off down below."

He helped Albina up the next flight. She suddenly turned at the landing and glared at him suspiciously. "How far? How far up?"

"All the way up to the top."

"You're crazy, man!" Jesus spat. "That's more than forty stories. We ain't ever going to make that. Mama can't make that!"

"You got a better idea?" Douglas asked coldly. "It's either go up or stay here and suffocate or burn. It's the only chance we've got. Take it or leave it." He turned to Albina. "You understand?"

She nodded, her face impassive. "Albina understand."

They started up the steps again. Behind him, Douglas could hear Jesus making vomiting sounds. Moments later, Douglas heard the scrape of his shoes on the stairs. It was going to be a long walk, he thought—and the air was already heavy with smoke

31.

It was a quarter to midnight when Mario Infantino turned into Elm Street, two blocks from the Glass House. Ahead of him was pure chaos: The street was a tangle of automobiles full of thrill seekers, police cars, ambulances, and fire equipment. Quantrell and the eleven-o'clock news must have brought half the city down to watch the fire in spite of the weather, he thought, disgusted. At the end of the block, the stream of fire buffs had finally been stopped by police barricades and forced to detour to the right.

He drummed his fingers impatiently against the steering wheel, his frustration building up with every bulletin that crackled from the car's two-way radio. It had been difficult getting there at all because of the weather and then the closer he got, the thicker was the sightseeing traffic. His siren had helped at first but now he was locked in; traffic was too jammed for it to get out of his way. Just ahead, he could glimpse the Glass House jutting into the overcast, almost lost in the driving sleet and snow. Heavy smoke was billowing from the seventeenth and eighteenth floors and behind the windows he could see an occasional smudge of orange flame. It looked as bad as his radio had described it.

A car to the immediate left suddenly stalled and he whipped the wheel over and edged into the gap, then broke into the empty lane and roared toward the road block ahead, scattering spectators who had wandered into the street. The sidewalks, he noted, were as jammed with sightseers as the right lane of the street was with cars. He'd have to get the police to move them back another block at least. That would make for twelve road blocks instead of four and require more police. But there was no helping it; the winds around the building were getting stronger and pieces of glass from broken windows could sail this far.

The police waved him through the intersection and Infantino pulled up behind Fuchs's official car on the opposite side of the street. The chief engineer had beat him there but then he had a head start. He reached in the back seat for his helmet and got out, buttoning up the collar of his turnout coat. The sleet seemed to bite right through the canvas-covered Neoprene. The temperature was still dropping—the worst thing they could have hoped for. The colder the weather, the greater the difference between the temperature indoors and out and the stronger the chimney effect. It was a condition firemen dreaded, particularly in multiple-story buildings such as high rises —and the Glass House was one of the tallest in the city. The one bright spot was the strong north wind. If he remembered the layout of the building correctly, it would help to keep one of the stairwells relatively free of smoke, though God help anybody trapped in the other one.

The street was a jungle of hoses leading from the city hydrants to the pumpers and then to the Siamese connections jutting from the side of the building, extensions from the standpipes in the stairwells. Aerial ladder trucks and snorkel units were helpless in any fire this high up; you had to fight it from the inside. The hosemen must have carried in their fifty-foot coils of two-and-a-half-inch hose and connected up to the standpipes by now. He saw only one salvage company and made a mental note to call up another one; water would cascade down the stairwells and the elevator shafts and even the poke throughs made by the utilities people. They'd best be prepared to handle the lobby and two or three floors at least.

"Hey, Mario, somebody said this is your baby. That

true?" Tom Bylson, chief communications officer, thrust his head out of the department's communications van at the curb.

"You heard right; what's the picture up there?"

"Hot as hell by the sound of things—heavy smoke and fire on the seventeenth and it's breaking through to the eighteenth. It's into the sixteenth, too. Flammable liquids flowing down the stairwell." He shook his head. "It's going up faster than anybody expected."

"Get a call through to the battalion chiefs. I want personal reports in fifteen minutes; make it in the lobby."

"Not a good idea, Chief; most of the tenants are camped in the lobby."

"Have they got a security room?"

"Right."

"Make it there."

Bylson ducked back into the truck, a brief babble of radio transmissions cutting through the cold night air before he closed the truck door.

Infantino jogged toward the lobby entrance, nodding at several familiar faces huddled around the Red Cross van where harried workers handed out cups of coffee to firemen and a small group of tenants in pajamas and overcoats.

The confusion in the lobby was worse than that in the street outside. Tenants still streamed from the residential elevator; they stood in small groups, waiting for someone to tell them what to do next. Some had suitcases and small stacks of clothes and valuables. One couple even had a small poodle on a leash; the dog, half crazed by the noise and commotion around him, was snapping at everybody within reach.

Infantino motioned to a young policeman nearby. "Get that dog out of here."

The policeman noted his rank and nodded. "What do you want me to do with it, sir?"

"I don't give a damn—lock it in a storeroom in the lower lobby, if you have to. I don't want it running around in here if it gets loose."

A small knot of tenants by the reservation desk were

arguing with one of the building's security guards, insisting that they be allowed to go back to their apartments to retrieve wallets and other valuables. Infantino strode over to the guard. "Nobody goes back up, absolutely nobody. Once they're down, they stay down. We have to have free access to the elevators."

At the elevator bank, he spotted Captain Miller of Engine Company 23. "Having any difficulty getting up?"

Miller shook his head. "Not too much. Electric locks on the stairwell doors; pried one open, then borrowed a key from a security man for the others." He stepped aside as a hoseman hurried onto an elevator carrying a fifty-foot coil of hose in a pack on his back. "We're getting as much hose up as possible. Heat's pretty bad; we've lost one section already."

"Elevators?"

"Two of the commercial elevators have a manual override; we're taking them up to sixteenth and then up the stairwell. Sixteen had started to go but we knocked it down pretty fast."

The manual override would eliminate the use of the elevators by any of the tenants who might have been working late, Infantino thought, but that couldn't be helped. If they were below the fire floor, they could use the other commercial elevators to come down. And if they were above . . . Well, God help them.

He glanced around the lobby again. A young woman in a nightgown and a flannel robe was trying to fight her way back onto the residential express elevator; several firemen and a male tenant, probably her husband, restrained her. He knew from long experience what the story was. He searched the crowd for the police officer in charge, finally locating him by the phone booth at the cigar stand. The officer hung up just as Infantino walked over.

"You the ranking police officer here?"

"That's right—until a superior shows up. You?"

"Division Chief Mario Infantino; I'm operating chief here."

The officer looked uncertain. "Chief Fuchs is here; wouldn't he be in charge?"

"It's been delegated to me; check with him if you want. In the meantime, better set your barricades a block farther out in all directions—there'll be glass and maybe masonry and aluminum panels dropping into the street. You know where the chief of security for the building is?"

"He's with some of the other building officials in their monitoring room. Want him?"

"So long as I know where he is; I'll get hold of him later." He nodded at the hysterical woman. "You'll need more patrolmen to handle scenes like that, too; there may be others. I can't detail firemen to do it."

The woman was screaming hysterically: *"Let me go, let me go! Oh God, he's still up there!"*

The police captain looked surprised. "I thought that was her husband standing next to her."

Infantino shook his head. "It probably is. Chances are she's hysterical because they've left a kid up there. If they have three or four, in the rush to get them out they either miscount or lose track of them; somehow, they always think they've got them all together. We usually find them when it's too late, hidden in closets or under blankets; if we go into a burning house or apartment and we know a kid has been left behind, that's the first place we look. It's hell when you find them afterward." He recalled the painful scene two years before when he and a man in his company had found two children in the second story of their gutted home. They had pulled pillowcases over their heads and crawled under the rug in their bedroom. They had died from smoke long before the fire had found their room.

A residential elevator on his left opened to discharge more tenants and several firemen. Some of the tenants were hacking badly from smoke inhalation. One of the firemen yelled, "Get a respirator over here!" He was half carrying another fireman; heavy strings of dirty mucus streamed from the nostrils of the unconscious man, smearing on his turnout coat.

Infantino watched them fumble with the respirator a moment, then muttered to the police captain: "Get this lobby cleared as soon as you can; we're going to be having a lot more of that." He walked away, brushing past two Red Cross men in blue hard hats talking with several tenants and taking notes.

He found one of the building's security guards, looking very young and very frightened, and had him act as escort to the security monitoring room. The room was already half full. Infantino introduced himself to the chief of security and his assistant—Dan Garfunkel and Harry Jernigan; they both looked worn and strained. Garfunkel introduced a worried-looking chief of maintenance named Donaldson. Garfunkel's suit and face were smeared with smoke; Infantino guessed he had headed up the building crew that had tried to put out the fire with hand extinguishers.

"Have you got a census of who's left in the building?" he asked.

Garfunkel shook his head, his face haggard. "No real way of knowing. There are maybe half a dozen tenants unaccounted for from the commercial floors. As far as the residential tenants go—no idea."

"Casualties?"

The security chief shook his head sadly. "Griff Edwards, senior engineer. He was with us when we first went up; it was too much for him. He's in the hospital; doctors suspect a coronary. I haven't had time to check back."

"Where's the building supervisor?"

"Vacation. His assistant went home this afternoon with the flu. Griff was third in line."

Infantino looked over at Donaldson. "What about your HVAC system? Can we use it to exhaust smoke from the building?"

Donaldson looked sour. "The fans should have reversed automatically. Two jammed, one with a motor burnout and another with frozen bearings. The others are on exhaust." His face suddenly reddened with fury. "I told the bloody bastards it was cheap gear the moment I laid eyes on it!"

Infantino glanced around at the monitoring tubes. "Any way we can use these for anything?"

Garfunkel shrugged. "Don't see how. They cover the lobby, the bank entrance, the Credit Union in National Curtainwall, and the restaurant lobby and sky lobby. The one for the Credit Union is out; the Union's on the eighteenth floor." He hesitated. "We have infrared personnel sensors set up in the stairwells. Several of them are gone, too, but just before one of them went, we detected some people in the south stairwell on seventeen."

"How many?"

"Three, maybe more."

The south stairwell, Infantino thought. The north stairwell would be relatively smoke free; the south stairwell . . . Well, good luck. The crippled HVAC system would help keep it partly free of smoke—but only partly.

By now, three of the four battalion chiefs on duty had shown up and he turned his attention to them. "Where's Captain Verlaine?"

"On the seventeenth floor; he's got his hands full," a voice said.

Infantino turned toward the door. "It's good to see you, Chief."

Fuchs nodded. "Gentlemen, in case you're not aware, Chief Infantino has complete charge of this operation. I know you'll give him every cooperation, as will I. I'm not abandoning my own authority; I'll be here all the time. But Chief Infantino's the best man for over-all command. I won't hide my own disagreements with him in the past, but for the moment they're irrelevant. It's a serious fire—one of the worst our city has ever had—and we're all here for the same reason—to knock it down. Mario?"

Fuchs retired to the back of the room. Infantino turned to Captain Miller, who had just taken over Engine Company 23. "Any ideas on origins and fire load?"

"It looks like it started in a storeroom near the utility core on seventeen. Heavy load of solvents, cleaning fluids, and the like. It spread from there down the hall to an interior decorating shop; bolts of fabric, bales of polyurethane foam for upholstery. There was a lot more than the standard fire load on the rest of the floor. Dropped ceilings on all the floors so the fire can spread unnoticed. It's a new building and consequently attracted a lot of wealthy commercial tenants, almost all of whom had their offices professionally decorated. You know the rule of thumb there: The more expensive the furnishings, the more flammable they usually are. The alarm system was apparently faulty and let the fire get a foothold. We have no record of it being logged in automatically at headquarters."

"Present status, Chief Fleming?"

"Seventeen is completely gutted, a few fires on sixteen which were minor and quickly darkened down. Situation on eighteen is serious; it looks like it's getting away from us. Smoke damage is heavy on nineteen and above —we don't know how far above except that smoke penetrated to the residential area." He paused. "There's going to be a lot of water damage on eighteen and seventeen and the floors immediately below."

Infantino nodded. "I've ordered up another salvage company, as well as rescue and wrecking companies. Chief Castro, what's our own position?"

"We need more men. We've been concentrating on seventeen but nobody can work in there for longer than ten, fifteen minutes at a time. The radiant heat will scorch your turnout coat and char hoses; we've lost one section already. The fire is spreading on eighteen and we don't have enough men to contain it."

"You'll get them. What about equipment?"

"Standard requirements so far—only more of it. The external standpipe is charged and working; the hoses in some of the stairwells are gone, of course—either burned through or vandals have hacked them through. We'll need more respirators and masks. And men," he repeated. "We need men."

Infantino caught Fuchs's eye. There was no smile of triumph on the chief's face.

"Casualties?"

"Four men to the hospital, smoke inhalation. We might

lose one—Murphy, Engine Company 25. Another man was badly cut; a rookie from Truck Company 33 tried to chop out a window to vent the fire on seventeen. He lost a thumb and two fingers."

The first thing you were supposed to learn, Infantino thought, was how to hold a hatchet. "All right, Chief Verlaine has charge of seventeen. The next engine company that arrives will be under his command. Castro, you take eighteen. You'll get another company as soon as possible. Miller, take care of the cleanup on sixteen. Fleming, contact Bylson in the communications van and have him set up a two-way communications system in the lobby for in-building contacts; that will take some of the pressure off him. I've asked for more police to help clear the lobby so working conditions down there should improve. Okay, back to stations—I'll be in touch with each of you as soon as possible."

They left, leaving the security men and Donaldson behind, as well as Captain Fuchs. Garfunkel was smearing the dirt around on his face with a handkerchief. He glanced up at Infantino.

"You've got another problem."

"What's that?"

"We've got a gas station in the basement."

Infantino stared at him. "What's the capacity?"

"Two one-thousand gallon tanks. They were just filled the start of the week."

"Those permits come over my desk. The Glass House never applied for one."

Garfunkel was sweating. "Harriman, the super, was going to; I remember him talking about it one day."

"So you people went ahead and installed it prior to the issuance of the permit? Who's your supplier, City Gas and Oil? Call up their night man and have them get a truck over here immediately and start pumping it out."

Fuchs interrupted. "You sure that's necessary? We'll probably have the fire knocked down before they get the gas pumped out."

"Maybe I'm playing it too safe," Infantino said slowly. "But I'm playing it safe. All right?"

"It's your show."

"We could pump it into the sewers," Garfunkel suggested.

Infantino shook his head. "No dice—gasoline floats on water. We'd fill the whole sewer system with fumes. A stray spark or a static discharge and we'd have more trouble than we could possibly handle."

He stood up to go and Garfunkel said, "What about the people in the restaurant at the top?"

"How many?"

"About a hundred and thirty."

"They'll be okay so long as they don't panic—and there's no reason for them to panic. The fire is forty stories away."

"Mr. Leroux and Mr. Barton are up there with their wives."

"Craig Barton?" Infantino said. Right now, both Barton and Leroux would be invaluable. Nobody would know the building better than its architect and Leroux was ready-made to fill in as building supervisor. "Get on the house phone and tell them to come down—immediately. We can use them both down here." He had a sudden thought. "Tell them to take the scenic elevator." To take others, he thought, suddenly depressed, might be murder.

"Yes, sir," and Garfunkel was gone. Jernigan and Donaldson followed after him.

Once they were alone, Fuchs eyed Infantino silently for a moment, then nodded. "You didn't ask, but I think you're doing all right so far."

"You're not hoping I'll fall on my ass?"

A tiny muscle jumped in Fuchs's forehead and his face froze. "That uncalled for, Infantino. You fail and a lot of people die. I would hardly wish that if my worst enemy were in charge."

"You're right," Infantino said. "That was uncalled for."

Fuchs smiled bitterly as he turned to leave. "Someday I'll tell you about the first real 'worker' I was responsible for knocking down." Infantino started to follow Fuchs when one of Bylson's communications men hurried into the room. He introduced himself as Bill Philtron. He was carrying a multiple handy-talky, a heavier version of the single crystal units in use among the fire crews. Infantino checked it out quickly, then went up to the lobby, followed by Philtron.

The floor was as crowded and confused as before, the firemen fighting their way to the elevators through milling crowds of confused tenants. Where was the goddamned police captain? Infantino thought. Why the hell hadn't the lobby been cleared? A young fireman hurried past him, his respirator mask dangling around his neck. Infantino recognized him and grabbed his arm. "How bad is it up there, Lencho?"

"Damned bad." David Lencho's face showed a dirty red pressure line from the mask; the rest of his face was streaked with soot. He looked older than his years. "The fire's breaking through to eighteen."

Infantino grabbed the phone from Philtron's walky-talky and called Verlaine. "Hal, Infantino—I'm coming up."

Verlaine's voice sounded tired and hollow over the phone. "It's your funeral."

Infantino handed the phone back to Philtron. "You're relay station for me while I'm upstairs. Stay on Verlaine's frequency." He turned to the elevators as one of the cab doors opened. A fireman stumbled out leading a small, red-eyed boy about four. The boy, crying and gagging, looked wildly about the lobby; he suddenly tore from the fireman's grip and ran sobbing toward the woman Infantino had noticed earlier. She swept him up and a moment later was joined by her husband. Some of the tightness in Infantino's stomach abruptly dissolved. The chance of two years ago repeating itself had been diminished by one.

He caught the elevator with two other firemen. A few moments later he was on the sixteenth floor. A steady stream of water drizzled from the corridor ceiling; the ceiling sagged in loose loops from the framing. Infantino's boots squished through the sodden nap of carpeting. The elevator opened directly on an office suite that took up the entire floor. The salvage company had spread canvas covers over most of the office space but part of the ceiling and carpeting by the elevator reception area was a total loss. Portions of the rug and ceiling were black and charred; Infantino guessed that some of the burning solvent had flowed down the elevator shaft from the floor above. It must have been hell stepping out into that, he thought.

Heavy water stains were spreading down the plastered walls; at one point expensive wood paneling had buckled and warped away from the wall. It would be much the same, though to a lesser degree, for at least several floors below. The insurance companies would be a lot broker after all this was over, Infantino thought.

Several firemen were on the stairwell landing; one of them leaned weakly against the railing, coughing up black phlegm while another tried to help him through the door. A fireman said to Infantino, "He got a lung full, Chief. Respirator valve failed." It was rare enough—every fireman was taught the care and cleaning of respirators until they could have assembled one in the dark, but on old equipment, valves still sometimes stuck.

"Get him below right away."

The landing on the seventeenth floor was slippery with water and the air was gray with smoke. Several firemen had retreated to the stairwell, smoke-streaked and coughing, while a fresh team edged past them with additional sections of two-and-a-half. Somebody tapped Infantino on the shoulder and handed him a respirator. "You can't go in there without a Scott, Chief." He helped Infantino strap on the cylinder and adjust the valve.

The main corridor was a maze of crisscrossing hoses, some of them snaking down side passages and others arrowing directly ahead. The smoke was dense and grew denser as he edged forward through the rapidly growing darkness. He could feel the heat now and occasionally see the red reflection of flames a few dozen feet ahead. He crouched by three hosemen; the lead man was directing the high-pressure stream toward the flames immediately in front of them. The water on the tile floor was an inch deep—and hot. Another hose team was a few feet farther ahead; Infantino waddled toward them. The stream from the nearby hose drenched the forward group with spray that cascaded down their soot-streaked turnout coats and puddled on the floor. Infantino felt a hand on his arm and turned; he recognized Lencho in spite of his mask.

Lencho leaned over, touching the face plate of his respirator to Infantino's ear. "It's bad," he shouted. "We've sent two crews down already. A lot of flammable stuff, plastic light fixtures and the like. And pieces of the false ceiling keep falling on us. It's a fucking mess."

"Whose crew is that up ahead?"

"Mark Fuchs's—he's working the nob." The chief's son, Infantino thought, getting his baptism under fire. Handling the nob of a high-pressure hose was a man's job; if you lost control, the heavy brass nozzle could swing around and brain somebody. It was the man on the nob who was most exposed to heat. Infantino had seen them come down after fifteen minutes close up on a fire with their faces red and the backs of their hands blistered right through their gloves. If it were hot enough and your turnout pants were tight against your knees, the flesh under the pants would blister.

"The fire loading is incredible," Lencho shouted. "Desks, open files, wall hangings, foam chairs and couches . . . all that paneling. The stuff goes up like it was drenched with kerosene."

Infantino nodded and started back down the corridor. He had just gotten to a cross corridor filled with dense, oily smoke when he heard a panicky *"Get down, get down!"* Heat flare-up, he thought; the differential between the ceiling and the floor could be in the hundreds of degrees and heat spread in waves. The first man to sense it would cry, "Get down!" so those behind him could flatten themselves against the floor. At that moment he heard a muffled explosion. The far end of the cross corridor flared a brilliant orange. Thick smoke suddenly boiled out at Infantino. He ran for the stairwell door and grabbed a walky-talky from one of the men there. "Philtron, smoke explosion on seventeen! Get a rescue company up here, on the double!"

There was a flurry of activity in the corridor. Two men stumbled through the door dragging a third. They pulled the mask off his face and dropped it on the concrete. The mask was filled with vomit; already blisters were puffing up the man's face. The man himself was coughing hard enough to turn his lungs inside out.

"Hot lung!" one of the men shouted. The man had breathed superheated air or even flames; he must have literally burned out a lung, possibly both. Infantino thumbed the walky-talky again. "Infantino here. Have an ambulance on stand-by; first casualty coming down. Notify the hospital emergency ward: hot lung case."

Two men carried the casualty down the stairwell.

"It's going to be an all-night wienie roast, Mario." Verlaine had appeared on the landing, his mask off and his lungs heaving. His face was red from the heat. "Ceiling temperatures have to be six, seven hundred degrees. We're inching the hoses along the floor." More men were staggering out on the landing now, several of them vomiting and gagging.

He was only in the way, Infantino thought. "Take care of yourself, Hal." He turned and walked down the steps, turning sideways halfway down to let another company come up. He rode down on the same elevator with the unconscious man with the ruined lungs, watching the faint pumping of his chest. He was going to die, Infantino thought; he probably wouldn't make it through the night. For a fleeting moment he wished to hell that all the taxpayers who had showed up at the last City Council meeting to protest pay increases for firemen could be here now. Why did a man stick with the department, he wondered blackly. Why did *he?* It certainly wasn't the money.

He pushed his way through the lobby and headed across the terrazzo plaza to the communications van. The door was partly open and he could hear the babble of Police and Fire Department transmissions crackling out into the cold night air. Fuchs was standing by the half-open door, staring up at the building, obviously lost in thought.

"We're not even holding our own," Infantino said grimly.

"Didn't expect we would; it's too soon. If we can keep it from spreading, sooner or later it'll start to die for lack of fuel."

"We had damned well do better than that."

"It's higher up than usual but we've handled fires like it before."

"I've never seen a fire like this before," Infantino snapped. "I don't think you have, either."

Fuchs looked at him intently. "Okay, Mario, what do you want? You didn't come outside just to enjoy the weather."

"I want to order some shape charges and blow through the floor . . . vent the fire from above."

"Forget it," Fuchs said flatly. "Central Supply doesn't have any."

"The department in Southport does; we could borrow some."

"Infantino." Fuchs paused to search for the right words. The snow cresting on his eyebrows made him look like a thin and haggard Santa Claus, Infantino thought. "You've had free rein so far but you can't have it on this. You're not detonating any explosives in that building. If you want to hole through a floor have your wrecking company do it."

"That would take time—and we don't have any."

"On the contrary, we have all night. We'll continue to use conventional methods; the unconventional ones are too damned dangerous. I see no reason why we shouldn't be able to control this fire with them."

Infantino felt the frustration start to build. "Do you know what shape charges are? How they work?"

"I'm familiar with them," Fuchs said. "But I also know the risk of using explosives in a building we know next to nothing about. Legally, it's risky; structurally, it's even more so. You prove to me that you're a building engineer and I'll listen to you. Otherwise, it's a flat no. You run the risk of weakening the whole structure to the point where it might have to be condemned after the fire."

"That's nonsense; I've handled explosives in the Army," Infantino persisted. "I know what they can do."

Fuchs looked up at the side of the building, ignoring Infantino. "I said no, mister," Fuchs said.

Infantino followed his eyes up the side, to the tiny spot of light crawling down the southern shear wall. The scenic elevator, probably with Barton and Leroux aboard. They might be able to provide both the information and the arguments that he needed. . . .

There was a sudden shout from firemen in the plaza. Far above him, Infantino heard a brittle, popping sound. One of the huge plate-glass windows set in the curtainwall at the eighteenth-floor level suddenly vanished. He caught a glimpse of something large and flat sailing out over the plaza; a moment later pieces of glass exploded from the terrazzo. He heard another popping sound; the neoprene gasket surrounding the adjoining window had softened. The glass, bowed outward, driven by the heat and internal pressure, then jumped from its frame. It knifed through the cold night sky, a natural airfoil.

"Get those men off the plaza!" Infantino yelled. Other windows were popping out now; they sailed out over the plaza. One fragment sliced through the top of a police car, another struck the side of a nearby ceramic planter holding a small conifer and shattered; shards of glass ricocheting against the communications van. Fuchs and Infantino ducked a fraction of a second too late. Infantino felt a sting in his cheek. He scrubbed his face with his hand; it came away, smeared with blood. . . .

He turned and stared down the street. A block away, a young girl and her boy friend stood by their car, watching the smoke and the flames. His arm encircled her waist; she snuggled closer for warmth. At the sound of the popping, she jumped. "What's that? Rick?"

"The windows," Rick said after a moment. "They're popping out of their frames and dropping into the plaza."

"I'm glad I'm not there," she said excitedly.

A shimmer like summer heat over pavement gave little warning. Glass exploded in front of them. Razor shards clawed at her calves. Behind them the tires of their car gushed air. She cried out, "Rick!" Rick was silent; his arm dropped from her waist.

She stared down at the sidewalk for a long moment; then she started to scream.

32.

The great thing about coming up to Consolidated Distributors, Krost thought, was that you could really pick and choose. And the very least any good drinker should be allowed was a choice.

He leaned back in his chair and, bleary-eyed, inspected the ten bottles he had lined up before him on the desk. He had intended only to steal a cheap bottle of brandy; it would never be missed. He doubted that they kept any kind of inventory check on their office samples. But a whole new shipment of liquor had come in, including a number of brands Krost had never heard of before. Naturally, the situation needed investigating.

He shook his head in an attempt to clear it but it wasn't much use. He was drunk, he thought. Too drunk. Daisy wouldn't let him in the front door and Donaldson would fire him. For a moment he felt tearful and maudlin: it was a cruel world for Michael Krost.

The moment passed and he glanced down the row of bottles again with a feeling of anticipation. He was very pleased with himself. He reached for the water tumbler, wondering which it should be now. . . . The Irish whiskey, an off brand with an intriguing amber color, a Kentucky bourbon in a holiday decanter shaped like a log cabin, or an eight-year-old imported scotch that he bet would cost a fortune in a liquor store.

Well, why not the Irish? He sloshed some into his glass, then realized with dismay that he had been trying it all evening, and now the bottle was empty. No matter; he could hardly put empties back in the display cabinet. Here's to me, Mr. Krost, he hummed, then downed the inch or so of whiskey in a few quick gulps. If only old pink-scalp Donaldson was there to see him now . . .

He had his face in his hands. Conjuring up an image of Donaldson stumbling on him right now really took the edge off the evening. He should be getting back to work; he didn't like the thought, but Donaldson might very well be looking for him. He glanced at his watch and whistled soundlessly to himself. Donaldson probably *was* looking for him. Well, if he called, Krost could always think of some excuse. But then there was the possibility they might meet face to face.

He abruptly felt like crying. Meeting Donaldson face to face wouldn't be fair, the damned Scotsman would know what he had been doing. It wouldn't matter what he said. . . . His mood changed again. Thinking of Scotsmen, he hadn't tapped the bottle of scotch yet, had he? Well, he had, but only a little. It deserved at least equal time with the Irish. The bottle was out of reach on the table and he stood up to get it, then immediately sat back down again. That had been a mistake. The whole room had shifted sideways. He'd have to edge over, little bit by little bit.

His fingers closed on the bottle and he dragged it back triumphantly to pour himself another shot. His hands shook so badly that some of the liquor spilled on the table top. Have to get a rag, he thought, glancing around the room. All the Christmas decorations were up and he felt his spirits soaring. 'Tis the season, he thought. The one time of the year when he and Daisy declared a truce in their constant bickering. It was the best season of the year, he thought, misty-eyed. Snow on the ground and a crispness to the air and everybody was happy and there were half a dozen grandchildren to lavish presents on. And there were Christmas carols on the radio and the Salvation Army people ringing bells and the church chimes . . . not like the damned sirens he had been hearing half the night.

There were more of them right now. He didn't like to hear sirens; he didn't like to think about them at all. They reminded him of something he had been trying to forget, something he didn't want to remember. Sirens and the sound of people shouting far below and noises like something breaking, actually more like Fourth of July firecrackers, big ones . . .

He sighed. He better take a look but he had a hunch it would mean more work and that meant running into Donaldson and if there was anything he didn't want to do right then, it was to run into Donaldson. He stood up, clutching the edge of the desk for support, then weaved over to a window and looked out.

Smoke was billowing out of windows several floors below; the street was jammed with fire engines and police cars. His hands tightened on the sill; he could feel himself sober for a second. Memory flooded back now, the incident he had never wanted to think about again. . . . The fire in the Melton Building, so long ago. They tried to pin that one on him, but Leroux had stepped in and saved his neck. He still didn't know why, at least he wasn't sure.

He squinted through the smoke and falling snow; he could make out ambulances far below. He caught his breath. There had been people hurt. He started to remember more then, and the panic started to build deep within him.

He turned away from the window and staggered to the office door. He had to get out, and get out fast. He hurried as quickly as he could down to the elevator bank, occasionally clutching at the corridor wall to steady himself. The smell of smoke grew as the memories that he had tried for a year and a half to repress boiled inside his head. Damnit, where was the elevator? He leaned against the call button, sweating, trying desperately to think of nothing at all. Finally one arrived and he half fell into it. He pressed the button for lobby, then leaned against the wall of the cab, sobbing.

He was almost sober now; the memories rushed back in force. The Melton Building fire was as clear in his mind as if it had happened yesterday. He had been relaxing in his combination office-storeroom, his feet up on the desk, reading and absently flicking the ashes from his cigarette on the floor. The storeroom had been dirty—Donaldson had been after him about it—and a streak of oily spill had ignited. It had gone up fast after that. Almost everybody had gotten off the floor but a secretary and her young daughter, who was a frequent visitor to her office, had been trapped. The mother had lived; the little girl hadn't. Krost had hit the bottle a lot more after that.

Krost leaned back, watching the floor numbers light up across the indicator. The air, he noted subconsciously, was growing uncomfortably warm and the elevator was unaccountably slowing. Nineteen, eighteen—what the hell was wrong? He had punched the lobby button. The elevator was stopping at seventeen. The cab jarred to a halt; the doors whooshed quietly open.

Krost looked out on hell.

Beyond the elevator doors was a solid furnace of flames filling the corridor, black streaks of oily smoke boiling through the sheets of fire. He stared in horror for a second, then frantically hit the "close" button; at the same moment the flames roared into the cab. The blast of heat struck him just as he started to inhale; the air was like hot lead pouring into his lungs. Then, abruptly, there was no more sensation.

The elevator doors oscillated back and forth; the smoke billowed past the electric eye beam holding them open. Krost tried to scream but there was no air in the dried sacs that had been his lungs. He felt the skin of his cheekbones and nose blistering, his eyelids and lips swelling. Thick mucus started to dribble from his nostrils.

He pressed the buttons on the control panel one more time, then started pawing at his blinded eyes with swelling hands as his hair and eyebrows burst into flame. He turned his back to the holocaust and sank to the bottom of the elevator, curling up into a ball of agony. The back of his workshirt and pants browned, then blackened, but Krost no longer felt the heat or the pain of the blisters.

His last memory was that the little girl's name was Bonnie and he had been very fond of her.

33.

Lex Hughes reached into the last cash drawer, deliberately ignoring the smaller bills and concentrating on the twenties. The brief case on the work ledge just below the drawers was already bulging. He had lost count of how much he had stuffed into it in his haste to skim the cream from the drawers, but he estimated he had at least thirty thousand dollars in twenties and fifties.

He debated taking tens and grabbed a banded stack of bills but the brief case could barely be closed as it was. Finally, he took the bills and the brief case into the outer office, slipped into his suit coat, and stuck the bundle of tens in his inner pocket. Then he paused for a moment in indecision. There were negotiable securities in the vault, but these could be traced. Besides, there was no way to carry them; the case was full. Well, thirty thousand dollars wasn't a fortune, but he could disappear and start a new life with it. He could buy a small business, and with careful management he could spend the rest of his years in reasonable comfort.

He left the brief case on a table and walked back into the vault area, slowly swinging the huge door closed. He automatically spun the tumblers and stepped back. Then the thought struck him that he should have left it open. If the fire penetrated this far, it could well destroy all evidence of his theft. Well, too late to think of that now; it probably didn't matter anyway. Once out of the building, by morning he would be far away.

He buttoned his coat and clutched the brief case in one hand. It was heavy, he thought, satisfyingly heavy. He hurried down the aisle of desks. At the corridor door, he paused, sniffing the air. Even with the door closed, he could smell the thick, resinous smoke oozing under the door. Alarmed, he glanced at his watch. He had spent a valuable twenty minutes in the vault; the fire may have spread too fast.

He took a breath, braced himself, and opened the door. The corridor was thick with smoke. He coughed as his eyes began to sting. Fearfully he wondered if he had delayed too long. No, the smoke wasn't that thick yet. He could hold his breath and make it to the elevator bank. Then he saw figures moving through the smoke and realized he had, indeed, delayed too long. The firemen had already reached this floor.

Quietly, he closed the door, leaving it open by only a crack. Voices came from the stairwell; he could see that the stairwell door was open. More figures labored through it, three of them lugging a thick hose that dribbled water. They got as far as the elevator bank and knelt down; the one in the lead opened the nozzle and a hard column of water at full force gushed forward. The firemen were directing it at the far end of the hall.

Hughes hesitated, then opened the door. Now he could take a quick look around the door, hopefully without being seen. The very far end of the hall was already wrapped in flames.

He backed inside the door, still leaving it open a hair. A wave of fear constricted his chest. He had waited too long, much too long. There was no chance of getting to the elevators now without being seen and the stairwells were out. He could simply walk out—but not with a brief case full of money. It depended on how much confusion there was in the lobby below. But it was risky, much too risky. Somebody was bound to be suspicious.

He slowly closed the door until it latched, feeling the terrible disappointment. His grand theft had ended before it had even really begun. He turned and walked slowly back down the aisle. There was nothing to do but return the money and go out into the corridor, empty-handed. The authorities might be curious as to what had taken him so long in fleeing the building, but they would never know of the bulging brief case. He stopped at the vault door, feeling suddenly ill.

He had locked it, he remembered. If it had been an ordinary lock, he could have worked the combination and reopened it, slipping the bundles of bills back into the proper drawers. But the lock was a time lock; he had set it so the vault couldn't be opened until eight o'clock the following Monday morning.

There wasn't much he could do, he thought. He sank into a chair in resignation. Suddenly the lights began to flicker; abruptly they went out, leaving him in darkness. The fire must have cut the electricity, he thought. Well, he would just sit there until they found him—found him and the incriminating brief case. The fire probably wouldn't get to him now since the firemen were on the scene. He coughed and amended the thought; the smoke might get thick enough that he would have to get out, leaving the case behind. He would get away with his life but he would still have to flee. Everyone knew that he and Carolyn were working late; she would tell the police that he had been the last one there with the vault door still open. The camera itself would have recorded that and the security men would know.

There was one chance, he thought suddenly. Most fires didn't last too long. When the firemen had left and the lobbies below would be relatively empty, he might make it. It was still risky but there was a chance. He might then make it down the stairwells to the lower lobby or the garage floor and then simply walk out.

He sat back in his chair and waited with rising hopes, ignoring the dead Eye overhead that no longer saw anything.

34.

Barton fought his way into the lobby past milling tenants. Firemen grimly pushed through to the elevator banks while a scattering of policemen ineffectually tried to bring order out of confusion. The lobby itself had changed drastically from when he had seen it a few hours before. Salvage covers, spread over the marble floor, were now slick with dirty water and lumps of melting ice. The chill air of the lobby held the faint, acid odor of something burning. Against the far wall by the doors to the bank, an ambulance team was bending over a stretcher, covering the figure on it with an army blanket. Barton stared for a moment before he realized what it meant. He could not tell whether it was a tenant or a fireman.

A few feet away two young parents held a sobbing boy while farther on, a woman cried hysterically, ignored by everyone around her. Only the crackling of a radio communication system cut through the general babble. He searched the crowd, finally locating several firemen standing by a comm system they had set up in the lobby cigar stand. Barton hurriedly threaded his way over.

"Who's in charge of the operations here?"

One of the firemen looked at him curiously. "Who are you, Mac?"

"Craig Barton—I was chief architect of the building; I'm also representing Mr. Leroux down here. Check it out; he's having dinner in the Promenade Room."

The fireman looked faintly impressed. "Division Chief Mario Infantino's the man you want—but he's too busy to talk to civilians now."

So Mario was running things, Barton thought; a sense of relief flooded through him. The building was in good hands. "Just tell him I'm in the lobby. If he gets a moment I'd like to see him—any way I can help, I will."

"Sure thing." The fireman nodded out at the lobby. "You might try doing something about that mess—the cops can't seem to."

"I'll give it a try." He turned back to the lobby. He saw Garfunkel and Jernigan, standing by the security desk in deep conversation; both looked haggard and worn. Garfunkel broke off the conversation when he spotted him, the strain in his face abruptly easing.

"When's Mr. Leroux coming down? Christ, we could use him right now—people are asking me fifty million questions and I don't know how to answer any of them."

"He'll be down later; you'll have to put up with me until he gets here." Barton pointed at the blanket-covered figure being taken out the front entrance by the ambulance team. "How many casualties?"

Garfunkel's face tightened. "One that we know of. The man they're taking out is Sol Jacobs, the seventy-year-old bachelor in 3214. The smoke got him." His voice dropped a notch. "And then there's Griff Edwards. He tried to help us when we first went up to the fire floor. Stroke—he's in intensive care. There probably are others."

To Barton, Jacobs was only a man. Griff Edwards he had met several times and liked; he assumed that Garfunkel was a close friend.

"How's Edwards doing?"

Garfunkel's voice shook slightly. "I talked to the doctors; they don't think he'll make it to morning."

There was no time for tears, Barton thought, either for himself, Garfunkel, or anybody else. He glanced back at the lobby; little clumps of tenants wandered aimlessly around or stood guard by their small heaps of possessions.

"Dan, open up the lunchroom downstairs. See if we can get volunteers to make coffee and sandwiches, then circulate among the tenants and tell them it's open. It will pull them out of the lobby. And detail one of the guards to call nearby hotels for rooms—it's the holiday weekend; chances are they'll have a lot of vacancies. Have him make reservations for the tenants who want one, either for the night or until such time as they can contact relatives or return here. Get hold of the night managers and explain the situation; tell them Curtainwall will pick up the tab." They'd have to make good with the lunchroom owner, too, he thought, but that would be a minor expense. It would also be in Leroux's bailiwick; let him worry about details. Then something else occurred to him. "Better call a cab company, too; have them send over all their free units . . . use the north entrance, so they won't interfere with the firemen. We'll have to use them to get the tenants to hotels. Then report back here."

He turned to Jernigan who was obviously ready for his own orders. "Harry, find the ranking police officer in charge and ask him to come over here."

Jernigan disappeared and Barton inspected the lobby again. At the elevator bank, two firemen, their faces smeared with soot, staggered out. Firemen nearby immediately slapped a respirator on the one; the other of the pair clung to the wall for support and started to vomit on the salvage cover. The doors to another elevator slid open; a rescue team came out lugging still another stretcher. The huddled form beneath the blanket was completely covered. Barton watched in morbid fascination as the ambulance crew, blank-faced, carried the stretcher toward the door. Maybe it was because their faces were too carefully blank, maybe it was because of the etched lines of strain. Barton was suddenly glad that the blanket was completely draped over the stretcher itself; the shape roughly outlined beneath it couldn't possibly be human. They passed him on the way out and he caught a whiff of odor. There were two smells that you never forgot, he thought, his stomach suddenly queasy. One was that of rotting potatoes. The other was that of burned flesh.

On the other side of the entrance, one of the guards was making a call on an outside phone; Barton guessed he was setting up hotel reservations for the tenants. Then, on the fringe of the crowd, he noticed Garfunkel in earnest conversation with some of the older women tenants. They listened for a moment, then followed him toward the escalator to the lower lobby. As soon as they had made coffee, the lower level restaurant would be open, Barton thought, and at least one problem would be on its way to being solved.

Jernigan suddenly appeared at his side with a slightly disgruntled police captain in tow; the snow just beginning to melt off his slicker. "Mr. Barton, Captain Greenwalt."

The captain didn't give Barton a chance to introduce himself. "I've got problems out there, mister; what's so damned important that you have to see me here?"

"Because you've got problems in here, too," Barton said dryly. "How come this lobby hasn't been cleared?"

The captain looked at him coldly. "I didn't catch the name."

"Craig Barton. I'm chief architect for the building."

"That's fine, I've got a mess outside to clean up." He turned to go.

"I'm filling in for Wyndom Leroux until he gets down here," Barton continued. "What's the situation outside?"

"Leroux?" The captain visibly thawed and said, "We're moving the barricades back another block around the building. Falling glass."

"Bad?"

"It's pretty windy; it's probably as bad as it can get." His face blanked for a moment at something he obviously didn't want to remember. "One fatality a block away. Pretty messy. Half a dozen others hospitalized. Maybe a dozen cars with slashed tops or hoods." He glanced at Barton sharply. "Was that all you want to know?"

"We're starting to evacuate the tenants. There'll be cabs coming in a few minutes to take them to hotels; they have instructions to approach from the north. Tell your men to let them through." He glanced at the lobby again and noted that more people were going downstairs. "We could use some more men here and downstairs to keep order. Can we get them?"

The captain shrugged. "I'll do my best. Outside it's a circus. All the television stations are carrying film on the fire; half the city is out there, weather be damned." Bread and circuses, Barton thought. Except there was no attraction half so fascinating as a fire.

"You have a walky-talky?"

The captain nodded toward the communications station at the cigar counter. "I'm hooked in over there; they can get me any time.'

The lobby crowd was gradually thinning out now. Garfunkel came back, his face less clouded than before. "The lunchroom will hardly hold them all, but the tenants can camp in the lobby down there; the coffee and the food's helping a lot—at least the level of complaints has dropped."

"Anybody sick or hurt down there?"

"No, most of those were taken out by ambulance crews before you came down. Mostly smoke inhalation." He hesitated. "We're making reservations in some of the nearby hotels, but a lot of the tenants don't want to leave."

"Any Red Cross people around?"

"They've got a van outside serving coffee. Some of them were in the lobby half an hour ago taking down names and addresses of relatives to be notified."

Barton turned to Jernigan. "Go out and contact their senior man—see if you can arrange for cots and blankets."

After Jernigan departed, Garfunkel said: "Craig, I told the chief—Infantino—about the gas station downstairs. He was pretty annoyed, particularly when I said we had just filled the tanks the first part of the week."

"What's he want done about it?"

"He's done it already—called City Gas and Oil; they're sending over a truck to pump out the tanks and fill them with water to force out the explosive vapors."

"Better call Greenwalt and tell him the truck will be coming through his barricades. North entrance again."

It wasn't very likely that the fire would ever reach the basement, but there was no sense in sitting on a time bomb, either. He had noticed the spillage and the fumes in the basement when he had parked. . . . "Oh, crap!" He turned and ran for the escalator stairs. Garfunkel had just finished giving instructions to the fireman at the relay station. He saw Barton forcing his way through the crowds and ran after him. "Mr. Barton, what the hell's wrong?"

In the lower lobby, Barton noted that the restaurant was filled; the hysteria and frightened looks had given way to a quiet murmur of conversations and discussions of what to do next. A few dozen of the tenants were leaning against the lobby wall of the restaurant, sipping coffee and eating sandwiches and stale doughnuts. The atmosphere was changed now, Barton thought. The survivors were beginning to enjoy the thrill and store up memories for reminiscing later. Barton ran past them to the stairway leading to the parking garage. He plunged down them, Garfunkel after him. "Where's the car hiker, Dan?"

Garfunkel bellowed, "Hey, Joe!" The young parking lot attendant came out of his booth, looking scared.

"Look, Mr. Garfunkel, how bad is it upstairs? I've been afraid to leave, but I don't know a damn thing about what's going on. How bad's the fire?"

"It may get worse. A truck should be here any minute from City Gas and Oil to pump out the tanks."

The attendant blanched. "It's getting closer?"

"It's precautionary," Barton interrupted. "We want to get the cars out, too. How many down here?" The floor looked half empty, probably because of the holidays, he thought.

"Seventy-three, Mr. Barton. Not counting my own."

"How many car jockeys do you know personally whom you could get over here in a matter of minutes?"

"Maybe half a dozen. The weather's lousy and the clubs in the area aren't doing any business."

"Call them up and ask them to come over. I want all these cars out of here as soon as possible." It was a remote chance, but if a fire started, the presence of the cars would be as bad as the full tanks themselves.

"Where'll we take 'em?"

"There's a city garage at Elm and Taylor, three blocks away. I'll have the police call and make the arrangements. Turn your tickets over to the garageman there."

He started back upstairs, Garfunkel trailing him. Mario Infantino was waiting for him at the communications desk, looking tired and grim. Barton felt his stomach begin to knot. Now would come all the questions he was afraid to ask and all the answers he didn't want to hear.

"How bad is it, Mario?"

"A lot worse than I thought it would be. You might as well have sprayed your walls with kerosene. So far as we can tell now, it started in a storeroom stocked with solvents and waxes. Once it got a foothold, there wasn't any stopping it."

"Casualties?"

"One of my men dead, three to the hospital—smoke inhalation and burns. Two tenants, maybe more, we don't know yet. Smoke may have caught a lot of them while they were sleeping. Carbon monoxide builds up slowly; you don't notice it. I understand one of your maintenance people is in the hospital with a coronary." He shrugged. "That's all so far."

Barton forced himself to ask the next question. "What about fighting the fire itself?"

Infantino hesitated. "A lot depends on luck. The seventeenth floor is gutted but it's also pretty much burned itself out. We should be able to contain it on eighteen. A lot of windows were broken on both floors; that vented the fire and helped a lot. For a while I thought we might have to hole through the nineteenth floor and try and get at it from above, as well as venting it. We don't have to do that now. There's been a lot of smoke damage—it'll probably cost Curtainwall a fortune just to clean its own offices."

"That's Leroux's worry. What about the floors above?"

Infantino seemed a little less certain. "I haven't been able to spare the men to check all the floors. There's been smoke as high as the thirty-fifth, probably much higher depending on what side of the building you're talking about. The wind's from the north so that side of the building is relatively free from smoke. One thing for sure, both the fire and the smoke spread fast. The building's like Swiss cheese, Craig. There're so many poke throughs in the floors and the walls, I don't think there's an effective fire barrier in the entire structure."

"The HVAC system should have changed over to exhaust once smoke was detected," Barton said slowly. It couldn't be that bad, he thought desperately.

"A lot of things should have happened that didn't, Craig. Part of your system did exhaust—but only part. One of your maintenance men can fill you in. We also should have received a smoke and fire warning at department headquarters automatically. We didn't; the alarm was phoned in." He caught the expression on

Barton's face. "Nobody's blaming you, Craig—you didn't build it."

It had started when he had noticed the cladding around the elevator banks, Barton thought. Since then, the building had been full of surprises for him, all of them unpleasant.

"You said the smoke spread fast—and so did the fire. Even if the HVAC system was only partly operating, at least it was either shut down or on exhaust. How come the fire itself spread so quickly?"

A fireman interrupted with a message for Infantino. He scanned it, then turned briefly back to Barton. "It depends on the fire load. On the seventeenth floor, it was exceptionally heavy—solvents and waxes in the storeroom, an interior decorating shop jammed with flammable draperies and upholstery materials, a number of very posh offices that were decorated like tinderboxes. What you end up with is a fire load that makes for a lot of smoke and a very hot fire." He turned toward the elevator bank. "Be back in a few minutes—I'll have to know about the fire loading on the other floors."

Barton was silent for a moment after Infantino left, then said: "Do we have any kind of a building census, Dan?"

"Not one that would be worth a damn."

"What about the commercial floors?"

"One of the cleaning women is missing; the others got out. So far as we know, a Lex Hughes who works in your Credit Union never left the building, though it's possible he got out during the height of the confusion. And there's one of the partners in Today's Interiors, Ian Douglas. He tipped us about the fire to begin with. We have no record of him leaving the building, either."

Today's Interiors was on seventeen, where the fire had started, Barton recalled. The upholstery and decorating materials that Infantino had mentioned were in his shop. Douglas probably didn't make it.

"Anybody else?"

"One of the maintenance men—Krost. Nobody knows where he is, either."

Jernigan snorted. "Nobody ever does."

"There's also a John Bigelow, a veep for Motivational Displays. We've been trying to raise their executive suite by telephone. He apparently was entertaining a client back there; he called Donaldson to have a refrigerator fixed. So far, nobody answers. It's a couple of floors above the fire floor so maybe he got out, too, though we have no record."

"What about the evacuation of the residential tenants?"

Jernigan shook his head. "It's been one mother of a mess, pretty disorganized, as you can see. Nobody really knew what to do, including me. None of us were ever told. But I think we got almost everybody out. The firemen got Mrs. Halvorsen and her husband down."

Barton vaguely remembered them—an elderly couple. She was a wheel-chair case.

"Did you try to notify everybody by phone?" Infantino had rejoined them.

Jernigan nodded. "The operators buzzed everybody in the upper floors, whether I had them logged out or not."

"Have the operators ignore all incoming calls and keep trying those apartments where you're not sure they made it down or aren't absolutely certain they've left for the weekend. Have them ring every fifteen minutes."

Barton felt curious. "Why have the operators keep trying, Mario? It seems like a waste of time—if they don't answer, they're not home."

"That's the wrong assumption," Infantino said grimly. "They might have been watching television when you called and couldn't hear the phone—or didn't want to answer if the show was exciting right then. Then there are the people who were taking a bath or a shower at the time or who turned the phone off for the evening or have taken sleeping pills and then hit the sack. As soon as I can spare the men, I'll have them check the upper floors personally with a pass key. If your phone operators *do* get a response tell the tenants to stay put and place wet towels around the door and over the ventilation grills. If they insist on leaving the room have them feel the door first to see if it's hot, though we don't think there's any fire above eighteen. If they leave, and the smoke is thick, have them head for the north stairwell as quickly as possible—it's relatively free of smoke. Under no conditions do they take the elevator—the sky lobby transfer point is right by the south utility core and the smoke is too thick there now. But have the operators keep trying the suspect apartments."

Jernigan suddenly looked stricken. "Mr. Barton, there's the Albrecht family in 3416."

Barton felt as if he should know something he didn't. "So?"

"They're deaf mutes."

Infantino whistled. "Okay, I'll get some men up there as soon as possible."

Barton had unconsciously glanced at the elevator indicator board when they were discussing floors. He suddenly tensed. "What elevators are your men using?"

Infantino followed his glance. "The two at the right with manual override. No need to worry."

On the indicator board, the red lights showed that the rest of the elevators had lined up neatly at the seventeenth floor; the lights read across in a single row. Then they suddenly flickered and went out. They were stalled there for good, he thought; the call buttons had fused, calling them to the fire floor. If there had been anybody on board trying to get down . . . It left them with three operating elevators, the residential express and the two commercial cabs which were equipped with manual override.

Infantino said, "Craig, we were talking about the fire loading before. Do you have any idea what's directly above and below the seventeenth floor?"

Barton shook his head. "Curtainwall takes up the eighteenth, nineteenth, and twentieth floors. The executive offices are on eighteen, probably flammably decorated by your standards. The other two floors are standard office floors, what you would probably call an ordinary fire load. I'm not sure what's on sixteen, ditto from the twenty-first on up." He paused. "Motivational Displays is on twenty-one; they've got a pretty large suite of offices and a storeroom that they keep most of their displays in. It's the holiday season so I imagine the storeroom is stuffed with polystyrene Santa Clauses, that sort of thing. Other than that, I don't know what's on the floor. This is the first time I've been in the building since the dedication. I also suspect there's been a heavy changeover in tenants."

"We can get most of the information from the building directory and make an educated guess at the contents. How about building blueprints? It would be nice to know where the numbers go."

"To the best of my knowledge, they're filed in our offices on eighteen."

Infantino looked frustrated. "We don't have a set, and you can't get at yours. Could you draw me a general floor diagram from memory?"

Barton felt around in his pockets, then walked over to the check-in desk where the girl had been making X's against the names on the Promenade Room reservation list. The small, black Magic Marker was right where she had left it. He picked it up, along with her clipboard, and hurried back to the cigar stand. He turned over one of the reservation sheets and drew a rough floor plan, then motioned Garfunkel. "You're been on fire patrols in the building, haven't you, Dan?" Garfunkel nodded. "Okay, fill in the numbers of the office suites and tell Mario about the furnishings—drapes, sofas, open filing systems, wooden desks or metal, anything he asks. If you can't remember all the offices, check with the building directory. Jernigan—" He glanced around. "Where the hell did he go?"

Garfunkel looked blank. "He was here a minute ago."

"When he comes back, see if he can help you any. I'll be down in the boiler room." In the lower lobby the Red Cross had started to set up cots; already some children were asleep under the heavy army blankets. The number of tenants had noticeably decreased; the switchboard and the security guard must be having fairly good luck in placing them elsewhere.

On the garage floor, the City Gas and Oil truck had arrived and was pumping out the two tanks. A little of the color had returned to Joe's face and he was shouting directions at the four parking attendants moving out the cars. Another half hour or so and the garage would be empty, Barton thought. When the diners started coming down from the Promenade Room, they would have to arrange for taxis to take them over to the city garage. More money out of Curtainwall's pocket—or some insurance agency's, depending on how the policy was written.

Donaldson was sitting at Griff Edwards' desk, looking tired and worn and on the verge of tears. Another good friend of Edwards, Barton thought. "Things going all right, Mr. Donaldson?" he asked gently.

Donaldson's face was dirty and his uniform rumpled. Barton recalled that he had been with the men from maintenance who had tried to put out the fire in the first place. "Things haven't gone right since I came on shift, Mr. Barton."

"I understand some of the fan motors conked out."

"One burnout, one freeze-up." He leaned back in his chair and was silent for a long moment. "Mr. Barton, this may cost me my job but I gotta say what I think. The lash-up down here is fine—for a building two thirds this size. As it was, Griff had to push it even under normal conditions. In an emergency, it just wasn't up to it."

"It met all the codes," Barton said stiffly.

Donaldson looked tired. "Did it? I sometimes wonder. It wasn't the gear that was specified."

The queasy feeling that had been building up in Barton's stomach grew stronger. "What do you mean?"

"I knew I was going to be transferred over and I talked with the architectural engineers when they first started construction. They had specified more expensive motors and generators, a more elaborate sensor system. What we ended up with does the job—but just barely." He ran dirty fingers over an already streaked scalp. "I guess it'll do the job all right, provided there're no sudden demands made on it or emergency overloading."

The equipment wasn't what the Wexler and Haines engineering department had recommended, Barton thought. What Donaldson was saying was that Leroux's accounting office had scrapped their recommendations and cut the heart out of the building. He felt the anger start to build in him, then. He had wanted to be site supervisor—a job that would normally have fallen to him. But Leroux had shipped him to Boston. Because Leroux had known he would fight for his building? Because Leroux had known he would quit before he would agree to the cost cutting that had gone on?

He started back toward the steps. "I'll be in the lobby if you want me, Donaldson."

He took a long break in the lower lobby lunchroom, huddled over a cup of coffee and trying to sort out his thoughts. It was his building, he kept thinking. It had been his baby. Leroux had had no right. . . . But of course, he did. Leroux paid the bills; Leroux paid his salary; Leroux had done the financing. Why had he cheapened it? There hadn't been any reason for it. . . .

"Mr. Barton, when do you think the fire will be over so we can go back?"

He vaguely remembered her; an elderly matron, her wispy hair done up in curlers, half lost in her soot-smeared silk bathrobe. "I don't know," he said honestly. "Maybe a few hours but then there'll be the cleaning up. We're making reservations for those who want to stay in a hotel until the building's all right for tenants to move back in. There'll be no expense on your part."

She shook her head and smiled somewhat wanly. "No, I don't think I'd care for that. This is such a beautiful building and it's home to us. My husband and I have been living in hotels for years."

There were murmurs from other tenants who were watching him; they didn't know him by name for the most part but knew that he must represent management. Some of them started to come over. He finished his coffee in a hurry and fled.

Back upstairs, Garfunkel had finished filling in several floors for Infantino. Barton had just bent over to study the sheets when there were quick bursts of light near the entrance. A small group of reporters started to crowd into the now almost-emptied lobby.

"Where's Leroux?" one shouted.

"Any statement from management?"

One of the reporters remembered Barton from the dedication. "What went wrong, Mr. Barton? The building's going up like it was a torch job."

"No comment!" Barton shouted furiously. He motioned to Captain Greenwalt who had come in to check at the communications station. "Get some men and clear the lobby. See that all reporters stay behind the barricades —it's dangerous within a block of the building and I'll be goddamned if I'll be responsible for anybody else's life tonight. No unauthorized personnel are to be allowed within a block of the building."

The captain motioned to several of his men standing nearby and headed for the entrance. "Okay, fellas, I'm sure everybody will have statements later on. Let's move on, let's go. At least a block and watch out for falling glass, we already lost one young man that way."

One of the reporters asked him what he meant; Greenwalt explained in brief, graphic detail. The reporter went white and the group backed quickly out, a few taking last-minute shots of Barton.

After the reporters were herded out, the captain came back. "There's a man from the insurance company by the barricades; he wants to talk to you. Also some people who claim they lease stores and offices and want to check their shops and empty the cash registers or else look over the premises."

"Nobody gets in," Barton said automatically. "Absolutely nobody."

"Some of them are pretty worked up."

"Tough." They wanted to complain to somebody, he thought, they wanted to confront somebody in authority so they could threaten to sue. But that was Leroux's job, that was his dirty laundry. "Greenwalt?" The captain turned. "Keep them out of my hair; I don't care how you do it. It doesn't matter if they're tenants or from the insurance company or what. Tell them . . ." He hesitated, then shrugged to himself. He had done enough, he had done more than enough. From now on, it was going to be Leroux's ball game. He had had it. And it didn't matter to him what Jenny was going to think.

"Tell them," Barton said slowly, "that Mr. Leroux will be down in a few minutes to talk with them."

Before he could get to a house phone, Infantino called him over. He was puzzled. "Craig, is there any way at all we can get blueprints? We need to know the distances between these offices and exactly which ones are above one another."

"No way, Mario, unless your men can get into Curtain-wall's offices."

"Okay, so we do without them. But it would help." He glanced up from the drawing in front of him. "I wish the hell you had designed in fire doors in the stairwells, too. It would cut smoke spread. It's not required by city code but it would have helped in preventing smoke spread— helped in evacuation, too."

Barton flashed in sudden anger. "I did design them, Mario! I knew they weren't required by the local code but I know the value of them."

Infantino shook his head. "They never bothered to install them, Craig." He laughed bitterly. "Looks like your baby was a breech delivery."

Barton stalked over to the house phone and savagely dialed the Promenade Room. He no longer trusted Leroux's reasons for having sent him down. It had been a setup, he thought. Leroux had known what he would hear and he didn't want to face it. So it was send down Barton as his patsy. Well, this was the end of it. He'd call Leroux and have Jenny come down with him. And when Leroux arrived, Barton would turn in his resignation on the spot.

He finished dialing and waited for the ring. There was dead silence on the phone. He dialed again and still nothing. Then he dialed the operator.

A moment later he hung up, feeling sick and tired—
and frightened. There was no phone contact to the forty-
fifth floor and above. Somewhere, the fire had cut the
coaxial for the bank of phones that served the Promenade
Room.

The restaurant was now cut off from all outside contact. And so was Jenny.

꧁

Nearly all of the offices in the area of the seventeenth-floor utility room, the birthplace of the beast, have now been gutted. Rugs and draperies are rich fuel for the fire, as are the heavy parquet floors installed by Psychiatric Associates half a corridor length away. The paint on the office walls and those of the corridor is a popular brand that advertises itself as "fire resistant." In the incandescent heart of the fire, it quickly bubbles, exposing the flammable surfaces beneath. The exposed metal studding glows and begins to melt; plaster decomposes and spalls in a rain of dirty white flakes.

In the washrooms, grouting crumbles away and tile walls buckle. Plastic water tumblers and hampers slump, then finally char and flame. The paint on the paper-towel dispensers blackens and the towels blaze, peeling away from the roll like the leaves of an onion. In various offices, the bottles in water coolers crack and shatter as their contents boil and turn to steam. In a lunchroom area, the glass front of a sandwich vending machine breaks and the sandwiches inside toast, then char as their plastic wrappings burn away. The front of a nearby soft-drink machine warps and buckles with the heat, then curls aside. The cans of soda explode in a continuing chain, like a string of giant firecrackers. In the offices of the collection agency next door, the fire sweeps the desks clear of correspondence and file folders, fuses staples and paper clips into solid masses of metal. It scorches the paint from a line of file cabinets and warps the drawers, then reaches inside to finger the contents. The records of a thousand debts go up in a rush of flames.

On the eighteenth floor, the fire has pushed its way through badly sealed duct holes to race across the carpeting in a dozen different offices. It climbs the wallpapered walls of an insurance company and penetrates into the

*air space above the acoustical tile ceiling. Here it dis-
covers a long air-conditioning duct that has accumulated
a heavy coating of dust and lint inside its walls. There is
just enough air within the confines of the duct for a hot,
incomplete combustion that chars the organic contents,
releasing flammable gases to burn in the limited oxygen.
The temperature of the resulting mixture of carbon
monoxide and resinous fumes approaches 1,000 degrees.
A hundred feet farther down, the duct fails at a plastic
joint. The hot, fuel-rich gases hit the open air. There is a
low-order, gaseous explosion that tears away whole masses
of ceiling tile. For a few seconds, the equivalent of a
massive blow torch flares over the wooden furniture below and plays against a wall covered with plastic paneling
resembling walnut veneer. The wall bursts into flame.*

*At the far end of the eighteenth floor, a portion of the
aluminum curtainwall outside has heated to the point
where it pulls away from the framework of the building;
this opens up a channel leading as high as the twenty-first
floor. Clouds of hot smoke billow up the resulting flue
and stream across the windows of the nineteenth, twentieth, and twenty-first floors, heating the metal frames.*

*On the twenty-first floor, a window suddenly cracks and
drops from its frame, plunging to the street below to
shatter between two cars. The draperies inside twist and
dance in the hot blasts of air, then start to blaze. They
lash back inside the office, flapping against a wall poster
that says simply "Motivational Displays Move Products."
A curling edge of the poster browns, blackens, and begins
to burn.*

*Three floors below the beast pauses as it realizes it has
almost run out of food. Abruptly something stings it on
one side and it retreats a few feet. There is another, more
painful hurt and it recoils farther. It is suddenly frightened; something is trying to kill it.*

*The pain is continuous now and it slowly but steadily
falls back upon itself. It senses a growing numbness.*

35.

Through the long early moments of the emergency, Wyndom Leroux sat silently, watching the diners. They were in no immediate danger and they seemed for the moment to know it. A sense of futility was settling over him, drowning his thoughts in a deadening blanket. He watched the diners and their reactions as though he were seeing them through the wrong end of a telescope. He was scarcely aware of Jenny or of his wife on his left.

For a while, after word of the fire had spread throughout the Promenade Room, the diners had treated the emergency almost as a lark. The roar of the fire engines below, the free wine on the house, the sense of danger and yet at the same time realizing they were far removed from it, the sensation of being suspended in the sky while the world below burned . . . all of these combined, evoking a mood of almost frantic gaiety. A few of the diners had quietly left, taking the scenic elevator down, but the others found themselves bound together by a tight camaraderie. A quiet night out now became a block party with people at adjoining tables joking and sharing the sense of distant danger, or else drifting out onto the promenade to try and see what was happening on the streets far below. They pointed out to each other the barricades and the police cars and fire engines, half hidden by the drifting snow.

It was great fun.

Then the ambulances pulled up to the edge of the plaza and tiny figures carrying rolled-up stretchers disappeared into the building; these reappeared a few minutes later bearing the same stretcher with a blanket covering it. From that distance it was impossible to tell whether the blanket completely covered the figure on the stretcher or not. The party atmosphere began to die as the entire dining room emptied. Nearly everyone crowded onto the promenade to silently watch the scene below. The smoke billowing from windows many floors beneath them and the driving snow made visibility difficult. Still they could see the oil truck drive down the ramp into the basement but few guessed the reason why. Shortly afterward a steady stream of cars began to leave the parking garage. At the north entrance, taxis picked up pajamaed tenants on their way to their lodgings for the night.

Moments later the windows on the fire floors began to explode outward. The tiny figures on the plaza scattered as the glass knifed downward, shimmering briefly in the falling snow. The diners became far more sober after that and the babble of cheerful conversation fell to an occasional murmur or whisper. A feeling of apprehension started to build in the room. Guests drifted slowly back from the promenade to drink and eat in silence, occasionally asking questions of the hostess. She seemed to have lost none of her self-assurance but she seemed disturbingly uninformed. Her calm had done a lot to reassure jittery diners earlier; now her calm seemed forced and her lack of information frightening.

Several of the more perceptive diners guessed that the phone lines to the lobby had been cut by the fire. A few more quietly paid their tab and drifted over to the scenic elevator, where a line began to form.

Leroux felt more uninvolved than at any other time in his life. He ate and drank mechanically and made small talk when it seemed to be expected of him. He could tell that Jenny was terrified and went out of his way to say all of the usual things to calm her. Thelma, he knew, was watching him carefully, trying to guess at his inner strain. There was no way that she could; his business affairs had been a part of his life that he had seldom shared with her and it was a little late to start now. Intellectually, he knew and accepted what was now going to happen: The public outcry, his personal crucifixion in the newspapers and on television, the investigations, the lawsuits.

He also realized that it hadn't hit him yet emotionally. Thelma and Jenny, the dining room, and the fire itself were remote from him; in a sense, they didn't exist. The fire was a catastrophe that he had yet to acknowledge, could not acknowledge. The worst that could happen had, but he couldn't grasp it, couldn't face what it meant. In the long war of Wyndom Leroux against the world, he had never found it necessary to prepare a line of retreat. Now it was necessary but there was no line. He had no plan of action.

"Wyn."

He looked up, startled. Odd, for a moment he really hadn't been there at all. He had been thinking of New Orleans when he had been a young man. His father had forced him to work on the docks so he would learn early what the world was like and what it took for a man to hold his own in it. The experience had been invaluable, but he had never forgiven his father for it.

Thelma started to say something to him, then stopped in mid-sentence, smiled, reached out and grasped his hand. He squeezed it, then drew back. He saw that she sensed his remoteness and was withdrawing. She turned her attention to Jenny instead. Jenny replied to her attempts at conversation in monosyllables. Odd, Leroux thought, we're both retreating, each from a different reality.

There was now a chill to the air in the Promenade Room and the faintest suggestion of stuffiness. Leroux sensed it first, probably because he was the least concerned with what was happening at the moment. The ventilation and heating system had been turned off, he realized, or at least the supply to the upper floors had failed.

"Mr. Leroux." Quinn Reynolds hurried to the table, sudden alarm showing in her face. "Some of the diners are trying to leave by the inside elevators. I've tried to dissuade them because I didn't think it was safe, but they won't listen."

It was like stepping out of a fog or coming up from a deep dive in a pool. This was something he could handle. "I'll be right there, Quinn."

Two couples were in the foyer, arguing with a frightened bellboy.

"Look, son, nobody here knows what's happening and

we're not waiting around to find out, not one more minute. There's no sense waiting in line for the scenic elevator; this one's just as fast."

The bellboy was white-faced. "I'm sorry, sir, I've got my orders and nobody's supposed to use these elevators."

"Sonny, I'm not paying the prices they charge up here to argue with the hired help." He started to push the boy aside, then suddenly felt a hand on his shoulder.

"The boy's perfectly right," Leroux said quietly. "The elevators aren't safe. You have to transfer at the sky lobby and from there the elevator will have to travel through the fire zone to get to the first floor. I doubt that it would make it—or if it did, that you would."

The man turned and glared at Leroux for a moment. Early thirties, Leroux guessed, about his own size, probably ex-football and out of shape. The other man was the same age, though somewhat smaller; probably played on the same team. Old college buddies taking their wives out for a night on the town. His eyes flicked briefly at the women. Suburban. Too much make-up, girdled and shellacked for the evening. The type of women whose lives didn't extend beyond their ranch house, two kids, and TV set; this sort lived vicariously through their husbands. They'd give him trouble.

"Frank, I'm not going to stay here one more minute!" She hung possessively on her husband's right arm and Leroux half smiled to himself. He waited impassively while the slightly paunchy husband debated his chances of intimidating Leroux. "Who the hell are you?"

"Wyndom Leroux, president of National Curtainwall. We own the building."

"Frank, we're leaving!"

Frank turned slightly. "Shut up, Gale." Then he faced Leroux, somewhat less belligerent now. The fear in his voice was unmasked and genuine. "I think we ought to get out, Mr. Leroux, as fast as possible. I think we're cut off—no firemen have come up here to evacuate us."

"Probably because the inside elevators aren't working or they're too dangerous to take," Leroux said quietly.

The man's wife paled and he nodded. "You're probably

right. So what do we do now?" He was automatically looking to Leroux for orders. Leroux welcomed it; it was a situation he understood, one that he could handle. The flash point for panic in the Promenade Room was probably only minutes away. They were in no immediate danger—the firemen on the scene below knew they were up here. Even though the phones were out and the inside elevators not functioning, the firemen would have taken the scenic elevator up to evacuate the diners if they had thought it necessary. The diners could still wait it out—it would be the smartest thing to do—but the man's fear was very real and probably everybody in the room felt the same way. Physically, they were safe where they were. Psychologically, the situation wouldn't hold together much longer.

"I think we ought to arrange our own evacuation," Leroux said. "If there's panic in the room people will get hurt, and it's even possible that someone in panic could jam the scenic elevator. If one of you gentlemen will get the hostess, we'll figure out a plan of action."

The smaller of the two men jumped at the chance to be a part of the action. "Sure thing, Mr. Leroux!"

Team spirit, Leroux thought cynically. You could play on it like you would an organ. The man was back with Quinn in seconds.

"Quinn, what's the capacity of the scenic elevator? I've never really noticed."

"Ten—though you might squeeze in one or two more."

"All right—circulate through the dining room and tell your guests that we're evacuating and remind them to pick up their coats from the checkroom. Start with the tables farthest from the elevator; the people sitting at them will feel the least secure, they're the ones most liable to panic when we start sending groups down."

He turned and motioned to the two men behind him. "I'll need your help in case there's any panic or somebody tries to rush the elevator."

"You can count on it."

Leroux glanced at their wives standing nervously nearby. "We'll send your wives down with the first load. My guess is that they've transferred all the cars in the basement to a public garage and your wives can pick them up for you." Their wives had probably pushed them into trying to take the inside elevators in the first place, he thought. Get them off the scene and the men would be easier to handle—if they had to be handled.

He stopped briefly at his own table. "Thelma, Jenny, we're sending people down on the scenic elevator. Get your wraps."

"What about you?" Thelma asked.

A smile flickered briefly over Leroux's face. "I'm running the operation."

Thelma settled back in her chair. "I'll leave with you whenever you're ready to go, Wyndom."

"What about you, Jenny? Craig's down there."

"I'd be in his way," she said stiffly, then managed a slight smile. "I'll stay here with you. It won't be long, will it?"

"Maybe half an hour, not much more."

"Just enough time to finish my wine," she said lightly.

Leroux hurried back to the scenic elevator whose entrance was just off the foyer. He introduced himself briefly to those in line, explaining the system of the farthest table first—after the people already waiting in line had gone down, of course. He could see Quinn at the far end of the dining room dutifully explaining the situation. One by one the farthest tables emptied, the diners going to the foyer checkroom for their wraps and then forming a line. There was no panic. Once people knew they would be leaving shortly and there was a plan and Somebody in Authority was present, the atmosphere in the room brightened considerably.

There were minor problems, however.

"I didn't come up the outside elevator," one woman announced, her face white. "I'm afraid of heights; I don't think I could stand it looking at the street from this high up with nothing but glass around me."

Leroux smiled and handed her firmly to her husband who was already inside the elevator. "Just close your eyes and when you feel the bump, that means the elevator's at the lobby stop."

A man in his mid-forties who looked like a wrestler was the next to hang back. "How do we know this will be safe? I heard you telling your friends here that the elevators were running through the fire zone. Why is this one safe but the others aren't?"

"The scenic elevator runs down the outside of a blank concrete wall all the way to the first-floor lobby," Leroux explained patiently. "There's solid concrete between you and the fire and absolutely no way the elevator can stop at a fire floor." He pushed the man inside and the elevator doors closed on his next question. He was probably actually afraid of heights, like the elderly woman had been.

"Mr. Leroux?"

The dapper little man who had been at the table directly behind them was standing in the foyer entrance, a worried look on his face.

"Yes?"

"You didn't notice Miss Mueller get on the elevator, did you?" Leroux looked blank and the man added, "She was my guest for dinner tonight. I went to the men's room a few moments ago and when I came back, she was missing."

Leroux turned to hand some more people into the elevator. Two loads had already gone down since the evacuation had started, but Miss Mueller had not been among them. "I'm sorry, sir, she hasn't left yet. Are you sure she isn't talking to friends at another table?"

The dapper man shook his head, for the moment looking inexpressibly sad. "No," he said slowly. "I've been through the room twice and she isn't here."

Leroux recalled the good time they both had been having and said, "Have Miss Reynolds check the powder room; she may be under the weather."

The man smiled faintly. "Her father was a brewer. She could probably drink us both under the table."

He went back into the room for another search of the tables and Leroux wondered briefly what could have happened to the woman. Then the elevator had come back for a third load and he forgot her.

It felt good to be immersed in the shuttle operation, but another half hour, Leroux realized, and he would be down in the lobby and it would be a different kind of reality. His mind couldn't face it now and he doubted that he could face it then. And he still had no alternative plan of action, he still didn't know what he was going to do.

And then he wondered what Barton was doing down below and how he was holding up. He was probably taking all the gaff that Leroux would have if he had gone down first. But it seemed like a practical idea at the time and might still prove to be.

He also knew that as soon as he got down, he would lose the best employee he had.

36.

Tom Albrecht stirred restlessly in his sleep. He had been very tired when he got home and after putting the children to bed, he and Evelyn retired early. Working late every night on the new satellite instrumentation for the Air Force took more out of him than he had thought. Tonight, fatigue caught up with him after a perfunctory few minutes of making love and his head had scarcely touched the pillow when he was sound asleep.

Now he was half awake. He punched his pillow and flipped it over, then buried his face in the cool depths of the other side, at the same time drawing close to the warm body of his sleeping wife. Sound slumber still eluded him. It seemed as if something heavy were sitting on his back, forcing his chest into the mattress. Still hazy with sleep, he coughed and rubbed absently at his nose. It was running badly, as if he were suffering from a heavy cold. He slowly became aware of growing discomfort. Then he was wide awake.

He turned on his back, staring up into the darkness above the bed. Beside him, Evelyn stirred fitfully and began to cough. The sense of discomfort gradually became more real. Suddenly he realized what was wrong. The air was thick and stifling; he sniffed and smelled the distinct odor of smoke. He fumbled for the switch of the reading lamp on the bed table and flicked it on. The room was filled with smoke, the bed lamp a small firefly in the almost complete darkness.

He sat bolt upright, sudden fear clutching at his heart. It was the wrong thing to do. The room was layered with hot smoke from the ventilator grill. He fell back on the bed, doubled up in a paroxysm of coughing; he was suddenly afraid that he might start to vomit.

Beside him, Evelyn began to cough violently. He couldn't hear her but he could sense the vibrations of the bed as her body shook it. For one of the few times in his life he tried to scream but no sound came out, as, indeed, no sound ever had. He shook Evelyn, trying frantically to wake her.

She responded slowly, too slowly. Still coughing, she blinked her eyes, then opened them wide as she recognized the danger. She opened her mouth to scream but even if she had been able to, Albrecht realized he could not have heard her. Before he could stop her, she sat up as he had. Immediately she gasped and began to gag. He pulled her down to the bed and then onto the floor.

The smoke was thinner close to the floor and the air was somewhat easier to breathe. His coughing lessened. He made frantic motions with his hands: *The building is on fire.*

The children, her hands replied.

The smoke was growing thicker and they both were starting to choke. *Don't get up,* his hands said. *Stay close to the floor.* Partly because of the tearing of her eyes and because of the steadily decreasing visibility, she didn't understand him. She struggled to rise and he pulled her back on the rug, touching her face with his to reassure her. She began to sob silently.

The children, her hands had said. He felt a terrible

panic. They were in the next room, but he had no idea if they were still asleep or if they had awakened and were crying for help. He began to crawl away from the bed, hugging the floor. He felt the lamp cord tangle in his feet and kicked to shake it off. The light went out abruptly; he was in complete darkness. He must have pulled the cord out of the wall socket, he thought. And then with despair: He was now deaf, dumb, and blind. Sightless in a soundless, voiceless world.

He felt quickly along the floor, touched his wife's arm and pulled her toward the door. They crawled rapidly forward and then he hesitated. Were they really heading for the door? In the darkness and the confusion of trying to locate Evelyn, he had lost his sense of direction. He reached out, sweeping his arm in a wide arc in front of him; his wrist hit against the leg of the bed. He could tell by the way the covers were tucked in that he was at the foot. They had been crawling parallel to the bedroom door.

Panicked, he rose to his feet and felt as if he had thrust his head into an oven. He threw himself to the floor. The level of heat halfway down from the ceiling must be close to boiling; the skin on his forehead felt tight and almost shriveled. He crouched low and half crawled toward the wall until he felt it in front of him. Then ran his hands swiftly over the surface, searching for the wall switch. Nothing. He moved a little farther down and suddenly his arm hit something. He felt around with his hand, encountered a doorknob, frantically tugged it open and bolted through. He would find the children and come back for Evelyn immediately.

If only he had the gift of voice, he thought, if only he could cry out to the children. Or if he could only hear them. . . . He sensed it was somewhat cooler in the room and stood up to fill his lungs. His face was immediately muffled by folds of cloth. A thin, metal object fell on him and when he put out his hands, he encountered smooth drapings of silk. He stumbled around blindly. An unseen hook that protruded from the wall raked across his forehead. Instead of the children's room, he had stumbled into the closet.

He whirled around, batting away the clothing in front of him. Coats, dresses, and suits slid to the floor. He found the doorway again and fell immediately to his knees. Where was Evelyn? He felt around on the floor, then found her near the bed. She was limp. Still on his knees, he gathered her up in his arms, his lungs desperately pumping for oxygen. He was too weak to crawl any farther.

The coughing wracked him again and mucus flowed like water from his nose. It seemed like there was no air in the world at all, only endless gusts of hot gases. Evelyn had already slipped from his grasp and he could feel himself collapsing on the floor beside her.

The children, he thought. Dear God, the children . . .

37.

"A toast?" Harlee Claiborne said. He held out his glass.

Lisolette smiled and held up her glass. They clinked and she took a sip. He was really very—continental? Or was that an old-fashioned word nowadays? She glanced around at the quiet diners who for the most part were talking in hushed whispers or simply not talking at all. Mr. Leroux had gone to talk to several couples standing at the elevator bank and they seemed to be arguing. She wondered what about and thought she could guess.

"I'm sure there's no reason to be alarmed, Lisa. The fire is more than forty floors below us and they must certainly be getting it under control by now."

"I'm sure you're right, Harlee. It does seem reasonable."

He looked at her shrewdly. "But something seems to be worrying you nonetheless."

"Yes," she admitted. "I am, though not for your safety or mine. It's something else and I'm not sure what."

Quinn Reynolds appeared at their table. "May I send over another bottle of wine?"

Claiborne beamed. "Why, thank you, Miss Reynolds. I can assure you we'll both enjoy it."

"Compliments of the management, of course," Quinn said and hurried away. A few moments later, their waitress approached with another bottle to fill their glasses. Her hand shook slightly as she did so and Lisolette glanced up quickly.

"I'm sure there's nothing to worry about, miss. The firemen arrived hours ago and they've undoubtedly prevented it from spreading, or we would have heard."

"The ambulance arrived hours ago, too, ma'am." She filled Harlee's glass. "I'm not even supposed to be on duty tonight. I'm filling in for a friend."

She left and Harlee lifted his glass to sip at it appreciatively. "Blast! I'm sorry, Lisa, I'm getting clumsy in my old age." The waitress had filled his glass too full. A few drops dribbled down his chin to spot the front of his white shirt.

Lisolette dipped her napkin in her water glass and daubed at it for a second. "I have an idea, Harlee. Why don't you take a salt cellar into the men's room with you? Sprinkle some on the shirt; the salt will absorb the wine and a bit of soap and water will complete the job. It will feel damp for a few minutes but it looks like the kind of shirt that will dry quickly."

"I swear, Lisa, there's nothing that you miss. I won't be a moment." He pocketed the salt cellar and rose to thread his way through the tables of diners to the rest rooms. Lisolette watched him as he went. He really is a very handsome man, she thought. So sweet and, more important, fundamentally honest. She wondered if it were really true that there were warrants outstanding for him in some states. Surely nothing that a good lawyer couldn't handle with sufficient time and patience.

She let her gaze wander around the room. It had been so enjoyable an evening until they had received word of the fire. Even then, for a time it had been something of a carnival. Until, as the waitress had said, the ambulances had arrived. A few of the diners were still on the promenade watching the activity below. She and Harlee had drifted out for a while, but the sight of the stretcher bearers and the sound of the windows crashing into the plaza below had taken all of the thrill out of it for her.

Even now there was still the distant whine of more sirens filling the air as additional trucks roared up to the building. She listened, imagining the ordered—and disordered—confusion far below. She hoped they were making good progress and that none . . . She wouldn't think about that, she promised herself. One of her students had become a fireman and she had never forgotten the shock when his name had appeared in the papers as a hero who had given his life to save some people in a slum fire. She stirred restlessly. Something was nagging at the edge of her mind but she couldn't quite put her finger on it.

The sirens, she thought. Of course. The sirens and the crashing of glass and the commotion in the street below and probably the telephone operators calling the rooms to notify the tenants of the fire. Enough noise to wake the dead, and very definitely the living.

Only there were people who would never hear the sirens.

People to whom such alarms meant nothing, people who lived in a silent, speechless world, who talked with their hands and read each other's lips.

Tom and Evelyn Albrecht. She knew they were retiring early, that he had been exhausted by many evenings of night work and had been looking forward to the holidays so he could catch up on his sleep. They wouldn't have heard the sirens of the fire trucks or the ambulances or the wail of the police cars. They wouldn't have heard the telephone, if the operator had tried to warn them of the fire. Little Linda had been taught how to use the phone, but she and the other children would have been put to bed before their parents. Even if Linda awakened when the phone rang, what would she know of evacuating a building, of fire alerts, or even of staying put and placing wet towels around the doors and over the ventilation grills? Linda was all of seven years old.

Perhaps she should tell Miss Reynolds, she would

know what to do. She could call down and alert the security people or the firemen. She caught Quinn's eye and motioned for her to come over and Quinn signaled that she would be there in a minute. Lisolette fidgeted, growing more worried and impatient by the second. If only Harlee would return. No—he was a dear but he was the sort of man who was at his best in a drawing room or at a formal dinner, not at all the type who could rise to an emergency.

Quinn had moved to another table of diners and was talking quietly with them, undoubtedly trying to calm them, Lisolette thought. There was no telling when she would come back.

Lisolette made up her mind then, rose and walked to the far end of the dining room where the house phones were. She quickly dialed security. But there was no dial tone, no subliminal garble of conversation in the receiver. She tried another phone with the same result. The phones were dead, she realized, and probably had been for perhaps half an hour or longer.

She thought of poor Schiller, trapped in her small apartment, then resolutely put him out of her mind. There was only one thing to do and it was taking a terrible risk. She had no idea that someone else might not have thought of the Albrechts and warned them by now, that perhaps they were quite safe or perhaps they had never been threatened at all. The fact that she was gambling with her life never entered her mind; the possibility that she was gambling with the Albrechts' did.

And there was also the thought of what her father would have done.

She glanced over at the elevator bank again. Mr. Leroux and the two couples he had been talking with had left; Mr. Leroux had gone back to his table for a moment and the two couples were standing by the entrance to the scenic elevator at the opposite end of the foyer. Nobody was looking in her direction. She hastily pressed the down button, then hurried to a nearby empty table, picked up a discarded napkin and drenched it with water from the table pitcher. She might need it, she thought, and hastened back to the elevator bank.

She remembered Harlee just as the elevator door quietly opened. He might think that she had deserted him in panic and be disappointed in her—the least he would do would be to worry about her. But it wasn't practical to wait and confide her plans to him; he would try to stop her. Well, perhaps she could make it up to him later. She quickly entered the elevator and pushed the button for the thirty-fourth floor. There would probably be smoke, she thought, though again, perhaps not. The fire was floors below and she wasn't even going as far as the sky lobby. The thought occurred to her again that she might very well be embarking on a fool's errand, but in one sense she hoped so.

The cab slowed and stopped. The moment the door opened, she detected smoke. The odor grew stronger as she walked down the hall; the air itself was hazy with it. It grew denser as she half ran toward the Albrecht apartment. Doors were open on both sides of the corridor now, indicating their hasty evacuation by tenants, and the interiors were thick with smoke. In one she saw smoke billowing from the ventilation grill and she automatically pulled the door shut. She was now genuinely frightened for the safety of the Albrechts.

They lived in a dead-end corridor where the smoke was thick and choking, harsh in her throat. She could feel her lungs begin to labor. She stopped briefly to tie the sodden napkin around the lower portion of her face so it covered her nose and mouth. It helped a little.

The door to the Albrecht apartment was closed and, predictably, locked. It meant nothing, she realized. It would be locked whether they were home or if they had left—unless they had left hastily, as had the other tenants along the corridor. She pounded on the door, hoping that the children inside might hear even if their parents couldn't. She knocked again, then realized she was wasting time when time might be very valuable.

She fished in her purse and pulled out her charge-a-plate from Grammerty's Department Store. How many times had she read about doing this in her favorite mysteries or seen it on television suspense shows? Pray to God that they had not shot the dead bolt. She knelt down and suddenly felt like crying. There was a thin metal molding running around the door frame, preventing direct access to the area around the lock. She hit the strip of metal in frustration and anger, then noticed that it gave slightly. The molding was tacked onto the frame by a relatively few small rivets. She felt quickly in her purse for her fingernail file, inserted the point between the molding and the frame, and drove it in for several inches, then wrenched it sideways. The file bent, and with a screech of pulled rivets, the molding gave slightly, the paint cracking up and down from the point of insertion.

She drove the file in farther and pried again, and the gap between the molding and the frame widened. One more time and there was room to insert the credit card. She could see the faint glint of brass where the lock's tongue slid into the striker plate in the door frame. She pushed the card in between the door and the frame, directly against the curved tongue. She couldn't tell whether the tongue was sliding back or not; then the card twisted out of her perspiring fingers. She wrapped a handkerchief around the end she held and tried again. For a moment there was no movement; then the tongue abruptly slid back. She turned the doorknob and pushed, almost tumbling into the apartment.

Inside the room, the air was heavy with smoke. For a minute she was caught up in a fit of coughing; then she readjusted the napkin over her face and crawled forward.

"Children!" she shouted. "Linda, Chris, Martin—it's Lisa! Are you here, children?"

She paused and listened intently for an answer. There wasn't any and for a moment she felt sick and foolish for having endangered her own life on a wild-goose chase. The smoke was getting unbearable. She shouted once more but there was no reply. Thank God, they had left already.

She was just going out the door when she thought she heard a faint cry. She turned back, almost hoping that she was wrong. "Children?" she shouted again. This time there was no mistaking it, there was a faint cry from the children's bedroom. She ran across the living room and pushed open the bedroom door. The smoke was less dense than in the living room, and she could see a little, once she had located the light switch.

The beds were empty.

"Children! Chris!" She turned to leave, suddenly fearful of what she might find in the rear of the apartment. Behind her, she heard a noise, a small child sobbing. Suddenly she realized it was coming from the bed clothing that lay in a heap on the floor. She crawled over and pulled the blankets apart. Little Chris crouched beneath them, his eyes wet with tears and smoke irritation.

"Chris! Chris, now listen to me! Where are the other children?" Chris pawed at his eyes and sobbed. "Chris, tell Lisa—please tell Lisa!"

"They're hiding," he said between sobs.

"Where, Chris? Tell Lisa where!"

He pointed to the closet. Lisolette ran to it and opened the door. The closet was dark and filled with hanging zipper bags for clothing. They stirred slightly and she parted them with a sweep of her hand. Linda and Martin, the baby, were crouched on the floor in the rear of the closet, holding on to each other. Linda was not crying, though her eyes were filled with tears from the smoke. She ran over to Lisolette and hugged her around the legs.

"Oh, Lisa, I'm so scared! I called downstairs but nobody answered. It rang and rang, but there wasn't anybody there! And I couldn't waken Mommy and Daddy, they had locked their door."

As parents with small children might do if they wanted to be alone for a while, Lisolette thought. And they had probably drifted off to sleep without remembering to unlock it. She ran her hands gently through Linda's hair. "There, there, don't be frightened. We're all safe. Just stay here and I'll be right back." She returned to the bedroom and stripped the cases from the pillows, then ran into the bathroom and quickly soaked them under the shower. Returning, she handed two to Linda. "Put one over your mouth and help Martin with the other. I'll help Chris with his. It will cut down on some of the smoke so you can breathe." She helped knot the cases behind their heads and started to lead them out when she suddenly remembered.

"Mein lieber Gott!" She had been so worried about the safety of the children, she had forgotten Tom and Evelyn. She would have to wake them up, signal to them what had happened. "You children wait right here!"

Lisolette gripped the knob of the bedroom door but it was locked. She looked about, then seized a heavy pedestal lamp from the table near the door. Three times she hit the lock before it shattered. She threw the ruined door open. Inside, it was like a blast furnace, the heat rolling out in waves. She crouched and fumbled for the light switch. The smoke was almost solid in the room and she had difficulty making out the two figures by the bed. She quickly crawled in. Both of them were unconscious, though still breathing slowly and heavily and occasionally gagging. She shook Tom but he only groaned. She would be wasting time trying to rouse them, she thought. Tom had fallen partially across the body of his wife. Lisolette rolled him off, then grasped Evelyn under the arms and dragged her across the floor. The thick carpeting made it difficult work and the few steps to the door took every bit of strength she could summon; she was also finding breathing more difficult.

"Linda, wipe your mother's forehead with your pillowcase. The rest of you children, lie down on the floor. You, too, Linda; you can do that while you're lying down. I'll go back and get your father."

It could have been her imagination but it seemed as if the air was even hotter and the smoke thicker back in the bedroom. She crawled over and grabbed Tom by the arms, pulling him toward the door. He must weigh around a hundred and eighty pounds, she thought; it would be so much easier if he were a little man like Harlee. He groaned and fell into a heavy spasm of coughing. For a brief moment Lisolette didn't know if she could make it to the door with him; the fumes from the ventilator grill were biting deep into her lungs. She gripped his arms tighter and gave a final tug; then they were out into the living room. She pushed the bedroom door partly shut behind her. The damaged lock prevented her from closing it completely.

"They're dead, aren't they?" Linda asked, dry-eyed. "Mommy's not moving."

"No, they're not dead," Lisolette said, feeling her own tears just beneath the surface. "But we've got to get them to some fresh air."

She tried mouth-to-mouth resuscitation on Tom; he suddenly groaned and coughed, then turned on his side. A thick mucus began to dribble from his mouth and he abruptly vomited on the rug. What was she to do? Lisolette thought frantically. She didn't have the strength to get both of them out of the building, unconscious as they were. She couldn't even manage Evelyn, who was considerably lighter than her husband. She would have to abandon the parents to the smoke and fire, she thought slowly. The children she could save.

"Come along with me, children; take each other's hands so we don't get separated."

Linda hung back. "What about Mommy and Daddy?" Her voice was beginning to tremble now, her tears just a moment away. Little Chris took his cue from the tone of her voice and started to cry.

"We'll send somebody back for them."

"I want to stay with them," Linda pleaded.

"No, no, *kinder,* you must come with me," Lisolette pleaded, almost in tears herself. Dear God, she thought, why me? Then directly to Linda: "Linda, would your mother and father want you to stay behind?"

Linda understood then and the tears rushed to her eyes. She nodded and held out her hands for Chris and Martin, then followed Lisolette toward the door, crying silently to herself.

The smoke was heavier now and Lisolette found the door as much by feel as by sight. Her eyes had started to tear badly and she was keeping them half closed to protect them from the stinging smoke.

"Miss Mueller, what the hell are you doing here?"

She thought she had heard footsteps in the outer hall but hadn't dared to hope. Her eyes flew open. Harry Jernigan loomed in the doorway. Behind him were two firemen in slickers and helmets.

"Gott sei' dank'!" She openly sobbed then, pushing the children toward the firemen. "You men help with these poor creatures!"

One of the firemen brushed past her and knelt by the figures on the floor behind them. He was very young, not more than twenty-five, Lisolette thought. But it was difficult to tell, his face was so red and smeared with soot-streaked sweat. He held Evelyn by the wrist for a moment, counting her pulse, then leaned close to Albrecht's chest.

"How are they, Johnny?" the older fireman asked.

"They're both in pretty bad shape—smoke inhalation. We'll have to get them out of here right away."

"Will they be all right?" Lisolette asked, fearing the answer.

"I'm not a doctor, lady. We'll have to get them down to the lobby where they have oxygen equipment and Pulmotors. Can you two handle the kids?"

Jernigan nodded. "Sure."

"I'll take the two little ones, you help with Linda," Lisolette said, taking both of the smaller children by the hand.

Linda was still crying and Jernigan said gently, "It isn't every day I can help a girl as pretty as you." She tried to smother her sobs.

The two firemen were in a hurry. "Johnny, grab the woman; I'll take care of the man." The younger fireman picked up Evelyn in his arms as if she were a child; the older one swung Albrecht over his back in the classical fireman's carry. "Okay, let's get the hell out of here. We'll see the rest of you downstairs. Don't take the elevators —the sky lobby is filled with smoke and the elevators aren't operating down from there anyways. Take the stairwell; doors are open from eighteen down to fifteen, you can get out on those floors. The rescue company will take the kids from there anyways to check them over."

They moved down the hall with their burdens, Lisolette following, and Jernigan bringing up the rear. She stumbled once and Jernigan reached out with a steadying hand. She was, she realized, weaker than she thought. The smoke seemed to have sapped her strength and left her lightheaded. Or maybe she was just growing old, she thought. She repeatedly had to tell the two children, clinging to her skirt on either side, to hold their damp pillowcases before their faces. Her own napkin had long since dried in the heat of the Albrecht bedroom and she found herself periodically coughing. She should have thought to wet it again before leaving.

The two firemen had already disappeared down the stairwell when they got to it. Jernigan pushed the door open and led the way. "Come on, Miss Mueller." She followed him in, the two children close behind her. Several flights down they could hear the scrape of the firemen's boots and Lisolette prayed that they would be in time. The stairwell was smoky but the air was relatively breathable; the pressure in her lungs lessened a little.

"They've made some progress against the fire," Jernigan said. "It's vented on the seventeenth and eighteenth floors and they're fighting it from the other stairwell, working their way in. It's cut down a lot on the smoke."

"It's also a little chilly," Lisolette said, then suddenly laughed at her complaint. If you could complain, she thought, everything was going to be all right.

Chris tugged at Lisolette's hand. "Are Mommy and Daddy going to be all right?"

"Of course they are, Chris. They're just sleeping."

"If I say a prayer will that make them wake up any sooner?"

"I'm sure it will, Chris. We'll both say a prayer—only very quietly, just inside your head."

The sound of the firemen's boots was receding even faster now. "They're beating us down," Jernigan said. He was almost an entire floor ahead of Lisolette.

"I'm glad they are," Lisolette said soberly. She was going to have to carry Martin, she suddenly realized; his

slow clambering down the steps was holding them up too
much. She couldn't have done it before, but she thought
she had enough of her strength back now. She leaned
over and swung him up in the crook of her arm.

The stairwell itself was strange to her, studded with
pipes that jutted from the individual floors and ran underneath the individual landings.

"Harry, what stairwell is this? I've never been in it
before."

His voice floated back from almost a floor and a half
farther down. "You usually use the one on the north side
of the building, Miss Mueller. This one's the south one,
it's right by the utility core—the hollow core holding all
the utility pipes and the inside elevators. The scenic elevator runs right up the other side of it."

She had more or less located herself now. A few more
flights would see it. "Hurry along now, Chris, we don't
want to lag behind."

"You need any help up there, Miss Mueller?"

"No, we can make it, Harry."

She started to move her lips in a silent prayer then, not
alone for Tom and Evelyn Albrecht, but for someone else.

It was only the second time that evening that she had
had time to think of Schiller, trapped in her apartment.

38.

It was the first major fire for rookie David Lencho and
despite the smoke and the frequently broiling heat, there
was a perversely exciting quality to it. The fire had become a personal enemy to Lencho, a kind of fiery
dragon whose existence had cast him in the role of St.
George. He was on the nob of the two-and-a-half-inch
hose, fighting his way down the corridor of the seventeenth
floor. Directly behind him were two more hosemen, one
of them Mark Fuchs, the chief's son. He knew that
Fuchs, too, felt the same kind of excitement.

Crouching down to avoid the layers of heat near the ceiling, he slowly worked the nob back and forth, spraying the hall directly ahead of him with a heavy stream of water under high pressure. He wore his helmet reversed so that the long brim normally in back would protect his face from radiant heat when he kept his head down. Visibility was poor but he could tell where the fire was by the heat. A dozen feet behind him a secondary hose team was playing a spray of water over him and the other members of the advance team. Half the time he felt like a drowned rat or, at the very least, one that was in hot water—and occasionally scalding steam when the water from the hose struck a really hot spot.

He edged a few feet closer to the beast, glanced back briefly at Fuchs and laughed in his excitement. Fuchs returned it as Lencho crept another foot farther toward the blaze. He would be good for about ten minutes up front and then he would have to be replaced. But that was enough for him to feel that he had gotten in his own personal licks against the fire.

He adjusted the spray on the nozzle slightly and played it over the ceiling, watching the tile turn black and pieces of it scatter under the force of the stream. Water rivulets coursed down his face from the cooling back spray. There was a particular satisfaction in fighting fires, and a definite pleasure in working with men he respected. The men with him on the hose team he especially liked: Jenkins, the third man on the team, and Mark Fuchs, the son of the chief, would normally be on the nob in a tight situation like this but had traded with him a few minutes before to give him the experience. Fuchs was his own age and they had gone to school together. A year after Fuchs had joined the department, so had he.

Somewhere along the line Fuchs had managed to get married and now had a small son. Lencho laughed to himself. Where the hell had Fuchs found the time? He supposed one day he would settle down with a nice Jewish girl. He'd have to talk to his mother about that; she had more time to look around for one than he did.

The nob almost got away from him again and Fuchs

yelled, "Watch what the hell you're doing, Dave!" Lencho nodded, his smile gone. The hose was delivering more than 250 gallons of water a minute at a tip pressure of better than fifty pounds per square inch. It took three men to handle a two-and-a-half-inch hose and if they lost control of it, the heavy brass nozzle could whip around and brain a man.

Forty feet ahead he could make out the warped door of the utility room where the fire was supposed to have started. On his left and to the rear, the charred remains of Today's Interiors still smoldered, although the major portion of the fire was out. Suddenly a piece of tile fell from the ceiling and landed on his gloved hand. He jerked his hand back in a reflex action; the hose sprayed erratically around the corridor walls as Fuchs and Jenkins fought it. Lencho lunged for the nob, caught it, and the three of them brought it back under control.

Fuchs leaned forward and shouted in his ear. "Do me a favor and don't let it go again, okay, Dave?"

Lencho nodded. He peeled away his cloth-asbestos glove and glanced down at his hand. The place where the tile had hit was raising a blister the size of a half dollar. It'd hurt for a week, he thought. The fire was not quite so exciting any more. His face felt burned and raw and his nose was leaking mucus and his lungs had started to ache. He coughed and tried to edge farther forward again, making a few inches before his muscles gave out. He suddenly felt a tap on his back and a voice shouted in his ear: "Okay, guy, you've had enough!"

The relief crew took over as he, Fuchs, and Jenkins dropped back to the landing. Chief Infantino was waiting for him there.

"You all right, Lencho?" It was the lead man that usually bore the brunt of it.

"Got my hand fried a bit; it's okay."

"Let's see it."

Lencho held it out; Infantino glanced at it professionally. "Okay, go to first aid in the lobby and get it covered."

"It'll keep."

"So it can get infected and keep you out for a week instead of a few minutes? Go to the first aid and get it covered, Lencho. That's an order. I'll let you know when we start giving medals for being dumb."

Lencho reddened. "I'll go right down, sir. Be back in a few minutes."

"Not here you won't."

Lencho stopped. "I don't understand."

"You've been beat more than you might think; you need a longer rest than just a few minutes. Send you back in right away and you wouldn't last half as long as you did the first time." Infantino's voice turned grim. "I heard that you lost control of the nob twice, endangering the men you were with. You've a brave man, Lencho, and you've got lots of energy—but it's a case of too much engine and not enough steering wheel. Knocking down a fire takes more than courage, it takes brains as well."

"It won't happen again, sir." Lencho felt like crying.

"You bet your ass it won't; I won't let it." Infantino eyed him for a moment, then partially relented. "When you get it taken care of, report to Captain Miller on sixteen. Get a pulldown hook and you and Fuchs help the crew down there check the halls. The main fire's out down there, but they'll be looking for flare-ups."

"Yes sir." Lencho felt like he had just flunked his orals. He turned for a last look down the corridor and said, "It looks like it's darkening down."

Infantino nodded. "With half the lake poured on it, I should hope so."

Lencho started down the steps to the fifteenth floor and the elevator for the lobby. It had been fun while it lasted, he thought.

39.

Barton could hardly wait for Leroux to show so he could wash his hands of the whole mess. But Leroux hadn't come down in the first elevator load of evacuees from the Promenade Room. Neither had Thelma nor Jenny. It occurred to him then that when Leroux finally did show up, there would actually be little left for him to do aside from facing the cameras. The lobby had been cleared and those tenants who hadn't taken advantage of the reservations made for them elsewhere were sleeping on cots set up in the lower lobby coffee shop and the corridor just outside. A few had gathered around tables in the lunchroom to talk in quiet monotones and congratulate themselves on having made the select fraternity of survivors.

There had been other problems in addition to those of the residential tenants. Barton had managed to locate repairmen for the ventilation fans in the machinery rooms. They promised him that in another hour all of the fans would be back in operation on exhaust to clear smoke from the building. Ductwork to the upper floors was still intact for the most part. Repair of the phone lines to the upper floors, however, would have to wait until the fire had been completely knocked down on the various floors.

Human problems had given him more trouble than the mechanical ones. A representative of the insurance company for the Glass House had somehow gotten through the police barricades. Barton had finished a cup of coffee in the lunchroom and when he came back up he discovered the man taping the operations of the firemen and the damage in the lobby with a port-a-pak TV camera. When he refused to leave, Barton threw him out physically.

He had also pacified some of the commercial tenants whom the police had brought in after getting Barton's permission. Most of them were desperately worried about

268

the records in their offices; a few about the actual physical furnishings. Barton had reassured the majority of them. To others he could offer little consolation beyond suggesting they contact their insurance companies once fire damage had been assessed. Access to their offices was denied everybody, Barton telling them they would be informed once the Fire Department had secured. There would be a lot of lease cancellations when it was all over, he thought, but that was Leroux's worry, not his.

There were a dozen tenants in the hospital with smoke inhalation and an equal number of firemen. And there were the missing who had yet to show up and about whom Barton felt an increasing anxiety. Douglas, Albina Obligado, Bigelow, Deirdre Elmon—whom Jernigan had insisted was still in the building, even though she had signed out—and a number of the residential tenants whom Barton didn't know.

And then there had been the fatalities. A tenant who had died of smoke inhalation. And Michael Krost. The firemen had knocked down the blaze on seventeen, helped by the fact that it had almost burned itself out. They found the doors of the stalled elevator still open. An ambulance crew had taken out Krost's remains, setting their stretcher down on the lobby floor to ask Barton for help in identification. It had taken a full sickening minute to place who the crisped heap had been. Barton made a tentative guess and the stretcher crew departed with their burden, the trailing edges of the covering blanket dripping dirty water that had collected on the lobby salvage cover.

All in all, Barton thought grimly, it could have been worse—much worse. The fire on seventeen had been knocked down, the few blazes on sixteen had been put out, and now eighteen was coming under control. Infantino's men were having problems with twenty-one—the fire had leapfrogged up the side of the building through a channel formed by warping of part of the curtainwall—but as yet it wasn't serious. But then, any fire was serious, or could be.

"Jenny down yet?" Infantino had come in from outside with coffee for the communications crew.

"Not yet—she and the Lerouxes will probably be in the last load from the Promenade Room." He glanced at the coffee cup in Infantino's hand. "Why didn't you get your coffee from the lunchroom?"

"Garfunkel asked for volunteers and Typhoid Mary was the first in line—that woman hasn't boiled water in her life. Any report from the hospital about Edwards?"

"Holding his own but still in intensive care. I told Garfunkel—they were pretty good friends." He noticed a few hosemen waiting by the elevator bank to go up. "What's the situation on twenty-one?"

"The fire's gotten a foothold in a number of the suites on the north side but we're making headway." Infantino sounded confident, then realized it, and immediately hedged his bets. "Don't get your hopes up; fires are unpredictable. Have a failure in one of your machinery rooms and all bets are off. Or if we've made a mistake on our estimates of the fire loading on the floors above eighteen, we could be in trouble. And I told you earlier the building was like Swiss cheese; the fire could have worked its way through a dozen different poke throughs and be smoldering away in areas we don't even suspect yet." He shouted instructions to a passing group of hosemen, then turned back to Barton. "Why didn't Leroux come down with the first load from the Promenade Room, Craig? I'm glad you're here, but it isn't going to look very good for him."

"Apparently he's running the evacuation up there, keeping them calm, preventing any panic, that sort of thing." He felt uneasy about the question. "Why do you ask?"

"There may be another reason—he's hot copy and you're not. The moment he sets foot in the lobby and the reporters hear about it, the cops will have a tough time keeping them away. They'll be hard on him, any way you look at it. I think Leroux figured all of that out."

"He could've," Barton admitted. "He could be stalling for time until he's thought of some answers to the questions they'll ask, though he could always say 'no comment.' In any event, that's his problem."

Infantino finished his coffee and crumpled the plastic

cup. "Let's go back to your maps again, I want to check on what's above twenty-one. How far can we trust Garfunkel for knowing the fire loading?"

"I'd stake my life on him."

"It won't be yours but it might be somebody else's. Let's give your drawings a double check."

They walked over to the cigar stand and the communications relay center. Barton noted that there were fewer transmissions now. Infantino had stopped sending out calls for more men, and in the rest of the city the functioning of the Fire Department had returned to near normal, with no more units being put on alert.

They were deep in a discussion of the fire loading on twenty-one when a policeman came up. "Mr. Barton, there's a man at the barricades insisting on seeing you."

"I'm not seeing anybody," Barton grunted, irritated at being interrupted. Then he sighed and put down his pencil. "Who is he?"

"He said his name is William Shevelson—that he used to be construction foreman or something on the building."

Barton caught his breath. Shevelson. His eyes met Infantino's. "Send him in."

Shevelson strolled through the lobby a minute later, an unlighted cigar in his mouth. He was half a dozen inches shorter than Barton and about the same number wider. They sized each other up for a long moment and Barton decided, as he had when he had first met Shevelson two years before, that he didn't like him. Shevelson had a belligerent attitude that was difficult to assess, an attitude that said he considered everybody else to be an incompetent.

"You're Barton." Shevelson studied him a moment longer. "I met you once, remember it now. A couple years back." He nodded at Infantino. "Where's Leroux?"

"He hasn't come down from the Promenade Room yet."

"If I were in his shoes I wouldn't either."

"You wanted to see me about something?" Barton asked stiffly.

"Yeah." Shevelson hesitated a moment, then abruptly thrust a roll of blueprints at Barton. "If the bastard was here I'd make him sweat for these, but he's not and I suppose you can use them."

Barton took them. "Thanks a lot." He wished he could put more feeling into the words, but Shevelson was a difficult man to be polite to. Then he caught Infantino's eye again and suddenly they both knew.

Infantino said it for him. "You were the one feeding inside information to Quantrell, weren't you?" There was hostility in his voice that he made no effort to disguise.

"He used me, too," Shevelson said calmly. "I was an innocent just like you. So now we're both wiser." He pointed to the blueprints. "If you want me to do penance there it is."

"I don't know if we need them now," Barton said. "Thanks anyway." It was a dismissal; the blueprints wouldn't tell him anything now.

Shevelson didn't move. He looked around the lobby, then glanced briefly overhead. "Oh, I think you'll need them all right." He waved at Barton's sketches spread out on the counter. "If I were you I'd toss those out and take a look at the prints. You might find them of interest."

"You forget, I designed the Glass House," Barton said.

"I haven't forgotten. You designed it and I built it and Leroux didn't do a goddamn thing but pay for it and that's the catch. He didn't pay very damn much."

Something in his voice prompted Barton to spread the prints out over his own drawings. He glanced at them quickly. They were familiar—all too familiar—and took him back three years to when he had been working on them. It had been a long time ago, he thought, a time when he had been happier, if less wise. The happiness he missed and the wisdom he was unsure of.

The prints were very much as he remembered and then he suddenly started noticing inconsistencies—changes that had been made of which he had been unaware. He suddenly realized he was looking at the actual working prints, not the original drawings he had labored over while at Wexler and Haines.

There had to be somebody responsible, he thought sickly. It couldn't have been Leroux alone. It was common practice for construction companies to suggest ways in which money could be saved, to suggest alternative materials and changes in specifications to the same end. And Shevelson had been the construction company's representative.

"You're right, Shevelson, I designed it and you built it and you did a lousy job. If you want particulars we can begin with the duct holes. Damned few were fire stopped; that's one of the main reasons the fire spread so fast."

Shevelson nodded affably and felt in his pockets for matches to light his cigar. Infantino took it out of his mouth. "I wouldn't want one of my men to slug you —they've seen enough of fire for tonight."

Shevelson shrugged. "That's right, Barton; the duct holes probably weren't fire stopped like they should have been. Sloppy workmanship, I agree. But you know better than to talk to me about it. Talk to the utility people—they're the ones who made the poke throughs. Or talk to one of the city inspectors from the Department of Building and Safety; he's the guy who should have raised hell about it. But maybe he had a heavy schedule that day and didn't have time for much more than a walk-through. And, after all, the city's not paying him enough for him to really bust his ass and find every little flaw, even if he had the technical expertise to know what he was looking for in the first place. Or maybe someone paid him to overlook every little flaw."

"There should have been fire barriers in the stairwells to prevent smoke spread," Barton said slowly. "That was your responsibility; we called for them."

"So you did. But the city fire codes didn't require them and maybe the developer considered them an expensive luxury. In this case, there was no maybe involved —he didn't want them. At the time of construction, the city code didn't require pressurized stairwells, either. Your original design called for them though, didn't they?"

"That's right, so why weren't they pressurized?" Barton asked angrily.

Shevelson took out another cigar. "You sure I can't

smoke, Chief? There's enough water in the lobby here; I don't think we need to worry about a few ashes on your salvage cover." He lit up without waiting for permission and turned back to Barton. "Look, Barton, why do you think I was fired? Because I approved of the changes that were made?" He shook his head. "I don't particularly like you but you designed a beautiful building. Everything considered, you also designed a fairly safe one. I didn't call for the changes; your boss did. I was just a flunky for the construction company."

"You're saying that Wyndom Leroux was responsible?"

"Who else? He paid the bills." He turned and blew the cigar smoke away from them. "Maybe he was just being a good businessman. You people draw up pretty plans and then somebody had to make an estimate and put it out to bid; or if it's a scope project, find a construction company that will at least be reasonable. If the project's up for bid it sure as hell better be a competitive bid."

Barton shook his head. "It didn't have to be. The construction company was a satellite company."

Shevelson raised an eyebrow. "Knudsen? I knew Leroux had an interest, but I didn't think it was that heavy a one. But it still doesn't change things. Leroux wouldn't stay in business very long if his own construction company couldn't built his buildings at least as cheap as anybody else."

He could imagine Leroux saying it, Barton thought: He was running a business, not a charity. He had settled for minimum compliance with the fire codes, cut costs to the bone, and eliminated all the "frills."

"You sound like you're defending him."

"You've got to be kidding!" Shevelson was suddenly bitter. "I was fired because I didn't agree with him, because I didn't believe in building firetraps no matter how pretty they look against the skyline." He suddenly changed the subject, his eyes narrowing in anger. "Where the hell were you during construction? You're pretty loose with your accusations. What were you doing? You were senior architect; it was your baby more than anybody else's."

"I was transferred to Boston during the primary construction work," Barton said tightly. "I was in San Francisco when they were working on the interior."

Shevelson was contemptuous. "Your work in Boston was really important, wasn't it? And have you really done anything more than spin your wheels in San Francisco? It never occurred to you that Leroux might simply have wanted you out of town during the construction? That if you had stayed here, you would have asked to be site supervisor, and if you hadn't gotten it you would have been over here every day anyways checking? Then what would you have done when you discovered that Leroux was cheapening it little by little? Blown your stack and quit? But Leroux got what he wanted. He got you—and he got you out of the way."

"You're right," Barton agreed angrily. "I would have blown my stack. But there's one difference between us, Shevelson: You knew. I didn't. Why didn't you go to the city officials or to the Fire Department? You knew what he was doing. You knew all the violations; what did you do about them?"

"That's the point," Shevelson said slowly. "There really weren't any violations. Oh, maybe a few minor ones here and there. But nothing major. And nothing I could prove. Some coincidences perhaps, like the sudden change in city fire codes eliminating pressurized stairwells. My case was essentially an emotional one so I took it to the papers and the television stations and nobody did anything but Quantrell. Now, God knows, I'm sorry about that."

Shevelson stood there for a moment, his face drawn, fighting to keep his anger on the inside. Barton and Infantino kept silent and waited. "Everything he did was perfectly . . . legal. A little chintzing here and a little chintzing there until finally the building was a weak version of what it was meant to be. Maybe it was no more dangerous than other buildings in the city, but this was one that I built." He cocked his head at Barton, the expression on his face that of a man who doubts that he's really being understood.

"You want to know who writes the fire codes in this city, Barton? Ask the developers. Ask the people who own the buildings; they're the ones who write the codes. The Fire Department inspectors come around and it's cut and dried. Are the valves set right? Do they work? Is the fusible link on a fire door installed properly? But there are other questions to be asked and nobody seems to be asking them. Why did this city remove the requirement for pressurized stairwells from its fire code? How come New York required neither pressurized stairwells nor smoke shafts until 1973? Why did Los Angeles allow shingle roofs—one of the greatest possible fire hazards —for so long? Who brings the political pressure to bear? This city isn't unique, Barton."

He was making an indictment and a plea for understanding all at the same time, Barton thought. And at least for the moment he could see beyond the façade and understand the contempt Shevelson felt for lesser men. He had met so many of them.

"Where's all this leading to?" Infantino asked impatiently. "We've still got a fire here."

And it wasn't out yet, Barton thought. But Shevelson had reminded him of something: The building was his; he was kidding himself if he thought he could walk away from it. He twisted the blueprints around so they were facing Shevelson. "What are the risks we don't know anything about? I could spend all night looking for them; you probably know them by heart."

Shevelson was suddenly all business. "Assume the worst. There are probably few of the duct holes that are properly fire stopped and the building is peppered with them. Dangerous and sloppy, but I'm sure it was fast, easier, and cheaper; the utility people had to make a buck and Leroux wasn't paying much. So they chintzed, too. You can assume the building has very little fire integrity. You can also assume that some of the main girders are exposed in places where ducts pass directly beneath them and are strapped to them for support. Or maybe conduits are strapped to them. In either event, the fireproofing would have been scraped off the beams and five will get you ten it was never replaced. It's standard practice—and in a big fire, it can buckle a floor on you. But your big worry is probably right here."

He took the cigar out of his mouth and pointed the lighted end at a portion of the blueprint. "The utility core. The old-fashioned method of building a fire-rated core wall was to make it from terracotta blocks and then plaster over that. What we use now is Pyrobar. It has a high fire rating but, structurally speaking, it's not very strong. The bad design feature is that there are some storage rooms, both those for the building itself and those for commercial and business tenants, that share a common wall with the utility core. Now remember that the gas, electric, steam, and some of the phone lines go directly up the core. It's conceivable that if one of the storage rooms should catch fire and burn out of control, you'd be in for trouble, depending on the fire loading. And in storage rooms, it's usually high."

Barton looked up at Infantino. "What are the chances?"

"Not very good." Infantino didn't seem impressed. "The one storage room fire we've had is under control." He glanced over at Shevelson. "But thanks for bringing the prints; it's a help to know where things really are."

Shevelson managed a quick smile. "I remember some professor saying a high-rise building is the biggest machine there is but nobody's written an operating manual for it yet. These were the best I could do." He stared down at the prints for a moment, then glanced around again at the lobby. "It's a beautiful building," he said quietly. "It's mostly yours, Barton, but a good piece of it is mine, too. I had to do what I could; I wouldn't even have held up Leroux, much as I despise him."

"You didn't despise him at the start, did you?" Barton suddenly asked.

For a moment Shevelson was lost in thought. "No, I didn't. At first, I thought he was one of the most capable men I had ever met."

Another load from the scenic elevator suddenly emptied

into the lobby. Barton searched the faces of the people getting off. There had been how many loads so far? Ten? Eleven? Leroux had to be on the next one.

And so did Jenny.

40.

For Ian Douglas the world had become an infinity of stairs that led steadily upward. Scramble up a dozen steps; rest for a moment on the concrete landing; then climb another dozen. Occasionally he would try a doorknob, hoping that one of them might not have closed completely, and they could gain entry to a floor. After a dozen attempts, he gave up trying.

And there was always the smoke—first the odor, then the slight haze in the air. The haze was building, and it was getting increasingly difficult to breathe. To add to his difficulties, Albina's twisted ankle had worsened on the thirtieth floor, and he had been forced to half carry her up the succeeding flights. He felt that he had long since passed the limits of his physical endurance; he stopped to rest more frequently. He would begin to climb again when he started coughing and saw that the smoke was getting thicker, slowly filling the stairwell.

They were on the forty-fifth floor when he realized he couldn't go much farther with the burden of Albina and with his increasing difficulty in breathing. Albina was coughing steadily now, and it was obvious that it was all Jesus could do to drag himself up the steps. Fortunately, he seemed to have shaken the withdrawal symptoms; the realization of personal danger must have flooded his system with enough adrenalin to overcome them. But they had to rest, Douglas thought, even at the risk of letting the smoke build up even more. He sat down on the landing steps and for a moment yielded to a fit of coughing.

"You go on," Albina said quietly. "Send firemen down

for me when you get to top. Take Jesus with you and go on."

He considered it, then rejected it. She was already weakened; she couldn't take much more smoke. And there was something else. For the first time Douglas was in a life-and-death struggle and he desperately wanted to win. All of his life the world had considered him weak, despite his muscle and bulk. He wanted to prove it wrong, but nobody would think it unusual if a man saved himself— he would have to see to it that all three of them survived.

Jesus and Albina were both coughing now and starting to gag when suddenly Douglas remembered something he had once read. "You two have handkerchiefs?" Jesus nodded and produced a dirty white piece of cotton. Albina fumbled in her smock and drew out a startlingly red bandanna. Douglas had a crisp, linen handkerchief in his suit-coat pocket, carefully folded into the appropriate triangle.

"What are we supposed to do with these?" Jesus asked, curious.

"Piss on it," Douglas said. Jesus looked at him, obviously not believing what Douglas had said. "Piss on it," Douglas repeated. "Then tie it over your nose and mouth; it will help cut the smoke."

Jesus looked shocked. "Man, you gotta be kidding!"

"I'm dead serious," Douglas said sharply. "Now do as you're told!"

"Who's telling me, man? You?"

The contempt in his voice was too much for Douglas. He slammed Jesus against the wall, then grabbed him by the collar and slapped him twice with the flat of his hand. The anger was bile in his throat.

"I don't give a crap what you think of me; you're going to do as I say! We've got another twenty floors to go and we're not going to make it if we can't breathe. You got a better idea? Now's the time to tell me. Otherwise, do as I say or I'll knock your teeth right down your throat!" He drew his fist back.

Jesus managed to straighten up even though Douglas had a heavy hand on his shirt. "You're taking it out on me, man." There was no fear in his voice but neither was there any contempt.

"Taking what out on you?"

"What you are." Jesus' eyes were steady. "I don't give a shit, man—I probably never really did. Junkie . . . queer . . . who gives a damn. Another ten minutes and nobody's gonna care one way or the other."

Douglas reddened and lowered his fist. For a moment, Jesus was the world, the sum of all the taunts and sneers and whispers that had piled up over the years. He felt ashamed of himself. "Piss on the handkerchief," he muttered. "It's the only thing that I can think of that might help."

"Do as he say," Albina said sharply. "Is he the only man here?"

Jesus turned without a word, the handkerchief in his hand. Douglas did the same thing, while on the stairs Albina turned and with remarkable grace repeated the action. Douglas helped her adjust the kerchief around her face. Then he hooked her arm over his shoulder and continued up the steps. Jesus followed.

They managed another two flights before Douglas realized the wet handkerchiefs were more a psychological help than real. The cloth was too thin to screen the small smoke particles and it was little help in filtering out the gases themselves. Douglas started to cough again as did Albina. Jesus tore his handkerchief off and dropped it on the steps. He said nothing and neither did Douglas.

At the next landing, Douglas noticed the fire hose behind the glass case. Suddenly he thought he saw an answer. He stopped while the others watched, untied a shoe and took it off. He hefted it, then brought the heel down sharply against the glass, shattering it. He picked shards of glass out of the frame, then reached in and tugged the hose out of the case.

When he had about twenty feet out, he turned to the landing window behind them. "Okay, stand back away from the window." Douglas lifted the body of the hose over his head so about ten feet of it, including the heavy brass nozzle itself, was behind him. Then he swung it forward and down, like a whip. The brass nozzle flew over his head and smashed against the window. There was a shatter of glass and a sudden blast of cold air. He did it twice more to clear the frame of large pieces of glass. The cold air poured in from the north now and spilled down the stairwell, effectively capping the rising smoke. He had created his own inversion layer, Douglas thought, by venting the stairwell. It might work.

They began to climb again. Another flight up and he shivered; the temperature of the stairwell air was dropping fast. But at the same time, it was getting considerably easier to breathe.

"I'm sorry about the handkerchief idea," he said suddenly. "I had read about it someplace; I honestly thought it would work."

Jesus laughed. "Don't sweat it, man. At least you thought of something. I didn't think of anything."

There was a sense of equality in his voice, of acceptance, and for a moment Douglas hated himself for responding to it. Who the hell did he think he was? But there had been no condescension. He suddenly wondered what Jesus thought of himself as an addict. Did he despise himself? Did he accept himself?

He looked at Jesus, thinking: It was hard but they both had learned to live in their own skins and accept it.

41.

The sidewalk and plaza in front of the Glass House were coated in a glistening sheath of ice. Infantino's boots slipped on the glaze underfoot; he held onto the open door of the CD comm van as he stared up at the building. In spite of the scars of the fire, it was still a thing of beauty with the banks of floodlights playing on its exterior. The queen of the city, he thought, but a tattered queen now. He could see the gaps in the curtainwall where the windows had been knocked out on the seventeenth and eighteenth floors. The thick mantle of ice ridged these floors and flowed down the outside of the building almost to the ground level. Perversely, the effect added to the building's beauty. The tower above was a glittering, golden gem swathed in a curtain of ice.

It hadn't gone too badly, Infantino thought. For a while he had feared the fire might spread and they would have to bring in helicopters for a rooftop evacuation. But the main fires on seventeen and eighteen were pretty well knocked down while the fire on twenty-one was now contained. They could look forward to a morning of pulling down the remains of walls and ceilings and searching for minor smoldering fires hidden in remote recesses of the various floors. Sometime before dawn the majority of his companies could probably secure, coil up their hoses and go back to their cold meals still sitting on the firehouse stove. They would try to forget that they had been part of one of the major near disasters of the city.

Infantino was surprised that there had been so few casualties. In a fire of this size, he would have predicted more. Out of a working crew of well over a hundred, perhaps a dozen had been sent to the hospital for smoke inhalation, burns, and cuts from falling glass. Some of the burns had been bad ones, both from the intense radiant heat and from some of the older turnout coats which had crumbled in the heat. But as yet there had been only one fatality—the man with the hot lung.

Shevelson's appearance on the scene was helpful but troubling. The blueprints were proving useful, though not as much as Shevelson obviously thought they should be. It was more helpful to learn, finally, that it was Shevelson who had been feeding information to Quantrell. Whether or not Fuchs would believe it, at least in his own mind Infantino knew he was free and clear. But Shevelson had impressed him in one area—the Glass House was a minimal building. The equipment in it was designed to serve sixty-six floors and not one more. There was no reserve, no back-up system. If there were any unpleasant surprises now . . . well, they could really be unpleasant.

He took one last look at the building, then walked over

to the Red Cross canteen truck where Chief Fuchs was having a cup of coffee. He took the cup offered by the girl inside, added cream, and ladled three heaping spoons of sugar into it.

"Sweet tooth, Infantino?"

"You burn up a lot of energy fighting fires." He studied the chief for a minute and decided to have it out. "Shevelson, the construction foreman for the Glass House, showed up a while ago. He brought along a set of the working prints."

"Oh?" Fuchs waited.

"He's your leak for inside information, if you were looking for one. He's been talking to Quantrell for weeks. Apparently he was canned by Leroux and still carries a grudge."

"That so?" Fuchs sipped at his own coffee without looking up. "Your friend Barton talked to me about that. He even introduced me to Shevelson while you were upstairs. Interesting fellow. Would have made a good fire captain, though I'm not so sure I'd care to work with him."

There was surprisingly little hostility in his voice and Infantino asked: "Any complaints so far?"

"About how you've been handling things? If I had any you would have heard about them. Pretty standard fire . . . larger than most, but standard."

"Seen one fire, you've seen them all?"

A little of the sharpness returned to Fuchs's voice. "I didn't say that."

"*I've* never seen a fire like this one," Infantino said. "And I don't think you have, either. It spread faster than any fire I've ever worked. And it was damned hot."

Fuchs nodded. "I'll give it that," he said mildly.

Again, the absence of hostility surprised Infantino. He took another sip of coffee, then suddenly said: "Why the hell are we fighting, Chief?"

For a long moment Fuchs said nothing; he stood leaning against the truck and gazing up at the building a few hundred feet away. "You've got your views, I've got mine. I didn't put you in charge of the high-rise problem because

I hoped you would agree with me. The only gripe I ever had was because I thought you were airing department business in public."

That was as much of an apology as he was going to get, Infantino thought, but it was enough. "I didn't think I was—but I can see where other people might have."

"Yeah," Fuchs agreed. "You know how some people are—touchy." He put his cup on the truck window ledge behind him and pulled his collar up closer around his neck. "Speaking of department business, I imagine you have some recommendations."

"I do. You probably won't like some of them."

"That's irrelevant."

"It will all be in a formal report."

Fuchs nodded. "I expect it to be, Mario. But I'd still like to hear your suggestions now."

"We need new equipment." Fuchs's face was impassive and Infantino added: "Mostly personnel equipment. High-capacity respirators would allow us to hang in there longer. And we could use lightweight bottles containing oxygen instead of compressed air. More comfortable masks, more reliable reducing valves. And new turnout suits; some of the ones we were using are so old they crumbled from the heat. And the advance hose teams could use aluminized cover suits—the kind they use in fighting oil fires—for close proximity work. Almost all burns were from radiant heat."

"Anything else?"

"I think every man working on a fire floor where the smoke is heavy should have a walky-talky. It's easy to get separated up there." Fuchs seemed lost in thought and finally Infantino asked, "Any comments?"

"Not many. You're right about the heat. It was greater than I had expected, though part of it may be because of the nature of the building—poor construction techniques, fire loading far above the norm, that sort of thing." He half smiled. "But you're not through in listing what you would like to have, are you?"

"Shape charges? We actually didn't have to use them tonight but they would be nice to have on hand."

"Speak to the department engineers and send me a memo. If they recommend it I'll look into it."

Fuchs started for the building and Infantino shouted, "I'm not through yet!"

"I don't know why I thought you would say that," Fuchs said dryly. "What did you forget this time?"

"I'd like to recommend the hiring of fire protection engineers, perhaps on a part-time basis, when it comes to the Fire Department checking out major buildings."

"Good idea if we can find them; there aren't many floating around. Put that in your memo, too."

Fuchs had taken a step back to the building when a voice said, "You gentlemen have anything to say for the tube?"

Quantrell approached from the other side of the Red Cross van, trailed by a cameraman, his sixteen-millimeter rig riding high on his equipment pod.

"Why don't you go straight to hell, Quantrell," Infantino said, suddenly acutely tired.

"I probably will, in due course," Quantrell said grimly. He glanced up at the ice-sheathed building. "Nice little fire; it probably could have been avoided if the developer had been more conscientious. Wouldn't you gentlemen agree?"

"Get lost, will you, Quantrell?" Infantino snapped. "The Glass House is no better or worse than half a dozen other buildings in this town. They're all alike; they all suffer from the same defects."

"Care to point out a few of the others? You'd be doing our viewers a public service. Now's the time to sound the alarm, now while the press is listening and watching." He cocked his head, half smiling. "Well, Division Chief Infantino?"

"It was a tough fire," Infantino said slowly. "A dozen of my men are in the hospital—some of them may not leave for months. One is dead. I'm not about to play games with you tonight; all I want is for you to get the hell out of here. It was probably a bastard like you that thought up the term 'body count' for the enemy dead in Vietnam. You cover disasters like they were football games; for you there's no difference between a man who gets tackled and one who gets killed. They're just numbers on a scoreboard."

Quantrell stepped closer to Infantino, the bantering smile gone. "Where the hell do you get off calling me names, Infantino? I've got my job just like you have yours. My job is to get the news out to the voters who just happen to pay your salary. I kick a few asses and I bruise a few feelings and nobody's ever going to vote me the most popular guy in the class. I don't deal in press releases and handouts; I get out there to see for myself. Buddy, you don't know this business—how much information do you think I would get with a sweetness-and-light routine? There isn't a department in this city that wouldn't like to brush me off with a couple of drinks and three pages of public relations bullshit. Well, if you don't like how I quote you, then stop being a gabby dago and keep your mouth shut."

"That's enough," Fuchs interrupted quietly. "You've had your say, Quantrell. Now get the hell out of here or I'll have you escorted out of the lines."

"Go ahead; it'll make a great story," Quantrell said sarcastically.

"If you don't think I'll do it try me."

Something in Fuchs's voice made Quantrell back off. "Okay, Chief, I've got my story anyway." He jerked his head at the cameraman and they walked away.

"That goddamned cameraman was picking all of that up," Infantino said, furious.

"Don't worry; they won't use it."

Infantino said, "I don't give a damn whether they do or not." But he did; Quantrell had really gotten under his skin.

Fuchs said, "Stay cool," chuckled, and started walking back across the plaza, the frigid wind whipping his coat around his waist. Infantino remained by the van a moment longer, staring at the Glass House. He was thinking of the men still in the building working at knocking down the last of the fire. Idly he watched the scenic elevator start down the side of the shear wall again; it looked like some slow-moving, phosphorescent waterbug. Then he spotted Quantrell and his cameraman running up the terrazzo steps to the lobby. Quantrell must have been counting the loads and realized that Leroux was in this one. They'd catch Leroux as he stepped out of the elevator, still dressed in evening clothes—a perfect contrast to the pajama-clad, weary and frightened-looking tenants whom Quantrell had probably already photographed in the basement lunchroom.

Infantino drained the last of his coffee. He could care less about what Leroux and Quantrell would have to say to each other. He'd read about it in the morning paper or watch it on the six-o'clock news tomorrow night.

The wind began to pick up again; the combination of sleet and snow pelted him like tiny little darts. He shivered, wanting desperately to go home. He thought of bed, and Doris' warmth beside him.

Another hour, he thought, perhaps in another hour . . .

42.

David Lencho rubbed his gloved hand against his turnout coat and swore quietly. The burn wasn't that bad, but it would be several days before it healed properly. The reddened skin hurt and the salved edges of the burn itself were beginning to itch. Probably an allergy to the ointment; he had a history of them as far back as he could remember.

The fire had only blackened part of the sixteenth floor, that portion of it directly beneath the original site of the fire on seventeen. Lencho and Fuchs and some of the other men under Captain Miller's command were going through the corridor with pulldown hooks and pry bars, pulling away charred paneling and ripping up sections of scorched carpeting, searching for any lingering traces of the fire. When they found any glowing embers, a man with a one-inch hose soaked them out of existence.

Mark Fuchs, just behind Lencho in the corridor, flashed his electric lantern around the hall, making sure they didn't stumble over any debris. The men before them had pulled down partitions, chopped through studding, and stripped off wallpaper looking for the last remnants of the fire. Fuchs occasionally spoke into his walky-talky, giving a progress report to Captain Miller on the landing.

The air stank of fire, Lencho thought. The particular acrid quality of burned wood and cloth and seared metal. The hall itself, except for the beam from Fuchs's lantern, was completely dark. Occasionally they passed an office with a battered door hanging on a hinge or leaning against a wall. He could see the night through the office windows, a framed portrait in deep blacks and purples with flakes of snow whirling past the glass. He rubbed again at his blistered hand.

"You pick up more burns than any rookie I know," Fuchs said. It was a flat statement, not a jibe; Lencho caught the irritation behind it.

"It could happen to anybody," he protested.

"I know, but it always seems to happen to you."

They moved cautiously down the corridor, constantly searching for smoldering sparks and embers. The previous cleanup crew had done a good job, Lencho thought; the floor seemed almost completely clean, except for an occasional glow that had rekindled after the other team had been through.

The corridor dead-ended and Fuchs said, "That wall marks the utility core; we've covered the whole floor." He thumbed his walky-talky, then hesitated a moment. "Did you check that mop closet?" He pointed at the last door on the corridor.

"Probably a utility room," Lencho said. "I'll take care of it."

Fuchs spoke into the walky-talky. "Captain Miller? Mark Fuchs—it looks like sixteen is completely cl—"

Lencho reached the door and turned the knob. He screamed suddenly in agony. The metal knob was incredibly hot. He pulled his hand back; part of the glove and the skin from the palm of his hand lay crisping on the knob. But the twist Lencho had given the knob was enough. The door swung open.

The utility room was directly under the two heavy fire loadings on the floor above. It hadn't caught fire but the heat from above had driven the oxygen off. Stored waxes and solvents had burst their containers, then vaporized in the oxygenless, superheated air. The door was remarkably tight. Very little air from the corridor had seeped into the intensely fuel-rich atmosphere. Nor had the room been cooled appreciably by the hosing of the corridor outside.

For a moment there was no sound but that of tile falling from the overhead ceiling, then the muffled sound of debris falling into the utility core itself where the explosion had ripped out the rear wall of the storage room. A quiet hissing followed and then abruptly . . . a second, louder explosion.

The corridor immediately filled with steam.

43.

Thank God, Leroux thought, it was the last load. The two men who had assisted in handling the evacuees had gone down the time before, leaving him, Thelma, Quinn, Jenny, and a scattering of the kitchen help—enough to actually overcrowd the small, scenic elevator.

Suddenly one of the women diners turned to Quinn. "I thought Harvey was in here," she said, panic in her voice. "He was with me until just a few minutes ago!" Leroux remembered both of them—a woman in her fifties who had been having dinner along with her teen-age son. The boy had made a pig of himself on the free wine and it suddenly occurred to Leroux where he was. He motioned to Quinn and they stepped back in the foyer for a moment.

"He's probably in the john," Leroux said in a low

voice. "Too much wine; he won't be ready to leave for a few minutes yet."

She bit her lip. "Mr. Leroux—when he comes back, there's no way we can squeeze him into the elevator. We're overloaded as it is."

Leroux swore to himself. "All right, I'll stay behind and wait for him."

Quinn shook her head. "I don't think that would be practical. Neither your wife nor Jenny will leave without you. For all three of you to stay behind is ridiculous. I'll wait for the boy."

"I can't let you do that, Quinn."

"Why not?" She looked irritated. "Because I'm a woman? That's ridiculous. We both know we're in no danger up here, even if the others don't. If we were we would certainly have known by now. Don't be foolish; go on down and I'll join you in another ten minutes." She laughed shortly. "I'll get some soda from the kitchen; the boy will need something to settle his stomach."

"All right, Quinn; you're the boss." He stepped back inside the elevator cage, and told the woman that her son would come down with Quinn in the next load, then he pressed the button for the doors to close before she could object. A moment later he felt the descent begin. He started to relax. He had made up his mind what to say to the reporters—which was nothing at all—and now he was anxious to get it over with.

"You can see the whole city below," Thelma said quietly to Jenny. They were all standing by the glass side of the cage. "With the snow falling, it looks like a jeweled fairyland."

"It's beautiful," Jenny agreed.

Leroux put his hand gently on his wife's shoulder. There would be investigations later that would be hard for him to take. He would need Thelma then more than he ever had. Suddenly he felt a sense of shame. He had kept her out of so much of his life. It hadn't been fair to her—or to him.

They were almost halfway down now; he could make out the ground below through the swirling snow. A few moments more and they would be in the lobby. And then the ordeal would begin.

At that point a muffled explosion rocked the cage. Someone grabbed at Leroux for support to keep from being thrown to the floor. Dimly he saw below them a flash of flame, reflected from the falling snow. The exterior bulbs that outlined the cage in a faint aura of light went out abruptly. There followed a ripping sound as the elevator plunged for an instant . . . then came to a sudden halt. The mechanical emergency brakes screeched against the side rails.

The inside of the cage became a screaming bedlam. Several people had fallen to the floor; they now struggled to their feet. Next to Leroux Jenny moaned, "Oh, my God, what's happened?"

Leroux, stunned, shook his head. It was obvious what had happened. Somehow an explosion had ripped away part of the shear wall of the utility core, twisting and bending the guide rails below them. When the electricity failed, the cage had dropped several feet. The emergency brakes, activated by a too fast descent, had automatically stopped their fall.

They were now suspended over the city, a good three hundred feet below.

Early

Morning

The beast has been weakening, growing older and more feeble. Water has sapped its strength and death is gnawing at its vitals. Its life span has been short, but in that length of time it has burned and blackened all of the seventeenth and part of the eighteenth floors. Now most of the fuel that fed the fire has been consumed. The flames on the twenty-first floor are being beaten back foot by foot. In a few short hours, the fire grew from babyhood through adolescence to become a lusty adult. Now it's past middle age and fast slipping into senescence.

Throughout the floors, firemen are working their way through the debris, their pry bars and pulldown hooks ripping out walls, exposing smoldering studding, smashing furniture to reveal the wormlike sparks nibbling along fabric seams. Whenever they are found, the sparks are deluged with water and quickly die.

But the beast is cunning; in small out-of-the-way rooms and closets it has hidden secret caches of food. One of them is in a storage room directly below the room in which the fire was born. It is a storage room for the executive offices of the Tops Supply Company, a large retail hardware and paint chain, and holds samples of various paints, varnishes, solvents, and the like. Many of the containers have been opened by salesmen to test the contents and then returned to the storeroom with their lids only loosely sealed. The Tops Supply Company is a recent tenant, having moved into the Glass House when a previous firm leasing the space had suddenly failed. Neither the inspectors for the Department of Building and Safety nor those for the Fire Department are aware of the new tenant or the contents of its storeroom. Both have been routinely notified, but the paperwork in each department is enormous; the notices are buried at the bottom of incoming correspondence boxes. Both departments will find them about a month after the fire is over.

The door of the storeroom has not been breeched during the course of the fire but inside, the solvents, paints, and waxes have melted and vaporized in the intense heat. The air in the room has been limited and most of the volatiles have gone through a first stage of combustion to yield hot carbon monoxide and various highly flammable breakdown products. Carbon monoxide is an extremely explosive gas and the temperature in the storeroom is well past its ignition point.

It is at this point that rookie Fireman David Lencho reaches out and opens the door. Cool fresh air rushes in to mix with the superheated fuel gases. The reaction is instantaneous. The explosion shatters the walls of the storeroom, blowing David Lencho's tattered corpse halfway down the corridor. It rips out the rear wall of the storeroom, which is also one of the walls of the utility core. Directly behind the wall a massive, high-pressure steam line carries steam up to the sixty-fourth-floor machinery room to power much of the HVAC system. The line itself has never been quite adequate to the task and tonight, the first really cold night in the city since the Glass House was opened, the line is operating over capacity. The steam in the pipe is several hundred pounds per square inch at a temperature of more than 500 degrees Fahrenheit. The line is already under strain and the sudden explosion in the storeroom hits it like a giant hammer blow. The line buckles and a brazed expansion joint, designed to allow for contraction and expansion of the pipe, abruptly fails; the line explodes. If the blast in the storeroom was violent this is far more so.

The force of the steam explosion rips through the outer wall of the utility core at a point where the rails of the scenic elevator are secured. Rivets tear from their mounting and the steel rails curl outward as if they are made of lead. The elevator slams to a halt, its emergency brakes wedges driven between the cab and the splayed rails. But the rails have been torn from their mountings and the braking power of the wedges is weak.

Inside the core, ductwork collapses as if a giant has stepped on its galvanized sheet metal. Electrical conduits are shredded. Power fails abruptly throughout the building, plunging the residential and the office floors into darkness.

Next to the electrical conduits and running the length of the utility core is the main gas line, carrying gas to the residential apartments and the public restaurants. It is held to the masonry walls by heavy steel strapping at the point where the gas booster pumps are positioned. The force of the steam explosion tears the gas main loose from the wall. It does not break at this point; rather its supports fail and the pipe itself bows away from the explosion. The shock is transmitted up the pipe and it vibrates like a plucked violin string. It is in the upper machinery floor, separated from the Promenade Room by the Observation Deck, that the pipe finally fails.

A heavy flood of gas gushes from the pipe and fills the machinery floor, billowing around the emergency electrical generators. The gas is lighter than air but, because the gas is relatively cold compared to the surrounding air, a good deal of it flows down into the floors beneath. There it seeps among the stacks of asphalt tile, plywood paneling, and other building materials stored on the still incomplete floors.

Up on the utility floor a relay suddenly snaps and a standby motor starts. The spark from the relay is enough. A low-order explosion rips through the floor. The armature of the motor is thrown off its shattered bearings and the armature begins to smoke. The motor overheats and the insulation begins to burn. Elsewhere on the floor, small fires have started near oil spills and in small open cans of grease. On a floor below, the gas-air explosion starts fires in several paint cans carelessly left open near a stack of paneling.

It is a modest beginning, but the beast quickly makes the most of it. The asphalt tile flows, chars, and ignites. Wooden studding and plywood sheets blacken at the edges and burst into flame. It takes only a minute or two for the beast to become firmly established in its new home.

Far below, the fire has been rekindled on the twenty-first floor and quickly finds its way through utility holes and ductwork to twenty-two.

The beast has a new lease on life and sends triumphant tongues of smoky flame up into the snow-filled night sky. It roars its rage and glares down at the city below it.

∽∾

44

The sound of a muffled explosion startled Barton. He looked over at Shevelson and was about to ask "What was that?" when there was a louder, sharper explosion. The makeshift table on which they had spread the blueprints trembled slightly; a second later the lights in the lobby went out. There was dead silence for a moment, and then the comm station in the cigar stand broke into an excited babble of transmissions. In the lower lobby, some of the women began to scream. Barton blurted, "What the hell happened?" Somebody turned on a portable electric lantern in the cigar stand. Shevelson was dimly outlined in the glow. He shook his head tensely and said, "Quiet."

Barton strained his ears and then heard it. A steady rain of debris falling down the elevator shafts, and then, suddenly, louder crashes thudding from the core bottom. "The core walls are going," Shevelson said quietly. "The explosions must have ripped right through them." Barton could imagine the chaos within the core itself: pieces of cinderblock and Pyrobar tumbling to the bottom from the floors far above, joined by crumbling bits of mortar, calcined plaster, lengths of cable and conduit, strips of piping, pieces of burning wood. . . .

"Let's get outside," Barton said, "we can't tell anything from in here." He ran for the door, followed by Shevelson and Garfunkel, who had groped his way up from the lower lobby. On the plaza, the wind cut through his suit coat like a scalpel. He shivered and turned up his collar, debating whether he should go back inside and borrow a turnout coat. Then he saw Infantino standing by the CD communications van and ran over.

"What the hell happened, Mario?"

Infantino seemed dazed, as if he were just coming out of heavy shock. "I'm not sure; there were two explosions —I don't know what caused them." He stared up at the building and Barton followed his eyes to the sixteenth floor. Flames flickered behind the windows almost the total length of the floor. He could see flames through the gaps in the curtainwall where the windows on seventeen had been. They were stronger on eighteen through twenty-two. There was probably little fuel for the fire on seventeen, Barton thought; most of it had been consumed. But the fires on the other floors looked serious.

"I don't know what caused the first explosion," Shevelson said slowly, "but I'm fairly sure the second one was the steam line going; it probably ruptured somewhere between the sixteenth and twentieth floors."

The steam line must have ripped through several floors and spread the fire upward, Barton thought. There was, as yet, no telling the extent of the damage to the utility core but all the main electrical and gas lines ran up it. There was no immediate way of knowing if their security had been breeched, but he couldn't risk it. He turned to Garfunkel. "Get hold of Donaldson and tell him to shut off all the main electrical circuits and the gas line. Right now."

"You're cutting all the elevators," Infantino said grimly. "I'll need them to get men up to the fire floors."

Barton slowly shook his head. "Mario, you're the boss here. But if the main gas line has been breeched, the upper floors will become a bomb, and even the flicking of a light switch could set it off."

"Do you know what a length of two-and-a-half-inch hose weighs, Craig? More than seventy pounds. Do you think you could carry one up sixteen or eighteen flights —or be of much use once you got it there?"

"Forget it," Shevelson interrupted. "The elevators are already out. The board was dead when we left. And I don't think you have to worry about the gas line being breeched. I'm afraid it already has been, but you won't like where."

"What are you driving at?" Barton asked. He started to shiver and jammed his hands in his pockets to keep them warm.

Shevelson didn't get a chance to answer. There were

faint popping sounds from far above and a second later
a sailing pane of glass shattered in the street a hundred
feet away. It hadn't come from the twenty-first or the
twenty-second floors, Barton realized with a shock. It had
come from higher, much higher. He craned his neck
and could make out the faint flicker of flames at the
very top of the building, a few floors below the roof. The
fire was in the machinery room, the point where the gas
line had probably ruptured.

He looked at Infantino, who shook his head. "There's
no way to reach that. It'd be murder to climb the steps
and even if we got there, with the electricity off, there's
no way of operating the booster pumps so we would
have a water supply."

Barton glanced back at the building and was shocked
to see the scenic elevator stalled a little below the
middle. It was difficult to tell because of the swirling
snow, but it looked like the tracks a few floors beneath
the elevator had been torn away from the side of the
building. Then he could make out the dark shadow behind
the twisted rails and realized that part of the shear wall
itself had been blown out.

My God, Jenny. . . .

Behind him he was vaguely aware of Infantino talking
to the communications officer in the van. "Call for
ambulances; there'll be casualties coming down. And
we'll need—" He cut off. Fuchs was running across the
plaza toward them. Infantino waited until he got there,
then started talking again, as much to Fuchs as to the
comm officer. "We'll need additional companies—a lot of
them. Call the department in Southport and ask for shape
charges and Primacord and a man who knows how to
use them. Also ask them if they can send a detachment
of men with proximity suits."

Barton said automatically: "I know how to use explosives."

Infantino didn't take his eyes off Fuchs, who had remained silent throughout his orders to the communications officer. "Forget it, you're not a fireman, Craig."

Then it suddenly occurred to Barton what Infantino

was talking about. "You set off a high-level explosion in there and you could damage the building structurally."

"What do you think has happened already?" Infantino said curtly. "There are no longer any chances that aren't worth taking." He was still looking steadily at Fuchs. "If you want to countermand my orders, you'll have to do it now," he said quietly. Fuchs shook his head and turned to look back at the building. He looked small and old, Barton thought. And beaten.

"Chief?"

A runner had dashed out of the building to report to Infantino. Barton listened intently. It was worse than he had imagined. The fire was raging on the twenty-first, twenty-second, and twenty-third floors. There were also reports that the upper machinery floor was on fire. Infantino silently pointed at the top of the building and the runner turned, stared for a moment, then continued with his report. "The explosion was on sixteen, sir—a storage room for a paint company. It blew out part of the inner wall of the utility core and apparently broke the steam line, or caused it to explode in turn."

"What about the salvage team on that floor?"

The runner licked his lips nervously, glanced quickly at Fuchs, then back to Infantino. "Most of the men are all right, sir, but rookie David Lencho and fireman Mark Fuchs are unaccounted for. We're trying to get a rescue squad in there now but it's pretty hot." His eyes flicked over again at Fuchs, who turned without a word and walked back toward the building.

"Anything else?" The runner shook his head and Infantino said, "Okay, report back to your company." After the runner had left, Infantino turned to Barton. "The Chief had three sons; Mark's the only one who followed him into the department."

"It's a rough night for all of us," Barton said quietly.

Infantino looked at the side of the building where the scenic elevator hung suspended halfway down. "Yeah, I guess it is." He started back toward the Glass House. "You coming, Craig?"

"Right behind you." The wind whipped around his

trouser bottoms and he was suddenly acutely aware of the cold, not only on his face and hands, but pressing against his back and legs. He began to shiver uncontrollably as his teeth started to chatter. There were more popping sounds from above, and he and Infantino abruptly broke in a run for the lobby doors. Behind them, falling glass slashed onto the plaza.

At least, Barton thought, most of the tenants had been evacuated and lodged elsewhere for the night, except for those in the downstairs lobby and luncheonette. And those who were still in the Promenade Room or trapped in the scenic elevator. But there was no point in thinking about the latter; there wasn't a damned thing he could do about it.

Shevelson had found an electric lantern and set it on one end of their table so they could see the blueprints. Barton walked over and leaned his knuckles on the table, staring blindly at the prints. He felt choked with a sense of futility, a feeling that there ought to be something he could do and the knowledge that there wasn't.

For a moment the lobby was silent except for the crackle of messages at the building's comm center behind them—the occasional thud from the elevator banks as more debris cascaded into the bottom of the utility core. The calm before the storm, he thought. In another few minutes, they would begin bringing down the injured from the upper floors and relief companies would start showing up.

"Barton?"

He broke out of his blue funk and glanced up at Shevelson. "Yes?"

Shevelson had an unlit cigar in his mouth and Barton noticed there were tears in his eyes.

"Our pretty building's a goddamned mess, isn't she?"

45.

John Bigelow was having a nightmare. He was being threatened by some terrifying danger. He struggled from sleep and lay half awake. The dream was lost; he couldn't remember what it was. He lay in bed, fuzzy from sleep, his mind still fogged by alcohol. He rolled once on his side and brushed against Deirdre. Automatically he nuzzled her hair, spitting out some stray strands that held the acrid taste of perfumed hair spray. Still half asleep, he could feel the press of love and pushed his face down on hers, then turned away, disgusted by the sick-sweet odor of her breath. After that, sleep came easy and he dozed off again.

The faint sounds of sirens far below pulled him back to a half-intoxicated consciousness. He coughed lightly, ignoring the faint, smoky taste to the air. The smoke from the grill was still light, thanks primarily to the heavy north wind that penetrated small chinks in the building and pushed most of the warning haze to the south end. In addition, he had smoked a great deal before they had gone to bed for a few desultory hours of mechanical love-making. His lungs were still filled with the biting tobacco tars and his mouth felt raw and seared. His nostrils were completely blocked and his breath rasped from his mouth as he wavered between a light sleep and heavy snoring.

It was minutes before his mind equated the sound of the explosions with reality. For a long time they seemed a part of the nightmare he had been having. Then he sat up, his mind still fogged, and stared about the darkened bedroom. It was another minute before he realized that he smelled smoke. The room, he realized with vague alarm, was getting warm. He was still very drunk but the sudden combination of the odor of smoke and the feeling of unexplained warmth sent a prickle of fear through his body. He fumbled for the lamp by the sofa bed and snapped the switch. Nothing happened. Unplugged, he thought. He threw back the sheet and staggered from the bed to the wall, groping for the overhead light switch. He found it but still nothing happened.

He was wide awake now. The electricity must have failed. He couldn't remember if they had a flashlight in the suite; he knew they didn't have candles. Then he remembered the electric lantern that Krost had left behind on the counter. He fumbled his way over to the counter, felt along it, and found the lantern. He turned it on and came back to the bed.

"For Chris' sakes, turn that damned thing off, will you?" Disgusted, Deirdre pulled the pillow over her head.

"Bitch," Bigelow muttered. He stumbled against the bar, almost knocking over his trophy. Then he saw the tendrils of smoke creeping from under the door to the outer office. He turned back to Deirdre. "Wake up, damnit! The place is on fire!"

"You're crazy," she said sleepily and burrowed deeper into the pillow. Bigelow set the lantern on the end table and yanked the sheets from the bed. "Johnny," Deirdre whined. "Lemme sleep."

"Come on," he insisted, kneeling on the bed and almost falling on top of her. He pulled the pillow away from her and dragged her half off the mattress. "Come on, put on something. We've got to get out of here!" He hopped from foot to foot, pulling on his trousers and hastily wriggling into his half-buttoned shirt. He ignored his socks and tugged on his Gucci shoes.

"What a creep," Deirdre said, solemn drunk, and crawled back into bed to lie there on her stomach. She had managed to put on a slip sometime during the night. There was a long tear in the rear, exposing her back and one buttock, and Bigelow wondered for a second how that had happened. He tucked his shirt half into his trousers and tightened his belt, then debated pulling her off the bed again and trying to slap her awake.

The smell of smoke decided him; he ran to the suite door and pulled it open. He staggered backward before the blast of heat and smoke and threw his hands up in front of his face. The outer office was the very substance of his nightmare.

On the far side of the storeroom, the banks of salesmen's small offices were blazing; their thin wallboard partitions blackened as he watched. The heavy floor-to-ceiling draperies on the other side were alive with flames while burning wooden office furniture added to the shimmering heat.

In the middle of the room where the displays were neatly piled, the fire-breathing gargoyles of his dream had become a reality. It took him a moment to realize that the long ranks of polystyrene displays were melting under the heat. The elves slumped as he watched, their features sagging and growing cancerous patches, their cheeks and noses becoming long and pendulous, evil in the orange-red light from the flames. The reindeer became frighteningly alive, their plastic coats gleaming wetly, their delicate legs and thighs oddly elongated, their tails sweeping the floor as they seemed to run swiftly forward. The Santa Claus figures were now humpbacked and bent, their knuckles brushing the wood below, their chubby, jovial faces now hollow-cheeked and vicious.

Bigelow slammed the door, shuddering. There was barely time, he thought frantically. He ran into the bathroom and drenched a heavy towel to wrap around his face. Then he did the same with a terry-cloth robe and pulled it on. Back in the suite, he tugged at Deirdre once again. "Goddamnit, leave me alone!" She pushed him away and snuggled under the pillow again.

Bigelow's eyes were stinging with the smoke. "Damnit, come on!" he shouted in panic and pulled at her arm. She rolled away from him, giggling. "All right, baby," he muttered. "It's your funeral."

He turned and ran for the door, then suddenly stopped by the bar. The only trophy he had ever won in a lifetime of competition. It weighed a ton, but he knew he couldn't abandon it to the flames. He tightened the towel about the lower part of his face, grabbed the trophy under one arm, and opened the door.

Outside amid the flames, the ranks of melting, threaten-

ing figures waited for him. He saw a clear path through the
terror to the inner door of the office reception room and
what he desperately hoped was escape. It probably
wouldn't stay open long, however. Then he looked more
closely at the wooden floor between the displays. It was
wet with the slick of melted plastic. He suddenly remembered the story of the Roman historian forced to walk
across a lava flow during an eruption of Mt. Vesuvius.
Well, his feet were a lot better protected than those of
a Roman. He walked to the edge of the slick and stuck
a foot tentatively into the melted plastic. The stuff was
sticky and formed thin, glistening threads when he pulled
his foot back. But his shoe protected him; he felt warmth
but little more.

He sucked in a breath of hot air, coughed at the smoke,
and started across the deadly slick. It was slow going.
He had to be careful not to spatter his legs with the stuff;
it would burn right through his pants. Step by step he
walked across the pool. He was finally beginning to feel
heat through the soles of his shoes. For a moment he
considered dropping the trophy; it was too heavy and the
metal was already warming from the radiant heat.

Then he realized he was only eight feet from the door.
A wild elation started to build within him. He could see
nothing through the frosted glass of the door to the outer
office. Perhaps it wasn't on fire yet; the door itself didn't
seem charred. A few feet more and he would be through
the door and to the elevators or stairwells. Only a few
more feet . . .

He could feel his right shoe sticking. He tugged at it
impatiently and his foot slipped from the loose shoe. He
was already off balance because of the trophy; for a
second he wobbled uncertainly on his left foot, then, un-
thinking, thrust out his bare right foot to keep from falling.
It touched the pool of plastic.

He cried out in agony as the scalding plastic spread
over his foot. He pulled it back, trying desperately to
master the pain; then he was off balance once again.
He fell forward, frantically clutching at the draperies
that hung on the storeroom side of the partition between

the outer office and the storeroom. He grabbed a handful of cloth, tried to pull himself up, then fell forward again as the draperies gave way. His trousered knee thrust through the folds of the wet bathrobe and slid along the floor as though it were on ice. Pain clawed through the trouser leg. He thrust out his left arm to keep from falling flat but his fingers found no purchase in the scalding slick as he slid face forward into the pool of plastic.

He screamed once and rolled over, trying to escape, still clutching the trophy and the handful of drapery cloth. The drapery rod overhead suddenly snapped under the pull. The rest of the draperies, including the folds that had started to burn at the far end, slid along the dangling rod and enveloped him. Where they touched the pool of plastic they flickered into flames that quickly danced over the surface, igniting the bundled draperies that covered Bigelow. It hadn't worked out, something within him thought sadly. It hadn't worked out at all.

The flames roared across the room. The walls became tapestries of fire, as the display figures slumped into the burning pool of plastic. Near the heap of charred draperies by the door, a blackened trophy jutted up into the smoky air of the room. The metal figures of the trophy were already beginning to flow.

46.

Deirdre was still drunk but a sense of terrible danger was sobering her fast. She sat on the edge of the bed and fought down an almost overwhelming urge to curl up beneath the blankets again. Her arm still ached where Bigelow had pulled at it. Absently she rubbed it. She wanted desperately to drift back to sleep, but it was so warm in the room, stuffy and hard to breathe. Something must have happened to the ventilation system. For some reason her eyes had started to water. She brushed at them, opened her mouth to yawn and ended up coughing.

The taste in her mouth made her gag. Bad liquor and something else. Smoke.

This time she managed to open her eyes all the way. The door to the storeroom was partly ajar and through it heavy masses of hot air billowed into the room. She coughed again and stumbled to her feet, her mind clearing very fast now. Bigelow had shouted something about a fire. She had to get out, she thought, beginning to panic. She slipped her feet into her pumps and ran to the door. At the other end of the storeroom, almost lost amid the wax-museum tableaux of melting elves and reindeer and Santa Clauses, she could see Bigelow walking slowly forward clutching his trophy. He moved with a peculiar lurch, as if his shoes were sticking to the floor.

Finally he stumbled and fell. Deirdre covered her face with her hands as he sprawled full length on the floor. He screamed once and between her fingers Deirdre saw the falling draperies cover him as the flames danced across the room and over the mound of twitching cloth. She slammed the door to shut out the horror, leaned against it, and began to sob hysterically. Gradually a deadly calm came to her; there was something very wrong and then she realized what it was. The door at her back was warm and getting warmer.

She ran through the living room, the electric lantern on the end table throwing terrifying shadows against the walls. She found herself boxed in the kitchen nook, frantically searching for another way out, but there was none. The hysteria had left her completely now. She turned and faced the door; the wood was browning from the heat on the other side. At the bottom, a thick stream of burning, melted polyester flowed sluggishly under it.

She ran into the bathroom looking for thick towels or another robe that she could soak and put on. Bigelow had almost made it that way. If it hadn't been for his damned trophy . . . But there were no more towels, no robes. She darted back into the living room. The door was blackening now. She was trapped; there was no longer any hope. She stumbled around the bed and pulled back the draperies from the picture window. Outside, the snow was drifting quietly down, gathering in little mounds of cotton on the narrow sill.

An immense calm mixed with a deep sadness filled her mind. The window, she knew, could not be opened. Even if it could, they were on the twenty-first floor and there was no fire escape. She could feel the heat behind her and turned to face it. The fire had burned through the door and flames now blanked the entire far wall of the suite. The smoke was thick and searing. She had to get air, she realized. There was a paperweight on the desk near the burning wall and she made a dash for it, scooped it up, whirled and threw it at the window. The glass shattered cleanly and fell out into the night. She ran to the window and leaned out, ignoring the pain as the tiny shards of glass left in the frame gouged the palms of her hands. The air was cold and flakes of snow whipped against her face. Far below she could hear the muted sounds of sirens and men shouting, their voices crisp and clear in the cold night air. She closed her eyes for a moment; somewhere from down below she imagined she could hear the faint murmur of bells and Christmas carols. It was her favorite time of year. . . .

Then she felt the heat at her back again and turned. The fire was halfway across the room and there was no escape now. She stood in the window, wrapped in a protecting blanket of cold air and snow and started to sob. In her mind, she could already feel the touch of the flames. And with that thought, her rational mind collapsed, leaving only a sheer animal need to escape.

She whipped the thin blanket of sheets off the sofa bed and pulled the mattress from the frame, then tugged it toward the window. It was the only possibility, it had to be of some help; it would protect her to at least some degree.

She stood in the empty window clutching the mattress in front of her, then hesitated. Perhaps someone would come, maybe right now the firemen were battling their way through the storeroom, knowing that she was there.

But nobody knew she was there, she remembered. She had made sure of that.

She waited a moment longer but no one came. Only the fire came, burning the desk and scorching the carpet and crawling along the painted ceiling. The upholstered arms of the sofa bed were blazing now and the varnish on the wooden coffee table in front bubbled and browned, then burst into flame. She couldn't stand it any more; her fingers where she held the mattress against the radiation of the fire began to blister.

She turned, her back to the flames; she felt a gentle tug at the bottom of her slip and something warm kissed the nape of her neck. She gripped the mattress tightly. In the next instant she was falling through the blessedly cold night, her only emotion one of a terribly deadening sorrow.

Her hair had caught fire in the last moment on the window ledge, as had the bottom of her slip. She didn't realize this as she plummeted the long, long distance down.

Her fall traced a long, flaming arc through the night sky.

47.

"Miss Mueller, are you all right?"

Lisolette looked over the railing through the narrow space between the flights of steps. She could just see Harry Jernigan on the landing below. "We're coming right away, Harry—little Martin fell down and his shoe came off." The three-year-old was busily trying to wedge his foot back into the tied shoe while five-year-old Chris looked on in disgust.

"Lisa, please hurry up." It was Linda's voice. Lisolette peered down over the railing again. Linda was holding onto Jernigan's hand, looking up at them, her mouth pursed in impatience. How like the very young, Lisolette thought—to so recently have been in danger of their lives and to have forgotten it already. "He'll try to put it back on by himself," Linda continued primly. "He always does and he's too young."

Jernigan's voice had a note of urgency in it. "Better hurry him along, Miss Mueller. We'll wait until you catch up."

Chris, quite unconcerned with all that was going on, was investigating the folds of fire hose locked in a frame bolted into the concrete wall. He started to play with the lock. Lisolette told him to stop and then knelt to help Martin put his shoe back on.

She was off balance when the explosion came. The blast threw her over little Martin, who cried out in sudden terror. She lay there for a moment, slightly dazed; then there was another blast several stories above her and all the lights in the stairwell abruptly went out. She heard a steady roaring sound for a moment and the concrete landing rocked beneath her. The roaring gradually stopped and she struggled to her knees. Chris was tugging at her skirts and crying, "Lisa! Lisa!" The air was filled with masonry dust. She couldn't see but fortunately she had her hands on little Martin. As she stood up, she felt the concrete slab that formed the landing quiver and cant slightly away from the wall behind her. She felt for both Chris and Martin in the darkness and hung on to them. The slight movement of the landing stopped. There was no sound but that of falling debris and little Martin, who was wailing at the top of his lungs.

"My God," she whispered to herself. "My God, what happened?"

"Miss Mueller!" Jernigan shouted up at her from the darkness. "Miss Mueller, are you all right?"

"I think so!" she shouted back. Her voice sounded odd; it didn't sound as it had before in the stairwell. There was, she realized with an abrupt sense of alarm, a lack of echo. "Harry, what happened?"

His voice was urgent. "The children—how are the children?"

"Frightened, but no one's hurt. My God, Harry, what happened?"

"High-pressure steam line explosion. When one of those

goes, it's like a bomb." There was sudden fear in his voice. "Miss Mueller, don't walk too near the edge of your landing."

The dust was settling now and where the wall had been on the other side of the stairwell was blackness. Air was blowing in at her, an odd mixture of cold air and drops of hot water. The condensing steam, she thought. But the cold air?

Her eyes were adjusting to the darkness now and she realized it wasn't completely dark. The wall that had stood between the stairwell and the utility core itself had vanished for a distance of three or four floors around her. The building wall remained behind her but in front there was . . . nothing.

It was then that she realized the explosion had shattered the flight of steps that led down to Jernigan's position. The stairs were concrete risers cast on a central "I" beam and for several floors the steps had disappeared, the beams themselves half torn from the wall. Lisolette, for all practical purposes, was suspended on a concrete platform some twenty feet above the one where Jernigan stood. In front of her there was a sheer drop to the bottom of the core itself.

"Take me down; I want to go down!" Chris screamed.

She held them both close to her. "Hush now. In a minute, Lisa will take care of you." The platform beneath her trembled again and she gasped involuntarily. Below her she could hear Jernigan say, "Linda, go into the corridor. I'll follow you in a minute."

"No, no," Linda sobbed. "What about Chris and Martin?"

"Do as he says," Lisolette shouted. "I'll take care of Chris and Martin."

She could see now by the flickering light in the well and looked around her. Behind her was the fire door leading into the building proper. She tugged at it and realized it was still locked. Then she thought with a feeling of panic that the fire must be just beyond; the doorknob was hot to the touch.

There was an ominous rumbling; she grabbed the two

children and huddled against the wall. Just opposite her, part of the shear wall of the utility core seemed to shake itself. As she watched, it suddenly dissolved and great chunks of masonry tumbled down into the shaft. Dust rose from the very bottom of the well and she began to cough. The children clung to her tightly, too frightened to even cry.

She stood quietly for a moment, then realized she had closed her eyes the moment the wall had started to fall in toward her. She opened them and gasped. Part of the external shear wall had collapsed for several floors and she was looking out into the night sky, her little landing platform now canting dangerously out into the void. Only the steel reinforcement rods that threaded through the platform into the inner wall saved them from plummeting down eighteen stories to the bottom of the well. And Jernigan and Linda?

"Turn around, children," she told the two boys. "Face the wall." She could not let them see that terrible drop. She forced herself to walk to the railing and look over at the landing twenty feet below them. It was canting now, too, and littered with chunks of debris, some of them the size of a watermelon. There was no sign of Jernigan or Linda.

She felt her own landing quiver again and concrete dust came up in little puffs from where the landing butted against the interior wall. She couldn't stay there, she realized. The platform would pull away from the wall soon, or perhaps part of the wall itself would go.

"Miss Mueller, for God's sake, are you all right?" It was Jernigan's voice and now he apparently had a flashlight and was beaming it up at her platform. She leaned cautiously over the railing again and glanced down. He was standing amid the debris, looking up searching for her, trying to find her in the beam of his flashlight. Behind him, there was light coming from the stairwell door. She guessed, correctly, that firemen were working in the corridor just beyond. Jernigan's landing must have been the one the two firemen had been heading for.

"Where's Linda?"

"Safe inside," Jernigan shouted. "I saw racks opening in the outer wall and we ducked just in time. Miss Mueller, we've got to get you and the children down from there. That landing won't hold much longer."

"How?" she called.

"Can you drop the children to me?"

She felt her breath catch in her throat. "It's twenty feet, Harry! And if you miss . . ."

"We'll have to chance that. Miss Mueller—I promise you I won't miss."

"It's too risky!" she cried.

"It's the only way!" Jernigan yelled back. Lisa started to protest and then felt the landing wrench slightly farther away from the holding wall. She turned quickly to Chris. He couldn't weigh more than fifty pounds, she thought, but what Jernigan expected her to do would tax her strength, to say nothing of his.

"Chris," she said softly, "can you close your eyes and make yourself very stiff, as stiff as a board?"

"You're going to drop me!" he accused.

She felt like crying. "Mr. Jernigan is very, very strong, Chris. He'll catch you. But you mustn't wriggle or twist. Can you do it?"

"Do I have to?" he asked rebelliously.

She could feel the tears gathering inside her. "Yes, Chris."

He nodded and clenched his fists and stood as erect and stiff as a soldier. "Close your eyes, Chris—that's very good. Don't open them until you feel Mr. Jernigan's arms around you." She tried to maintain the calm in her voice. Then she picked him up as if he were a statue. She could feel his body quivering with the tension and for a moment she felt the heavy thump of his heart against her chest.

She looked over the railing to where Jernigan stood twenty feet below with his arms outstretched over the abyss. She prayed silently to herself as she lifted Chris up and over the railing. Her arms fought his weight and she remembered the past with the *Turnverein* in St. Louis. Thank God for the residual strength from those grueling days. She held Chris suspended over the void, positioned him as carefully as she could, and dropped him.

He fell as though in slow motion. She saw Jernigan flex his knees and then the boy's body struck his arms. For a brief moment it seemed like they were both going to go over. Then Chris was a wriggling mass of flesh, clutching frantically at Jernigan. He sank to his knees, holding the boy around the waist while Chris clung to his neck.

"He's okay!" Jernigan shouted triumphantly. A fireman appeared behind him and led Chris away. Jernigan straightened up and rotated an arm. "Christ, I think I pulled a muscle."

"Can you catch little Martin?"

"I think so—I have to."

After that, Lisolette thought, the situation would become very grim indeed. She could hardly jump as the children had done and hope that Jernigan could catch her. Somehow, she would have to get down on her own. She turned to Martin.

"No!" he screamed, wriggling out of her grasp. "I won't! I won't!" She grabbed for him and he struggled hysterically. Beneath them, the concrete landing shuddered and dipped slightly farther toward the yawning core.

"Harry! I can't drop Martin, I'll have to bring him down myself!"

"Miss Mueller, there's no way!" Jernigan shouted from below.

She glanced frantically around the landing, then suddenly saw the racked fire hose. The frame was now loose in the wall. "Yes, there is!" she shouted to Jernigan. She left Martin sobbing on the floor and ran to the hose. The wind was driving snow into the utility core and she could feel dampness spread over the back of her dress. She wrenched at the rack and it came free from the wall. She pulled the hose away from its retainer rod and began to feed it over the railing. Jernigan grabbed it from below and began to pull. In seconds, the full length was played out. Lisolette eyed the coupling that held the end of the hose and decided it would be strong enough. It had to be;

she didn't have time to devise another anchor in any case.

She began to rip strips of cloth from the bottom of her dress. Her nice dress, she thought; the one she had bought especially for the dinner with Harlee. But there was no way out of it; the dress was ruined anyway. As soon as she had half a dozen stout strips of cloth, she called to Martin. "Come here, son."

"No!" he cried.

"Come over here and put your arms around Lisa's neck," she coaxed. "That's a good boy. But stand behind me and do it."

Martin dubiously walked behind her and before he could wriggle away, she grabbed his wrists and bound them with one of the strips. He jerked back, nearly choking her. As he struggled, she reached behind and circled his body with two of the strips tied together, then brought them around to the front and knotted them at her waist. It was crude but when she had finished, Martin was firmly bound to her back.

She walked to the railing and ran her fingers over the rough surface of the hose. Her palms were wet with perspiration and she wiped them on the front of her dress. Martin was struggling on her back, crying with fright. She eased herself carefully over the railing, concentrating on looking at the hose rather than at the pit that opened beneath her feet. She turned and gripped the hose, transferring their full weight to it. The first few hand over hands were an agony with the boy bucking and struggling against her.

"Please be quiet, Martin," she pleaded. "Lisa will take care of you."

She slowly let herself down the hose, clutching at the rough fabric with her knees. Thank God she had torn some of the cloth away from the bottom of her dress or she wouldn't have had complete freedom to use her legs. She was halfway down when she heard the high-pitched screeching from above; the reinforcing rods that held the platform next to the interior wall were giving way and bending. The edge of the landing dropped a frightening two feet. Lisolette's heart pumped violently and for a moment she closed her eyes. Then the movement stopped and she started to let herself down the hose again, trying desperately to master her panic. All the old instincts were coming back now and she could feel long-unused muscles bulging beneath her skin. She felt a sudden wave of pride. She could still do it; she would make it.

Martin had become very still. The sense of power and competence that she now felt seemed to have been communicated to him. Then she felt strong hands on her ankles, guiding her down. The next moment she was standing beside Jernigan and a fireman who helped to free the now quiet Martin.

"Come on," Jernigan said urgently and pulled the two of them through the door where Linda and Chris waited. Once inside, Jernigan looked at her proudly in the light of a nearby lantern. "You were tremendous," he said quietly.

Lisolette smiled. "Thank you very much, Harry." Before she could say more, there was a high-pitched rumbling sound. Lisolette darted one quick look behind her, then grabbed Chris and Martin and hastily pulled them back into the safety of the corridor.

The concrete landing she had been standing on moments before pulled away from its supports; with an almost unbelievable slowness it fell toward their landing. It smashed with an explosion of concrete shards and then that landing, too, gave way. From the safety of the corridor, Lisolette and Jernigan watched the two concrete slabs tumble end over end down the utility core.

It was some seconds before they heard them strike the bottom, nineteen floors below.

48.

At the moment of the steam line explosion, four firemen were descending from the twentieth floor in one of the manual override elevators. There was no longer a dangerous fire zone on floors seventeen or eighteen, and the fire on sixteen had been knocked down for at least an hour. The men were tired and dirty and leaned against the walls of the cab without speaking. Ron Gilman, who had been lead hoseman earlier in the evening, had a badly scorched nose that was now a burned red and beginning to peel. Nick Pappas' eyes were red and watering and every few seconds he had a fit of coughing. Sam Waters and Jake Lapides were in slightly better condition; they had served on the backup crews.

After a moment of silence once the doors had closed, Lapides said, "Christ, I hope all the tenants got out."

"They didn't—they never do," Gilman said sourly. "The smoke was too heavy, even with the ventilation system on reverse. When we start going through the apartments on the south side of the building, that's when we'll start finding them."

"I don't think I'd care to be part of the cleanup detail," Waters said slowly.

"Weak stomach?" Pappas accused.

"You're absolutely right," Waters agreed sarcastically. "I've been in this business for ten years and I've still got a weak stomach. The day I don't, I'll—"

The steam explosion came at that moment. It must have been close, for the elevator cab shook violently and plunged downward. The lights went out abruptly. "Oh, my God!" Lapides yelled. A few feet farther down the wedge brakes jammed between the side rails and the cab and the elevator screeched to a halt. In the silence that followed, they could hear the thud of falling masonry as it hit the bottom of the elevator pit far below. Overhead, something that sounded like gravel rattled against the top and sides of the cab.

"For Christ's sakes, somebody got a lantern?" There was a fumbling in the back of the cab and then a glow from a lantern held by Pappas.

"What the hell happened?" Lapides asked. His voice was shaking.

"Explosion," Gilman said softly. "I think it snapped some of the hoist cables—did you hear that thudding sound? It sounded like the counterweight hitting the bottom. The rattling could've been caused by the steel ropes brushing the cab as they fell."

Waters automatically punched the call board, with no response. "We can't stay here," he said after a second. "If the ropes are gone, we can't depend on the brakes holding forever. Who wants to take a look around?"

"I'll need a hand," Gilman said. Pappas gave his lantern to Lapides and stepped under the escape hatch at the top of the cab. He thrust a knee forward and made a sling of his hands. Gilman placed his right boot in the cupped hands and held onto Pappas' shoulders for support. Pappas grunted and heaved upward while Gilman fumbled with the overhead panel, finally pushing it aside. He clung to the edge of the access port. "Give me a boost, Nick." Pappas pushed upward and Gilman muscled his way through the opening.

There was a long silence from above and finally Waters shouted, "What the hell's wrong up there?"

"It's a mess," Gilman yelled back. His face appeared in the opening. "Four of the hoist ropes have been snapped and the counterweight's blown off the other two. There must have been two explosions—five or six floors around us are blazing and about a hundred feet up it looks like half the outside wall is gone."

"What the hell are we going to do?" Lapides asked. He was the youngest man of the four and close to panic.

Gilman hesitated, then called down: "Everybody up here."

"You're crazy," Pappas said.

"You heard the man," Waters grunted. "You want to

stay here and roast?" The temperature in the cab was already noticeably warmer.

Lapides stepped in Pappas' locked hands and jumped upward at the same time Pappas heaved him toward the port. Gilman caught his hands and a moment later he scrambled out on the roof of the cab. Waters followed almost immediately. Then they both leaned through the port and caught Pappas' hands and swung him up when he jumped. They pulled him through and he looked around and muttered, "Jesus Christ!"

Two of the hoist ropes lay coiled like black snakes on top of the cab; several more hung limp over the side. Two floors above them, flames roared from a breech in the utility wall while bits of crumbled mortar and construction block dribbled down from the shattered wall. Flames were spraying directly from the floor in front of the cab and shooting up over the edge of the elevator's roof, while opposite them and perhaps a hundred feet above, a mammoth break in the outside shear wall exposed the core to the cold air and snow. Bits of flaming debris were falling past their stalled cab, with an occasional piece landing on the roof itself.

"We've got to get out of here," Gilman said quietly.

Waters smiled sardonically in the fire-lit gloom. "No shit—you got any ideas?"

"Yeah, we'll have to make it down the hard way."

"What are you guys talking about?" Pappas demanded.

"A couple of guys from the East Coast did it once," Gilman explained. "We go down one of the cables."

Lapides began to stutter. "Hand over hand? Those ropes are covered with grease!"

"We'll take a couple of hitches around them with our belts," Gilman said. "And we can wrap our legs around the rope. But we'll have to get rid of our coats and helmets and any binding clothing."

There was a moment of silence. Then Waters took off his heavy turnout coat and dropped it over the edge of the elevator cab. It billowed open as it fell and then disappeared into the chasm below.

Lapides backed away from the edge of the roof. "You're

nuts, Gilman; it's a good eighteen floors to the bottom of the pit."

"Pappas, hand me your pulldown hook," Gilman said. He took the tool and lay flat on top of the cage. He extended the hook, sagging one of the steel ropes that was free of its counterweight. There was sufficient slack in the rope so he was able to haul it close to the cab. "Okay, who's first?"

"I don't think I can make it," Lapides said in a frightened voice.

"Then you'll have to go first. If you go last and slip, you'll take the rest of us with you." Gilman shook his head sadly. "Sorry, kid, you didn't leave yourself an out—it's got to be you."

Lapides edged close to the rope and looked over the side of the cab. The core below was smoky and lit with flames from the burning floors. Below that, it was pitch black; he couldn't see the bottom.

Waters said, "Well, shit or get off the pot, Jake. We haven't got all day."

Lapides could feel the sweat drip off his upper lip. "Don't rush me."

"Wait a minute," Gilman said. "Tie the lantern to your waist so we can see." He added, "Don't slip—the rest of us are depending on you."

"Take a double hitch with your belt around the rope," Pappas said. "I'll help you down."

"I can do it," Lapides said, suddenly angry. The front of his pants felt wet. He wiped his gloves on his trousers and pulled hard at the belt he had looped around the rope, then lowered himself over the edge of the cab roof. He slipped a few feet, then clutched the rope with his legs, his turnout pants acting as a further brake. He started to lower himself down the rope.

"Don't look down," Gilman warned, then noticed that Lapides had closed his eyes.

"It's slippery as hell," Lapides said in a strained voice, "but I think I can do it."

As soon as Lapides had cleared the lower edge of the cab, Pappas followed, then Waters, and finally Gilman.

Above them, flaming debris rained down from the ruined floors.

"Remember, don't look down!" Gilman yelled once more. He let go of the hook and grabbed the rope as it swung out from the cab. He slipped a foot before he could clutch the rope between his knees.

"It's a piece of cake!" Lapides yelled. His lantern was bobbing twenty feet lower down the rope.

"Some cake," Gilman grunted. Of the four men, he was the one who suffered the most from a fear of heights.

49.

"Get a vertical shot past the hose trucks!" Quantrell yelled. Kimbrough, the cameraman, broke into a shambling run toward the street. Quantrell held his breath. If the bastard slipped on the water-covered ice five grand worth of camera equipment in the pod on Kimbrough's shoulder would go all to hell. Kimbrough got into position and Quantrell turned to Zimmerman, the young reporter. "Al, see if you can get a short interview with the cop who was standing near the young couple when the kid got hit by the flying glass. Don't let it get too clinical— play the youth-on-a-thrill-trip angle."

"Right," Zimmerman said and was gone. Good man, Quantrell thought briefly; at least he knew who was in charge. He looked back at Kimbrough; he was in the middle of the street behind the hose trucks, using them to frame the building for the shot. He knelt down and pointed the camera up to get more of a tower effect to the building; Quantrell automatically followed the angle of the camera, trying to imagine what the shot would look like on screen. It was then that he spotted the thin streak of flame tracing its way across the night sky. He followed it down as it resolved itself into the figure of a partially clad woman, clutching a mattress. Halfway down the mattress was torn from her hands and he could see her flaming hair and nightgown streaming behind her. She was going to hit in the plaza, very close to him. The small army of firemen in the plaza also spotted her and scattered wildly.

Quantrell watched with almost hypnotic fascination, the seconds seeming like hours in his mind. Then his eyes were on a level with the huge aluminum and Plexiglass light sculpture, caked with ice but still lit, before the building. He barely had time to think *not there, not there.* He turned his head; there was a sound like a thousand crystal glasses shattering.

He yelled to Kimbrough, "Get that!" The men on the plaza were shouting. Two men from one of the trucks ran forward with a tarpaulin. Kimbrough was already whirring away and Quantrell wondered if there would be anything usable in the footage—probably nothing beyond a quick scan of the broken sculpture and the two firemen racing toward it with the canvas cover.

Quantrell himself hadn't taken a closer look, hadn't been able to force himself to. There had been that time years before when the kid in the university town had set fire to himself in front of City Hall to protest the Vietnam war. Quantrell had been a guest lecturer in the journalism school at the time and had gotten close enough to the corpse to recognize it as one of the students in his lecture class. The one who had asked the most questions, who had seemed the most deeply concerned about the impact of the media on society . . . He would find out soon enough who she had been; he could dub in an excited "on the spot" commentary later.

"Jan, got a fresh cassette?" The blond girl who was with him dug in her equipment bag and pulled one out for him. He dropped it in his tape recorder and began to dictate commentary as harried-looking firemen ran past him. A brief description of the thick layer of ice on the plaza and the sidewalk with the thin slick of water on top, the steadily falling puffy flakes of snow that kept turning the scene into a Grand Guignol Christmas card, the wind and the acrid smell of smoke in the cold, sharp air, and the bottom third of the Glass House sheathed in a thick mantle of ice—a palace right out of a fairy tale. And, of course, the flames and smoke pouring from the upper stories . . .

While dictating, he glanced occasionally over at Jan who was jotting down her own notes on the scene. Quiet, efficient, in her early twenties, and a stunning looker. If Sandy left him, he thought, he might not have nearly as many regrets as he had imagined. Jan was a reporter who could do things that Sandy could not. Maybe a lot of things that Sandy could not—or would not.

Kimbrough came back and Quantrell quickly collared a young fireman who was hurrying past. "Hey, Mac, got a minute?"

The fireman muttered, "What do you think?" He tried to sidestep him but Quantrell kept getting in his way. "Can you at least tell us your name?"

The fireman looked uncertain, then paused and said reluctantly, "Jim Artaud."

Kimbrough was getting the action now as Quantrell started talking rapidly into his microphone. "We're talking with Fireman Jim Artaud in the plaza before the blazing National Curtainwall Building. Jim, how many floors are involved in the fire now?"

Artaud looked uncomfortable, realizing, too late, that he was trapped. "I've got to go," he protested.

"Just one minute, Jim," Quantrell said smoothly. "You can spare that."

"Well, at the moment floors sixteen through twenty-five are heavily involved. Sixteen and seventeen had been pretty well knocked down before and the fires on eighteen and twenty-one were being contained—then the explosions occurred. After that, all hell broke loose."

"What about the fire at the top, Jim?"

"That's a gas fire—at least it was when it started. The gas lines serving the upper floors ruptured after the explosions and that set it off. I'm not sure how bad it is now."

"What plans does Chief Infantino have for fighting a fire on the sixty-fourth floor?"

Artaud looked at him as if he were stupid. "Look, man,

the electrical system is completely knocked out, which means the building's booster pumps aren't working. There's no way to fight that fire, no way at all—we can't get water up that high."

For a moment Quantrell just stared. He hadn't thought of that. He had imagined it would be difficult, a difficulty that would make for an even more sensational story. But he hadn't thought it would be impossible. He was suddenly aware of his own silence and quickly said, "You mean that the fires on the top floors will simply burn out of control?"

Artaud nodded. "That's right, unless they can figure out some way of jury-rigging it so there's juice for the boosters. Look, mister, I've got to go." He turned and ran for the building. Quantrell faced the camera head-on.

"That's it for the moment, ladies and gentlemen. While the major portion of your city's fire-fighting force is still embattled on the eighteenth through the twenty-fifth floors, the fire also rages at the very top of the Glass House with no immediate prospects of either fighting it or containing it. I—"

He paused as Zimmerman hurried up and handed him a note. Quantrell glanced down at it and then looked grave as he faced the camera once more.

"Ladies and gentlemen, as you recall from our bulletin of ten minutes ago, an explosion of a high-pressure steam line in the Glass House rekindled the fire on the lower floors as well as starting a new blaze at the very top. I have just been told that it did considerably more than that. The explosion has destroyed a good portion of the south facing of the building's utility core. In doing so, it wrecked the guide rails of the scenic elevator being used to evacuate diners from the Promenade Room lounge. The elevator with its last load of passengers was on its way down when the explosion occurred and is now stranded at about the twenty-fifth floor with an unknown number of passengers aboard. Whether any of them were injured in the explosion is also unknown at this time. We will continue live coverage of the fire at the National Curtainwall Building—the worst fire disaster in our city's history—throughout the night. This is your KYS reporter, Jeffrey Quantrell. Please stay tuned."

He turned to Kimbrough. "That's enough of me for now," and called Zimmerman over. "Kimbrough, get some shots of the elevator. We can handle the commentary with voice over. Al, try and find a cop or a fireman who saw the explosion from the outside, from the plaza." As Kimbrough walked away, Quantrell called after him: "And try and get some footage of the cascade of ice on the west face—it makes the building look like a popsicle."

He stood for a moment staring up at the Glass House. He was shaken from his reverie by Jan. "It's a beautiful building, isn't it?" she asked.

"It was," he corrected.

"I've seen film clips of a high-rise fire in São Paulo, Brazil. All forty floors were on fire; it was one solid torch. Even the buildings across the street were going up from the radiant heat."

He nodded. "I've seen them, too."

"Can you imagine the Glass House going up like that?" She shivered.

He was suddenly wary. "I'm not sure I ever thought of it."

She laughed. "You're lying, it would be impossible not to."

She was right, he thought. In his mind's eye, he could see the Glass House in flames for its full sixty-six stories. It would be a frightening, exciting, and, in its own way, beautiful sight. A part of him shied from the horror while another part contemplated it with a morbid fascination.

"You trying to tell me something?"

She smiled without much warmth. "You're getting too involved."

"And that's bad?"

"Not for tonight. A week from now, yes."

"There're always stories," he said quietly. "They may take some digging but they're there."

She looked at him curiously and he had the feeling

that she was studying him like he was a dying species. "Not like this one. Is there anything particular you might want me to do?"

"Talk to some of the tenants," he said dryly. "Get some on-the-spot interviews." He watched her walk away, noticing the slight, confident swing to her hips. He had misjudged her, he thought. She wasn't the Girl Friday type after all—she was future competition. And she would use her assets—all of them—quite as coldly and dispassionately as he used his. He was staring at the future and as far as she was concerned, the issue was already decided.

He turned away and checked his tape recorder. Infantino would be reluctant to talk but there were ways of making him. A few judicious goads and Infantino would blow up. A little editing—well, it was ingenious what you could do with a taped interview and a splicer. He had no desire at all to misrepresent Infantino's views, just heighten them dramatically by removing the redundancies and qualifications. It was a tight moral line to walk, but news was first of all drama, a fact of life that Quantrell had learned long ago.

He found Infantino standing by the CD communications van, talking with another man. When Quantrell got closer, he recognized Will Shevelson. What the hell was he doing here? But, of course, he couldn't stay away. Quantrell pulled the fur collar of his coat up around his ears and shivered as a sudden blast of cold air raced through the canyon streets. He felt uneasy running into both Shevelson and Infantino at the same time; by now they must have compared notes and probably elected him villain of the year. He looked hastily around for Kimbrough and spotted him in the lee of one of the fire trucks, reloading his camera before he caught the elevator shot. Well, the elevator could wait; it wasn't going anyplace. He caught Kimbrough's eye and motioned at the van. Kimbrough nodded.

There was no sense trying to be social; neither one of them would buy that. Get in, ask his questions and get the answers, and then get out.

"I understand it's impossible to put the fire out on the upper floors," he said to Infantino.

"You didn't hear it from me," Infantino said curtly.

"Can you confirm or deny the report?"

"I don't have to make a choice," Infantino said coldly. "The department gives out press releases after the fire is over, not during."

"In your opinion, would you say this is the work of an arsonist?"

"I'm not saying anything in my opinion," Infantino said sharply. He pointed at the cameraman. "Get your man out of here or I'll have him thrown out; he's in the way of the fire-fighting crews."

Quantrell glanced quickly around. "I don't see any."

"You've got to have twenty-twenty vision for this job," Infantino said. "I can see them coming along any minute. Now beat it."

Kimbrough circled around to the left of Infantino, getting more of Quantrell and less of the division chief.

"Wasn't the filling station in the garage against fire regulations?" Quantrell persisted. Let Infantino throw him out; that would look great. And he knew that Infantino realized it as well. "Or did your department approve it?"

"No comment," Infantino said dryly. "Whatever I could say might prejudice negotiations between the owner and the insurance company."

"What about casualties from the fire so far?"

"No comment pending notification of next of kin."

"I think the public would be interested in knowing how many persons have been hurt or have died by this time," Quantrell said, not bothering to hide his annoyance.

Infantino smiled thinly. "I think the public would condemn any interviews by me at this time," he said dryly and turned his back.

The bastard was learning, Quantrell thought. He turned to Shevelson. "How do you feel about your predictions on the Glass House coming true, Mr. Shevelson?"

"Stuff it, will you, Quantrell?"

It took an effort but Quantrell kept his voice reasonable. "It seems to me that you would be pleased to see a perfect demonstration of your charges against Leroux's skirting of good building practices. I don't mean," he added hastily, "that you feel anything but dismay about those who have been killed or wounded."

"There's another casualty," Shevelson said tightly. "The Glass House itself. I helped build her—she's part mine, with all her defects. I'm sorry, it doesn't please me that she's going up in flames."

Quantrell motioned to Kimbrough and shoved the microphone toward Shevelson. "Do you have any other comments?"

Shevelson took the cigar out of his mouth and looked thoughtfully at Quantrell. "Yeah, you can kiss my sweet ass," he said softly. He dropped his cigar on the ice where it sizzled briefly. "I think the chief told you to leave the area. If you need any help I'll be glad to give you some."

Quantrell motioned to Kimbrough and backed away. "You called me, Shevelson, I didn't call you. You were the one who wanted to spill his guts. You wanted revenge and I gave it to you—because it served the public interest. You'll have more to say all right, but you'll be saying it in the courts. Leroux's a lead-pipe cinch for indictment and you're slated to be the chief prosecution witness. Or you will be when I tell the authorities you were my source."

Shevelson spat on the ground, part of his spit splashing on Quantrell's boot. "Get the hell out of here, Mac—and I don't give a shit if you get this on film or not." He took a threatening step forward. Quantrell turned and walked away, with Kimbrough trailing behind. He couldn't use the exchange on the air, it would only corroborate Clairmont's charges of a vendetta. But his face burned and he felt like he was back in the sixth grade when the school bully had challenged him to a fight and he had run away. For twenty-five years he hadn't been able to make up his mind whether he had backed down because he had been a coward or simply because it had been the smart thing to do. He knew at the time that if he fought, he would be badly beaten. But for years now he wished he had been a dummy instead of the brightest one in the class—dumb enough to get the crap beat out of him back then so he wouldn't spend the rest of his life doubting his own personal courage.

And then the wind came up and there were other things to think about and do. He walked back to the station's mobile van to talk to the unit director who was handling the station's live coverage of the fire.

"Jeff, we're getting some beautiful shots from the helicopter. You want to go on camera to handle them?" He gestured at the master monitor in front of him. The yawning image on the screen was an overhead shot that took in the whole side of the building, including the shattered utility core.

"Sure, give me about five minutes, will you? Kimbrough, get some footage of the elevator, will you? How many times do I have to ask?"

"Twice is enough," Kimbrough protested. "With a dozen other requests in between. Why the hell didn't you slug him, Jeff? He would've creamed you but you would have felt better. Who knows, you might even have gotten in a lucky punch."

Quantrell stepped outside with Kimbrough and watched him jog toward the side of the building. Quantrell turned, absently lit a cigarette, and stared into the snow-filled sky. His gaze traveled over the light-washed plaza and stopped for a moment on the crumpled aluminum and Plexiglass sculpture. A tarpaulin had been pulled over the shattered base and the snow around the edges was only slightly pink now. *Above thy deep and dreamless sleep, the silent stars go by. . . .*

Poor creature, he suddenly thought. Poor, desperate creature. He wondered who she had been.

50.

Lex Hughes had been almost dozing in a chair in the inner office, waiting patiently for the firemen to secure so he could steal down the stairs. The explosions jolted him from his seat and threw him sprawling across the floor. The far wall of the Credit Union, facing the outer corridor, abruptly crumbled into shattered debris. Hughes clutched at the floor desperately as the surface seemed to jump and dance and heavy desks tried to walk across it. From somewhere close by a hissing sound filled the air and a hot mist rolled into the room. Then the sound rapidly died down and it was quiet, except for the incidental noise of dribbling plaster and the more distant fall of masonry.

He lay on the floor for a moment, dazed, then slowly got to his feet. The office was a shambles. The area around the vault was still intact, but the wall separating the office from the outside corridor was gone—the thin partition actually blown in and lying in pieces across nearby desks. The far wall in the corridor bordering the utility core was also shattered, the reinforcing rods showing through the broken concrete. The lights were out and what little he could see was illuminated by the small flames that now seemed to flicker almost everywhere. Most of the corridor outside was hidden by black, curling smoke.

He rubbed his face and was shocked to find blood on his hand when he took it away. He could feel a large, ragged cut across his left cheek where flying glass or debris had slashed it. He dabbed at it with his handkerchief to try and stanch the flow of blood, then gave up.

The initial shock was now wearing off and a feeling of panic setting in. Something more terrible than the fire had happened—and it had happened close at hand. He had to get out, he couldn't wait any longer. He hesitated before taking the brief case, then decided to risk it; he grabbed the precious case and stumbled down the aisle toward the outer corridor, picking his way around chairs and file cabinets that had been toppled by the explosions. The glass was gone from the outside door, shards of it lying on the floor. It was probably a flying piece of glass from the door that had cut his cheek, he thought.

Heavy clouds of smoke now boiled through the corridor, laced with occasional tongues of fire. He started to cough. Christ, the whole place was going up. He pulled at the door from force of habit and jumped back as it fell from its hinges, almost trapping him under it. In the hallway, the dense, black smoke bit into his lungs, starting another fit of coughing. Every now and then a puff of hot, wet air condensed on his face and he realized the steam lines in the building must have broken. Far away, he could hear the cries of firemen coming from one of the stairwells to which they had retreated. A thin beam of light from a flashlight cut momentarily through the murk and he dodged to one side. He would try and get to the other stairwell; chances were all the firemen were at the nearest one. He knew where it was; he could feel his way to it.

He stooped low to avoid most of the smoke and held out his hand in front of him; the light from the small fires in the corridor was becoming stronger now and he would have to hurry to avoid being seen. He ran forward, doing his best not to cough, and in the next instant sprawled over an abandoned fire hose, the brief case spinning out of his grasp. Its catch snapped and packages of bills held together by rubber bands bounced across the corridor floor.

He grabbed at them, then realized he was on the edge of hell itself. A few feet beyond the shattered wall of the utility core, part of the floor itself was gone, the rest of it sloping gently down into the gap in the wall. Through the breech he could see the stark utilitarian outlines of the interior of the utility core itself. For a moment he was paralyzed with fear and hugged the floor, staring at the bundles of bills and the brief case lying just beyond his fingertips.

For a long moment he lay there; then he sensed a slow draft of air in the corridor flowing toward the open utility core. Scattered bills from a broken bundle of fifties stirred slightly with a life all their own, then tumbled like wind-blown leaves into the chasm beyond. Hughes whimpered and crawled forward, grabbing frantically for the bills. A clump of them caught on an exposed section of wire mesh and reinforcing rods where the concrete floor had been shattered. There was fire on the floor beneath, and in the rising heat some of the bills began to blacken and then burst into flame, setting fire to the other bills on the mesh.

Freedom, the Adriatic coast, a new life were burning up just beyond his reach. It was too much for Hughes. He got to his knees and clutched for the money, frantically trying to beat out the flames. One packet of bills rolled toward the mesh, smoldered while he was trying to beat out the flames on individual bills, and started to burn around the edges. Hughes grabbed for it, then suddenly realized his hands were blistering and his face was raw from the heat. The hot air began to sear his lungs. He tried to roll back, away from the jagged mesh and the chasm beyond. Suddenly the small section of floor that he was on tipped and crumbled. He toppled forward and caught the full strength of the heat from the fire below. For an instant he was looking straight down the core for the entire eighteen floors.

He tried desperately to pull back, his feet scrabbling on powdered concrete. For a brief moment he was poised on the edge, like a figure in a freeze frame of a motion picture. Then the floor beneath him was gone and he plunged into the smoky darkness of the utility core.

Time slowed and he could feel himself tumbling in the strong drafts from the bottom of the shaft. He felt a touch of heat and as he turned looked up to see the final bundle of burning bills falling toward him. The fiery packet of money looked for all the world like a great flaming eye set in the face of some terrible, avenging God.

51.

Douglas was completely unprepared for the explosions. The stairwell lights went out immediately after the first blast. There had been two explosions some floors below and then a more muffled one somewhere above them. It was the last one that worried him the most. He had hoped they could reach the Promenade Room and then take the elevators back down, or else simply wait while the firemen put out the fires on the lower floors.

The explosions shattered his hopes and with the sudden darkness came new fear. Albina had been terrified at first; now she had simply withdrawn. She obviously did not expect to live out the night and was resigned to it. Jesus had immediately gone to pieces and Douglas had to slap him out of his hysterics. After that, they had followed him in silence up the shadowy stairwell; the only light was that which came from the windows at the various landings. Albina needed more and more help and the rest stops became more frequent. There was little smoke at this height, however.

Douglas was now halfway up the landing to the sixty-fourth floor. He turned to wait for Albina, who was half pulling herself up the stairs with one hand on the railing and the other on Jesus' shoulder. She stopped to rest; both she and Jesus were breathing heavily.

"Come on, come on," Douglas called impatiently. "Do you need help?"

"Go to hell, man; we'll make it." Jesus sounded exhausted and Douglas felt sorry for him. From pride, Jesus had taken over the task of helping his mother up the steps. He had continued to help her through sheer grit and gutter courage, though Douglas also admitted that part of it may have been due to his own constant ragging and shaming of Jesus. Now the kid was trembling with fatigue.

Douglas walked back down a few steps and held out

his hand. "Here, Albina, grab hold." Jesus started to brush his hand aside, then shrugged as Albina clutched Douglas' fingers. Between them, they supported her for the last few steps.

"How much farther?" Jesus asked. In the dimly lit stairwell, he looked almost green.

"One more flight and we'll be at the Observation Deck," Douglas said. "We should be able to get in there." The stairwell was open at the top and the bottom and from what he remembered, the top was the Observation Deck. They could get up to the Promenade Room from there but that was by an interior flight of steps that connected only the deck and the restaurant itself.

Jesus nodded, then suddenly looked up at Douglas, his face twisted with anger. *"You dumb son of a bitch!"*

Douglas reddened. "What the hell are you talking about?"

"The electricity, man! All the lights went out when we heard the explosions, right? We should've tried the doors right then, the locks must have gone out, too!"

Douglas stared, then turned to the door behind him. Sixty-four. The machinery-room floor just below the Observation Deck. He reached out and touched the knob, then jerked back. "Not this one," he said grimly. "Let's get up to the Observation Deck right away."

Jesus hung back. "Not me, man. I'm getting off right here. I'm not going to walk up one more goddamn flight of stairs if it kills me."

"Come on," Douglas said shortly. "We're in danger here."

As Jesus started for the knob, Douglas grabbed his arm and pulled him back. "Go ahead and touch it," he said softly. "But just touch it, don't try to open the door. Okay?"

Jesus looked annoyed, reached out and touched the knob, then yanked his hand back. "All right," Douglas said. "Upstairs and fast." They both grabbed Albina and half dragged, half carried her up the stairs. They reached the next landing just as there was a soft explosion behind them. The door they had just tried blew off its hinges into the stairwell; a blast of hot air and flames followed it. Douglas had expected it—the knob had been hot and there had been the faint odor of gas. There had probably been one gas explosion earlier, the explosion they had heard above them. Another pocket of gas had probably built up by the door.

What that meant, he thought slowly, was that they had outraced the fire by forty floors only to find it waiting for them. "Come on," he said, fighting for calm. "One more flight to go." He felt his voice shake and hoped that Jesus wouldn't notice.

Jesus shook his head dumbly. "What's the use, man? I'm beat. We come this far and the fucking fire's kept right up with us." He sounded near tears. Douglas inspected the boy's face in the light from the landing window. Before he had seemed older, perhaps eighteen. Now he knew that couldn't be true. He was maybe fifteen, at best sixteen. Fatigue and defeat had dissolved the hard look. He was just a kid, Douglas thought. But then, they aged fast on the street. Thank God that the adrenalin in his system had countered the earlier withdrawal symptoms.

"What are you going to do?" Douglas asked. "Just sit there? Wait until the fire gets to the Observation Deck and you're trapped here? No way up, no way down? You'll move fast enough then, but it won't do you any good. Now come on, help your mother—we're almost there."

"Okay, man, sure. We're almost there. Almost to where?" Jesus stood up and gripped Albina by the arm. "Come on, Mama, one more flight."

They staggered up the stairs to the red-painted door. Douglas touched the knob and turned it. The door opened easily and a moment later they were on the Observation Deck. The deck itself was U-shaped, surrounding both sides of the utility core and a large, completely walled-off room in the middle. Douglas had never been inside it but knew that there had to be a door and that someplace inside that room was the interior staircase leading to the Promenade Room.

He had been on the Observation Deck before, when it

was noisy with parents and their kids peering through
the coin-operated telescopes or buying postcards and
souvenirs from the small souvenir stand. Now they were
the only ones there, standing alone in the dark and the
silence with the snow swirling just beyond the huge plate-
glass windows that lined the floor.

Jesus found the door leading into the large, central
room and they crowded through it. Inside were the massive water tanks that served the wet standpipe for the
sprinkler systems in the commercial areas below, as well
as Freon tanks for the air-conditioning systems. These
were directly under the penthouse that took up one part
of the roof, separated from the Promenade Room by small
gardens.

The metal staircase to the Promenade Room was at the
far end of the floor. Douglas walked toward it, then suddenly leaned against the side of the water tank. All at
once he felt both sick and dizzy and the staircase seemed
miles away. He hadn't realized how exhausted he was,
how far he had pushed himself. The climb and the energy
necessary to keep up Albina's and Jesus' flagging spirits
had completely drained him. Now that they were almost
there, he suddenly felt on the verge of collapse. He was
getting too old, he thought, getting too fat. It was no
wonder that Larry . . . No, strike that; time enough to
think about that later. His knees began to tremble and
for the first time he seriously doubted that he could go any
farther.

"Tired, man?" Jesus was looking at him and there was
the faint trace of mockery in his voice. He was a young
man, Douglas thought, and young men got second winds.
Now it was his time to rag. Douglas forced his knees to
quit shaking and stood upright.

"Yes, but I can make it to the stairs. You'll have to
help your mother, I don't think I can." It was Jesus' turn
now, he thought; he himself was played out. He limped
toward the steps, bringing up the rear. The Observation
Deck was a floor and a half in height and the steps broke
at a landing. Douglas wanted to rest but Jesus shook
his head. "Stop now, man, and you won't make it.

You're too big for me to carry." He craned his neck. "Besides, the door at the top is open. Another minute and you can sit down. How'd you like that, huh?"

He'd like it fine, Douglas thought; he'd like it just fine. He grabbed hold of the railing and half pulled himself up a step at a time. His knees started to go again and the muscles in the front of his legs passed from the aching point to the painful stage. Then they had pushed through the door into a carpeted alcove. To the left were the rest rooms that Douglas had missed that time, weeks ago. To the right, through the curtained doorway, he could see people. He gritted his teeth and followed Jesus and Albina into the room beyond.

The dining room that had once been so elegant and filled with soft light and the murmur of diners was now nearly deserted. Half-eaten meals were still sitting on the tables, the busing carts in the kitchen hallway loaded with dirty dishes. Crumpled napkins, partially emptied bottles of wine, scattered silver, and wilted roses littered the tables. The only light in the room came from decorative candles on each table top.

A cluster of people, many of them in night clothes, huddled at the far end of the room. Tenants, Douglas thought. They must have come up via the residential elevators or by the stairwells, as he and the Obligados had. Some of the tenants he recognized. An older man— Claiborne, Harlee Claiborne. He had wanted Modern Interiors to decorate his apartment. Likable personality, but that had been his sole asset. His first check had bounced.

Douglas looked around, found a nearby chair and collapsed into it. Jesus and Albina had already done the same. Douglas stretched out his legs and lightly massaged them a moment, then turned his attention back to the group. The leader of the group was obviously Quinn Reynolds, the hostess. He knew Quinn because of the business lunches he frequently held in the Promenade Room with prospective clients. She spotted him and came hurrying over, turning her attention first to Albina, who had closed her eyes and seemed to be hardly breathing.

"Is she all right?"

"Mostly exhaustion," Douglas said. "And a possible turned ankle." He explained what had happened to them.

"You walked up all those flights of stairs?" Quinn looked at him in amazement. He nodded and she abruptly turned to a table behind them and poured several glasses of wine, handing one to each of them. Albina gulped at hers, choked briefly, but waved Quinn away when she started to take the glass from her.

"Thank you, thank you very much."

"Miss Reynolds!" a man called. Douglas and Quinn turned. Nearby an older man was holding a small girl in his arms. She was crying and coughing; the coughs were deep and racking.

"Pardon me a moment," Quinn said, and disappeared with them toward the kitchen. She came back a minute later. "We keep a first-aid kit in the kitchen for the help and for diners who suddenly get sick." Her face was drawn and she looked worried. "There's not much in it that's good for smoke inhalation."

Douglas had been glancing around the room, a terrifying thought slowly forming in his mind. "Miss Reynolds, how come you people are here? Why haven't you left?"

Quinn looked surprised, then said, "That's right, there was no way for you to know. The explosions knocked out the scenic elevator as well as the electrical system so the residential elevators are also useless. Probably the smartest thing to do is to wait here while the firemen put out the fire down below." She hesitated. "I suppose we could leave by the same way you came up—the stairwells. It would be much easier going down."

"That's impossible," Douglas said slowly. "You can't do either."

Quinn correctly read the tone of his voice and paled. "I'm afraid I don't understand."

"You can't do either one," Douglas repeated. "Even if the stairwells weren't filled with smoke, I doubt that you could get to them now. And you can't stay here, either."

"I still don't understand," Quinn said. "Why not?"

"The fire," Douglas answered, feeling the weariness sweep over him again. "It's on the machinery floor, two floors below us. And it's spreading."

52.

It was a longer, harder climb to the sixteenth floor than Chief Fuchs had anticipated. The smell of seared metal and burned wood was heavy on the air and the concrete steps were slippery with water. The stairwell itself was ordered confusion, with hosemen and salvage crews pushing past him in the dimly lit shaft. Nobody noticed his rank in the semidarkness. Once he stepped aside as two men, supporting a third, stumbled down the steps. The face of the man in the middle had that beet-red look that told Fuchs more than he wanted to know. He must have been caught in the steam explosion, Fuchs thought, and wondered just how badly he was burned. One thing for sure: He would be making trips to the plastic surgeon for years to come.

He didn't let himself dwell upon it but in the back of his mind was the thought that Mark might be in the same fix. Or worse.

He got to the landing at sixteen and glanced quickly around. Just inside the smoke-filled corridor, Captain Miller was giving instructions to a hose crew about to go into action. Fuchs waited until he was through, then walked over. Miller recognized him and said, "I'm sorry about Mark, Chief. We've got a rescue crew in there searching for him now. It's tough going."

"Where'd it happen?"

"The last feeder corridor off the main one, by the utility core. We think the explosion may have blown him quite a distance down it."

"Think I'll take a look," Fuchs said calmly.

Miller suddenly stood in the way. "You're being foolish,

Chief, and you know it. You're the head of the department and you, of all people, know you can't let your emotions get in the way. You can't do anything more than is being done right now. If you were no more valuable here than a backup hoseman that's what you'd be. But you're not and in there is not your place."

"Nice speech," Fuchs said. "Thanks. As far as this fire goes, Division Chief Infantino is in charge, you know that. I'm not very valuable looking over his shoulder."

Miller hesitated. "If it were my son, especially without a backup man, would you let me through?"

Fuchs shook his head. "No. But if you were me and it were your son, you'd go." He pushed past the protesting Miller and strode into the smoky corridor, turning on his lantern a few feet in. It didn't help much in cutting through the smoke. He had borrowed a respirator, one of the newer ones with an automatic demand regulator that would deliver all the air he needed even under heavy work conditions. He slipped on the mask, adjusted the tank on his back, and started down the charred corridor toward the fire. Once he paused as part of the false ceiling in the corridor ahead gave way and tumbled to the floor in a shower of sparks.

The smoke was getting heavier now and it was more difficult to see. Then he rounded a corner and the smoky flames were a few dozen feet ahead. A backup team was spraying the primary crew that was battling the fire. The smoke billowed down the corridor and sought the natural vent of the elevator shaft on his left. The elevator doors were open to one of the cabs; the interior was blackened and charred, the flocked paper that had covered its walls hanging in soggy, scorched strips.

The corridor dead-ended just ahead and he backtracked. Miller had said the last feeder corridor. . . . He went back a few yards, found it, and walked down it, trying not to stumble over debris that littered the floor. The smoke was thicker than in the main corridor and visibility was almost zero. The corridor seemed deserted and he could sense the smoke closing in behind him, hiding him from view of anybody in the main hallway.

The mask felt warm on his face and Fuchs suddenly realized he wasn't getting enough air. He could smell the smoke penetrating the outlet valve of the mask as well. He felt down at his side for the main-line valve. Demand regulator, my ass, he thought. Then he felt for the mask itself. The outlet valve wasn't functioning properly. He heard it pop as it bowed under the pressure of his exhaled breath but the valve itself wasn't opening. Instead, the pressure was building up inside the mask and his exhaled breath was escaping about the seal on the sides of his face. He struggled with the mask but couldn't open the valve.

Don't panic, he thought dispassionately. You've been through this before. Hold your breath and take the goddamned thing off. Now. Thirty to sixty seconds to free the valve.

Only it wouldn't free. He jiggled the valve, his breath pushing against his lungs. He used to be able to hold his breath for several minutes, but that was a long time ago. He was feeling panic now and could hear a ringing in his ears. The respirator was a dead loss; he'd have to make it back to the main corridor and the landing in a hurry. He turned, stumbled over a piece of fallen tile, and fell forward. He broke the fall with his arms but the effort drove the air from his lungs and he involuntarily inhaled.

The next instant, his lungs filled with a thick oily smoke. He coughed and pulled in more air, then desperately tried to hold his breath. It was too late; convulsive coughing seized him again and he took in more lungfuls of the corridor air—a thick, resinous smoke with far too little oxygen and far too much carbon dioxide and carbon monoxide. He struggled to his feet, still coughing, took a step, and was suddenly too weak to continue.

It was too much for him; he was too old and too tired. He should have listened to Miller. He sank back down to the floor, hoping that the rescue team would find Mark before it was too late. Before he lost consciousness, he thought: What a stupid way to go.

53

A dozen emergency lanterns had been set at straight points in the lobby and Barton could now see his way around without tripping over the folds in the salvage covers or bumping into the furniture. Donaldson was trying to locate a mobile emergency generator. If he succeeded they could start stringing lights up the stairwells for the firemen. Most of the tenants in the lower lobby lunchroom had elected to transfer to nearby hotels after the explosions. The lobby now reminded Barton more than ever of a ship at sea stripped for action.

"Mr. Barton?" Garfunkel had returned from an inspection tour of the basement garage.

"How is it downstairs, Dan?"

"It's empty now—the tanks are pumped out and all the cars have been transferred. There was one casualty."

Barton tensed. "What do you mean?"

"It was a car," Garfunkel added hastily. "When the lights went out, one of the hikers smashed into a pillar —totaled the front end. The car's already been towed. Incidentally, Joe wants to go home. Says he's freezing his balls off down there."

Barton nodded. "Let him go—and tell him thanks. I'll see to it that Leroux says thanks in a more substantial way."

"He could probably use it, but I think he'll appreciate your thanks more."

"See how Donaldson's doing on that generator, will you, Dan? And if there's any coffee left in the lunchroom, bring me a cup. I don't care whether it's cold or not."

Garfunkel disappeared and Barton went back to his blueprints, staring at them but not actually seeing them. Shevelson was down in the lunchroom and Barton was by himself when Infantino came up.

Barton looked up at him. "Bad?"

"Sixteen through eighteen are gutted, nineteen through

twenty-five are on fire, and it's going to be slow going on them. I've asked Southport to send all the men and equipment they can spare, including shape charges."

"Got any plans for them?"

Infantino shrugged. "Not really, but if we want them, we'll have them on hand."

"And the fire in the sixty-fourth-floor machinery room?" Barton asked slowly. "There's no way of getting to that; is there? We just stand here and let it burn, right?"

Infantino looked tired. "Wrong, Craig. Southport's sending a Seagrave pumper that's a monster—it's a new model that will deliver more than fifteen hundred gallons per minute at over 400 p.s.i."

"That's Greek to me, Mario. What's it mean?"

"It means we don't need the booster pumps—we can hook it up to the dry standpipe and we'll have usable water pressure to more than eight hundred feet. The pumper was one of the items in disagreement between Fuchs and me; he couldn't see any use for it except maybe once in a blue moon. By his lights, he had a point. Neither of us expected a blue moon so soon." He glanced around the lobby, then noticed several hosemen disappearing into the stairwell. "I've already started to send hosemen up in relays so they can connect up as soon as the pumper gets here. Between now and then . . ." He shrugged.

"Any more casualties from the explosion?"

Infantino looked strained. "A rookie named Lencho. The puppy-dog type that you rag a lot; I knew him pretty well. The first explosion killed him instantly."

"Young Fuchs?"

"They haven't found his body yet, so I guess there's still hope. I'm more worried about the chief. Miller tells me he went in on sixteen looking for his son and nobody's seen him since. Five, ten more minutes and he'll be out of air."

Barton started to ask another question when there was the distant rumble of a muffled explosion. Infantino said, "Oh, Christ!" and ran over to the comm center in the cigar stand. He came back a few moments later. "Another gas explosion on sixty-four—it's really going up now." He hesitated. "One of the hosemen was almost up there and he had a walky-talky with him. He reports that the stairwell is filling with debris blown out by the explosion. It'll be more difficult to get men up there now."

The Promenade Room was two floors above, Barton thought, and it would be a while before the Southport pumper got there. Whoever was in the Promenade Room was now directly threatened. And if Jenny wasn't in the elevator, she was there. For a moment he felt his emotions start to buckle, then deliberately throttled his feelings. You did the best you could, and for the rest you hoped. And prayed.

Shevelson came up from down below and handed Barton a cup of coffee. "Compliments of your security chief —says he warmed it with his lighter." He looked at Infantino. "Didn't know you were here, Chief, or I would've brought you one as well."

Infantino nodded. "Thanks anyway." He turned to Barton. "Can we get Donaldson back up here? He'd know the fire loading on the floors just below the machinery room, wouldn't he?"

Shevelson interrupted. "So do I." He shrugged at Barton's questioning look. "I've never lost touch, Barton. I was curious how they were going to fuck it up and I've got lots of friends in contracting. They kept me informed." He riffled through the blueprints until he found those of the upper floors. "You've got five floors of unfinished apartments—"

"Infantino?"

Quantrell had walked up behind them, minus his cameraman.

"I told you to get the hell away from my working crews," Infantino said tightly. "You can consider this a working crew."

Quantrell ignored him. The faintly mocking look was gone from his face. "We've got our news helicopter up there and they've made a few passes past the Promenade Room. The pilot says there's maybe twenty or more people in the room—it's hard to tell since it's lit only by candles." He glanced at Barton, paused a moment, then continued. "He also took a pass by the scenic elevator. He swore it slipped a little while the photographer was taking his footage. He thinks the emergency brakes may be going."

It was Barton who said "Thanks" in a soft voice as Quantrell walked away. Infantino touched his shoulder briefly, then turned to Shevelson. "Five floors of unfinished apartments," he repeated. "What's on them?"

Shevelson started to methodically list the contents—the stacks of tile and lumber, the sheets of plywood, the five-gallon cans of paint and varnish, cans of sealer and adhesive, wallboard, rolls of carpeting and wallpaper, cartons of kitchen appliances packed in excelsior, a dozen other items. Barton caught Infantino's eye. The upper floors were a tinderbox.

"Once they start to go," Shevelson finished quietly, "I don't think you'll be able to stop them."

There was silence for a long moment afterward. Suddenly Infantino looked puzzled and held up his hand for quiet just as Barton was about to speak. Barton heard it then. A faint pounding from the doors to the elevator shaft, far too regular to be debris falling into it.

Infantino shouted over to the comm center: "Get a couple of men in here with pry bars!"

A moment later several firemen lumbered in and Infantino motioned them over to the elevator shafts, pausing by the doors until he located the one from which the noises came. Barton and Shevelson walked up as the men wedged their pry bars between the shaft doors and slowly muscled them open. For a moment all they could see was the darkness of the shaft with a faint glow from the bottom where burning debris had hit. Barton found a lantern and held it close to the doors. Three men were hanging on a cable about five feet in. One of them held a pulldown hook with which he had been tapping on the shaft doors. Infantino grabbed the extended end and pulled the man and the cable slowly toward the doors until the firemen in the lobby could grab the hands of the others hanging to the cable and swing them onto the floor.

The three men collapsed on the salvage covers and one of them immediately vomited. The other two just huddled on the floor, their faces strained and blank. Barton got a quick look at their hands and felt like turning away; their palms were black and bleeding.

"What happened?" Infantino asked after a second.

The youngest of the men was the first to speak. His eyes looked wild. "Four of us were trapped in an elevator about the eighteenth-floor level. There was no way out but to come down the cables."

Infantino said, "You say there were four of you. What happened to the fourth?"

"He was Ron Gilman," the young man said. His voice started to break then. "He never got a good grip to begin with and he couldn't hold on. He was the last one on the cable. When he felt himself slipping, he jumped to one side so he wouldn't take us with him." The tears were leaking down his face now, mixing with the grease and the soot and the mucus from his nose. "He made me go first because he was afraid *I* would slip. Oh, Jesus Christ!"

He broke completely then and started to cry.

54.

The scenic elevator was halfway down the side of the building when the explosion ripped away the wall below it. The elevator bucked and dropped for an agonizing second. There was the harsh squeal of metal on metal and then the car jerked to a halt. The overhead lights flickered out and Jenny Barton was left in semidarkness, surrounded by the elevator's hysterical passengers.

"What happened? What happened?" somebody kept yelling. There were shouts and screams and the sound of somebody close by sobbing. And then over all the babble was the bellow of Wyndom Leroux's voice shouting something unintelligible.

Oh my God, Jenny thought, we're going to fall the rest of the way. She sank to her knees, fear knotting her stomach. For a moment she couldn't breathe. Beneath her, the floor of the car shuddered as the elevator slid an additional foot down the rails before stopping. For a moment she wasn't sure whether the floor was slightly canted or whether it was her imagination. No, she decided, the floor now had a distinct tilt to it.

Leroux's voice roared out again over the babble of shouting and crying. "Listen to me, listen to me, everybody. Don't panic—we're perfectly safe!"

"What happened?" a man's voice demanded once more.

"Explosion down below!" Leroux shouted. "It bent the rails outward. We're jammed in the rails or the friction brakes under the cab have been activated. In either case, we're safe."

"Safe?" The man sounded incredulous. Looking up, Jenny could see him outlined against the glass walls of the cab. She remembered him from the dining room—a big man who had been drinking far too much and whose loud voice had set everybody in the restaurant on edge. "Safe? What happens when the brakes let go, mister?"

It was quieter in the cab now, the passengers listening intently to the exchange between the questioner and Leroux. "Nothing happens if the brakes fail," Leroux said calmly. "If they do the cables will hold us. There are six of them and any one will be sufficient. The hoist motor has braked automatically—the brakes go on when the electricity is shut off."

"That's great," the man said sarcastically. "So how the hell do we get down?"

"We don't," Leroux said. "We wait out the fire and then they hoist us back up."

Jenny recognized Thelma's voice next. "We can't get down, Wyn?"

Leroux spoke directly to her. "I'm afraid not, Thelma. The rails are gone below us. We'll have to wait until they can activate the hoist motor. Right now the power is out—the explosion must have cut the electric lines."

"Just great," the man muttered sourly. "We hang out here and freeze." Jenny suddenly realized two things— the cab was noticeably cooler and the man seemed more calm. She wished that she was; she was still shaking. In her mind's eye she could see the cab falling into the night to scatter her and the other passengers over the terrazzo plaza below.

"Are you all right?" Thelma Leroux asked, kneeling beside her. Jenny started to get up and Thelma motioned her back, then tucked her own skirts beneath her and sat down. "There's room enough; we might as well be comfortable since we're going to be here awhile." Jenny detected the nervousness in her voice but admired the effort to keep it calm. The passengers standing around them loomed up like a wall, sealing them into a little world all their own. "It's a matter of waiting," Thelma continued. "To let yourself be afraid won't help anything at all."

Jenny tried to shut out the fear but she couldn't keep from trembling and she couldn't control her voice.

"I'm scared stiff," she said, and bit her lip to keep back the sobs she felt within. She fought them back for a minute, acutely aware of the passengers around them. She now knew what it meant when they said a dog could smell a person's fear—the cab stank of it. "I guess I don't have your fortitude."

Thelma was silent for a moment, then laughed a little. Her voice was easier now, even more in control. "I'm being unfair. Perhaps I feel less fear because I know I've lived the most of my life and you've yet to really start yours."

It wasn't philosophic, it was personal, Jenny suddenly thought. The idea caught at her for a moment and she became slightly less aware of the people pressing around them. "You mean Craig and I," she said flatly, not quite sure whether she welcomed the chance to talk about it or resented the statement as an intrusion of her privacy. "We've been married two years."

"Really?"

For a moment it seemed like the car was moving again and Jenny caught her breath, then forced herself to talk, anything to take her mind off of being suspended in space. If she let herself think about it she was deathly afraid she would come down with screaming hysterics.

"No—not really, I guess. I have competition. Craig's job." She realized what she had said as soon as she had said it, and whom she had said it to. But it was true and she had been wanting to say it for two years.

"I know," Thelma said quietly. "Jobs have a way of being more demanding than any mistress. If they had a choice I sometimes think a new wife would prefer their husbands have a mistress. At least their time demands are predictable."

Jenny flushed. It had been common gossip in the company.

Thelma laughed quietly in the dark, in contrast to the muffled sobbing around them. "Of course I know. I'm hardly that isolated. And it's not the sort of thing a man can keep from his wife."

"I could never tolerate that," Jenny said stiffly.

"Any more than you can tolerate Craig's present mistress—his work?"

Somebody had started praying in the darkness of the cab above them. Jenny felt her mind start to wander back to the reality of their situation and forced herself to return to the conversation. One thing was true—there was something about Thelma that invited confidences. "All right—it's true that we're not doing very well. That's easy enough to guess."

Thelma placed her hand lightly on Jenny's shoulder. "It's not what you expected of marriage, is it? But then, most women are raised with romantically outrageous ideas of what marriage should be like. At least my generation was. We were never taught that men are human and have weaknesses just as women do. Perhaps more of them."

Thelma was probably just as frightened as she was, Jenny thought; talking probably eased her fears as well. The idea suddenly lent her a sense of equality. "I don't know if you would call it a weakness to lead two lives —his professional one and his home life. I'm not invited to participate in the one and there's very little of the other left to me."

"That sounds like a damaged ego," Thelma accused. "The sudden realization that you are not the center of his whole life. Men need to be dedicated to something. I learned long ago that there was only a part of Wyn's life in which I could play a role. The rest was forever closed to me."

"That's inhuman."

"No, it's very human. Why should Craig devote his every waking moment to you? He's a person in his own right."

"I'm a person in *my* own right," Jenny protested fiercely.

There was a babble of shouting above them and then the sound of a sudden, hard slap. "Get control of yourself," Leroux suddenly said in a loud voice, his tone icy. "There's not a damned thing you can do."

"Build a world that centers around you," Thelma said quietly. "There are a thousand things that can go into that world. Only save a part of it to overlap with his. He can't think of you all the time and you must grant him the privilege of neglecting you occasionally."

"Doesn't he love me?"

Thelma was silent for a moment, then said "Only you can answer that. But first I would consider carefully exactly what you mean by love."

Jenny was about to reply when there was another distant, muffled explosion. Something heavy clattered to the roof of the elevator and the cab shuddered and slid downward a few inches.

"That was an explosion!" the big man shouted. "Where the hell was it?"

"Higher up," Leroux said in a strained voice. "I don't know where."

"Look!" somebody shouted.

Through the glass side of the cab, Jenny saw two thick snakes coil past and drop into the night, slamming back against the elevator itself.

"The cables!" a man yelled. "Two of the damned cables have been cut!"

Life was suddenly frighteningly real to Jenny again. *Please God,* she thought, *don't let us fall. Please.*

55.

Quinn Reynolds pushed a lock of hair out of her eyes and realized that her hairdo had collapsed. Her formerly neat dress was wrinkled and stained in a dozen places. Not that anybody had noticed or that she herself cared —there were far more important things to worry about. Smoke had started to seep into the restaurant and several tenants who had straggled up from the lower floors reported, as had Douglas, that the machinery floor below the Observation Deck was ablaze. She couldn't imagine how they had managed to get past the machinery-room landing which was open to the flames but they had. Probably held their breath and ran, with all the risks that that entailed. One of the older men was badly burned on his right arm and two of the women were coughing badly. The kitchen first-aid kit had been of some help in treating the burn but useless when it came to smoke inhalation.

There were now almost fifty people in the restaurant, the majority of them tenants who had come up from the floors below. Several of them had minor burns and a few had inhaled too much smoke. The one that worried her the most was the little girl. Her father had brought her up shortly after the explosion on the machinery floor. She was having a great deal of trouble breathing and was only half conscious at the time. Quinn had done what she could for her and then the interior decorator . . . Douglas . . . had taken over. At one point, Quinn saw that he was giving the girl artificial respiration, using the old method.

Odd, Quinn thought, she had known Douglas from the numerous times he had had lunch in the room but had never figured him as one who could take over in an emergency. But that seemed to be exactly what he was doing. He was working with the girl now, looking up only to give brief orders to the olive-skinned boy who hovered nearby. She watched as Jesus went into the kitchen with boxes of candles and began to replace the ones that had burned down at the various tables. He would glance at Douglas occasionally, his face a study of conflicting emotions, and Quinn wondered what their relationship might be. She had known other relationships of *that* sort and inevitably it was the boy who held the whip hand. This seemed to be much more even-handed.

There was nothing she could do elsewhere in the room at the moment. Quinn walked over to Douglas and knelt beside him. "How is she?"

"She's taken in a lot of smoke," Douglas said, worried. "I was afraid she had stopped breathing there for a moment."

"Is there anything I can do?"

"No—Jesus will help you with the other diners if you need him. Just tell him what you want to do." He sniffed the air. "It's getting pretty stuffy in here; we may have to break out a window for ventilation." He looked back down at the girl and shook his head. "We've got to get her out of here."

The father standing nearby asked, "Are you sure there's no way down?"

Quinn shook her head. "All of the elevators are out and it's impossible to go back down the way the others have come up."

Douglas returned to ministering to the girl. She was coughing more weakly now. He felt her pulse and bit his lip.

"Just too much wine, Quinn." She turned. Harlee Claiborne, who had been taking care of the youth in the men's room, had now returned. He said with a wan smile, "He'll live, though right now I don't think he wants to. In any event, he'll think twice before he touches wine again. Where are his parents?"

"They went down in the last elevator load," Quinn said.

"The one that's stuck?" He frowned. "I think it would be better if we didn't tell him that just yet. Is there anything that can be done about it?"

"Not while the fires are burning; the people in the cab will just have to wait it out. The brakes held, thank God, though somebody here said the cables would hold it anyway. Actually, I'm afraid we're in more serious trouble than they are."

"It looks like it," Claiborne said. A shadow crossed his face. "I wish I knew what happened to Lisolette. I have a hunch that she went below to try and help some of her friends get out."

"Maybe she succeeded," Quinn said, trying to cheer him up. "She's probably down in the lobby now, worrying about you."

"I certainly hope she's down there, though not necessarily worrying about me." He hesitated, then added wistfully: "The world would be a much drabber place without her—at least for me."

"Quinn," Douglas asked suddenly, "are you sure there's nobody here with any medical knowledge?"

"I've already checked—I'm afraid not."

He motioned her closer and she knelt down on the floor. "We're going to lose her, you know," Douglas said, his voice shaking. "We *have* to get her down."

"There's no way," Quinn said sadly.

Douglas looked back down at the girl. "No, I don't suppose there is," he muttered. Suddenly he raised his head and said: "Listen!" Quinn strained her ears and over the mumble of conversation in the room heard a beating sound. The sound wavered in intensity as if it were approaching and receding from the building, or as if the sound itself was being carried away by the gusts of wind.

"Helicopter?" Quinn asked. "What would it be doing out there?"

Douglas stood up, said, "Jesus, take care of the girl," then grabbed Quinn by the arm and half pulled her across the restaurant, weaving through the scattered tables until they were at the glass expanse of the outer wall. It took her a few seconds before she made out the running lights of the small helicopter. It had a plastic bubble passenger compartment, the sort that could carry just two people, and as it hovered outside the windows she could see the stenciled news logo of KYS-TV on its side. Inside the bubble, she thought she could see a man with heavy camera equipment on his shoulder but she couldn't be sure.

"How do we get to the roof?" Douglas demanded.

"There's a service ladder in the kitchen."

"Let's go."

Quinn led the way and Douglas followed her. He grabbed a white tablecloth from one of the tables as he went, scattering the dishes and silverware over the floor. The ladder was a permanent steel one bolted to the rear wall of the kitchen. Above it, in the ceiling, was a small trapdoor.

"It will be cold and windy outside," Quinn warned. "Chances are the roof will be covered with ice, as well."

"We don't have any choice," Douglas said hurriedly. He climbed swiftly up the ladder and pulled back the latching bolts on the trapdoor. The last one gave him some difficulty and he pounded on it with his fist. Then he shoved the door back flat on the roof. Quinn had followed him up the ladder and was suddenly chilled by the blast of cold air and snow that roared through the opening.

"Don't try to follow me!" Douglas shouted. He pushed through the opening. Quinn ignored his warning to the extent that she could peer out through the trapdoor opening, the wind icy against her face and hair. The roof of the Promenade Room was white with a thin sheet of glistening ice and over that a mantle of snow. To the left she could make out the penthouse and the small gardens that surrounded it, the snow-covered conifers in their redwood planters oddly cheerful, a reminder of the coming holidays. To the far right was the black mass of the shed that housed the elevator motors; the rest of the roof was pocked with a scattering of ventilator shafts.

Douglas had crawled to one of the ventilator tubes and held on to it while he stood up. Once on his feet, he braced himself against the shaft, unfurled the white table-cloth, and began to wave it back and forth. Quinn could hear the flop, flop of the 'copter blades but for a moment she couldn't locate it. She looked up just as it passed directly overhead. The plastic bubble threw back a dull red reflection—the reflection of the fire two floors below, she realized with sudden fear.

The helicopter was now poised over the roof, swaying back and forth as it was buffeted by the heavy winds. Douglas redoubled his signaling. Finally the helicopter settled on the roof, its backwash blowing away the snow from the ice covering beneath. Slipping and skidding on the ice, Douglas ran toward it. As he got close, the bubble swung open and Douglas began to shout, the wind carrying away his words before Quinn could hear them.

But even though she couldn't hear what Douglas was saying, it was obvious he was getting angry. Suddenly he reached inside and began to struggle with the cameraman, apparently trying to pull him out of the bubble. Quinn could see that he was belted in and for the moment it looked like he was succeeding in pushing Douglas away. Then the camera and equipment pod on the man's shoulder came loose and Douglas suddenly grabbed it and jumped back. The cameraman immediately unbelted and leaped out of the bubble. Douglas held him off for an instant, then heaved the camera equipment toward the edge of the roof. It landed on the ledge and hung there for a second while the cameraman raced for it. Then the wind caught the equipment pod and it tilted and slid over the edge just as the cameraman was about to grab it. In the meantime, Douglas, in a frenzy, had pulled out several cases of camera equipment and jettisoned them over the side of the building.

Quinn held her breath. The cameraman had turned and lunged at Douglas. The big man grabbed the camera-man's arms and pinned them behind his back while he talked rapidly for a moment. The cameraman finally nodded. Douglas let him go and he climbed back into the passenger bubble. Douglas turned, hunched himself against the wind, and beat his way back to the trapdoor.

"Goddamned idiot!" he yelled at Quinn. "Thinks more of his camera equipment than of a dying child! Well, there's nothing to argue about now. But you'll have to help me."

"They're leaving!" Quinn cried. The helicopter had begun to rise.

"They're just getting closer," Douglas explained. "Let's get the girl."

They hurried through the kitchen back into the dining room. "Jesus, give me a hand with the girl."

Quinn watched while he picked the girl up in his arms and Jesus, with surprising tenderness, wrapped a heavy tablecloth around her. "She don't look good, Mr. Douglas." She was having trouble breathing and moaned once in Douglas' arms. They half ran back to the kitchen and the trapdoor ladder. Douglas hurriedly climbed it, then turned and leaned down through the opening. Jesus had followed him halfway up the ladder. Quinn held him from below, her arms wrapped around the boy's legs to keep him from falling, while he handed the girl up to Douglas. Then another set of hands reached past Douglas to help him. Douglas disappeared and Quinn followed Jesus through the trapdoor opening up onto the roof, wincing as the cold wind bit through her dress.

The helicopter was only a few feet away. The cameraman was bundling the girl into the rear section that had once been occupied by his precious equipment. "I won't be coming back!" he shouted. "It's too dangerous; the 'copter's too light in this wind."

Douglas nodded. "Just get her to a doctor as soon as you can!"

"Come on, come on!" the pilot shouted. "This damned wind's going to blow us right off the roof!" The cameraman climbed in and closed the bubble. The 'copter rose, bobbled in the wind for a moment, and then soared off into the night.

"They won't be coming back?" Quinn shouted to Douglas.

He shook his head. "No, Quinn, it would be too dangerous. But at least we got one off."

Jesus suddenly slapped her on the back, grinning. "What're you worried about, lady. We're gonna be okay!" He jerked a thumb at Douglas. "He'll take care of it!"

Quinn's teeth began to chatter and they ran for the trapdoor then. She desperately wanted to believe Jesus.

My God, how she wanted to believe him.

56.

Harry Jernigan closed the ambulance door and stepped back, watching quietly while the white vehicle with the huge red crosses on its sides disappeared into the confusion of other emergency vans filling the street. Its red light started to flash and the wail of its siren filled the still night air. Then he walked back across the street to where Lisolette was standing with the three children. They were bundled up in blankets while Lisolette looked lost in an oversized man's overcoat.

"I think they'll make it," Jernigan assured her. "I talked to the driver and he said they'd had far worse tonight that were doing okay."

"I pray to God that they'll be all right," Lisolette said softly. She wrapped an arm around Martin who had started to cry.

"Well, let's not stand around out here," Jernigan said. "Donaldson got hold of an emergency generator and there's light and heat down in the lunchroom now. One of the firemen told me the Red Cross has set up a field kitchen down there for the men. We might talk them into giving us a cup of coffee. Want to try?"

Lisolette couldn't help smiling. "I guess I'm brave enough for that." She shepherded the two smallest children in front of her while Jernigan took Linda's hand and they started across the plaza.

The lunchroom was surprisingly quiet; half a dozen

firemen gulping mugs of steaming coffee and a few tenants huddled in the corner. "You sit here," Jernigan said, pointing to a table by the wall. "I'll get us some coffee and cocoa for the kids." He hurried off. Lisolette found a handkerchief and blew Martin's nose.

"I didn't cry," Chris said proudly. "Only babies cry." He looked at Martin accusingly.

"Martin is younger than you, Chris," Lisolette said. "But you *are* a brave boy and I'm very proud of you."

"Boys," Linda said, disgusted. "All they can talk about is how brave they are. Both of them cried. I saw them."

"I did *not!*" Chris protested, paradoxically near tears.

"You were *all* very brave," Lisolette said in a tone of voice that settled the matter.

Jernigan returned with the top of a paper box holding two cups of coffee and three cups of cocoa. He gave the children the cocoa and then offered Lisolette a cup of coffee. "You'll have to take it black; they're out of cream and sugar."

He sipped at his coffee for a minute in silence, then said: "I suppose we should consider getting the children to bed. I can get someone to drive you to a hotel. Or maybe you've got relations in town or friends. Want me to try them?"

"Harry." She hesitated. "I have no relations in town and I guess I'm not the type to make many friends. I have no one close to me, I haven't had for years." She looked up at him. "Please don't feel sorry for me; that's not why I said that."

He shrugged. "I know that. Frankly, if you could stand a mob of kids and in-laws, I'd be delighted to put you up at my place. I've told Marnie so much about you that she's been dying to meet you anyway."

"Why, thank you, Harry," Lisolette said, smiling with genuine pleasure. "I know we really should do something about the children but . . ." She hesitated, then continued in a quieter voice: "I think I would like to stay here a little while longer, at least until everyone is down from the Promenade Room." She glanced over at the chairs with the three children in them, all of whom had gone to sleep in the middle of drinking their cocoa. "There's no real hurry."

Jernigan suddenly remembered. "You were dining up there tonight with Mr. Claiborne, weren't you?"

She nodded. "I've looked all over down here for him and I haven't seen him. I asked Mr. Garfunkel and he thinks that Harlee may still be up there—or possibly on the elevator." She shook her head sadly. "He's such a fine man; I just hope he's all right."

"The fire is pretty bad up there," Jernigan said slowly. "It's just one floor beneath the Promenade Room and they're having trouble getting to it."

"They'll find a way," Lisolette said firmly. "They will; I know they will."

"Miss Mueller." Jernigan toyed with his cup, hating himself for what he was going to say and knowing that if he didn't say it, the day might come when he would hate himself even more. "Mr. Claiborne had credit difficulties with the management here. Rosie did some investigating—all right, call it snooping—and Harlee might be a nice guy but he's not, you know, on the up and up."

"He's what they call a con man," Lisolette said quietly. "I've known that for almost two weeks now. I know it and it hasn't made that much difference to me." She laughed quietly. "I suppose that makes me a foolish old woman."

Jernigan suddenly reached out and took her hand. "I don't think it does, Miss Mueller. I think all it means is that you like him a lot."

"Thank you," Lisolette said, squeezing his hand very tightly. "Thank you so very, very much."

57.

His worries about what might have happened to Chief
Karl Fuchs had preyed on Infantino long enough. His
first stop was at the emergency first-aid station that had
been set up on the eighteenth floor near the stairwell. It
was here that Infantino discovered Mark Fuchs, his clothing ripped and torn from the explosion itself and from
subsequent burial beneath the resulting debris. Fuchs had
been dazed and semiconscious for half an hour and was
just now coming out of it. Except for second-degree burns
and severe lacerations about the face and shoulders, his
chief injuries stemmed from shock.

Infantino found him sitting on the edge of a cot, staring
into space. He took one look and turned to the rescue
man in charge. "Why the hell hasn't this man been
evacuated?"

"Chief, we don't have that many men to help the injured down the stairs. And except for a few burns, he's in
far better shape than the rest of them. Besides, he refused
to go."

Infantino turned back to Fuchs. "Mark, you're as bad
as your old man—stubborn as they come. Look, you
want to go downstairs by yourself? Do I have to order
you down?"

Fuchs's face was without emotion. "What happened to
Dave? They won't tell me."

"Dave?"

"Lencho. He was just ahead of me when the blast
occurred. He probably touched it off when he opened
the storeroom door."

Infantino stalled, trying to figure out Fuchs's state of
mind and how much bad news he could stand. "How'd
you survive?"

"An overhead beam fell over me and the rest of the
debris piled on top of it. You didn't answer my question."

362

Infantino felt uncomfortable. "I'm sorry, Mark. He was right in front of the blast."

"Bad?"

"He's dead. It killed him instantly."

For a moment the younger man seemed on the verge of tears and then, with obvious effort, controlled himself.

"That's too bad." Softly, with pity: "He was a lousy fireman."

"We'd better get you to the hospital for a checkup," Infantino said.

Fuchs didn't move. "They told me the old man was nosing around on sixteen after the blast."

If he told him why, Infantino thought, young Fuchs might never leave. "That's his privilege," he said gently. "Theoretically I'm in charge but I'm not about to put a bridle on an old war horse." He tried to change the subject. "Look, you're in no shape to be hanging around up here. Get down to the first-aid station below and if they want to send you to the hospital, go. It'll probably only be for a short while. Besides, it's free."

Fuchs's eyes were chilly and old. "Quit bullshitting me, Chief. The old man came looking for me, didn't he? And nobody's seen him since, have they?" His voice trailed off. "It was a dumb thing for him to do."

"And you're waiting for them to bring him here, right?" Infantino asked.

"You've got it." Defensively he added: "He's my father."

He was wasting precious time, Infantino thought. He'd wanted to avoid talking about it altogether and if he had, to break it to young Fuchs gently. But there wasn't going to be time for that.

"Okay, Mark," he said coldly. "You're right, the chief came up looking for you. He pulled rank on Miller and got on the floor. There's been no word from him since, and if he started with a full bottle for his respirator the air in it must be gone by now. There's a rescue squad looking for him; I came up to help—there's not much else I can do until the new equipment arrives from Southport. One way or the other, I'll find your father. We had our difficulties but besides being my superior, he was also my friend. I'll make a point of getting word to you just as soon as I find out anything, regardless of what it is. If it's good news you'll be among the first to know. If it's bad I'll let you know just as soon."

He stood up from the box he had been sitting on. His voice was now icy. "You're cluttering up the rescue station here, Fuchs. They've got men more seriously hurt than you to worry about. Go downstairs and let the doctors look you over—that's an order."

He turned to go and Fuchs suddenly said, "Chief Infantino."

"Yes?"

"Don't try being a nice guy. Just be professional. It's easier on the rest of us that way."

Infantino said quietly, "You've got a point."

Fuchs let himself be led out into the stairwell and helped down the steps. Infantino followed as far as sixteen, then turned in at the stairwell door. The corridor was slippery with water and cluttered with a tangle of hoses that led from the stairwell standpipe. The smoke was light at the landing entrance but thickened rapidly a few feet farther in. Boiling clouds of smoke churning at the far end of the corridor, past the elevator shafts, marked the present extent of the fire. Occasionally the dull orange flicker of flames could be seen through the smoke. Infantino started to cough, slipped on his mask, and picked his way down the corridor until he ran into a hose crew. He knelt and tapped the rear man on the shoulder, bellowing into his ear: "Where's the rescue team that went to look for Chief Fuchs?"

The man turned slightly and shouted back: "Second feeder corridor off this one. They've covered the others and have been working their way in."

There were two ways of doing it, Infantino thought, and that was the wrong way. They had assumed that Fuchs had started searching the feeder corridors closest to the stairwell landing, which was easier and quicker but hardly logical. Chances were the old man had gone directly to the farthest corridor, the one at whose end the explosion had occurred. He had probably been knocked out or pinned by falling debris, or else . . .

Infantino turned and ran back to the stairwell landing. "Who's got a spare respirator? Any bottles with pure oxygen? Okay, give them to me." He ran back in past the hose crew, cutting off into the feeder corridor just before the fire itself, catching the spray from the nob full against his side before the crew could turn the hose away. Then he was past it and into the no-man's land that was the battlefield for the wars fought between fire and men, the burned-out areas that were desolate marshlands of ash and water. It was a land of charred walls and studding, of thick, greasy smoke, of burned-out offices, of twisted, half-melted skeletons of fire-blackened typewriters and adding machines, of shredded draperies dripping water on smoldering carpeting. Farther down the corridor, the fire had consumed most of the combustibles, and the active blazes had been extinguished. He passed a salvage crew pulling apart the smoking remains of a pile of office furniture. The offices in the area had been completely gutted, sagging metal wastebaskets and half-melted hangers drooping from warped coat hooks indicating how intense the fire had been. The smoke was considerably heavier now.

At a cross corridor, Infantino hesitated, considering his next move. He could hear the salvage crew moving up behind him, dampening down the last of the smoldering debris. To his left, an entire section of acoustical ceiling had collapsed as its supporting walls had buckled. Here the debris was surprisingly free of the touch of fire. The collapse had apparently denied air to the fire in this section and only occasional tendrils of smoke drifted up from the heavy mass of wreckage. He was about to turn to the right-hand corridor when his eye caught a gleam of rubber and canvas.

He knelt and scrabbled away at some of the fragments of tile. What he had seen was the tail end of a fireman's slicker. He heaved a section of the debris to one side and uncovered a booted foot. He started to work feverishly now, tugging desperately at the hot wreckage and prying away hunks of plaster and tile and lengths of partially burned two-by-fours. In a few minutes he had tunneled part way underneath the pile, exposing the man below up to his waist. Suddenly the stack of debris he had pushed to one side began to slip. He grabbed a length of metal pipe that had fallen from the ceiling area and used it to prop up the wreckage. It was some minutes before he could grab the man about the waist and gently ease him out from under the remaining mass of tile and charred studding.

He turned him gently over on his back. Chief Fuchs. For a moment, Infantino thought the old man was dead. His respirator mask was lying to one side and his skin was a cyanotic blue. Then he noticed Fuchs's chest moving slightly. He quickly removed his own mask and tried giving mouth-to-mouth resuscitation. After a moment, the chief's chest heaved spasmodically and settled into a more normal breathing cycle. Infantino scrambled back into the corridor where he had left the spare respirator and the tank of pure oxygen. He had forgotten to put his own mask back on but that could wait a minute. He accidentally took a lungful of acrid smoke and started coughing. He forced himself to stop while he tightened the mask on Fuchs's face and carefully adjusted the oxygen flow. Then he quickly strapped his own respirator back on and tried to lift Fuchs to his shoulder. Jesus, what was wrong, a little smoke and some exertion and he was dizzy as hell. . . . He tried to half carry, half drag Fuchs down the corridor.

Suddenly he felt other hands taking the chief from him. The salvage crew had abandoned their hoses and ran to help him. Two men carried the chief down the corridor and the third put his arm around Infantino and helped him down the hall toward the stairwell. Once on the landing, he took off his mask and sat down on the steps for a moment to let his head clear. He started coughing again but it wasn't too bad, not serious enough to require attention. A moment's rest and some fresh air . . .

He craned his neck and watched the salvage crew carry Fuchs down the steps. He hoped desperately he had found

the stupid, obstinate, brave old bastard in time. He
watched a moment longer and automatically started to
move his lips in the old familiar litany: *Holy Mary,
Mother of God . . .*

58.

Thelma had instinctively clutched at Jenny at the sound
of the explosion and the clatter of the cables as they fell
on the roof of the cab. Then she abruptly loosened her
grip, fearful that Jenny could feel her own trembling.
The situation was bad enough as it was; there was no
sense in communicating to Jenny her own fright. She
wondered briefly how it would feel if the last cables
snapped and they plummeted to the ground. What would
she think about, and then the crash on the plaza below. . . .

She couldn't, she wouldn't think about that. Instead
she concentrated on her husband's voice roaring above
the hubbub in the cab: "We're perfectly safe! As long
as even one cable holds, we're safe!"

Jenny was on the verge of hysterics and had started
to cry. Thelma reached over and touched her shoulder
gently, as she might to reassure a child. "Don't be afraid
—Wyn knows what he's talking about." She believed
Wyn, she believed him implicitly, and at the moment she
was proud of him. He was the steadying influence in the
darkened cage, the voice of sanity and courage that kept
the rest of the passengers from panicking. Twice now the
emergency brakes had slipped briefly and Wyn had calmed
the fears of those in the cab each time. She knew that
Wyn was actually as confident as he sounded—and fortunately he could communicate that to those around him.

Funny, she thought. In a situation like this, he could
be so brave. What worried her was how he would react
in the months to come, when the challenges were of a
different sort.

Jenny had huddled closer to her in the darkness, partly

for warmth and partly for the sense of security that
Thelma knew she radiated. A sense of false security,
Thelma thought to herself. But the mere effort of trying
to remain calm for Jenny's sake was helping herself as
well.

"You're very close to him, aren't you, Thelma?"

"Close?" She thought about that for a moment. "I
suppose so. You might say that Wyn and I depend on
each other."

"You're actually content to let him have his outside
interests?"

There was a slight jiggling to the cab now; the wind
was catching at it, Thelma thought. She forced her mind
back to the question. "You mean his having a mistress?
Tolerate would be more accurate, I suppose. But what
can I do? Nag? Issue an ultimatum? It might be effective
for a while, but eventually he would look for considerably
more than he does now. And . . . I don't think it would
do me any credit. Besides, if I . . . pushed it, I might lose
Wyn. And I don't want to lose him."

"If it were Craig I would have to tell him to get out."

"That's confidence without considering the conse-
quences, Jenny. And I think it shows you want to own
him." Thelma was surprised at her own obtuseness. Another time, another place, and she would be considerably
more diplomatic. But their own immediate situation hardly invited diplomacy. "I don't want to own Wyn; I don't
think I could stand to live every moment of his life along
with him. Much of his life has no appeal to me and there
would be no point in pretending that it does. He gives
me a great deal of himself. I need him—and he needs
me."

"He'll need you more than ever after this is over,"
Jenny said.

That was very true, Thelma realized. There would be
inquiries into the fire, attacks in the newspapers, all sorts
of innuendoes. Now, more than ever in his life, Wyn
would need her. For a moment she had a strange feeling
of satisfaction, then dismissed it as being unworthy of her.

"Jenny, I said I depended on Wyn but you can't carry

that too far. There's a difference between love and de-
pendency. I think if a person does not live their own life
that they eventually end up with no internal strength at
all; and without that, a couple would have nothing to give
each other. A man and a woman live their own lives and
their gift to each other is the sharing thereof. I think . . ."

At that moment the cab shuddered and the air was
filled with the screeching of the emergency brakes on
the outside rails. People began to scream and once again
Thelma threw her arms about Jenny, half to comfort her
and half to comfort herself.

The cab began to sway like a pendulum, dropping as
it did so. Some of the passengers were thrown to the floor
and Thelma winced as somebody fell heavily across the
lower part of her legs. But there was no time to cry out
at the pain. The brakes, she thought. The cab must have
gradually slipped to the point where the guide rails had
been spread and the emergency brakes had now released
their saving grip. She realized with horror that they had
started the long drop toward the street below.

Then, suddenly, the cab jerked short. For a moment
it was completely quiet, except for a faint, swaying motion.

The cables had held, she thought, slowly releasing her
breath. But the cab was no longer braced against the side
rails. They were now dangling in midair, held only by the
four remaining cables.

59.

Barton and Infantino were outside on the plaza, staring
up at the shear wall, when the scenic elevator broke loose
from its rails. It slipped a few feet, then suddenly plunged
from its seating on the steel tracks. It came to an abrupt
stop when the remaining cables broke its fall. The cab
bounced a few times, then settled down to swaying gently
in the wind, occasionally brushing against the side of the
building. Barton slowly let his breath out. He could

imagine the panic inside the darkened cab. He wondered again if Jenny were in it or if she were still up in the Promenade Room. If she were in the cab she had taken quite a jolting. And if she were in the Promenade Room . . .

Infantino watched his eyes traveling up the side of the building to the smoky red haze that hung around the sixty-fourth floor. "When the Southport pumper gets here, we can do something about that, Craig. I already have men and hoses in the stairwell on the sixty-third-floor landing and below."

"The fire will have gotten quite a foothold by then."

"Sorry, Craig—we do the best we can."

The night had been full of tragedies, Barton thought. Certainly Infantino had his: Lencho, who had been from Infantino's own division and something of his personal protégé, probably because he needed babying. And Chief Fuchs, now in intensive care, with the first reports anything but encouraging. Plus Gilman, the veteran under whom Infantino had once been a rookie. But tragedies were something you were selfish about. And Infantino's had already happened; Barton was still waiting for his to occur.

There were more sirens cutting through the crisp night air now. There was something strange about them to Barton's ears; partly the number of them and partly the slightly different pitch to their sirens. Then one of the firemen was racing across the plaza to Infantino. "Chief, the crews from Southport have just passed the barricades!"

Infantino turned and shouted to Barton, "Let's go!" and took off across the plaza to the street. Barton followed. The winking red lights on a small parade of new pumpers and salvage trucks were now plainly visible as they slowly drove down the crowded street.

A red command car was the first to pull up. The man who bounced out was small and wiry with a weather-beaten young face, the type of face a professional surfer might have after a few years of riding the waves on the ocean. A younger version of Chief Fuchs, Barton thought.

"Chief Infantino?" Infantino nodded. "Battalion Chief Jorgenson from Southport."

They shook hands and Infantino asked, "How many companies did you bring?"

"More than you asked for. We've got a number of high-capacity respirators, heat shields, and several dozen proximity suits."

"What about the shape charges?"

"Fifty one-pound charges and a dozen or so ten pounders. About a thousand feet of Primacord to go along with them. You can't get a simultaneous detonation without connecting the charges with Primacord." He looked at Infantino curiously. "You thinking of holing through a floor with the charges?"

"Yes, we were thinking about it."

Jorgenson shook his head. "I'd think twice if I were you, especially if the building is structurally weakened."

Infantino was shouting against the wind now. "We've got some serious problems on nineteen through twenty-five, but I think we can contain them without explosives —most of the windows have blown out and pretty well vented the floors. It's the fire topside that really worries me." He described the situation to Jorgenson. The Southport chief whistled.

"When you big city people have a fire, you really pull out all the stops, don't you?"

Southport didn't have the problems that their city did, Barton thought. It was primarily an industrial shopping-center town; their fire chief hadn't had to do the budget balancing that he suspected Chief Fuchs had had to contend with. And the tax base was such that money was no problem.

"We stand a chance now that you're here," Infantino was saying. He suddenly turned toward the street and scanned the Southport equipment lined up against the far curb. Already men in aluminized suits were getting off the trucks. "Chief, where's the Seagrave pumper? None of those at the curb have the capacity."

Jorgenson looked grave. "She'll be late. She skidded

off the freeway coming in; we've got tow trucks trying to pull her out of the ditch now."

"For Christ's sakes!" Infantino shouted. "How long is that going to take? We don't have the time, man—we just can't sit here and wait!"

"I feel as bad about it as you do," Jorgenson said. "There's no way of telling. Maybe in the next half hour, maybe not until morning. I didn't stick around to see how deep she was mired in."

Infantino turned away in disgust and Barton asked him, "What's it mean, Mario?"

"It means we can't count on her," Infantino said bitterly. "It means that you may be right—we just stand here and watch the Glass House burn. There's not another pumper that size in a hundred-mile radius."

"Chief Infantino, how do you want my men deployed?"

Infantino turned back to talk to Jorgenson. Barton stood, staring blankly up at the building. No way to put out the fire at the top, he thought dully. She would burn and keep burning until eventually the fire would engulf the Promenade Room, the roof would collapse and with it the elevator housing for the scenic elevator, and the cab itself would take its final plunge to the plaza below. The scenario was already written; all it needed was time for the acting out.

Shevelson had come over and read his face. "That bad?"

Barton nodded. "The big Southport pumper is in a ditch; no telling when she'll be out."

Shevelson said: "The grapevine claims you and Infantino are thinking of bringing in explosives. Any experience with them?"

"Some—in the service." Barton felt annoyed. "The grapevine doesn't waste much time."

"When you're not getting your skin burned off or drinking coffee, you might as well gossip." Shevelson hesitated. "The utility core's not in very good shape."

Barton thought for a moment. "The steel skeleton will hold. You could drop part of a floor, probably without fatal results. If the building were reinforced concrete you would run the risk of pancaking the floors. Not so here."

Shevelson lit another cigar. "I'm not so sure it would matter; the building's a mess now anyway."

"Give a few million and it can be repaired," Barton said bitterly.

"By Leroux? It would be rebuilt with all the same old mistakes if he had his way. But this time he won't have his way; by the time the courts and the papers get through with him, plus the civil suits that will be brought against him, he'll be out of business for good."

Revenge must taste sweet to Shevelson, Barton thought. Unfortunately, it was a revenge compounded of a number of personal tragedies besides the destruction of the Glass House itself. There had been the deaths among the tenants and the firemen and then there was Jenny, condemned either to die in the restaurant at the top or to plunge to her death in the elevator cab. It was difficult for him to keep a sense of perspective and right then he didn't feel like trying.

"Shevelson, you've got a right to your revenge but don't gloat about it around me. I don't give a crap what you think about Leroux and I don't care what happens to him. Tonight I've seen too many dead people and in a few minutes my wife may become one of them. If you want to brag about how right you were tell somebody else. I'm not in the mood."

Shevelson looked faintly ashamed of himself. "Look, Barton, I'm sorry about your wife. I'm sorry about the others, too. Not that it matters, but people have been killed by the building since the day it started to go up. My best friend worked in high steel on it; a crane operator accidentally knocked him off a beam one day. Another bought it when they were pouring the foundations; he's still down there, they chipped off a couple of hunks of concrete and buried them in a symbolic rite."

"All right," Barton muttered. "So everybody's been a loser." He turned to go back inside the lobby when Quantrell appeared in front of him, his cameraman a few feet away.

"It looks like you're going to lose the entire building, Barton—any comments on that?"

Barton whirled. If nothing else, Quantrell was a target he could take a shot at, unlike the others of the evening. "If your trained seal points his camera at me just one more time, Quantrell, you'll both be picking up your teeth off the sidewalk!"

Behind him, Shevelson said calmly, "Need help, just holler. Always glad to help a friend—particularly in this case."

Quantrell bared his teeth and Barton had a momentary image of the cornered weasel. "They call it freedom of the press, gentlemen, in case you haven't heard. It's guaranteed me in the Constitution. Barton, I understand your wife is either in the Promenade Room or on the scenic elevator, is that true?"

"What do you want me to do?" Barton gritted. "Spill my guts so your viewers get ten seconds of wallowing in my problems and they can forget theirs? Get the—"

Overhead there was the sudden beating of helicopter blades and all four of them glanced up to see the bubble craft lowering toward the plaza. Infantino, who had been in urgent conversation with Jorgenson a dozen feet away, ran over to Quantrell. "That's a KYS 'copter—who the hell gave you permission to use this plaza as your private landing pad? We've got equipment coming in here!"

Quantrell looked startled. "What the hell, I didn't order them down!"

Barton and Infantino ran toward the helicopter, Shevelson and Quantrell trailing after. The door of the bubble opened and a man carrying a young girl climbed out. "Somebody give me a hand!"

Barton took the girl from him and Infantino folded back the edge of the tablecloth that had been tucked around her throat and face. "Smoke inhalation—pretty bad."

Quantrell turned to the cameraman. "Get her downtown to one of the hospitals; I can have a photographer waiting to get some pictures and maybe a reporter to interview the doctors."

Infantino held the cameraman from taking the girl back. "Sorry about your scoop, Quantrell, but she wouldn't make it without Pulmotor help." He turned and waved at some of the white-clad attendants in one of the ambulances. The men got out of the cab and ran over. "Get her on a 'motor." He glanced again at the girl's mottled complexion and the slight motion of her chest. "Maybe we're not too late." The attendants took the girl's still form from Barton and ran for the ambulance.

"We got her off the roof," the helicopter pilot said, leaning out over the passenger side. "Pretty tricky with the winds up there; this craft's too light for that sort of thing."

The cameraman who had gotten out with the girl shook his head. "Things are pretty bad. The fire's directly below the Promenade Room now and there are still a lot of people up there."

"What about the elevator?" Barton asked. "Did you notice it on the way down?"

"It's off the rails—you should be able to see that from here. The wind is damned strong and it's swaying back and forth; two more cables have frayed through and so far as I could make out, there're only two left holding it. If you're going to get those people out of there it'll have to be pretty soon. You'll have to make it soon at the top, too."

"Could you help us?" Barton asked the pilot.

"Take them off one at a time? You're crazy, man—it was rough enough this time, we were lucky as hell."

"Take her back up!" Quantrell ordered. "You're missing some beautiful shots."

The cameraman suddenly laughed. "What'll I take 'em with, Jeff? Some madman up there threw all my gear over the side."

"He *what?*"

"Yeah, I was carried away with the shooting—didn't realize what he was saying about the girl at first. We would have had to lighten the 'copter anyway if we were going to take her so he did it for us."

"That was five thousand dollars' worth of equipment!" Quantrell screamed.

The cameraman shrugged. "Don't yell at me, Jeff—I didn't do it. We're insured, aren't we?"

One of the attendants came back to report to Infantino. "The girl's in bad shape. We'll have to get her to a hospital fast—heavy monoxide poisoning."

"Don't waste time asking me—take off. If we have other casualties, there'll be other units." The attendant ran back to the ambulance, with Quantrell and his photographer trailing after. Barton continued to stare up at the building, watching the smoke billow out of the windows on the sixty-fourth and sixty-fifth floors.

Infantino said, "We don't have any choice, we'd better call in the 304th."

Barton started running to the SD comm van. "Let's see if we can shake up Colonel Shea at the Squadron. He's got five Bell UH-1's under his command—seven-passenger Model D's, as I recall."

"We can get a Boeing from the Coast Guard," Infantino added thoughtfully.

"Fine, we'll need every rescue unit we can get. Which leaves the problem of the elevator." A partial answer to that suddenly suggested itself and Barton snapped his fingers. "We could put in a call to the helicopter shuttle service at International Airport. They've got a Sikorsky F-106 that they lease out for industrial use—lifting heavy air-conditioning units to the tops of buildings, that sort of thing. It should be big enough to handle the elevator."

Where the hell were Garfunkel and Donaldson, he thought. They'd have to start clearing the plaza of the planters holding the conifers; the little news helicopter could set down between them but a seven-passenger Bell was too damned large.

He took a deep breath of the night air and glanced once again at the top of the building. They would have to hurry.

The fury of the fire on the lower floors is now waning. Most of the readily available fuel has been consumed and the added influx of additional men and equipment from Southport has begun to have its effect. Numerous crews of firemen with hoses and fire shields are steadily pushing back the fire's boundaries, slicing off small sections of the beast to drench them with water. The salvage crews follow after the hose teams, ripping out walls and pulling down stringer ceilings, seeking out the last faint spark to destroy it. The beast gives way foot by foot, fighting for its existence, but realizing that it is slowly dying.

Forty floors up, the beast is very much alive. On the machinery room below the Observation Deck, it greedily feeds on drums of grease and oil. At one end, a stack of wooden pallets on which recently installed machinery was strapped is blazing, heavy drafts sweeping the flames into storeroom and equipment bays.

Oil and grease have flowed through the various poke throughs in the floor to the unfinished apartments below. The drizzling strands of oil are flaming and spatter on the stacks of asphalt tile and the sheets of plywood below. They catch fire and the flames quickly spread to the cans of paint and varnish and the excelsior-filled cartons of appliances. In some of the apartments, the windows expand in their frames, as they did on the floors far below. The first one pops from its frame and sails out over the city. Its range is much greater since the launch point is more than seven hundred feet above street level.

Firemen have started to rig electric lines from the emergency generator to the booster pumps in a utility room halfway up the building. But it is a task that will take time. The beast is unaware of it and knows only that while below it is dying, it has found new life on the upper floors—an incredible supply of food is close at hand

and there is no indication at all that anything will impede its progress.

It has poked a tentative finger into an unstopped hole in the ceiling of the sixty-fourth floor, which is also the floor of the Observation Deck. There is little fuel immediately at hand, but it suspects there may be more in the restaurant on the next floor above and claws its way up along the painted stairwell walls.

The beast may have lost much of its vitality on the floors below but here it is very much alive—and growing.

~~∽⌒∽~~

60.

There were lights strung throughout the lobby now and Barton found the blueprints much easier to read. Buried someplace within them had to be at least the suggestion of an idea. But then, it was only magicians who pulled rabbits out of hats, he thought.

"Give it up, Craig," Infantino said after Barton flipped back to the first of the drawings and started to go through them again. "Within another hour or so, they should have the booster pumps hooked up on emergency power."

"Within another hour, the whole top of the building will be a torch," Barton said.

"There's still the Southport pumper—that might still arrive in time."

Barton hit the table with his fist. "I don't believe that and neither do you, Mario."

A runner came over and told Infantino that the last of the lower floors was now under control. Shevelson relaxed visibly. "You won't have to use any explosives then, right?"

Infantino shook his head. "That's right, though I really doubted that we would've right from the start. It was just nice to have them on hand in case we needed them. Why? I thought you said there was no danger?"

"I'm no engineer," Shevelson said. "That was an off-the-top-of-my-head answer. If I had to gamble I'd still stand by it, but there would always be an outside chance if the structure were weakened enough you might end up dropping an entire floor."

One of the men from the CD comm van came running into the lobby then to report to Infantino, "Chief, Colonel Shea just radioed that the UH-1's are airborne. We should be seeing them in fifteen minutes."

"What about the Sikorsky?" Barton asked.

"Still trying to locate the owners—the shuttle 'copter service is closed for the evening."

"Keep trying and when you get through, light a fire under them. We need that dinosaur pronto, ten or more lives depend on it."

"Can't we use the winches on the UH-1's?" Infantino asked.

Barton shook his head. "Doubt it. Certainly not while the birds are airborne and I don't know how to anchor them on the roof for enough purchase."

"Colonel Shea also said he was sending over half a dozen pyrotechnic torches," the comm man added.

Shevelson looked at Barton, puzzled. "What the hell are they?"

"Essentially self-contained solid rockets," Barton explained. "They give you an oxygen-rich flame, burn for about one minute, and will cut through almost any metal. I wanted an oxyacetylene torch, but these will be less clumsy."

"I still don't get it," Shevelson said. "What do you want them for?"

"In case we have to cut through elevator cables."

Shevelson stared at him for a moment. "I don't know what you're planning, but I'm glad it's your responsibility and not mine."

"Don't worry about it," Barton said curtly. He turned to Infantino. "That leaves us only the fire at the top, right?"

Infantino nodded and spread his hands. "That's right, Craig—but beyond waiting for the pumper or the booster pumps to be hooked up, there's not much that can be done."

"There're five more floors of unfinished apartments for the fire to spread to in the next hour or so," Barton said. "What do you think your chances of saving the building will be then?"

"We'll probably save the building," Infantino said calmly. "The top floors will be gutted, of course."

"And if there are further explosions in the utility core?"

"All bets are off then, you know that." He paused a moment. "You've got an idea, haven't you?"

Barton shook his head and pointed to Shevelson. "It's

not my idea, it's his." He flipped through the drawings to one of the machinery room just below the Observation Deck, and then to the Observation Deck itself: the large Freon tanks, the huge water reservoir for the wet stand-pipe, the HVAC system on the machinery floor, and the piping to the rooftop evaporator next to the untenanted penthouse.

"I know what you're thinking," Infantino said. "It's too dangerous."

"You don't know how much damage explosives will do to the structure of the building itself," Shevelson objected.

"None of us are sure," Barton pointed out. "But we know how much damage the fire is doing, don't we?" He pointed at the drawings of the Observation Deck with its massive water and Freon tanks. The supporting metal beams were clearly outlined in the print. "We can take measurements right off the drawing and assemble a Primacord/shape-charge lattice down here. Position three of the charges at beam connections and the others will automatically be in place when the cord is taut. That means we can rupture every supporting member in the floor at the same time when we detonate the charges."

"What about the structural integrity of the building?" Infantino asked.

"Shape charges are highly directional. So long as we don't damage the outer skeleton, the floors above will remain intact. They'll take some beating from the Prima-cord shock wave, of course. The PETN in Primacord is pretty potent. I hope the lower floors can take the impact load; that's a helluva mass of water."

"For what you want, the shape charges will have to explode almost simultaneously," Shevelson objected.

"That's why we use Primacord," Barton explained. "The shock wave travels six thousand or so yards a second along it. That means the charges will go off within a split second of each other."

Shevelson gaped. "Christ, if you blow the Observation Deck floor, that means . . ."

"All the water and Freon tanks on the Observation Deck will be dumped on the machinery-room fire below."

Shevelson shook his head. "It probably wouldn't stop there, Barton. At least in spots; the explosions and the sudden weight of water dropping down will shatter the machinery-room floor, too."

Barton nodded. "That's the point. A lot of water will cascade through the broken flooring onto the sixty-third floor below, the untenanted apartment floor that's on fire. I'd expect that; I'd hope desperately for it. But I also figure that's where it will stop—a lot of water will have flowed down the stairwells and the elevator shafts by then."

There was silence for a long moment and Shevelson asked: "What about the rooftop evaporators and the water they hold?"

"Drop the floor, you break the pipes and that water will drain down on the fire, too." He turned to Infantino. "What about it, Mario? You're in charge."

Infantino shrugged. "It's a great idea—if it works. If it doesn't I guess I'm out of a job."

61.

The smoke in the Promenade Room was getting thicker. Fifty or so tenants were huddled in a corner, near one of the windows. Someone had managed to break out the thick glass with a chair and there was some ventilation, but the wind outside was coming from the opposite direction. Only an occasional gust blew in through the shattered pane. Douglas watched as Quinn moved among the tenants trying to reassure them, but her words seemed to be having less effect. Several of the women were in hysterics and their husbands were close to it.

Douglas was seized with a sudden attack of coughing. He managed to gain control as Quinn walked over and said quietly, "We can't stay here much longer."

Douglas loosened his collar. Despite the broken window, it was appreciably warmer in the room. "I know,

Quinn." He thought for a moment. "What about the penthouse? Is there a way over to it?"

"There's a staircase hidden just off the corridor to the kitchen. It made it easy for anybody who was renting it to take an elevator up here, then slip into the corridor and walk up."

Jesus had come up behind them and heard part of the conversation. He shook his head. "No way, man. I been looking around and if it joins the same staircase, it's solid smoke. You ain't gonna get these people to go over there." He turned as Albina, who had been sitting quietly in the corner, hobbled over to him and mumbled something in Spanish. Jesus' face turned grave. "Mama's not feeling well; says her leg hurts and she's getting sick to her stomach."

"I think we all are," Quinn said.

Douglas watched Jesus for a moment, who was huddled with his arm around his mother. It had taken Albina a long time to find her son, he thought. And for him to find his mother. He turned back to Quinn. "There's only one way to go, Quinn—up to the roof. We'll have to take them up through the trapdoor."

"It's an iceberg up there!" Quinn protested. "Ten minutes and we'll be suffering from exposure!"

Douglas spread his hands helplessly. "We can stay here, Quinn, but if we do, we'll die from smoke inhalation—or worse." He pointed at the rear stairwells, hidden around the corner from the foyer. Heavy smoke started to drift up from down below and every few seconds there was the dull reflection of flames. "If we go up to the roof at least we'll live a little longer. And if it's a choice between freezing to death or burning to death, at least freezing is pleasanter."

She nodded. "All right. Is there anything I can do?"

"Gather up all the tablecloths, the coats in the cloakroom, aprons in the kitchen—anything that might serve as a windbreak. We'll pass them out among the tenants, then help them onto the roof."

Quinn shook her head. "I doubt they'll follow you, Mr. Douglas."

Douglas pointed at the stairwell behind her. She turned and could see the occasional lick of flames. "They can argue, Quinn, but after five minutes or so, the argument will be strictly academic." He turned to Jesus. "Help her gather up the tablecloths, Jesus—and look for anything that's heavy plastic; it'll help against the wind."

"Sure, man," Jesus said and followed Quinn to the checkroom.

Douglas walked over to the group of tenants, who had been intently watching his conversation with Quinn. "The restaurant's getting too filled with smoke and the fire's about five minutes away," he began without preamble. "We're going to have to go up to the roof."

"In the snow and that wind?" a man demanded. "You're out of your mind!"

"Miss Reynolds is getting coats and tablecloths and anything else that might help ward off the wind."

Somebody laughed. "A tablecloth up there? What are we going to do, dine out?"

The first man said: "I'm not going anyplace, buddy. When I see the fire, that will be time enough."

"When you see the fire, it will be past time," Douglas said quietly. "The only way to the roof is up a ladder in the kitchen. Once the fire gets here, there's no way in the world all of us could make it up the ladder in time."

There was silence then. "Can I help Miss Reynolds?" a pale-looking teen-ager asked. Douglas recognized him as the boy who had drunk too much wine earlier in the evening.

"She'd appreciate that; she's in the cloakroom."

"What happens when we get to the roof?" a woman asked sarcastically. Quick change, Douglas thought; she had been having hysterics a few moments before. And then he realized that unless he lied, few of them would leave. But there was always the chance that it might not be a complete lie.

"The only way to get us off is by helicopters," Douglas said smoothly, remembering the small KYS-TV news helicopter and the little girl. "When they land, we'll have to be up there waiting. It'll be a little late to try and scramble up the ladder from the kitchen then—provided you haven't passed out from the smoke or been burned to death."

"Look, Mac, I'm not going!"

Douglas smiled grimly. "Suit yourself, I can't force you. You've got about five minutes before the fire hits this floor." He turned and walked toward the checkroom, most of the tenants trailing after him. He could hear the man and his wife argue whether or not they were going to go up to the roof. They'd go all right, he thought.

At the checkroom, Quinn and the young diner were handing out coats, tablecloths, and plastic table liners. From somewhere Quinn had found several thick blankets and had cut them roughly into two. "Follow Miss Reynolds into the kitchen—she'll show you the ladder and trapdoor leading to the roof." Most of the tenants lined up silently and followed her into the kitchen hallway. Douglas looked around. Albina was still sitting in a chair; Jesus came out of the checkroom with a fur coat and wrapped her in it. Well, he could hardly blame him, Douglas thought. He looked at the fur. "Looks like a good fox," he said noncommittally.

"Nah," Jesus sneered, "synthetic—but a nice one."

"How can you tell?" Douglas asked curiously.

Jesus laughed. "Just something I picked up, man. If it was the real thing you could feel where they sewed the skins together underneath the lining. And you take a good look at the quality of the tailoring—the buttonholes and how they sew the buttons on, the details, that sort of thing. It's like cars, the more expensive they are, the better built they are. They got cheap customers up here; this was the best coat in the whole room."

Boosting, Douglas thought. Jesus had his talents, all right.

He turned for one last look around the dining room. It was empty—no, it wasn't. Not quite. At a far table, an elderly man was sitting by himself staring out at the flakes of snow swirling down. Douglas hurried over. "Mr. Claiborne? It's time to leave."

Harlee Claiborne didn't move and Douglas could see

his eyes were bright with tears. "I thought I'd wait until Lisolette came back," he said. "I'll have to tell here where you've all gone."

Douglas stood there and searched his mind for the right thing to say. Finally he said, "Do you think Miss Mueller would want you to wait?"

Claiborne thought about it for a long moment, then got to his feet, shaking slightly. "No, I guess she wouldn't," he said in a sad voice.

He followed Douglas toward the kitchen hallway. Douglas noticed that just before he left the dining room, Claiborne took the carnation out of his buttonhole and dropped it on the floor behind him.

Douglas pretended that he hadn't seen.

62.

There had to be room for the helicopters to land and discharge their passengers. Barton instructed Garfunkel and Donaldson and the few security and maintenance people still on duty to clear the plaza of its ceramic planters. He watched for a few moments while they struggled to tip them to break the ice seal at the bottom, then slid them over to one side of the building. He estimated the size of the area they would be able to clear, then ran back into the lobby.

The next ten minutes Barton worked cutting the Primacord to the proper lengths. Then one of the comm men ran over to Infantino. "Chief, the lead 'copter is on mike."

"Be right with you," Infantino said. They were just finishing the last of the complex web of Primacord and shape charges, using the measurements they had taken from Shevelson's prints. The web was in two sections so that two men could carry the bulky charges. "Pack those up in two musette bags," he instructed a fireman who had been helping. "Let's go, Craig."

Barton jogged after him toward the comm van, asking the runner: "Any sign of the Sikorsky?"

"Three or four minutes behind this group."

They climbed into the van and Barton heard the crackling hiss of a voice transmission as they entered. "This is Burleigh. ETA one minute." Barton grinned. Burleigh! The one stroke of good luck during the whole damned night. He couldn't have asked for a better man. Burleigh, a crazy Texas chief warrant officer who could put away more scotch than any man he'd ever met. One of the mainstays of their reserve unit, a man with two years' combat duty in 'Nam. "Mario, let me speak to him."

"It's your mike, Craig."

"Tex, this is Craig Barton."

"Didn't know you were down there, Captain. Where do you want us?"

"We've got about fifty people in the restaurant on top of the Glass House and we can't get them down. Can you bring in your birds and land on the roof?"

"How much clearance do we have?"

"There's a penthouse and some gardens adjacent to it, the air-conditioning evaporators, and a shed that houses the scenic elevator hoist. I'd say you might get two UH-1's onto the roof. Certainly you can get one in."

"Any television antennas?"

"No commercial ones; there's a community receiving one."

"Let's hope for the best, though that could make it tricky. Okay, we'll move in one at a time."

"Tex," Barton added, concerned. "Do you see any sign of a Sikorsky F-106? We asked City Shuttle to dispatch theirs."

"Just a minute, it's so goddamned dark. . . . Why the hell didn't you have your fire at high noon? Yeah, there's the bird. A couple of miles away, unless I'm watching the wrong lights."

"You've got the pyrotechnic torches?"

"I do," Burleigh said. "Where do you want them unloaded?"

Barton's voice turned grim. "Tex, that's part of the

problem. I'll need your help. Let the other crews handle the evacuation. Have your copilot drop you on the roof."

"What the hell for?"

"Give me a minute and I'll tell you." Barton talked rapidly, explaining his plan.

Burleigh sounded dubious. "I don't know, Captain. I've got the hardware Colonel Shea asked for. Three splicers, if we can get that many on the cables. One should do it, though."

"Can you make the linkup?"

Burleigh paused. "I think so. But in this weather, it will be touch and go."

"There are at least ten people aboard that elevator," Barton said slowly. "I have reason to believe one of them is my wife."

Burleigh whistled. "I'll give it everything I've got, Captain."

He signed off and Barton said to the comm man, "Get me that Sikorsky pilot as soon as you can." He clicked off the mike and leaned back in his chair, fatigue suddenly washing over him. If anybody could do it Burleigh was the man.

"I hope it will work," Infantino said quietly.

"If you've got a better idea tell me now," Barton said. Then, desperately: "Look, Mario, it has to work—we don't have time to try anything else."

63.

They weren't going to make it, Douglas thought. They didn't stand a chance. They couldn't go back down the ladder to the restaurant; the smoke was far too heavy for that. But twenty minutes or half an hour on the roof would finish them off from exposure, even if the fire didn't claw its way up there and eventually force them over the edge.

The plastic table liner he had wrapped around himself was stiff with the cold and little protection against the wind. Some of the tenants had tried to seek shelter in the penthouse, but the smoke had driven them out and they had returned to the roof, huddling against the near wall of the penthouse as partial protection from the wind. At least Larry would be provided for, Douglas thought. His insurance would take care of that, perhaps even give Larry a second chance if he wanted to remain in the business.

One of the tenants struggled to his feet and walked over to Douglas. "What the hell do you expect us to do, sit here and freeze?"

Douglas shrugged. "You can go downstairs and burn. It's your choice."

The man turned to the group. "Anybody with me? We'll go back to the restaurant and take the stairs down on the other side."

Several of the tenants got to their feet to follow and the others looked uncertain. Douglas swore and stood up. "You'll have to go down past the fire floor!" he shouted. "You'll never make it!"

"What about the helicopters?" another man yelled. "You said there would be 'copters coming!"

So he had, Douglas thought, and he'd give five years off the end of his life to have been right. It had been a gambler's lie and it looked like he was going to lose the gamble.

The first man looked at Douglas slyly. "You know, fat man, I think that's a lot of bullshit. I don't think anything's coming." He turned. "Come on, Martha." A heavy woman in a thick fur coat waddled out of the group and they went to the trapdoor and disappeared down into the smoke-filled kitchen.

"You're killing yourselves!" Douglas shouted after them.

A few of the other tenants ran to the trapdoor, looked down at the smoke, hesitated, and then walked silently back to the lee of the penthouse.

Douglas had started to shake from the cold. Jesus walked over to him. "Mr. Douglas," he said quietly, "you never lied to me tonight. Does anybody know we're really here? Are there really helicopters coming?" He read the answer in Douglas' eyes before he had a chance to reply.

"Man, people have lied to me all my life but this time I know why. At least that's something."

"I'm sorry," Douglas whispered hoarsely. "I didn't know what else to say—"

Somebody in the group yelled, "Listen!" In the distance, Douglas could hear a dull *whop-whop-whop* sound.

"It's a helicopter!" somebody shouted.

Douglas listened closely. It was a 'copter all right— and there were more than one. They'd have to have a place to land. He glanced quickly around. "They can't land with that television antenna in the way!" he yelled. "We'll have to flatten it!" He grabbed the nearest brace and started to pull on it.

Jesus glanced at the wires, said, "Back in a minute," and ran for the trapdoor to the kitchen. He disappeared inside and came back a few moments later, carrying a huge cook's cleaver and coughing heavily. "You know those two people who went down earlier?" Douglas nodded. "They couldn't have made it, man, you can't breathe down there." He chopped at the wires of the antenna that Douglas was tugging on. A moment later the tenants had pushed it flat, just as the first 'copter appeared at the edge of the building.

It touched down on the rooftop and the side door slid open on greased rollers. A lean, rangy man with a thick mustache and dressed in fatigues jumped from the interior. The crowd surged forward and he shouted, "Wait a minute, folks, just a minute! We can only take seven at a time—there'll be another bus along in a minute, just have your transfers ready!" He turned and dug a tool bag and two long boxes from the inside. "How about some help here?"

Douglas and Jesus ran forward. The crowd was starting to push again and the man yelled, "No more than seven, damnit!" He turned to Jesus. "Count them as they get on, kid. No more than seven, there're other choppers right behind this one. If you have any trouble just holler."

Jesus half smiled. "There won't be any trouble, man."

The soldier turned to Douglas. "Name's Burleigh. How about helping me with these boxes a minute?" Douglas helped him carry the cartons away from the crowd. Burleigh quickly tore them open. Inside were tubelike devices with nozzles. They looked very much like two-foot-long rocket motors. "Got any idea where the motor housing the scenic elevator is?"

Douglas glanced quickly around the roof and made a guess as to the approximate location of the scenic elevator. The shed there had to be it. "Over there," he said, gesturing at the edge of the roof a hundred feet away. Burleigh jogged over toward it.

Douglas started running after him, then heard Jesus shouting: "Hold it, man, wait your turn—women first and you don't look like you're wearing a skirt!" There was something mumbled about a "fucking PR kid" but nothing more was said. Douglas looked quickly around before following Burleigh. Jesus was standing at the door to the 'copter, helping women aboard with one hand. In the other, he still held the cleaver. There would be no trouble there, Douglas thought. He turned and trotted after Burleigh.

The shed that housed the motors and the idler sheaves over which the cables passed was of aluminum sheeting, riveted to an aluminum frame. The door was locked with a flimsy-looking lock. Burleigh pried the lock loose and kicked the door open. He stepped inside, glanced around in the darkness, and said to Douglas, "We've got to knock this down so the cables are exposed to the air—how tight's the siding?" He kicked at one experimentally and it came partly loose at the bottom from the rivets that held it to the frame. "Help me with the others."

Douglas started kicking at the panels at the bottom, then wrenching them away where they were riveted at the top. Most of the panels he let lay where they fell on the roof. A few slid over the edge of the building and spiraled away into the darkness. Burleigh took a heavy wrench from his bag and started hammering on the overhead roof panels. Within a matter of minutes, there was nothing left of the shed but the thin frame. Inside was the control panel, motor generator set and starter, and the gearless machine beneath which the secondary idler sheave was suspended. Fortunately, the skeletal frame would not interfere with their work.

Burleigh looked for a long moment at the motors and the idler sheaves, suspended out from the building's edge, and the cables disappearing down below into the darkness. He shook his head. "This is going to be a bastard."

Douglas glanced back at the tenants gathered in the middle of the roof. The first 'copter was taking off with its load, disappeared into the sky, and a second one settled in its place. The rest of the tenants had dutifully queued up under Jesus' shouted directions. Somewhere, that kid had to fit in, Douglas thought briefly.

Then there was a heavy chopping sound overhead and he glanced up into the night to watch the biggest heli-copter he had ever seen settling toward them, a heavy cable dangling from its recessed midriff.

64.

Barton and Infantino were waiting as the first of the heli-copters descended out of the night to land on the broad plaza surrounding the Glass House. The landing area had been cleared of planters and the fire hoses shifted. The 'copter settled to the ground and the door opened as the blades idled. Several policemen and ambulance attendants rushed forward to assist the passengers as they stumbled out. A few were coughing badly; all looked chilled and wet.

Infantino bellowed at the ambulance personnel: "Those that need treatment for burns or smoke inhalation, take them directly to the hospital—the others go to the first-aid station in the lower lobby!"

Barton searched the faces frantically as the people left the helicopter. "Quinn! Over here, Quinn!" She turned and smiled wanly. Barton hurried over. "Where's Jenny?"

The smile faded. "I'm sorry, Craig. She and the Lerouxes were in the last elevator load that started down."

She glanced quickly around as if looking for someone, then said: "How bad is it?"

"Very bad—though there's an outside chance we can get to the elevator."

Reporters and cameramen had started to surge around them now. Barton caught a brief glimpse of Quantrell and his assistants talking to some of the tenants as they were being escorted to ambulances. Then he felt somebody pushing behind him.

"Quinn! My God, Quinn!" A tall man, somewhat younger than himself, pushed past and then Quinn was in his arms. For a moment Barton watched them; Quinn's eyes were closed, but he could see the tears streaking down her face.

"Leslie, please get me out of here."

"Sure, Quinn, my car's half a block down—the police let me through." He took off his coat and wrapped it around her and started to lead her off. She glanced back once, said, "Good luck, Craig," then huddled against the man at her side. The poise and self-reserve were leaving her very quickly now, and Barton could see that she was sobbing.

Barton briefly thought of Jenny, then turned back to the milling crowd and shouted at the police, "Get these people back, get them out of here! Another 'copter will be landing here in a minute or two!"

Infantino had talked briefly with the helicopter pilot and now hurried over to Barton. "Burleigh turned the bird over to his copilot; he's handling the elevator up there."

"Let's wish him luck," Barton said quietly. Then the 'copter blades started to turn as the helicopter rose from its improvised landing pad. Far above they could see a second one descending.

"It's our turn as soon as Number Four comes in," Infantino said. "It will probably take us that long to get ready." A runner ran over and handed him a slip and he glanced at it, then turned to Barton, his face grim. "Casualty report. You remember that salesman you couldn't account for? Bigelow? We found him." He spelled out the details and Barton felt as if he were going to get sick.

"What about his girl friend, the one Jernigan thought might be with him?"

"Elmon?" Infantino shrugged. "Three guesses," he said, and nodded at the canvas-wrapped sculpture before the building.

Behind them, the second UH-1 settled softly to the plaza and began to discharge its tired passengers.

65.

"Come on, you mother!" Tex Burleigh swore violently to himself as he hurriedly pulled down the last of the elevator housing. The cables that wound over the sheaves were now exposed directly to the elements.

"Four of them must have snapped," Douglas said, holding Burleigh's flashlight on the cable drums.

Burleigh glanced over at him, trying to estimate how much muscle there might be beneath the man's bulk. Big men had a way of fooling you, he thought, but something told him there was a good deal of power under the man's flab. "What'd you say your name was? Douglas? Well, look, Douglas, can you stick it out here for a little while? I know you're freezing your ass but I'm going to need your help." He was shouting now, trying to make himself heard over the noise of another UH-1 setting down on the roof and the roar from the giant Sikorsky overhead.

"You've got it!" Douglas yelled. "What do you want me to do?"

Burleigh pointed above them at the Sikorsky and the long cable that dangled from her middle. "We've got to splice the cable from the F-106 to one of the elevator cables and then cut them free from the sheaves." He pointed at the two rocketlike tubes. "That's what the torches are for."

"What if the splice doesn't hold?"

"Mister, it's got to!" Burleigh began to pull out various tools from the bag at his feet. Finally he took out three

arge, slotted steel bars, each with two heavy, hexagonal
olts protruding. "These are our splices and we damned
well better make one of them good!"

Burleigh gripped a ten-inch wrench and began to loosen
he hexagonal bolts. One end of the splice bar fell open
as he withdrew one of the bolts. "You'll have to hold
nto me while I get this around the elevator cable," he
old Douglas.

"Will it fit?" Douglas asked.

"The bolt tightens the jaws of the splice. They're
errated; they'll bite into the cable like teeth. After we
plice onto the Sikorsky cable, then we'll have to cut the
levator cables free. But before that, we'll have to wrap
he cables with wire to keep them from splaying. They
ould take your head off otherwise. And if the splice
oesn't hold, that's the end of the ball game." He reached
nto the pocket of his jacket and pulled out a walky-
alky and extended its antenna. "City Shuttle Two, come
n."

"Loud and clear, Tex—where the hell are you?"

Burleigh nodded at Douglas. "Give them a wave with
he flashlight."

Douglas moved back from the shed and started to
wave with the flashlight, then felt himself start to slip and
icked out with his foot. He felt it hit something and then
ound purchase on part of the shed platform. He flicked
he switch on the flashlight several times and waved it back
nd forth. The Sikorsky spun on its rotor thirty degrees
nd moved forward, settling lower as it moved, the single
able trailing slightly behind it in the wind.

"Okay, hold it," Burleigh said into the walky-talky.
Then: "Give me about ten feet of cable."

Above them, the 'copter's winch made a distant whin-
ng sound and the cable slowly dropped. It whipped
cross the roof once, then came back. Burleigh threw
Douglas a heavy mechanic's rag. "Grab it with this; don't
se your hands—it'll cut them to ribbons." Douglas took
he rag, then caught the end of the cable, feeding it into
he shaft opening at his feet. The cable continued to lower.

"Okay, hold it for the splice." Burleigh slipped the

walky-talky back into his pocket, picked up the wrench and glanced about the roof for one of the splices. "Hey what the hell—?"

Douglas lowered the flashlight so the beam hit the rooftop. Only two of the slotted metal rods were there. The big man had slipped on the roof for a moment, Burleigh recalled; he had probably kicked one of them over the side. Douglas thought of it at the same time and for a moment looked like he was going to come apart.

"Christ, I didn't mean—"

"Forget it," Burleigh said. "I told you one would hold." He picked up a splice and said, "Okay, grab my legs. I'll be leaning over one of the sheaves. When I give you the word, feed me the 'copter cable."

Douglas found a purchase and gripped both of Burleigh's legs. Burleigh leaned far out over the shaft opening. The wind whipped about his head, tugged at his fatigue cap, and blew it out into the void. The elevator cable was cold and coated with a thin slick of ice. For a second Burleigh felt as if his hands might stick to the metal. He brought the open latch of the splice around and secured it onto the cable. Then he inserted the bolt and began to tighten it with the wrench. The snowflakes melted on his hands and made the wrench slippery and suddenly it started to slide out of his grasp. He grabbed for it with the other hand and heard the splice riding down the cable.

He wriggled back up and sat on the roof, breathing hard for a minute. "All right," he said finally, "that's one for each of us. Last try, and this time we've got to make it good."

Burleigh leaned into the hole again, Douglas holding onto his legs. The man was a helluva lot stronger than he had thought at first; he was probably really suffering from the cold, too—with absolutely no complaining.

Again, Burleigh brought the open latch of the splice around the cable. The going was slow as he tightened the bolt and once more the wrench almost slipped from his grip. Finally the teeth bit tightly into the cable. He then estimated where he was going to cut it and wrapped the cable on each side of the projected cut with steel wire he had brought along, using the wrench to tighten the tourniquet of steel around the bundle of wires that made up the cable. Then he yelled, "Feed me the 'copter cable!" Douglas loosened one hand for an instant and a second later the 'copter cable snaked down past Burleigh's face. This was the difficult part, he thought: The cable had to be threaded through the other end of the splice which didn't open. The cable was cold and writhed in his hand; he could even feel the vibration of the 'copter's motor through it. They had given him enough slack so the bucking Sikorsky in the heavy gusts of wind didn't give him too much trouble. He found the end of the cable and after two false starts succeeded in threading it in a "U" through the other end of the splice. After that, he wrenched down the second bolt until it bit into the 'copter cable.

He pulled himself back onto the roof, smiled triumphantly at Douglas, and took out his walky-talky again. "Okay, take it up slowly—very slowly, just enough to take up the slack." He waited until the cable drew taut. "Okay, that's it. Hold it there. When I cut it loose, we don't want the damned thing to drop too far."

He slipped on a pair of safety goggles, picked up one of the solid propellant torches and yelled at Douglas, "This is dangerous—stand back a little." He pulled the safety pin and then the igniter wire, aiming the nozzle out into the night. The torch took fire with a swoosh and jetted out a burst of flame for a foot. The flame sparkled with burning aluminum power while a heavy white cloud boiled from the jet. Burleigh moved around the shaft opening so he could get at the one cable that had not been spliced. The flame slowly cut through it in a violent shower of sparks. When the cable parted, the snapping sounded like a firecracker going off. Even with the wire sizing wrapped around them, several strands of the cable popped loose and whipped about like striking snakes.

The cutting of the last cable was easier. The metal strands glowed red, then white, and finally erupted in a shower of sparks. The metal sagged for an instant and then he was through. Above him, the 'copter cable sang under the tension.

Burleigh pulled himself back and spoke into the hand radio again. "It's snug down here, start winching it up. When I give you the word that you're clear, move out and up. Whatever you do, don't let the cage bang against the building."

He motioned Douglas back onto the center of the roof —no point in both of them being in danger. The Sikorsky was winching the cage up now, sliding it along the face of the utility wall. They had some three hundred feet to go and progress was slow. Now he could hear the distant scraping. It sounded closer, then finally very close. He glanced over the edge of the building and could see the top of the cage approaching the floor below. That would ordinarily be the limit of its travel.

He flicked on the walky-talky again. "Okay, swing it out now." He walked back to the middle of the roof where Douglas was standing. The Sikorsky was rising and moving slowly away from the building. Suddenly the elevator cage was in the clear, swaying back and forth in the wind and finally settling into a gentle oscillation as the cable shortened still more.

"You're on your own," Burleigh told the pilot and signaled with the flashlight. The Sikorsky rotated and started the long descent, lowering the elevator cage to the roof near a UH-1 that had just landed.

Douglas was suddenly laughing and pounding Burleigh on the shoulder. "Well, what do you know," Burleigh said, suddenly aware of the sweat oozing from under his arms. "We did it."

"You didn't think you would?"

"Mister, that's something I'll never tell anyone, not even on my deathbed," Burleigh said fervently. He started running toward the elevator cage. "Come on, we've got to get those people out of there!"

66.

It was quiet in the darkness of the elevator cab, except for the sounds of one person sobbing. It was a full minute before Leroux realized that it was a man crying—the same heavy-set man who had been so belligerent a few moments before. He shivered; outside the snow and sleet spattered against the glass walls of the elevator and he could feel the cold penetrate his thin tuxedo. Somebody was pressing up against him and he knew by the faint fragrance of her perfume that it was Thelma.

"What will happen, Wyn?"

He hugged her gently and kissed her on the ear. "I don't know—just hang here for a while, I guess."

Thelma lowered her voice. "We don't stand much of a chance, do we?"

He let just the right note of annoyance creep into his voice. "I know what the cables can take, Thelma. If I thought we were going to drop, I wouldn't have tried to reassure people. Everybody should have a chance to make their peace with God without any kibitzing from me."

He could feel her relax and thought to himself that the Almighty would forgive him that one white lie. She was absolutely right; they didn't stand much of a chance.

The heavy winds suddenly caught the cab and swung it away from the building a short distance, then let it swing back against the concrete wall behind him. The cab twisted on its cables as it did so and crashed slightly askew. One of the glass side walls cracked and a woman standing near him was thrown off her feet, her cry lost in a sudden burst of screaming. Leroux tensed. The cab couldn't take much of that, let alone the cables. There were only a few left.

"Listen!" somebody shouted. There was a sharp clatter from overhead and Leroux strained his eyes to peer out into the night. Seconds later heavy debris fell past the glass walls. Leroux wasn't sure but it looked like aluminum sheeting and maybe thin angle iron. He was mystified for a moment, then suddenly remembered the scenic elevator's housing far above. My God, if it was coming apart . . .

He suddenly felt Thelma's grip on his arm. "What's that, Wyn?" Leroux cocked his head, then picked up the faint sounds. The distant *chop, chop, chop* above them. Not one of the light helicopters he had seen a few minutes earlier, but probably a big mother, maybe a Sikorsky F-106 they had used to lift some of the heavier equipment up to the restaurant during construction. Trust Barton to think of that. They'd probably try a cable splice and swing them up. He raised his voice.

"Everybody quiet and listen to me! They've brought in a sky-hook helicopter and I think they're going to use it to pull us up. It'll be bumpy and I'd suggest all of us lie down on the floor."

"What the hell do you know?" the heavy-set man suddenly shouted. "You haven't guessed right on your building so far!"

The other passengers had begun to ease themselves to the floor. Somebody mumbled, "Watch your damned knee," and finally they were all down except the heavy-set man who was still standing, braced against the one cracked glass wall.

"Get down!" Leroux warned. "This cab's going to crash into the wall a dozen times before they get us to the top."

"Screw you," the man said.

He couldn't get to him, Leroux thought. He couldn't force him down. "Suit yourself," he said shortly. He and Thelma were lying together, and he suddenly put his arm around her and pulled her closer. They would either make it or they wouldn't, and if they didn't he wanted to feel her body against his one last time.

"Listen," Thelma whispered. The cables overhead were singing in the wind. Suddenly one fell past the cab. The elevator sank an inch and Leroux tightened his hold on his wife. A second cable lashed past the cab and disappeared into the night.

"The next one will be the last one they'll cut," he said quietly to Thelma. "Let's pray their splice is good."

The last cable parted and the cab dropped for half a foot. Somewhere in the mass of bodies on the floor a women choked off a half scream. The car swayed alarmingly for a moment and then began to inch up the side of the building. There was a frightening scraping and banging sound and Leroux felt his own heart start to beat uncontrollably. It wouldn't be long now, he thought. They were almost there. What incredible irony if in the last moment . . . No, he mustn't think of that.

They were abreast of the utility floor now and he could see the smoky red of the flames. Then they started to swing out from the building until they seemed to be floating over the city below, wrapped in pounding snow and driving wind. The cab swung loose in the wind and then a particularly strong gust swung it far enough away from the building so there was a perceptible tip to the floor.

It occurred to Leroux then what was going to happen and he screamed, "Get down, get down!" They had begun to swing back now and they were still in line with the building. There was an abrupt jolt and a shattering sound and almost immediately afterward a scream that quickly faded away into the distance. A voice shouted, "I'm cut!" and a sudden gust of cold air told Leroux what had happened. They had hit the building on the side again and the one glass wall had shattered; the heavy-set man who had braced himself against it had nothing to hold onto and had fallen out.

Leroux closed his eyes and whispered to himself, *"Oh, my God."* Then the cab had stabilized. He could feel it still ascending as the helicopter continued to lift it, then the slight swing as the cab was positioned over the roof and finally he could sense it slowly dropping. He was tired —too damn tired to even watch.

A moment later the cab touched down heavily on the roof. Leroux tumbled forward with the impact, his head hitting the cage wall and momentarily stunning him. Then everything was silent except for the whistling of the wind.

They were safe, he thought. Safe.

There were the sounds of men outside now, gently pulling the remnants of broken glass out of the one side wall. Then people were struggling to their feet and helping hands were pulling them out of the cage. Thelma said, "We're safe, Wyn," and suddenly she began to cry.

He wrapped his arms around her for a moment and then they were stepping through the shattered side wall. His mind was already on other things.

They were all safe, he thought. All but himself. On the ground below would be the reporters and the fire inspectors and probably a team flown in from Washington.

All safe, he thought again.

Except for himself.

67.

Barton was still struggling into his aluminized proximity suit when the evacuation UH-1 settled down on the plaza to discharge its passengers. Infantino was already into his suit and impatient for Barton to finish.

"Any more information from the Sikorsky?" Barton asked.

"Just that Burleigh is working at the linkup. By the time we get up there, maybe they'll have beat us with the elevator. One thing for sure; we can't blow these charges with people on the roof. Here, let me help you with your respirator." He stepped behind Barton and adjusted the straps.

"Did you get your men out of the stairwells?"

"The upper floors have been cleared—I don't think we need to worry about the lower ones."

"What about the streets below?"

"The police have been given their orders." He frowned. "I shouldn't be letting you go on this one."

"You have somebody else who knows how to handle explosives—and who knows the building?"

The copilot of the waiting UH-1 ran up. "Okay, they're all off but the elevator passengers. You men ready?"

Barton nodded. He recognized the copilot from his weekend reserve work when he had been with the squadron but couldn't remember his name. He'd won thirty dollars from him in a poker game one night—that he recalled. But the name was a blank. He gathered up the heavy canvas satchel containing the explosive charges connected by the Primacord. Infantino finished the adjustments on his own respirator, then picked up the other satchel. Once they were on the Observation Deck, they would have to connect the two explosive arrays together.

They walked clumsily across the plaza toward the waiting UH-1, its blades cutting cleanly through the snow-thickened air. The copilot helped Infantino and Barton climb inside and then belted into his own seat.

The pilot glanced back briefly at Barton and said, "All comfy, Captain? Here we go." Barton nodded and the pilot felt for the four antitorque pedals with his feet. Then he checked the position of the collective, a two-foot stick centered in its left-hand panel, and the cyclic stick above him. He nodded at the copilot who was now on radio, and moved the collective. The 'copter rose and hovered for a second, slowly turning as he corrected the torque. Then they were airborne, rising quickly into the black night.

"I can't set it down too close to the restaurant," the pilot yelled at them. "They're loading another UH-1 up there and that Sikorsky is still overhead—its downdraft would rip us apart."

"Try the penthouse," Barton shouted back. "There're some gardens separating it from the Promenade Room—you won't be able to set down there. You'll have to use its roof." He turned to Infantino and said in a musing voice, "That was going to have been the best address in the city. Got any idea what that penthouse would have rented for?"

Infantino didn't look impressed. "Right now it's only

good for one thing and after that, it won't be good for much of anything."

"We're coming in!" the pilot yelled. The 'copter slipped sideways toward the glistening rooftop, sailing over a loading UH-1, and then settling down on the small, snow-covered roof of the penthouse. Infantino and Barton unbelted and Barton tugged open the door. They got out quickly and Barton glanced back at the Promenade Room roof in time to see the Sikorsky swing the elevator cab in and slowly lower it toward the roof. Two figures ran over to it and pried the doors open. People straggled out to clamber on the waiting UH-1; several of them had to be carried.

Even at a distance he could recognize Leroux. The commanding figure and the white hair, caught for a moment in the spotlights from the rescue craft, were unmistakable. Barton's heart suddenly leaped with relief. Behind Leroux was Jenny, and she was looking over at them. Probably wondering who they were and what they were up to. There was no chance that she would recognize him, dressed as he was in the mirror-bright proximity suit. He started to wave but she and Leroux had already disappeared into the waiting rescue 'copter. Another UH-1 was hovering alongside the building to take off the last of the passengers.

Infantino was busy pulling the satchels out of their own 'copter. The last item he took out was an electric lantern, which he flicked on. "Got everything?" he asked.

"Everything," Barton said. He reached to put on his respirator, then paused a moment. "Be sure the Primacord fits into its slot under the charge backoff. These charges have to be level on the floor and they need the backoff space to concentrate their punch."

"Understood," Infantino said, slipping on his facepiece. He motioned Barton to do the same. Now Barton felt like he was in a world of his own, his breath sighing through the respirator valve. Heavy winds beat across the roof, and for a moment the 'copter behind them teetered, then righted itself.

"You guys better hurry!" the pilot yelled at them. "We

can't hold here under this wind for very long." The copilot rolled the door shut and the pilot pulled back into his seat. Suddenly the rotors stopped. That was stupid, Barton thought. You didn't kill your engine under these circumstances. Then he heard the high whine of the starter and watched the blades begin to slowly rotate again. The pilot had lost his fire. Well, that was his problem, he'd have to get it started again.

Barton and Infantino picked up their heavy canvas bags and trudged across the penthouse roof. It would be murder to try and climb through the restaurant trapdoor and down the ladder into the kitchen, Barton thought, even if they could make it across the gardens to the icy Promenade Room roof. Not with their bulky suits and satchels of explosives. But inside the penthouse was a staircase that led to the kitchen hallway and from there they could get to the Observation Deck. They pushed through the door of the rooftop entrance and carefully descended the steps to the penthouse anteroom.

The inside door was locked. Infantino tried it one more time, then stepped back and kicked it open with his heavy boot. They stood in the gloom of the penthouse for a second trying to orient themselves. The air was thick with smoke, which explained why the tenants hadn't sought refuge there. Infantino slowly flashed his lantern around, the light cutting through the smoke to the paneled walls and splashing off the parquet floors. Like the other upper apartment floors of the building, the penthouse was still unfinished and the inside was a confusion of supplies and building materials, with sheets of wallboard and lumber stacked against one of the walls.

Infantino located the stairs with his lantern and started to walk toward them. Suddenly Barton reached out a restraining hand and signaled for quiet. He stood there for a long moment and listened, with his feet as well as with his ears. Beyond the distant shriek of the wind, there was no noise, no sense of the pulsing life that had been the building. Even with the insulation, there should have been the subliminal feel of throbbing life in the building below—it was impossible to completely mask the vibrations of powerful machinery, he thought.

But now there was no noise, no vibrations, no feeling of the power and life that had once filled the building.

"What's the matter?" Infantino asked, his voice sounding muffled from behind his facepiece.

Barton shook his head. "Nothing—let's get on with it." They walked over to the carpeted steps that led down to the kitchen hallway, and then climbed down the smoke-filled stairwell to the Observation Deck. The smoke was blinding them now and Infantino motioned Barton to hug the wall.

It was in the stairwell where they stumbled across the two bodies. A man and his wife, probably. She had on a heavy fur coat and he had a tablecloth wrapped around his head and shoulders. Barton guessed that they had been two of the tenants on the roof who had changed their minds before the helicopters showed up. They had tried to get back down and died of smoke inhalation on the stairs. He pulled off a glove and knelt down to check for a pulse. Nothing. He looked up at Infantino, who shook his head and pointed at their bags. Barton stood up and they stepped over the bodies and continued down the stairwell.

Once on the Observation Deck the air was somewhat cooler, though the smoke was just as thick. Barton pulled the canvas bag from his shoulders and Infantino did the same. Barton was the lead man in positioning the charges and he searched for the corner he had chosen from Shevelson's blueprints. He set the first charge in position and carefully measured out the distance to the second charge. With these two in place, they needed only to stretch the Primacord taut to position the other charges. Infantino linked into his array and placed his charges on the other side of the central room. Barton checked quickly to make sure all the charges were upright in their positioning sleeves, then taped a length of Primacord from Infantino's array onto a lead cord from his own. They had three charges left and Barton began to unreel the remaining Primacord toward the central room. Infantino wedged the door open and once inside, Barton set one of the charges at the base of the Freon tank and the remaining two on opposite sides of the water reservoirs.

After he had finished, Barton signaled Infantino and they went back to the Observation Deck proper. Barton taped a detonator cap onto one of the lengths of Prima-cord and inserted a delay fuse. He took a pair of crimping pliers from the canvas satchel and crimped the soft copper sleeve of the detonator cap onto the fuse. Once the charges were set off, they stood a good chance of collapsing the entire floor; certainly there would be vents for the cas-cading water and Freon to reach the floor below. And with any luck at all, the fire floors might pancake one onto the other.

For a moment Barton couldn't find the butane lighter in the bottom of the canvas bag and searched frantically through it, then located it in a partially ripped seam of the satchel. He thumbed it and played the flame over the fuse until it started to sputter and then roared into life. He and Infantino ran to the stairwell and seconds later were in the penthouse and racing for the ladder to the penthouse roof.

Outside, a UH-1 was waiting for them, the copilot standing by the open door. Above, the slowly revolving blades quivered in the heavy wind and the 'copter rocked slightly. Barton fumbled at his facepiece and hastily climbed in. "We've got about fifty seconds—let's get moving!" Infantino followed him in and they belted down.

The pilot grabbed at the collective stick and increased power. There was a heavy sputtering and then silence as the 'copter blades wound down. "Must've got water in the ignition," the pilot grunted. He keyed the starter motor. It coughed and the blades twisted once more.

"We've got thirty seconds before all hell breaks loose!" Barton said tensely.

"I'm doing my damnedest, Captain." The slight film of sweat on the pilot's face glistened in the light from the instrument panel. He tried again and Barton sighed with relief as the motor caught and the blades began their accelerating dance around the rotor. The 'copter shook itself in the wind, rose several feet and rotated slowly. Then a gust of air caught it and it rose faster. The cabin rotated and stabilized as the pilot worked the antitorque pedals. They were five hundred yards away from the Glass House now, heading east.

Barton glanced back. At that moment the shape charges and their connecting lines of Primacord detonated simultaneously. The Observation Deck filled with fire and boiling smoke. The windows around the side of the deck abruptly flew out in jagged shards that sailed over the streets below. The roof bowed slightly upward from the pressure wave and then sank in the middle along the line that bordered the garden area. Sheets of aluminum curtainwall puffed outward, split and peeled away from the steel frame.

Inside the building, the concrete floor of the Observation Deck rumbled and cracked away from its supporting beams. Huge sections of it fell to the machinery room below. Clouds of steam and half-vaporized Freon blew out through the window holes under the pistonlike pressure of the falling floor sections. The fires on the machinery floor puffed out instantly. The weight of the falling masses of concrete and the sudden deluge of thousands of gallons of water in turn shattered portions of the machinery-room floor, which caved in toward the center. The water and the Freon plunged down the slope to the flaming apartment floor below, smothering the fires and then flowing down the stairwells and the elevator shafts.

It was over in fifteen seconds. In the 'copter Infantino and Barton had watched the disaster in silence. Barton suddenly felt sick. The building looked as if a giant claw had raked across it, tearing at its skin and muscle and digging deep into its vital organs.

It had been his baby, Barton thought. He had conceived it and seen it delivered from his drawing board into the hands of Leroux, who had served as midwife.

And now he had just helped to murder it.

68.

The UH-1 settled slowly to the terrazzo plaza, bounced slightly; the pilot cut the power and the rotors slowed. Infantino said, "We're here, Craig," and Barton blinked and unbelted. He felt old and tired and desperately in need of both a bath and a bed. He pushed back the 'copter door and stepped out into the cold. Small flakes of snow were still falling, the winds still whipping across the plaza.

"It's all over," Infantino said quietly.

"Not completely," Barton said dryly. A group of reporters and cameramen had surrounded the helicopter and surged forward as the blades came to a halt. Flash bulbs lit up the night and the questions tumbled at them one after the other, half of them torn away by the wind. "Later!" Barton shouted. "Later! There's still a lot we've got to do!" He pushed through the crowd of newsmen, who now turned their barrage of questions on Infantino.

At the edge of the crowd, he sensed somebody at his side. "Mr. Barton?"

He glanced around, ready to fend off another reporter, then relaxed. "Hello, Dan—how's Griff?"

"The doctors say he'll make it." Garfunkel nodded at another group of reporters and evacuees a hundred feet away. "Your wife and the Lerouxes came through okay. They're shaken up and Leroux has a sprained wrist, but nothing worse than that."

"Thanks, Dan." Barton took a breath. "Is there a final census on the building? Anybody still unaccounted for?"

"The firemen have pretty well gone through it floor by floor," Garfunkel said slowly. "There were more casualties than we had thought—thirty-one deaths from various causes, mostly burns and smoke inhalation. Thank God, it was the start of the long weekend. We haven't been able to account for Lex Hughes, one of the accountants at National Curtainwall, and several others. I suppose they'll

find them when they go through the ruins." He gestured a
the tarpaulin-covered sculpture. "There hasn't been a
positive identification of the woman yet, though we're
pretty sure we know who she was."

A conservatively dressed man walked up and suddenly
interrupted. "Mr. Barton," he said smoothly, "I'd like to
have a moment with you. Brian of International Surety
We—"

"Mr. Brian," Barton said carefully, "you really don't
want to talk with me and, to be frank, I don't want to
talk with you. I'm not even sure I work for Curtainwal
any more. The man you want to see is Wyndom Leroux."

"But it will only take—"

"Mister," Barton said, his voice thick with exhaustion
and annoyance, "I'm too damned tired to be polite, to
you or anybody else. Now get lost. Go see Leroux—it's
his building."

The man stared at him for a second, then abruptly
turned and half ran, half walked toward the far group
that included Leroux. Barton glanced around for Infantino, then noticed that Mario had torn himself away
from the reporters and was over at the comm van, struggling out of his proximity suit. Good idea, Barton thought
and started to undo the latches on his own. In it he had
felt like an aluminum-clad Santa Claus looking for his
stainless steel reindeer. *'Tis the season,* he thought sourly. . . .

It was winding down, Infantino thought. Crews would
still be at work through the early morning but they would
be primarily salvage companies. The bulk of the companies had completed their mission and were draining
hoses on the plaza and rolling them up. Others were
stowing tools and respirators while still others were in the
basement cafeteria catching a quick cup of coffee before
returning to their firehouses.

He contacted his battalion chiefs one by one, taking a
brief moment for small talk and compliments before giving them their final orders. Chief Jorgenson came out of
the lobby clutching a cup of coffee and a candy bar he
had filched from the cigar stand.

"Chief, how do we thank you?"

Jorgenson managed to smile. "Don't worry about it; the city will send you a bill. Then there's always the possibility we'll have to ask your help someday." They shook hands and Jorgenson was gone.

Infantino found Captain Miller in the lobby and asked for a casualty report. Miller took a notebook from his pocket and began to go through the depressing details. Who was it who had said it? Infantino thought bleakly. *The brightest and the best* . . . Gilman, Lencho, a dozen others. "What about Chief Fuchs?" he asked at last.

Miller shook his head. "Both legs crushed; he'll probably lose a lung. He'll be in intensive care for . . . Well, better ask the doctors, they didn't know when I talked to them a few minutes ago. He'll make it, but it'll be strictly a desk job for him from now on in. He'll never go near a fire again."

The old man should have known better, Infantino thought bitterly. But if it had been him and it had been his son, who knows. . . . "What about young Fuchs?"

"Minor injuries; they'll probably hold him a day and release him." Miller added automatically, "Good man, by the way."

"Yeah, I know—he learned it all from his father." A department inspector came up and handed him a note. He read it slowly, thanked the man, and walked outside to the plaza. His car was at the curb. He took off his helmet and wiped his eyes, wondering how she had talked her way through the police lines. Then he noticed that Doris was a passenger and that one of the rookies was driving. He walked over and she saw him and rolled the window down.

"You should be home in bed," he said quietly. His eyes were drinking her in.

"You, too," she said.

"There's still some winding down to do, but I think they can do it without me. Worried?"

"Not too much," she said, but Infantino could tell she was lying. He reached through the window and squeezed

her hand, then opened the rear door and got in the back
seat. She came back to join him.

"You got anything to eat at home?"

"There's a steak in the refrigerator."

"That'll do," he said softly, "that'll do just fine." He
suddenly spotted Barton crossing the street and rolled
down the window to shout, "Hey, Craig, can I see you
as soon as you're free?" Barton yelled, "Be back in a
minute," and Infantino leaned back in the soft seat.
"Christ, I'm tired." He leaned over into the warmth of
his wife's body and was dozing in seconds. Doris put her
arm around him and didn't move, even though the position was a little cramped and awkward for her. She ran
her fingers lightly through his hair and watched the parade
of tired men roll up their hoses on the plaza and climb
in their trucks and silently roll away. An ambulance a few
cars ahead caught her eyes and she watched it curiously
for a moment. A woman—one of the cleaning women, by
the look of her dress—was being loaded into it, while a
heavy-set man in his forties and a young boy were watching. She wondered idly if they were related somehow. . .

The ambulance doors closed and Douglas turned to
Jesus and said, "Don't worry, she'll be all right. A little
smoke and a sprain; they'll probably let her out in a day
or two."

"Sure, man, I know," Jesus said. He didn't meet
Douglas' eyes. He was beginning to shiver again.

"You riding with us, buddy?" the driver called from
the front seat.

"Yeah, I'll be coming along," Jesus shouted. He turned
back to Douglas, suddenly looking him straight in the
face. "Look, man, would you come along? Mama would
like it and so would I."

"I'd like to," Douglas said, "but I can't. I have to
meet someone."

Jesus' eyes flicked away again. "Sure, man, I understand."

They stood there in silence for a moment, Jesus looking
small and slight in the old turnout coat that a fireman had
given him. "The street's a crappy place for a human

being," Douglas said at last. "It's none of my business, but I'd like to see you off of it."

"It *is* your business, man!" Jesus suddenly said violently. He shook his head, trying to say something. "Okay, okay, I'll try."

"I know people who can probably get you a job—" Douglas started.

Jesus interrupted. "You were really great, man." He suddenly squeezed Douglas' arm and Douglas reached out absently and grabbed his hand. He stood for an instant, holding it, then gave it a firm handshake. There was a fleeting return squeeze and Jesus walked around the ambulance and started to climb in. He turned and yelled, "You take it easy, fat man."

And then Douglas had it. "I know a furrier," he shouted. "He needs somebody to help out around the shop."

Jesus paused, half in and half out of the ambulance. Douglas could see his withdrawal symptoms were returning, now that the excitement was over. Jesus managed a smile, his eyes bright. "Hey, you mean it, man? I can tell fox from rabbit at a hundred feet! I'll see you tomorrow, no, I mean Monday! Next time I'll even knock!"

"I'll be expecting you!" Douglas shouted. Then the driver reached out and pulled Jesus inside. The ambulance roared away.

Douglas waved and watched it go. Not Monday, he thought. The kid would be looking for a fix again. Maybe in a week? In a month? He turned to leave, then glanced back at the receding ambulance. It wasn't that easy; you didn't turn your back and just walk away. There were doctors he knew, welfare workers who could get Jesus into a methadone treatment center or a halfway house. What Jesus really needed was somebody to give a damn.

He smiled to himself. Concern. That was the only real requirement for a self-elected foster father. Everything else was minor.

Then the excitement and the euphoria drained away and he suddenly realized he was all alone—alone with the twin disasters of a bankrupt business and the collapse of

a relationship he wasn't sure he could live without
Which wasn't quite true; he could live without it, but
the question was whether life would be worth living. He
walked away slowly back across the plaza, stepping over
the tangle of hoses and unconsciously making a wide
detour around the canvas-sheathed sculpture.

"Ian! Ian Douglas!" He turned. Larry was running
toward him, the smile on his face one of intense relief
Then he was up to Douglas and hugging him. "My God
Ian, they told me all about it. They told me all about
you!"

Douglas took a breath. "They didn't tell you everything," he said sadly. He explained what he had almost
done and that the firm was bankrupt.

Larry looked puzzled. "Ian, there was no need for that
In the first place, we would have gone into Chapter Eleven
not bankruptcy. The second thing is there was no need for
it in the first place. We're not bankrupt, we're not anywhere
near it. At least we won't be."

He had to have it out, Douglas thought. If it tore him
apart in the middle of the plaza, he had to have it out
"Look, Larry, I'm getting older. It's a tough thing to
admit; I don't suppose it's anything that anybody likes
to admit. It's natural that you should—well, become interested in somebody else."

Larry looked puzzled. "Ian, I don't understand, I don't
know what the hell you're talking about."

"I saw you at lunch," Douglas started. "Oh, it's none
of my business, but . . ."

"You mean Mitch," Larry said finally. "The guy I had
lunch with at Belcher's one day. He's an old friend . . .
friend, Ian. He's happily married and he's got four kids
He manages a motel chain and we were talking about the
decorating contract for the Midwest." He suddenly slapped
Douglas on the back. "And we got it, Ian! If we don't do
anything else for the next two years we'll make a fortune!
He paused and quieted a little. "Ian, for as long as I can
remember, you've been carrying the weight for both of
us. I thought it was about time to do my share."

"I wish you had told me," Douglas said. He felt slightly miffed.

"Do you begrudge me a surprise, Ian?"

Douglas smiled. "No, I guess I don't." He suddenly remembered something and reached into his pocket and pulled out the netsuke of the water buffalo. "I tried to save the 'Minotaurmachie' and I couldn't. But I managed to save this. I guess I've always liked it—and it's one of a kind."

Larry took it and turned it over in his hand for a moment, half caressing it. "One of a kind," he repeated. He suddenly looked up at Douglas. "Ian," he said quietly, "why did you doubt me?"

"Jealous, I guess," Douglas admitted. He looked away and his voice suddenly cracked. "I guess I'm getting old."

His friend's arm was suddenly around his shoulder. "Ian, I've got news for you," he said softly. "I don't know anybody who's getting younger. The car's down this way."

Larry had parked just ahead of Jernigan's distinctive Mustang with the broad blue racing stripe; Douglas would've known it anywhere. Jernigan's wife was behind the wheel. Douglas knew her only slightly but nodded to her as he passed. As they pulled out, he could see Jernigan walking toward his car, along with Garfunkel. . . .

"It's been a helluva night," Garfunkel said. "There's not too much more that we can do here; you get on home with your wife."

Jernigan nodded. "Thanks a lot, Dan—sure you don't need me here?"

"Yeah, I'm sure." He paused. "Something I want to ask you. You ever play pro ball any time?"

Jernigan looked surprised. "No, why do you ask?"

"I heard about the catches you made. I figured—you know—that you had pro experience or something."

"Sorry to disappoint you, Dan. I may look it, but the only thing I ever caught in my life was a cold."

They stood awkwardly by the car a moment, Jernigan waiting for Garfunkel to say something more. Garfunkel picked idly at a piece of dirt on the door, then said:

"That woman who works with Marnie—she don't really have to be a knockout or anything. I mean, you know like she's pleasant to be with? I'm getting a little old for the foxy ones."

Jernigan grinned. "Marnie's told her a lot about you. I think you'll like each other a lot. Just don't get upset at Leroy. I figure we won't eat until early evening so you'll have time to catch a nap before you come over." He suddenly reached out and squeezed Garfunkel's shoulder. "Marnie's a damn good cook, man, you've got no idea!"

Jernigan opened the door and slid into the right-hand seat. "You drive, Marnie, I'm bushed."

"I figured. What were you and Garfunkel talking about?"

"I'm sorry, should've told you right off. You've got an extra mouth to feed tonight. Mr. Garfunkel's giving us the pleasure of his company. And don't get a big head about your cooking—I think he wants to meet your friend."

Marnie sighed and started the car. "Make that three more mouths to feed."

"Three?" He was suddenly wide awake. "What do you mean, three?"

"Jimmy and his wife were evicted. He showed up with all his baggage and said he was willing to ignore his intense natural dislike of you and honor us with his presence."

"That's all I need," Jernigan said, tired. "Where the hell you going to put them?"

"I'll find a place."

"Just so long as they don't wind up sleeping in our bed."

Marnie chuckled quietly. "Not a chance!"

"Then I really don't give a damn," Jernigan said. He yawned, nuzzled closer to his wife, and fell immediately asleep. She keyed the starter and moved slowly out into the street, beeping once at Garfunkel as he trudged slowly back to the building. He turned and waved and then disappeared down the steps into the lower lobby. . . .

Garfunkel helped himself to coffee, ladled in the cream and a couple of spoonfuls of sugar, and looked around the lunchroom for a place to sit. Most of the tables were taken up by firemen and policemen going off duty, then he spotted Donaldson at a table by himself, his pinkish-red hair streaked with soot and no longer neatly combed over his bald spot.

"Mind if I sit down?"

"You already are," Donaldson pointed out. "Hell, you'll be somebody to talk to besides the hose and hatchet boys. What've you heard about Griff?"

"He'll live," Garfunkel said shortly. "It wasn't as bad as we had feared. He'll even be able to come back to work."

Donaldson cheered up. "It'll be good to see his fat face around, telling me how to do my job."

Garfunkel gulped at his coffee, then suddenly noticed Lisolette Mueller and an older man—what was his name? Claiborne?—at the next table over. They were, he noticed, holding hands on top of the table. He nudged Donaldson. "I guess you're never too old at that."

Donaldson followed his eyes. "Christ, I should hope not," he said fervently. . . .

At the next table, Lisolette said quietly, "I'm sorry I worried you so much, Harlee, but I was afraid that nobody would think of the Albrechts."

"I didn't know where you went," Claiborne said, trying to act put out but not quite succeeding. "I was . . . quite concerned."

"I couldn't leave a note," she said. "It would have taken too much time. And if I had stayed until you returned, I was afraid you would tell me all the logical reasons why I shouldn't do it."

"It was a very brave thing to do," he said quietly.

The strain and the fatigue now began to catch up with Lisolette and tears started to leak down her face. "Do you think they'll be all right, Harlee?"

He pulled his chair around so he could put a comforting arm around her. "I'm sure they will," he said softly.

"I'm quite sure they will." He paused. "Their uncle came for the children. They didn't want to leave you."

She nodded and then got a little control of herself. "What will you do now?"

"I'm not sure," he said thoughtfully. "I have no relatives to hold me here, and very few friends. . . ."

Lisolette drew back, her face puzzled. "What about me?"

"Lisa," he said slowly, "I tried to take your money. They call it 'conning' someone. I give people some charm and in turn they give me some money. It's not a nice way to make a living."

"Did you never . . . like your 'ladies'?" Lisolette asked.

"Lisa, I liked them all!" he said proudly.

The sparkle was suddenly back in her eyes. "A gentleman can be forgiven his indiscretions."

"Gentleman?"

"Yes, gentleman." She leaned back in her chair and was suddenly all business. "Harlee, I have a friend in the travel agency business who would be absolutely delighted to have such a charming man as you among her employees." She put a hand to his mouth as he started to object. "It's hardly charity. There are tours to be arranged for retired people, schoolteachers who may be more interested in the ruins of Greece than where the 'swinger' spots in Athens are, that kind of clientele. They have no faith in a younger person, in somebody who's never seen the world as I'm sure you have."

"Thank you very much, Lisa," he said sincerely. "But there are little legal matters . . ."

She smiled. "I doubt that any of your ladies would have her heart more set on revenge rather than restitution."

"And you?" he asked.

There was a hint of a smile on her face now, the sort of hint that made her seem years younger and suddenly a little opaque to him. How long had it been since he had felt quite uncertain around a woman? he wondered.

"Hey, fellas, look what I found wandering around the thirty-fifth floor!"

Lisolette. and Harlee automatically turned toward the door where a fireman stood holding a spitting, slightly drenched cat.

"Schiller!"

The cat bounded over and Lisolette scooped him up, her nose wrinkling at the smoky, slightly singed odor to his fur.

The fireman came over and took off his helmet. "I'm glad he's yours, lady, though my kids would've loved him. I figure he's only got one life left anyway—he must have used up eight of them just surviving up there."

"Thank you *very* much," Lisolette said. She stood up and Harlee followed after her to the line of cabs on the far side of the plaza.

"We might as well stay in the same hotel until we can move back in," Harlee said. He added firmly: "I have no intention of losing track of you, you know." He held the cab door open for her and nodded to two women passing by. They had been with the party sitting behind them up in the Promenade Room. . . .

Thelma Leroux acknowledged the greeting and continued talking intently to Jenny. "I hope I haven't been too forward. There was a lot to be said tonight and it seemed as if the opportunity might never come again."

"No," Jenny said quietly. "Somebody should have said it to me a long time ago. It's very hard for someone like me to see life in that way—but I'll try."

"It's not all that bad and you have a good husband. He's worth trying to hang on to."

Impulsively, Jenny hugged the older woman. "Thelma, thank you so very much." Thelma smiled and said, "I'd better get over to Wyn—the reporters have cornered him and he'll need moral support." She walked quickly away, turned once and waved, then disappeared into the crowd.

Jenny looked around for Barton and spotted him at the edge of the plaza, in deep conversation with a burly-looking man, somebody she didn't know at all. She hesitated a moment, not wishing to interrupt. . . .

Will Shevelson said, "Well, Barton, I guess you won't be needing me any more."

"What can I say, Will? Without the blueprints . . ."

Shevelson shrugged. "Do me a favor and don't send them back." He glanced up at the building briefly. "Whatever I felt for it is gone now. It's just another photograph on the wall of my den." He laughed a little. "Just another pretty face." He turned away. "Take care of yourself, Barton."

"You, too, Will."

Jenny came up then and Barton silently put his arm around her shoulder and walked over to the crowd. Leroux had broken away from the reporters for a moment, the police holding back the cameramen. Barton said quietly, "I want to speak to him alone for a moment, Jenny. Be right back."

Leroux noticed him at the same time and left Thelma to meet him. "I can guess what you're going to say, Craig."

"That I'm quitting? You're right. Any reason why I shouldn't?"

Leroux was abruptly intense and for a second the plaza and the night fell away, leaving the two of them isolated from the rest of the world. "Lots of reasons, Craig. Good professional reasons. Good personal reasons. Probably the most important one is that right now I need you more than I ever have."

Barton was quiet for a long moment and the world gradually came back. The snow struck, melted, and ran down his face. The sharp wind was cold against his back and the plaza stank of smoke and fire and death. The man in front of him suddenly seemed shrunken in stature, a man who pleaded rather than offered. A man growing jowly and old who had been too anxious for just one more cast of the dice.

"We're quits, Wyn. I'm tired of working for a pyramid builder. Maybe I think pyramids are out of style. I'd like to build places for people to live in, rather than warehouses in which to store them."

"She was your baby," Leroux said softly. "She can be rebuilt—rebuilt the way you want her. She's still structurally sound. You know we can do it."

Barton stared up at the ice-encrusted building behind Leroux and for the first time could see nothing of himself in it. It was a different building than the one he designed, he thought. There was no reason to pretend an attachment that no longer existed.

"I'm sorry, Wyn, I'm not interested."

Leroux's face became that of a stranger. "All right, Barton. I hope you never regret it because I'll never take you back."

He turned to go and had gotten about three steps away when Barton suddenly asked: "Why did you do it, Wyn?"

Leroux hesitated, then turned back to him. "Some of our interim financing fell through at the last minute," he said calmly. "We couldn't find additional financing in time and it was either cut the size of the building or pull in our belt as far as it would go. Too much depended on it, Barton. I didn't build the building you wanted—but if it's any satisfaction to you, I didn't build the one that I wanted, either."

Barton watched him walk across the plaza to where Thelma stood. He couldn't be sure but it looked as if Leroux were leaning on her as they walked away.

Jenny was at his side now and said quietly, "Was it difficult?"

"To quit?" He shook his head. "No, it was easy." He thought for a moment. "He's not unique, Jenny. He cut a lot of corners but then most builders do. The real tragedy is that he's not the man he thought he was."

They walked slowly along the line of parked cars toward Infantino's. Through the window, Barton could see Infantino dozing on his wife's shoulder. She started to wake him up and Barton made a shushing sound with his finger, then reached through the partly opened window and gently shook Infantino's shoulder. "Hey, smoke-eater, wake up!" Infantino shook himself awake, glanced at Barton and started to say something, and then suddenly frowned.

Behind them, Barton could hear Quantrell shouting: "Something for the wrap-up, Chief? Any indication it was arson or what might have started the fire?"

It took a moment for Infantino to focus his eyes and then he said calmly, "There'll be a statement from the public relations department later in the morning. If you get there early maybe you'll be fourth in line."

Quantrell stared at him steadily for a moment. "I've got a long memory, Infantino."

He turned on his heel to leave and Infantino shouted after him: "You've got a big mouth, too!" He turned back to Barton. "Craig, can you make it down to the department later today? We'll need a statement."

"Sure thing," Barton said. And then: "Mario, any idea how it started? Was it arson?"

Infantino shook his head. "I talked with the inspectors —they don't think so. Earlier this evening, they found part of a broken brandy bottle in between some half-burned mats in one of the utility rooms on seventeen. Funny, you would've expected it to be completely consumed but part of the label was even intact. Matted cotton burns, but I guess in this case, it acted partly as insulation. Anyway, they presume somebody stashed the bottle, lit a cigarette, and probably stubbed out the match on the matting before leaving the room. Just a guess, it's hard to really tell."

"Brandy?" Barton said slowly. "I can imagine who put it there." He told Infantino about Krost and his constant tippling. "Poor, stupid, incompetent bastard."

Infantino yawned. "There're plenty of those in the world, Craig. It's full of grown-up kids playing with matches. There's always one of them ready to do the one stupid thing that ends up in this kind of disaster."

"It could have been anybody," Barton said. "Or any building."

Infantino nodded. "And it could happen again. It *will* happen again." He laughed cynically and rested his head again on Doris' shoulder. "It's like death and taxes, Craig. It's inevitable."

"And that's why we have firemen."

"That's a real comforting thought, Craig. Thanks a lot." He suddenly smiled, said, "See you around, buddy," and signaled to the driver. The car started up and Barton could see Infantino's head loll suddenly to one side. He was asleep already.

He watched the car turn slowly into the traffic, then glanced down at Jenny. "Where to now, Jenny?"

"Home," she said simply.

He frowned. "Southport's a long way away."

"I didn't mean Southport," she said quietly. "I mean home—any place where you are." She looked up at him. "The nearest hotel will be fine. We both could use some sleep and after that"—she paused—"I think we ought to try and get to know each other."

He gripped her arm and they started walking toward the string of cabs.

~⦿~

The dark clouds are closing in now, wrapping th
wounded building in the healing embrace of cold ai
and pelting snow. It is early morning and the salvag
crews are seeking out the last sparks of the fire and de
stroying them. In one corner of the penthouse, which th
salvage crews have not yet reached, a spark glows brightl
in a shattered section of expensive walnut paneling. A
breeze fans across it. The spark flares, touches a splintere
piece of wood, and for a moment the pale ghost of th
beast is outlined against the cold morning air. Then t
chilling wind blows through the opening, driving rain and
sleet before it. The small flame sputters and blackens, a
tiny wisp of smoke marking where it had been.

The beast is dead.

~⦿~